' 'Twould be error to suppose that my sentimental education commenced on that sunny morning in May, 1815, when, sent back from church to fetch my lady's forgotten purse from her bedroom in Alcovary House, I came upon my master's youngest son rogering his sister in their mother's bed.'

Thus begin the saucy adventures of a young lady and gentleman of leisure, whom Fate casts adrift in the English countryside in Regency times. Their amorous exploits will defy even the most jaded imagination . . .

Eros In The Country

Or The Adventures of a Lady and Gentleman of Leisure

Anonymous

HEADLINE

Copyright © 1988 Derek Parker

First published in 1988
by HEADLINE BOOK PUBLISHING PLC

10 9 8 7 6 5 4 3

ISBN 0 7472 3145 1

Typeset in 10/11 English Times
by Colset Pte Ltd, Singapore

Printed and bound in Great Britain by
Collins, Glasgow

HEADLINE BOOK PUBLISHING PLC
Headline House
79 Great Titchfield Street
London W1P 7FN

**For the convenience of the reader
we here record a note of
IMPORTANT PERSONS APPEARING IN
THE NARRATIVE
in the order of their appearance**

Master Andrew Archer, our hero.
Master Frank Franklyn, a young gentleman.
Miss Sophia Franklyn, our heroine.
Sir Franklin Franklyn, Bart., of Alcovary.
Lady Patience Franklyn, his wife.
Horace Gutteridge, a flaybottomist.
Spencer Franklyn, Esquire, a young gentleman, later a
Lieutenant in H.M. Navy.
Master Ffloyd, a schoolmaster.
Mrs Tickert, a housekeeper.
Mr Caister, a butler.
Tom, a footman.
The Third Earl of Rawby.
Mr Haddon, an insignificant personage.
Tabby, a maid.
Ellen, another.
Sir Walter Flount, a lecher.
Mr Nelham, a scholar.
The Lady Elizabeth Rawby, a lady.
The Lady Margaret Rawby, another.
Signor Giovanni Cesareo, a musician.
Henry Rust, Esquire, an ancient Beau.
Jack, a lascivious undergraduate.
Coln, another.
George, a third.
Will, a strapping bumpkin.
Rosanna Vanis, a Gypsy.
The Honourable Misses Glaistow, two lascivious sisters.
Derai Bovile, a *dimber damber*

Sam Vanis, a Gypsy.
Anna Soudras, a Gypsy.
Miss Sarah Wheeler, a young lady.
Mrs Hester Muster, her aunt.
Major Willoughby Fawcett, an unworthy officer.
Major Constant Hawtree, his friend.
Captain Dawkin, an inconsequential soldier.
Dean Runciple, a cleric.
A Handsome Fellow of Winchester.
Sergeant Hardy, a pugilist.
Mr Charles Finching, a country gentleman.
Mrs Finching, his wife.
A Highwayman.
Mr Harry Grose, a rich merchant.
Mrs Grose, his wife.
Miss Patience Grose, his daughter.
Bob, their servant.
The Honourable Frederick Mellor, suitor to Miss
Patience.
An enthusiastic Rustic.
Mr Edmund Weatherby, brother to Mrs Finching.
A number of rude sailors.
Mrs Esmerelda Plunkett Cope, an actress.
Miss Cynthia Cope, another.
Samuel Prout Higgens, an actor.
David Ham, another.
Nathaniel Grigson, another.
Miss Jessie Trent, a school mistress.
Dolly, her maid.
Eight young ladies.
Ned Farkin, a jester.
Miss Meg Tamblin, a whore.
Mr Harry Rockwall, a young gentleman.
Thomas Bidwell, a rogue.
Sir Ingle Fitzson, a magistrate.

Chapter One

The Adventures of Andy

'Twould be error to suppose that my sentimental education commenced on that sunny morning in May, 1815, when, sent back from church to fetch my lady's forgotten purse from her bedroom in Alcovary House, I came upon my master's youngest son rogering his sister in their mother's bed.

To be sure, being at that age unversed in the singularities of amorous play, I was somewhat perplexed that Master Frank should have been partially clothed in one of Lady Franklyn's finest Empire dresses, while upon the upper body of his sister I recognised the uniform coat of a lieutenant in one of His Majesty's naval vessels, doubtless the property of Master Spencer, then newly promoted and attending Matins with the remainder of the family.

'Twas not, I say, the start of my education in matters of love. No person whose early years are spent in the same bed with four brothers and three sisters can long remain ignorant, if not by performance then by observation, of the mechanical purposes for which man and women are differently formed. Yet the tangle of pleasure I glimpsed that morning marked a turning-point in my life, as the reader will discover.

I was born the second son and fifth child of one Jonathan Archer, sometime gamekeeper, sometime poacher, of the parish of Bedmoretonham, in the County of Hertfordshire, on the twenty-seventh day of May in the year of Our Lord 1800 and the fortieth of the reign of His Britannic Majesty King George III.

Of my childhood I need say little, for 'twas no different than that of a million other young creatures of our times – spent in a mud cottage of two rooms, one for day use, one for night, where the whole family huddled together in comfortable if fetid warmth. In addition to childish pleasures and play, I was early educated in poaching game, setting snares by the time I was five or six, and learning to break a rabbit's neck almost as soon as I could walk.

It was through my adept capturing of his game that I came to the notice of Sir Franklin Franklyn of Alcovary, a gentleman of independent means and the owner of a large estate which he administered with care, riding out often to see his tenants, interfering regularly in their business, and governing them with more enthusiasm than knowledge of the land. We lived just outside his walls, which I often surmounted in pursuit of apples, pears and medlars as well as more profitable meat.

One summer day when I was seven year old, I had released a rabbit from a snare in a wood not far within his park gates when, emerging from the thicket, I found myself faced by the squire himself, accompanied by two servants and his lady wife. Turning to run, I found behind me a pair of keepers, each smiling broadly – for they knew me as a waster of Sir Franklin's property, and were happy to see me face to face with a painful fate.

Sir Franklin was a portly, red-faced bull of a man, a villain to any thieves who came before him (for he was a local justice, complete in his hatred of any offender who crossed him: he had hanged a man the year before for stealing twelve pence from a man of his).

What took me I know not, for before I could be seized, I fell on my knees before Lady Franklyn and offered the rabbit to her as a parson might offer the host at the altar.

I had chosen the gesture well, as it turned out, for though she was not a woman of uncommon kindness, she was susceptible to flattery.

'What, now,' she said, smiling, 'tribute from so tender a babe?'

'Ay, my lady,' I piped. 'I found this fine fat cony in the wood, and was bringing it to the house for your la'ship's table.'

Out of the corner of my eye I saw Sir Franklin scowl, for not only was I clearly not going towards the house, but the ragged back leg of the beast betrayed the wire of the snare which had been its death. But happily my lady was caught in a snare of another kind; I was a pretty child, and despite my dirty state and ragged clothes – such as they were, for I was shirtless and my breeches, which had covered several arses before mine, were mere threads – she stepped forward and reached out her hand to tousle my hair. Thinking better of the action, which indeed might have resulted in her acquaintance with a number of small animals who had their habitation therein, she drew back at the last moment, but said, 'Franklin, you would not be harsh with so young a culprit?'

Her husband drew in a breath, as I drew mine, for I had heard many tales of the whipping almost to death at the cart's tail of children no older than me. But she continued: 'Something, I think, can be made of him. Pochett, take him up to the house and clean him, and we shall see what we shall see.'

One of her servants seized me by the collar before I could run and marched me off to the hall, where I was wiped all over with a wet cloth, and a shirt and pair of breeches belonging to one of her ladyship's sons were placed upon me before I was taken again to her, when she questioned me at length.

I cannot now remember what she asked, or what I replied, but native wit must have won me favour, for though I was sent packing to my father (who whipped me soundly when he heard my story – not for my capture of the cony, but for allowing myself to be caught) a week later there was a message for him to attend Lady Franklyn, and soon I heard that she had readily persuaded him to allow me to take lessons at the big house with his own children – Sir Franklin's that is – Mr Spencer, the eldest boy, then aged eleven, young Frank, two years my senior, and Miss Sophia, of an age with me. My father was all too pleased that there should be one less hungry mouth to feed in our small cot, and my mother the same. My only elder brother at twelve years of age was already working on the land of a neighbour farmer and had no notion of jealousy of my good fortune, believing that nothing came of book learning, while my sisters, though they looked at me with envy, could do little other than sometimes cuff or scratch me in revenge for having been picked out for favour.

As for me, I was by no means entirely satisfied at being plucked from freedom into the prison of the schoolroom; neither was I pleased when Mr Gutteridge, the schoolmaster (who, as I now know – and as you shall later judge, for he plays some part in this story – was a most ignorant man and most unfit for his position), demonstrated that his chief pleasure in life was in whipping, for I had not been in the schoolroom for more than a day when he tore my second-hand breeches from my body to belabour my bum with a birch he kept for the purpose.

I believed at the time that this was a lesson he reserved for me as an ignorant newcomer to his rule, but on the following day, she not knowing her Collect, he divested Miss Sophia of most of her clothing and, making her brother Spencer hold her arms as she leaned over the back of a chair, raised great welts upon the white cheeks of her backside while she screamed most pitifully. Note that he only ever attacked his pupils in such a manner when sure that his master and mistress were out of hearing, and though the children complained, their parents were reluctant to take to task a tutor they had obtained for a trumpery sum and who was a mark in the neighbourhood of their gentility and superiority, for no other gentleman within many miles employed a tutor for his sons and daughters.

For three years I and my fellow pupils suffered – and without the compensation of knowledge gained, for this master knew almost as little as we; the daily Collect was drubbed into us from the prayer book, and that was all. This cruelty had what was for me an excellent result, drawing us children together in a way which mere propinquity would scarcely have achieved, considering the difference in our rank. I soon picked up their manners, which though not those of the greatest in the land were at least finer than what

I would have learned from my ragged fellows in the village. Frank and I soon became the closest of friends, while little Sophie, who even then seemed to me to possess charms altogether superior to those of my sisters, showed me always the greatest kindness. Master Spencer, perhaps because of his position as the eldest son and heir of Sir Franklin, was cooler towards me – but also towards his brother and sister – though not unkind.

Oppressed in the classroom, I spent many happy hours outside it, Frank and I together exploring the countryside far beyond the borders of Alcovary Park, he eager to learn from me such wiles of country life as the setting of snares and the disabling of man-traps (to which engines Sir Franklin was much addicted), while he taught me how to swim in the nearby river. Our young bodies cleaved the waters between March and September, and being altogether naked turned from white to brown, so that by the by they resembled rather the pelts of wild animals than of human beings. My life became even happier when, on my reaching the age of eight, I was brought to live at the big house. This was the result of the intervention of Lady Franklyn who, seeing how fond her children were of me, approved heartily. She called me 'pretty child' and employed me to fetch and carry for her as a sort of page-boy, when I was not at what she innocently believed were my lessons.

The servants of the house, though at first jealous of the favour her ladyship showed me, soon grew my friends. Sir Franklin kept twenty men and women in his house – clerk of the stables and clerk of the kitchen, baker and bailiff, butler and groom of the chambers, and below them the coachman and footmen, park-keeper and gamekeeper, provision-boy and foot-boy. My lady was served by her chambermaid, and she, with the other maids, was my particular friend.

As we grew in years so my companions and I became more and more discontented with the violent temper of our master; scarce a day passed when one or other of us was not more or less violently beaten, and many an afternoon after lessons we would retire to a private place to comfort each

other as best we might. I found a peculiar pleasure in suc-
couring poor Sophie, whose soft skin broke more readily
than ours under the birch. She found the application of
saliva to her wounds most comforting, and nothing loath I
would often apply my tongue to her backside, cooling the
stripes and affording her much ease. The reader will credit
that, though innocent of any sensual intention, I found this
activity most pleasant – partly because of her expressions
of content and partly because the proximity of her nether
region was peculiarly interesting to me. (My sisters and I
had often explored each others' bodies, as a matter of
course, but the closeness of our rooms at home, together
with a lack of fresh water and the disapproval with which
my mother regarded any application of it to the body – it
was, she believed, especially weakening to the female sex –
rendered their persons noisome in the extreme, and I had,
then as now, a misliking for dirt which made it impossible
for me to enjoy the closeness of those subject to it.)

But to return to my narrative, one day in the summer of
1810, Mr Gutteridge finally achieved his own downfall. It
was a peculiarly hot season and he had ordered us, for the
good of our health, to undress to our shirts, while he himself sat clad only in breeches and a shirt which fell open to
the waist disclosing a chest covered with coarse black hairs
and a bulging, pale stomach which seemed barely confined
by his belt. Upon Frank's failing to complete the recitation
of the day's Collect without prompting, the master reached
– as he had so often done – for his birch, and instructed the
boy to remove his trousers. Bending him over a chair, he
began to lay about him until Frank wailed again.

Finally, seeming to complete the punishment, the master
threw his cane to the floor, but rather than striding from the
room as he usually did, ordered myself, Sophia and Master
Spencer to leave the room for he wished to speak seriously
to the still crying Frank. We went ill-humouredly enough
into the yard which lay outside the schoolroom (once part
of a stable). Soberly waiting there for Frank to join us, we
heard a cry of alarm quite distinct from the sound he had
made when being beaten. Clambering onto a water-butt,

Master Spencer and I looked through the window of the schoolroom, where the sight met our eyes of the naked bottom of our master, who had thrown his breeches from him and was moving with a peculiar violence upon the back of our schoolmate, still bent over the punishment chair. He was holding Frank's shoulders the better to enable him to maintain a position whose significance was then unknown to us, for at that time we were ignorant that one man could dance the goat's jig with another, by use of the windward passage.

Frank's cries of pain and alarm were enough to make us instantly leap from the barrel and rush into the room. Master Spencer was by this time a strong youngster of fifteen, and I was for my age possessed of a certain wiry strength. Together we thrust ourselves upon Gutteridge, sending him reeling back from his attempt at bum-fiddling to fall to the floor, where with amazement I saw that part of him I supposed to be constructed merely for the act of urination was in a state of vast erection – so much larger than I could have imagined by comparison with that of Spencer, which he had been proud to display to Frank and me since it had begun to swell in obedience to his increasing age.

Frank, meanwhile, was sobbing and clutching his backside, still bleeding from the birch. Enraged by Gutteridge's attack, though little we understood it, we soon took our revenge. Seizing the birch, which lay upon the floor nearby, Master Spencer caught his master a whack upon that part of his anatomy which, while it had begun somewhat to shrink, still presented an accessible target. With a cry Gutteridge leaped to his feet and, followed by Master Spencer and me, ran in a state of nature from the room and was pursued across the yard before the astonished eyes of Miss Sophie, and out into the gardens where Mistress Franklyn was showing a spinster neighbour a new strawberry bed. The ladies were more than somewhat disconcerted at the sight of a plumply naked, hairy schoolmaster pursued across the lawns by two boys clad only in their shirts – and those to a large degree torn from them in the excitement of the chase. While the master hid behind a nearby bush, Master

Spencer explained to his mother the circumstances which had led to the sudden apparition and his mother, pausing only to tell the quaking Gutteridge to go to his room, accompanied us to the schoolroom where she comforted young Frank and the frightened Sophie. Sending them back to the house with Master Spencer, she turned to me and congratulated me on the part I had played in the affair. I never had much conversation with the lady, simply receiving instructions to fetch or carry; now, I found it disconcerting to be standing before her almost without covering while her cool grey eyes seemed to see every part of me, including that part which my hands and the remnants of my torn shirt were attempting to conceal. To my surprise, she placed her hands on my shoulders, drew me towards her, and kissed me, before sending me off to join her children. If, as it seems now to my recollection, her bosom was rising and falling with peculiar interest, it surely could only have been under the pressure of events, although even at eleven my figure was already somewhat manly, brown as it was through exposure to the sun, and muscular through my enjoyment of outdoor exercises.

After the departure of Mr Gutteridge, which followed instantly, there was a period of freedom until a new master made his appearance – Master Ffloyd, a young Welshman of twenty, as kind as he was handsome, whose interest in us and in learning was married to a charm which made him immediately not so much a master as a companion. Besides introducing us to the mysteries of Latin grammar and arithmetic, he spoke to us of Napoleon and Wellesley, of Sir John Moore at Coruna and the taking of Martinique, read to us from the poems of Lord Byron and the novels of Sir Walter Scott, and in general brought us towards the beginning of an understanding of what was civilised life.

As he came to know us more, he grew especially fond of Sophie, and was seen by me to cast many a lascivious glance toward her as, the months and years passing, she grew more a woman. Yet, whether for fear of his master or from natural backwardness I could not tell, he made no open declaration of his feelings – which I approved, for apart from the youth of the object of them, he was altogether too poor a man to be entertained as a lover even by so inexperienced a person as my sister.

Master Spencer, in two years' time, left us to go into the Navy, but Frank, Sophie and I continued our studies for some time, although I was increasingly given duties by my mistress which took me from the schoolroom into the house. I was still more a member of the family than a servant; not only was my mistress almost over-kind to me, but I shared a bed with Frank and we became almost brothers, exchanging confidences and partaking together the pleasures of growing to manhood. This included, of course, much discussion as to the proper employment of those instruments with which nature had provided us for procreation, and which to us at our age soon came to be used for pleasure, and were so used in the manner of young boys throughout the centuries in the way of stroking and playing. We talked much of finding a girl whom we might persuade to inform us of the true nature of the carnal act, but the daughters of the neighbourhood were coarse and unappetising to us both, our tastes being shaped now by higher living than the village provided, while the house itself had little communication with its neighbours except on special occasions which were rare and ceremonial. And for me, Sophie, while infinitely delightful, must clearly be unobtainable.

As we grew increasingly conscious of our needs, so the opportunity to satisfy them seemed to retire. In Sir Franklin's library – of which I had free run – I discovered between the shelves of religion and philosophy a cabinet containing a number of books which at once informed and inflamed me. Some elaborately lascivious etchings showed me what could be done between a man and a maid without indicating how I could acquire the opportunity to perform it, while as I puzzled out the language of M. Chorier's *The Delights of Venus* and Mr Cleland's *Memoirs of a Woman of Pleasure* my impatience to practise knew no bounds, and the relief which could be afforded either in solitary pleasure or in play with Frank grew less and less satisfying. He also, I noted, grew less inclined to play, and after a while seemed to grow entirely uninterested, though I little suspected the reason of it.

But now we come to the accident with which I opened my narrative. I had, as usual, accompanied my master and mistress to church, with Lieutenant Spencer in all his glory, while Frank had pleaded to remain at home to complete a task Mr Ffloyd had given him, and Sophie because she desired to finish a dress she was sewing. I had no reason to suppose that either excuse was anything but the truth – until, that is, I opened the door of my mistress' bedroom, where her reticule – as she told me – lay on the bedside table, and saw before me the spectacle of my two friends in a transport of pleasure. It was Frank who saw me first, for he lay upon his back with his head upon the silk pillows, the green muslin of his mother's dress rumpled about his chest and shoulders, while Sophie sat astride him, the black cloth of Master Spencer's uniform coat making even whiter the skin of her lower back, where it flapped as she moved like a girl on horseback, trotting.

Frank seemed not one whit disturbed at my entry. Indeed, he smiled, and said: 'So, Andy, you find us out at last!' – at which Sophie looked around, and as she did so the coat fell from her shoulders displaying that pair of breasts whose presence I had often noted beneath her thin summer dresses, but had never thought to see unencumbered and as they now presented themselves, swelling gently to roseate buds brushed by the fair hair that swung over her shoulders and halfway to her waist.

Even at that moment I felt some chagrin that Frank should have been enjoying his sister without communicating the fact to me – as I was later to find, they had begun to console each other over a year before the *tableau* now before me, and it was Sophie who, with a modesty which did not preclude her enjoyment of the act, had persuaded my friend to keep their secret. Even now she was more abashed than he at my discovery, though my sudden appearance seemed to have an effect upon her of extraordinary excitement, for as she saw me a strong blush spread to her cheeks and even her upper arms, while her body positively quivered, her buttocks clenched, her eyes rolled, and she was for a moment unable to speak. But then she relaxed and, panting, raised herself to recline at Frank's side, his tool still standing and seeming disproportionately tall, from the slimness of his body.

'Why, don't stand there, Andy, but come and join us!' he cried.

All thought of prayer and purse forgot, I did not hesitate, but threw off my Sunday coat, shirt and small-clothes and mounted the bed at their side. Still shy of the unknown, my first instinct was to lay hold of my friend, who however pushed my hand away and indicated his sister: 'Here's Soph',' he said. 'We've often spoke of you, and though she's shy you'll find her willing!'

Indeed, she lowered her eyes as I gently dared to place my hand upon her breast, for the first time feeling beneath my palm the limber, supple weight of that loveliest part of woman. But soon I felt her own hands stroking my flanks, and then Frank, with a laugh, thrust at my shoulder and sent me tumbling upon my back, with a cry of 'Let the purchaser see the goods!' – and nothing loath, her curiosity stronger than her bashfulness, she bent over me, and I felt her finger tracing my thigh and weighing my cods, while her eyes devoured the part my mother only, among women, had seen – and not to the advantage to which it now showed in its eager readiness for enjoyment.

'Now come, sis!' cries Frank. 'Poor Andy's a dry-tail, and must be allowed to bob!' and drawing his sister upon her back between his legs, his arms about her, reached down to draw her legs apart and display to me a mark to which I was drawn as the arrow to the target. Neglecting in my eagerness more than to glimpse the mark, I immediately let fly at it.

Ah, that in later years we could recall with each new mistress the pleasure of that first encounter! Innocence and freshness endowed my joining with Sophie with a pleasure rarely echoed since then. Though – as will be amply shown – my encounters have been numerous and delightful and my passions often more strangely and generously excited, the sensation as my tool passed without stay into the soul of my young partner was one which still remains in my memory as the most charming. She too, by her expression, enjoyed, and as with that instinct which needs no tutelage I began those movements which excited us towards our goal, her eyes sparkled and her lips parted to meet mine in a rapture communicated by our flickering tongues and the gentle nipping of our teeth. Frank the while clasped my shoulders to draw me more closely to his sister, while the friction of our bodies brought him soon – but not much sooner than ourselves – to the culmination. In youth, haste provokes no reproach, for boy and girl most often race together to the post.

Satisfaction stayed us for a while, and we lay upon the bed in a pool of sunlight from the high windows, our arms about each other, with no constraint nor trouble in the world until Frank, ever eager to renew, leaned to lap at Sophie's breast, while she, stroking with her fingers, tried – and not without success – to rouse me towards a second pleasure. Needing little encouragement, I soon presented Sophie with a renewed proof of my admiration while Frank, jealous of my success, knelt to offer himself to her lips – a meal to which she made no objection.

But in our pleasure and the interest of the situation we had been unconscious of the passage of time. Frank and Sophie had succeeded so far, by ingenious contrivance, in escaping notice of their meetings, whether by me or any other member of the household at Alcovary. But on this occasion in their enjoyment they lost account of passing minutes, until the sound of an opening door followed by a shriek announced the return from church of my mistress. Abashed, we drew apart, and Lady Franklyn ordered Frank and his sister to their rooms, whence they proceeded, white and trembling, clutching their clothes to them. I made to follow, but when my lady ordered me to remain I moved to take possession of my clothes, which lay upon the floor. But Lady Franklyn pushed at them with her foot, sending them to the other side of the room, and made with her hand a gesture which rooted me to the bed.

She was clearly in a passion, though its nature at first deceived me, for I took the flushing of her face and the panting of her bosom (which rose and fell with a peculiar rapidity) to be signals of extreme anger. In my fear, I nevertheless had room for admiration; the fashionable ladies of that time wore excessively little clothing, and through the lawn of her dress I could see the entire shape of her body, more voluptuous than that of her daughter, rather offering the pleasure of a bower in full, dark leaf than a spinney of young green trees.

What was my amazement when I saw her raise her arms and begin to undo her dress! As her bosom fell free of the material that hemmed it in, her breasts swung like ripe pears on the bough, gathered to dark nubs like acorns at their centre. Falling to her feet the folds disclosed a still slim waist, with below it a generous, black bush disguising the entry to love's channel. Yet still so astonished and incapable of response was I that she, now completely naked, had moved towards the bed and thrust me prone upon it before I realised that what I was to suffer was to be far from the chastisement I had anticipated.

My apprehension had naturally brought about my collapse and the speed of events prevented my recovery. But when in silence she lowered her head and applied her lips to that shrunk appurtenance of my manhood which lay fallow upon my thigh, it was not long before the resurrection occurred, and I was ready – so generous is the vitality of extreme youth – for a third bout.

If my education had been started by the daughter, it was continued by the mother, for the attentions she paid me were very different from those I had received from the girl – and, of course, from those I had exchanged with Frank in our mutual explorations of our changing bodies. Youth is centred on self; here, for the first time, in the arms of a woman twice my age, I enjoyed a partner who desired not only to take her pleasure but to enhance my own. Her lips drew upon my body as though parched, while her hands caressed me with a freedom which offered joys of which I was previously unaware.

In truth, under these ministrations it took no long time for me to recover both my confidence and my vigour, and within minutes I was clasped by stronger, more experienced – but no less engrossing – thighs than Sophie's, while half sitting I took between my lips one of those nut-like nipples, my attentions to which were evidently keenly approved by their recipient, who soon began to rise and fall upon me so that my tool was embraced along its full length by lips which, rimmed with dark tresses, were soft as those other lips through which we utter speech. Seeing, no doubt, on my countenance the signal of my imminent decease, she lifted herself from me and placing herself at my side threw up her legs, offering freely that delightful notch into which no man could but hammer a peg – which I swiftly did, setting my plug tail directly between those plump thighs, now lifted so that they embraced my sides, the knees rested beneath my armpits. It was a position I was familiar with from my library studies, but had not thought a woman of my lady's considerable age (for she was certainly thirty years old) capable of; not for the last time was I surprised at the lissom dexterity of passion.

But then as I dug my toes into the bed, raising myself the better to plunge into my mistress – whose dark eyes sparkled with the mutual pleasure of our joy – I suddenly felt a searing pain across my exposed parts, and heard a roar of anger – which emanated, as I found upon turning my head, from the throat of my master, Sir Franklin Franklyn. His unannounced (and as I later learned, unaccustomed) entrance into his wife's bedroom was as a result of the untoward expressions of delight from her lips, loud enough to be heard in the neighbour passage.

To be brief, Sir Franklin's apprehension of my encounter with his dame was not as sanguine as her view of my connection with her children. There was no appeal. Driven from the room by renewed blows from his riding crop on every area of my all too exposed body, and despite my lady's tearful excuses – though what these could have been

I cannot now conceive! – within an hour I found myself walking through the gate of Alcovary House, a small bundle upon my shoulder containing the one spare suite of clothes I could call my own, and in my pocket three shillings which, wrapped in a piece of paper, were thrown to me from a high window at which the face of Lady Franklyn appeared briefly as I left the back door of the house. If the world lay before me, I speculated, it seemed unlikely to offer, in the immediate future, as comfortable a place as that I had left. Yet I turned a brave face towards it, and set out in the opposite direction from the village, towards the open country.

Chapter Two

Sophie's Story

That a lady should set down in print a story as little suited for drawing-room reading as mine might bring a blush to the cheek of modesty, were it not for the fact that I am fixed in my mind that 'twill discourage others of my sex from trusting too much in their emotions rather than their reason – a propensity which has always been my downfall (though as often my delight).

I cannot complain of my birth or upbringing; my father, Sir Franklin Franklyn of Alcovary in the county of Hertfordshire, was a man of independent means who lavished upon his family every luxury save affection; that, he altogether lacked the capacity for – whether for his wife and children or for others. But he in no way hindered us from the pursuit of pleasure, which in a large house in a small neighbourhood was not perhaps so grand a freedom as the reader might at first apprehend. Nor can it be said that he was a willing expender of money, though having no means of discovering the extent of his fortune we had no reason to consider him a miser.

I was the youngest of three children: first, in the earliest year of my parents' marriage, was Spencer, named for my father's father on whom the house's fortune rested, and who showed his gratitude for the compliment by dying three days after the christening. That was in the year of '96, that of the mutiny at Spithead. Two years later, in '98, followed my brother Frank; and in the first year of the new century, myself, christened Sophia Venetia Lavinia after three paternal and maternal relations, none of whom showed the merest attempt at affection or financial endowment.

To my family of brothers was soon added a third – though not of blood – Andrew, or Andy as we called him, the son of one of my father's former gamekeepers, to whom my mother had taken a fancy. This was after my father had engaged a tutor for Spencer and Frank, chiefly to prepare the former, then eleven year old, for his entry into the Navy. On hearing that a boy from the village was to attend lessons, I immediately requested – nay, demanded – that I should also be permitted attendance, for why was I to be excluded from what I innocently believed to be play? I quickly regretted my eagerness, for this tutor was a large and unprepossessing man, a Mr Gutteridge, as lacking in personal graces as in knowledge for, as I was later to discover, he had no Latin and less Greek! And he would not for a moment have deceived any person more learned than my father, or less eager to impress his neighbours at the least possible expense (for Gutteridge was paid a mere pittance, nor even provided with clothing at our cost).

We quickly found our master keener to impress our bodies than our minds, for on the very first day he beat Frank fiercely upon his naked back, and for no good reason, choosing him no doubt because he lacked the conviction that my father would permit him to beat me. However, lack of interference and the realisation that Sir Franklin was interested in nothing so little as our wellbeing, encouraged him, and almost every day after, one or other of us had to strip to the birch, for he was no less ready to beat me than my brothers. They tried as best they might to shield me from pain but since Mr Gutteridge beat us without rhyme or reason, knowing my daily Collect or repeating the Lord's Prayer without error was no protection to me; nor did the boys have the physical means to stop him.

Out of school, Frank and Andy in particular became great friends. Spencer, being the elder, though always courteous considered himself to be more worthy of respect than of friendship and rarely entered our play – indeed, I often felt that he was somewhat jealous of Andy's presence. Nor did Frank at first favour me, but Andy was always pitiful of my cries beneath the whip and many a time I saw him regarding me with tenderness.

After one such day when we had all felt the birch, Andy and Frank, as was their custom, made off across the fields, and Spencer to his rooms. I, limping and sore, took to follow the two younger boys for want of something better to do, and from the sounds of splashing – for it was a summer day – easily found them at an inlet or pool of the river which lay in a hollow below the hill on which our house stood, protected by a fringe of trees. As I approached through these, I saw through the low branches the boys swimming in the dark water, their bodies, though naturally brown from the sun, white against the blackness whence their vigorous strokes struck a sparkle of drops. Soon, as I watched, they climbed the bank. They had so often been stripped of their breeches by Mr Gutteridge in course of his attacks that I was neither dismayed at their nakedness nor specially interested; nor did I consider it strange or unusual that they should display their stripes to each other, though I must admit to some surprise when, as Frank lay upon the grass, I saw Andy approach his face to his friend's fundament and lick the red bands, upon some of which dark spots of blood still appeared. This clearly gave Frank much pleasure, and he wriggled again, till jealous of the attention I burst upon them with a cry of 'Me too, Andy, lick me too!'

At first the boys were no less angry than surprised at my intervention but then had pity. It took me little time to strip and lie down, and soon I felt Andy's tongue cooling the welts on my skin, an activity which appeared to please him no less than it comforted me, though we were quite innocent and childish in the matter for we were not of an age to take any further the pleasure we felt, rooted though it was, as I have no doubt, in that instinct which was at once the pleasure and the curse of our ancestors in Eden.

Our familiarity continued no more and no less intense for some years, until that day when Mr Gutteridge particularly wished to punish brother Frank, for no reason other than whim, and sent Spencer, Andy and me from the classroom. Hearing Frank's cries, my two brothers mounted the water-

butt, and what they saw I know not – only that on a particularly piteous exclamation of Frank's they descended
with one leap and in a moment were into the room. Then I
heard a cry from the master, who in a brief time appeared,
naked save his shirt, and rushed into the garden so quickly
that my glimpse of a huge, monstrous something below his
belly seemed a vision I might have dreamed.

That afternoon I followed the two younger boys again to
the river but something held me from announcing my
approach, and indeed what I saw was more an education to
me than anything I had learned in the tutor's class. My
mother had by then impressed upon me the necessity to be
less free in the presence of my brothers, for being much
together with them, I had taken on somewhat of a tom-
boyish manner, until being free with a joke upon farting in
the presence of Mrs Tenkerton, Parson Tenkerton's wife,
she whipped me – though more gently than Mr Gutteridge.
And later she told me to mind my ways and become more of
a lady, though since she was the only lady I ever saw, 'twas
difficult to know her meaning, for she was herself always
very free with the servants, joking among them as if she was
one of them. Particularly lately, when my breasts had
begun to swell and my body become more a woman's, she
insisted that I cease to go off with Frank and Andy on their
rambles, and introduced me to the pleasures of sewing,
which bored me so much I could have yelled.

But after the affair with Gutteridge I followed them to
the river, being intent to find why they had suddenly been so
violent. As I came upon them, I saw indeed that though
they were engaged in the same comforting activity as previously, there was a difference – or more properly, two dif-
ferences, for between their legs there was now not the small
thing which I had seen, but not noted, on previous
occasions, but something much more wonderful to me –
something like a large extra limb, which I marvelled they
could conceal beneath their clothes.

Andy was, as before, applying his tongue to the stripes on
Frank's buttocks, the latter kneeling before him. But at the
same time one of his hands was playing between Frank's

legs, while with his other hand he was caressing himself. As I watched, he withdrew his hands and gently applied them to Frank's fundament, drawing its cheeks apart to reveal, indeed, what seemed to be a bruise or complaint, but as he was about to minister to it, Frank drew himself away with a shudder and a cry and threw himself into the water.

After a brief pause, Andy followed him, and in a short period they were frollicking happily, the dappled sunlight flashing between the leaves onto their bodies as they cleft the dark water. After a while they climbed onto the bank and threw themselves down upon the grass in a patch of sunlight. From my vantage-point I looked down upon them, and a pretty picture they made even to my then innocent eyes, their slender limbs disposed wantonly and carelessly, open to the view, as I had often seen them. Golden drops of water lay upon their skin and trembled as they breathed, before drying in the heat of the day. They lay so still I thought they slept, and was about to leave my place and go down to them to offer my solicitude to my brother, when I saw him reach out and begin to stroke Andy's thigh gently, his hand wandering then down to the spot where his tool – as I had heard them call it – lay quaggy and small below the slight bush of hair that now sprouted at its base.

To my surprise, the flesh almost instantly stirred beneath Frank's hand and began to grow, and as I strained my eyes I saw it become as it had been ten minutes before, long and thick, and at its end what seemed a darkly pink bud appeared within a fold of skin. I had thought Andy asleep and unconscious of the liberty my brother took, but now I saw his eyes were open, and he reached out to pass his hand between Frank's thighs. As the latter took hold of his tool and began to work it vigorously he too pulled at my brother's as though 'twere the teat of a cow he was milking – save that no cow but would have protested at the violence he seemed to offer, but which his friend was amorous of, for he began to buck his arse with pleasure. In an instant I was amazed to see a quantity of undoubted milk spring from both organs – after which the boys laughed and lay back, their parts recumbent on their bellies, still a little oozing.

I withdrew, having much to think of, and forbore to accompany the boys to the river in future, though on occasion they requested it, and I thought they showed an interest in those tender protruberances which now began to swell the bodice of my dress. But they lacked opportunity to explore them, for I was now in the ordinary course of events with them only at lesson time, with a new master, a Welsh man who was kindly disposed and from whom I learned much. I longed to ask him about that strangeness of my brothers' milking each other but some natural caution warned me against such a freedom, which I was later grateful for.

Full four years passed without any incident worthy of recall. They were years of pleasure for me, for I had a natural desire to learning which had been far from satisfied by our former master. Mr Ffloyd, our new teacher, was happy to supply me with all the information I required, for he was a well-educated man, with a knowledge not only of numbers and the fluencies of the English language, but of French, Greek and Italian, book-keeping and drawing, and even of dancing and music. Dark and with a white, smooth skin which marked him out from the brown-skinned house servants, he had a kindness of manner which made him a favourite with us all and as we grew older, he seemed to lose the power of a master, rather becoming an older friend – and not so old, either, for we learned in time that he was still below the age of twenty when he came to us. He roused in me a love of music, of which I had formerly been entirely ignorant, and sounded again the notes of the ancient harpsichord which for many years had lain unused in the drawing-room. He also infected me with his own love of reading, a delight which has lasted my lifetime. Finally, informing me that no educated woman who wished to take her place in society could be ignorant of dancing, he instructed me in some figures, though I had little opportunity of practice for my mother declined to take me even into such slender society as our district offered. Lessons with Mr Ffloyd made the hours fly speedily and these were indeed the last years of my life to pass without the regular tumult of sensual pleasure, which has its rewards but is also exhausting to the senses.

'Twas in the summer of 1814 that I passed my brother's room, and between the crack of the door saw him upon the bed, his shirt thrown up, and at his milking. Andy had gone for a day to see his mother, and after a hesitation which depended more on fear of Frank's disapproval than on want of curiosity on my part, I threw open the door and marched in, whereat Frank hastily drew the sheet over himself and pretended to be reading a book. However, I was not to be shrugged off.

'Tell me, Frank, how 'tis that a boy can give milk as well as a nursing mother?' I enquired.

At first he pretended ignorance, and that I was asking a mere silly conundrum, till I explained that I had seen him and Andy at their work by the river, and confessed that I thought much of asking Mr Ffloyd to unriddle me the matter. At this he hastily said no, he would save me that trouble, and explained that one morning some months before the adventure with Mr Gutteridge he had woken early in the bed he shared with Andy, the clothes thrown off for 'twas hot, and had seen as his brother lay asleep that that part of him wherewith he pissed, and which had been used to be small and pliant, was standing up from his belly and was many times larger than its habit. He had stretched out his hand and touched it to find it was hard as horn, and as he handled it he felt a disturbance between his own thighs and found that his own tool was swelling to match his friend's in dimension.

By this time Andy had woke and they both felt an irresistible itch which they lost no opportunity of assuaging – for rubbing their tools, when in that enlarged state, was, he said, more pleasant than anything they had theretofore experienced. The pleasure mounted (he explained) until he fear'd he had done himself some injury, for there was what seemed more than anything else like the bursting of a vein, whereupon the milk had broken from the head of his tool, and shortly after the same experience was shared by his brother.

They at first feared that they had done themselves damage and for some days watched lest they suffered some calamity as a result, but no such thing showing itself and, recalling the pleasure, they set to their practice again. Soon it was their custom to satisfy the itch whenever it occurred, which was sometimes several times a day, at which, he said, the flow of milk was sometimes lessened in the repetition.

By this time I was most curious to see this phenomenon and invited Frank to shew me the engine which so interested him, which he was loath to do, until I again employed the name of Mr Ffloyd as oracle, whereafter he reluctantly drew aside the sheet and I saw, to my dismay, only the small, limber thing I had so often seen before. At my disappointment, Frank began to fondle it, but 'twas reluctant to stir, whereupon, I put my hand to it and for the first time began with interest to examine it, for modesty had prevented me heretofore from doing so. 'Twas a perfunctory instrument indeed, with a little bag beneath which seemed to contain two small, soft stones, tender to the touch for Frank expressed pain when I pressed one to see how hard it was.

As I continued to press this bag with my hand, I saw his tool begin to swell, and as I drew back the skin at its top to examine the tiny hole there, it grew still more. Then I felt Frank's hand creeping beneath my skirts, and he ask'd whether 'twould not be reasonable that he should examine me in similar fashion. Nothing loath, I threw off my clothes and we lay naked upon the bed, head to tail. By now his tool was of truly surprising size, and bore little resemblance to what it had been before. So large was it, indeed, that the bag beneath was for want of skin drawn up tight at the root which, I felt, ran firmly behind it to the very fundament.

The limb which I now saw was white and smooth, firm to the touch as he had said, though as I passed my hand up its length I could feel the skin move upon it as if 'twere an ivory column clad in velvet. At the top it swelled out, the skin stretched, it seemed, to breaking point – though when I pulled it back it slipped over the rounded edge to lie below it, revealing a bulb brightly pink, the skin caught up at one point to its head, just behind the small aperture which gaped there.

It was clear that Frank derived the utmost enjoyment from this instrument's being caressed and smoothed; at the same time I was conscious of some pleasure derived from his explorations of my lower parts which, at that age, I had scarcely myself explored, but now found not ill-conceived for sensual enjoyment, though as he endeavoured to thrust his thumb within my most intimate part I felt a pang of pain as it encountered some obstruction. But he did not persist, for I was now making with my hands the motion I had seen Andy employ, with a view to producing the flow of milk, and indeed within a short time, as my brother panted, his chest rising and falling as though he was a-running, I felt the instrument leap between my fingers, and a copious flow spurted from the aperture, falling upon both our bodies. Consumed with interest, I took a drop upon my finger and conveyed it to my mouth, but it had by no means the taste even of milk, much less of cream, but merely of a slight saltiness.

This, as the reader may guess, was by no means the last time that Frank and I met to explore our bodies and to begin to tune them to that appreciation of pleasure which became to both of us a great – though secret – satisfaction. At night, he and Andy shared the bed and Frank kept our secret, though, he said, Andy had wondered at his being disinclined so often now for the pleasures they had previously enjoyed. 'Twas because during the day we had entertained ourselves, either in one of the attics of the house or, in summer, in some corner of the woods where there was little chance of discovery, though on one occasion our father passed just behind the bush where we were lying, naked and in a sweat doubled by a pleasurable fear of discovery!

The reader who may exclaim at my shamelessly relating such incestuous pleasures must remember that we had no means of knowing either that such joys were to be condemned, or indeed that it was uncommon for a boy and girl to explore each other without restriction. Indeed, I am told that there are few families in which such pleasure has not formed a part of the childhood of siblings, though the schools have recently taken to discouraging them as dangerous no less to morals than to the health of families where offspring result from early and illicit unions.

But to return to that first scene of delight, 'twas not long before Frank, tiring of simply testing with his fingers that aperture which he found so interesting, suggested that a larger instrument might enjoy exploring it. This was a surprising proposal, for it had never occurred to me that such a thing could be managed, nor, I dare swear, to Frank (though later I found that a book which he had found in our father's library had given him the notion). And so it was that on one afternoon I felt that best part of man make its way, not without pain, into that part made for its reception. Frank was struck with fear at the blood which he drew from my body but after the first fright of it, I was soon able to assure him that the concomitant pleasure was entirely superior to the slight discomfort, and our enjoyment of each other became complete – so naturally so that we completely lacked the clumsiness which I have marked in older lovers whose inhibition inhibits pleasure.

Indeed, so accustomed were we soon to the pleasures of love that 'twas not long ere we aimed to increase them by other play. This included the imitation of adults, Frank dressing up in our father's coats and myself in our mother's clothes, until I expressed the desire to see what sort of girl he would make. At this, without demur, he placed one of our mother's gowns upon him, the brownness of his shoulders looking most strange, but not stranger than the thing which stood out under the gown below his waist, like a barber's pole upon which someone had hanged a drapery! Meanwhile, I tried waistcoats, shirts, top-coats – anything above the waist, for Frank was insistent that my lower parts should always be open to his enjoyment, nor did I demur.

So we were enjoying ourselves in the great bedroom one Sunday morning, I sitting astride him and riding him like a horse – a sufficiently strange occupation for a lieutenant in the Navy (for it was brother Spencer's coat that I wore) – gripping his slender waist between by knees while riding upon his tool as 'twere a broomstick when, hearing a noise from the doorway and looking round, I discovered Andy whom we had thought to be safely at church.

To cut the tails of the story short, Frank invited our brother to enjoy us and he was not slow to do so. Nor was I dismayed, for he was a kindly and dear fellow, and apart from that I was curious to see whether all men were similarly fashioned. As – I should assure my less experienced sisters – is not the case; Andy's tool was thinner and longer than Frank's, with a darker coat and a cluster of almost black hair about its root, while Frank's was almost ginger. Neither colour had much similarity to the hair upon their heads and was, moreover, liker to wires than to flax.

No time was spent in mutual exploration for, throwing me upon my back without ceremony, Frank drew my thighs apart and directed Andy immediately to the seat of pleasure, whereupon he set himself to it like as the end of the world might come before he could experience the joys of love. And it would have had to come quickly, for almost as soon as he entered me, and I felt or seemed to feel the end of his instrument knock truly at the seat of my belly – so long it was – I felt his cheeks quiver beneath my hands and within me distinguished the first flood of his pleasure. Half pleased by the delight, half sorry for the speed of its accomplishment, he lay for a while unsmiling, but I had learned from Frank how to recover the small man to a great one and in a few minutes he was once more able to enter me, and this time our pleasure mounted slowly to its apogee. Frank, meanwhile, knelt at our side, and in a moment offered his staff to my mouth, an offer I accepted, as I always did in later life, with pleasure, its full smoothness lying upon my palate like a fruit.

'Twas as we were at our pleasures that I heard the door open, and a shriek announce the appearance of my mother, who ordered Frank and me immediately from the room. The servants later told me that they saw Andy walk from the house, dismissed, it seems, by my father, to whom my mother no doubt confided her disapprobation of his actions. My brother himself, it was announced, was to be sent to Oxford to continue his education until some occupation could be found for him, for Spencer was the only one of us who could count on an income sufficient for him to live upon, should he not achieve rank at sea. And as for me, my father summoned me to the library that same evening and announced that I was to be married.

Chapter Three

The Adventures of Andy

For some hours I walked through well-loved lanes without determining whither to direct my way. Then I found myself in unfamiliar countryside and before long came upon a main road leading, as far as I could guess, to the north. Growing up in the countryside around my native village I had had no cause to travel further from it than the house and, established there, than the walls of Sir Franklin's estate for on the rare occasions when he or his wife travelled abroad (which was not often) I was never one of the party.

But now the darkness began to close and, already beginning to be hungry, I made for myself a hole in the hedge where I curled up, and nursing my growling innards as best I might, eventually fell into a sleep made the deeper by the excitements and confusions of the day.

It was broad daylight when I awoke – not from the sun striking, as it did, upon my face, but by the sound of the rumbling wheels of a cart, and the noise of a rough song:

> *These London wenches are so stout*
> *They care not what they do;*
> *They will not let you have a bout*
> *Without a crown or two.*
>
> *They double their chops and curl their locks*
> *Their breaths perfume they do;*
> *Their tails are peppered with the pox,*
> *And that you're welcome to.*

Without losing a moment I broke from my warm burrow onto the road, sufficiently startling the plodding horse to bring it momentarily to a halt, its great head nodding, and the song broke off. 'Twas a cart laden high with a great quantity of logs and driven by a great hulk of a man, rough red hair sprouting from his head, his chin covered with several days' growth of beard, and wearing the clothes of a man who paid more attention to the contents of his belly than wherewith he covered it.

'Well, princox!' he cried. 'And what do you do, leaping out upon a fellow like some box-jack on a summer's morning?'

I bade him good day, and begged he would give me a ride to some town where I could buy a crust of bread. I made a more presentable figure than himself, for I had been allowed to dress in those clothes of Master Spencer's which had been passed to me in course, during the past few years, and though these were somewhat threadbare they at least gave me the appearance of worn gentility.

The carter was puzzled. My appearance, and even my speech (for, correcting this, Lady Franklyn and Mr Ffloyd between them had succeeded in giving me an intonation not unlike that of a gentleman) were cultivated. Yet here had I leaped from a hedge in which, from the sticky buds adhering to my clothes and the grasses stuck about me, I had clearly spent the night.

However, 'Ay, and welcome,' he said, whereat I climbed up beside him and, he clipping his horse with a switch, we set off to a new verse of his song:

> *Give me the buxom country lass*
> *Hot piping from the cow,*
> *She'll take a touch upon the grass,*
> *Ay, marry, and thank you too!*

> *Her colour's fresh as a rose in June,*
> *Her temper as kind as a dove,*
> *She'll please the swain with a wholesome tune,*
> *And freely give her love.*

After which he fell silent, and reaching into a bag at his

side fetched out a crust of bread and some cheese, broke a piece off and offered it to me. It vanished very quickly, for at the very sight of it my belly, which I had managed to quieten by dint of not thinking of it, set up a clamour which was not to be denied.

On the carter's questioning me, I admitted that I was a servant who had left employ.

'And suddenly, I'll warrant!' he cried. 'I thought you were a natty lad and no bumpkin. Your master caught you a-bilking, no doubt!'

When I had got from him the meaning of his words, which might as well have been spoken in French for all I knew, I assured him that I was no thief, nor had I stolen the clothes I had about me (nor the money, though that I did not mention), and on his questioning me further I admitted to him that I had been dismissed for over-familiarity with the daughter of the house, though to what degree I did not confess. On hearing Sir Franklin's name he cursed for, he said, that man had made a friend of his, a walking poulterer, dance at the sheriff's ball – which I learned was to be hanged, and that a walking poulterer was a fellow who stole chickens from one man to sell them to his neighbour. (But I shall give no more examples of his strange language, which was that, I soon learned, of a city man, he having left London a few years before to live in the country, where he made a living by carrying goods, of whatever kind, from place to place.)

In relating my history – or such portions of it as I deemed fit to convey – I had neglected to discover whence my inter-locator was directing his journey, which he volunteered to be the city of Cambridge, where he hoped to gather some trade at the summer fair. He was content to carry me there on condition that I helped him to unload his logs at Rawby Hall, some miles to the south of the city, where he was to deliver them. The Earl of Rawby, he explained, was so proud of his estate that he would have no timber felled within its walls and the fallen branches were insufficient for the use of a huge household.

The size of the estate soon became plain for we followed a

great wall for five or six miles before reaching tall iron gates wrought in fantastic shapes, between two pillars atop which stood carvings of two strange monsters, each belaboured by the club of a naked Hercules. A shrill whistle from the carter brought a liveried gateman to open to us and we turned into a long, straight avenue of elms which ran for what must have been at least a mile towards the Hall. As we drove up, my friend enlightened me about its owner, the third Earl of Rawby, a widower of some half-a-century in age who lived there with his two daughters. Rawby dedicated himself entirely to the life of the Hall – not only to country pursuits (being a great hunter) but to entertaining the nobility and gentry of the country at feasts, routs and balls over which his daughters, though yet young, presided. It was rarely, I learned, that there were less than thirty guests about the house, either in winter or summer, and a great number of servants, both resident and visiting.

It was at that moment, as we came in sight of the house itself, that I decided to try for employment there; I had no taste for poverty, and if my life had recently been pleasant enough, surely so grand a house as this would offer even greater luxury? For it was a fine place indeed; as we took a path leading around the side of the building, I glimpsed through the trees wide smooth lawns before the main entrance, the dew yet on them, and the front of the house itself, perhaps fifty yards across, with tall windows reflecting the slanting, early rays of the sun, and a great double staircase curving up to the front door.

Soon we rattled over cobbles into a yard where – unlike the front of the house, where no-one stirred – all was bustle: maids drawing water, carrying pails, scouring cauldrons and pans, men with baskets of produce, three old women plucking birds in a flurry of feathers in a corner . . .

Without exchanging a word with anyone, my friend backed the cart up to an open shed door and, leaping to the ground, threw down the back flap of the cart.

'Come, young put!' he called. 'And let's see the size of your muscles!'

Meaning to impress, I jumped to it, and we were both

soon at work throwing the logs onto a pile already lying in the shed. In twenty minutes all was done and the carter wiping his brow with the back of a hand, for though the chill was scarcely off the day, we were both in a muck of sweat. He beckoned me to the back door and in the scullery a buxom maid brought us a full tankard of ale, which we made short work of. Through the open door of the kitchen I took an idea of how great the house might be, for it was much larger than the one at Alcovary; here was an enormous fireplace where, though now only a small flame flickered on a bed of ash, there must be a great fire when time came for cooking meats, and before it was what I had never seen: a spit for turning a roast. When first I saw it I doubted its purpose, for at our house meat was cooked simply by placing on a grid near the fire. Then over the fire hung a huge kettle for the provision of hot water, and at the side a great cauldron for boiling meat. From the ovens came a smell of baking bread, the night-fire having been sufficient for that purpose. As we drained, the scullery fell quiet and looking round I saw a tall, bustling woman had entered. Skinny and sharp-faced, and with the manner of one who would brook no nonsense, she was calling for one Ellen.

'She be gone to village, Mrs Tickert, for the redcurrants for the jelly, Mrs Munce having sent only seven pound when ten pound was asked.'

'Right, girl, right! But there's milady's salon not yet cleaned. Find Tabitha and turn her onto that, and – who's this gawping boy?'

Realising that she could only be referring to me, I drew myself up and made my best bow.

'Forgive me, ma'am,' I said, 'I hope not to incommode you,' and gave her a smile, though she looked unlikely to be softened by it. However, she paused for a moment, and then nodded.

'Ah,' she said, 'Mr Caldwell's offering, no doubt. You start this morning?'

She must have seen that I was oblivious to her meaning for 'Is the boy foolish?' she asked anyone who cared to answer. 'Has he no brains in his noddle?'

'I'm sorry, ma'am,' I said, 'but I know not . . .'

At which I was interrupted by a great lubberly fellow who burst in through the door and knocked over a chair upon which someone had set down a bowl of hot water in which some eggs were poaching. The china splintered on the pavings, half-cooked eggs smashed and curdled on the floor, and the boy hopped as some scalding water splashed his legs.

'Hor! Hor!' he cried, and Mrs Tickert threw up her hands in horror.

'Out! Out!' she cried. 'Lummux, silly, nazy, stupid damber!'

'But Missus – Master Caldwell sent me, I was to ask for 'ee . . .'

Standing not on ceremony, Mrs Tickert seized a broom from one of the girls and made to stab him with it, whereon he rapidly ran from the room. Meanwhile, I had taken a wooden trug and was on my knees piling the broken china into it while a giggling maid wiped up the water. As I straightened up Mrs Tickert, panting slightly, handed me the broom.

'So where have you sprung from, if not from Mr Caldwell?' she said. 'No, I've no time to hear endless tales,' (as I opened my mouth to tell her). 'Anyway, he could not think such a lubberly fellow as that could suit! But how did you hear I wanted a man?'

The maid at my side scarcely repressed a giggle, but at a glance from Mrs Tickert ran immediately from the room.

'Well, boy?'

'Ma'am, I am at a disadvantage,' I said, 'I know not . . .'

'You mean you are not come for a footman's place?'

'Ma'am, I was not aware,' I said, 'but the truth is that I have some experience . . .'

'Well, you look pretty enough,' she said, 'and what I can't teach you, Mr Caister will. Fifteen pound a year, and you'd better go and see about your uniform.' Whereat she swept from the room.

My carter friend, who had been making himself insignificant in a corner, came forward and took me by the hand.

'Well, rascal,' he said, 'you've tumbled upon your feet. You'll not get rich here, but there's plenty of food and plenty of ale, and if you've served Lord Rawby you'll be fit to serve any man in the country!' At which he said farewell – without my having so much as learned his name – and left me to myself. The maid who had witnessed the scene was still hanging by the doorway, and still giggling, and I learned from her that I had stepped into a place of footman, one of six in the house, that Mr Caister was the butler, and that it was to him I must apply for my livery.

She conducted me from the scullery through the kitchen and along a passage to a small, dark room where I found Mr Caister, a short, dark man in rusty black, who dismissed the maid.

'Mmmm – where do you – mm – spring from – mm – boy?' he stammered. 'Mm – mm – Mr Caldwell sent you?'

I explained that Mrs Tickert had engaged me upon sight, and said that I had formerly served in the house of Sir Franklin Franklyn ('Mm – never – mm – heard of him!' was the ungracious response), and that I had been sent to be fitted with my livery.

He nodded somewhat grudgingly, and went to a door in the corner of the room, which led into a small room or large cupboard where enough livery hung on rails to dress, as I thought, the whole of Hertfordshire. From one of a number, having eyed me shrewdly, he took a handsome livery comprising breeches of strong, grey cloth and a black coat trimmed with silver braid.

'Throw – mm – this on,' he said, and watched me with what seemed uncommon interest as I removed Mr Spencer's breeches and pulled on the others.

'Ay, not a – mm – whit too tight,' said Mr Caister, and passed his hand over my thigh. 'They do not pinch your – mm – privities?'

Nay, I assured him, they were a perfect fit. The coat too hung well from my shoulders. He then pulled a line, and a distant bell brought a boy of my own age to the door. 'Tom,' he said, 'this is . . .'

'Andrew,' I told him.

'Andrew. Before the house is about, take and show him the ground. And you,' he turned to me, 'you know your duties?'

'I do,' I said with confidence. If I could not copy my fellows closely enough to pass muster, I was less sharp than I thought myself. Mr Caister waved his hand, and Tom led the way from the room and turned to go up the stone steps which led to the main floor of the house.

I cannot swear that I was much the better off after Tom's speedy tour of the Hall than before it, for – as though I stood still and saw a vision – there sped past me a number of great rooms each of which seemed to be the size of the whole of Alcovary House. First, at the top of the stairs and so within easiest reach of the kitchen, was a great dining-room with a long table which appeared to me to stretch to infinity. Beyond it lay a long gallery with paintings and sculptures so prolific that they peopled the empty room in a crowd. Through a door and along a corridor, Tom indicated, were the dressing rooms and sleeping apartments of the two daughters of the house, Lady Elizabeth and Lady Margaret – 'Still abed, I'll warrant, and no knowing in whose company!' he winked.

Turning, he retraced his steps through the gallery and the great hall within the main doors of the house, beyond which a fine circular room rose to a splendid dome. Beyond this again, a saloon gave onto a spacious drawing-room which looked over a pleasant courtyard, covered to my astonishment with glass and decorated with strange plants the like of which I had never seen (brought, Tom told me, from countries over the seas). Across the courtyard he pointed out the windows of My Lord's bedroom. Next the drawing-room was a smaller anteroom (as he called it) and beyond this a range of guest bedrooms and dressing rooms, including a state bedroom only used when royalty stayed at the house ('Prinny came four years ago,' he said; I knew enough to recognise that he meant our Prince Regent, always spoken of at Alcovary with the greatest respect, but here as I was to find regarded by My Lord and his fellows as a creature only fit for jokes and scorn).

Briefly, he showed me the chapel, sombre with dark wood panels, gold gleaming dully from the altar, then led me by another stair down towards the kitchen again, but half-way down, opposite the laundry (from which I heard a splashing and girls' laughter) was a most curious compartment: a door led to four steps which descended into a great stone pit with a contrivance like a four-legged stool hoisted above it and the pit was filled with water. Tom, seeing my amazement, proudly said that it was a bath and that when the men of the house had been a-hunting, and returned muddied, they made their way here to wash themselves, while onto the high legs of the machine a pail was hoist containing hot water which, by use of a string, was released through the bottom of the bucket to shower upon the man standing beneath. This had only been installed for a year, and when it was first placed the mistake had been made of placing boiling water in the pail and badly scalding the inventor, Mr Standing of Cambridge, who personally demonstrated it to My Lord.

By now it was almost ten o'clock and Tom hastened me to the kitchen, for it would be time to serve My Lord and his guests, who were going a-hunting and therefore would be eating large. 'Twas late in the season, I protested; Sir Franklin never allowed hunting over his land after the end of April. At which Tom scoffed, and said My Lord was a law to himself, and let Sir Franklin do what he might, at Rawby when the Earl wished to hunt, he hunted. This year he had started late, having been on envoy to the Low Countries, so he had decreed the season extended until the middle of May. And so food was today required early – usually a draft of ale sufficed to break fast, when nothing was eaten until dinner at three in the afternoon. Today there would be simple food to send them out with their bellies full: twenty rabbits or so, some joints of pork, pigeon pie, and of course ale from My Lord's own cellars.

The kitchen was by now all a-bustle; a fire was blazing and the smell of roasting and boiling flesh rose to us as we entered. The two cooks were contending at the table, the girls preparing platters and setting out meats, and two other footmen whom I had not yet met were bringing the ale from the cellars in great wooden vessels and placing them on trays with tankards ready.

Careful to imitate the others, I served the breakfast easily enough. And if I had wondered whether I would be noticed, I need have had no concern, for My Lord and his fellows had no interest save in their food and drink and their plans for the day – though there was not much talk, and I perceived that several of them suffered from the distemper of too much wine the night before, which was now followed with a great quantity of ale to cure the sickness. My Lord finally rose, a great, fat man with a stomach upon him like a pregnant ewe, and an old-fashioned curled wig which he wore (Tom said) to disguise a bald head upon which there was a great purple disfiguring mark he had had all his days, and was jealously secretive of. Therefore he did not take to the new habit of wearing his own hair, having none to boast of.

'Come ye,' he said, 'we start for Poulton's Brake, and if we don't find there, over towards Baldock. Haddon' (addressing a small, thin man next him at table) 'if ye'r head stay upon ye'r shoulders this morning, it won't be for want of all ye'r efforts last night!'

At which Mr Haddon nodded carefully, as if indeed his noddle might fall into the greasy dish of boiled rabbit he had been cautiously addressing. Then 'Here come the cattle!' said My Lord, and the party all rose and made for the door. Looking out of the window from where I stood against the wall with my five fellows, I had seen a procession of beautiful horses making its way across the grass from a spinney beyond which some gates announced the stables, and in a few minutes the party was mounted, and followed My Lord towards the drive and out of sight.

The rest of the morning was spent clearing the dishes and doing the work of the house which, at midday, included Tom and I carrying two great baskets of bedclothes to the laundry-room, which entering without ceremony we found three girls – one of whom I had seen already in the kitchen – all in steam, pounding at the linen in two great tubs. It being a warm day, the water hot and the effort great, they had stripped to their shifts which consisted of little but loose gowns hanging from their shoulders, and as Tom and I tipped the dry clothes to join the others in the wash, it took but little contrivance for him to slip the thin ties from the shoulders of one of the girls so her shift fell to her waist, disclosing a fine pair of bubs which she made no effort to conceal, but gave Tom a push which sent him reeling backwards into the other two, who laughed with a will.

'Now, Tabby!' cried he. 'Don't show your temper before young Andy – he'll think the worse of you.'

Unblushing, she looked at me, her fine eyes alive with fun.

'And who's Andy when he's at play?'

'Well, now, hasn't he been gifted to us from a great house in the neighbour county, where he got the mistress and her seventeen daughters all with child, and him not yet fourteen!'

The three girls fell anew into giggling, whereupon Tom took his advantage and coming up behind Tabby grasped a breast in one hand while with the other he raised her shift, showing a long white leg which reminded me strongly of the pleasures I had enjoyed with Sophia.

'See, his young eyes are walking up your thigh! Lock your door tonight, little Tabby, 'gainst all save your Tom!'

Tabby leaned back against him and gave him a quick kiss, while he gently tweaked the brown nipple of her breast, and his other hand was at what work I knew not.

Later, while the ladies' maids were caring for their mistresses, upon which I had not yet set my eyes, Tom and I sat with Tabby and Ellen in the sun in the yard enjoying a pot of ale, a crust and some cheese. The other footmen, being older than the two of us – one in his forties, one about thirty, and two I guessed in their middle twenties – were at dice elsewhere. I now learned more about the house. Mrs Tickert's bark was less than her bite; Mr Caister's hand would certainly sooner or later make its way into my breeches (but, said Tom, he was an impotent old man, and what harm? – moreover, he had the provision of ale below stairs); and if I wished to dip my gingambobs, Tabby was the girl for me (at which she fetched Tom a great blow upon the side of his head, wherefore he kissed her soundly).

Meanwhile, Ellen, much quieter than her friend, was silent. She was slimmer and darker, somewhat chicken-breasted. Or so I guessed, for she was modester than Tabby and kept her dress carefully gathered to her neck, while Tabby made no god of decorum and if a titty happened to fall from her bodice, only replaced it when she had first completed what task she was at whether finishing an apple or draining a tankard. While she had laughed with the others at the riot in the laundry-room, I believed Ellen to be less ready than her friend to be a bawd or play at rantum-scantum. Which apprehension was sharpened by the blush which came to her cheeks when Tom rallied her and said that she had surely shared a bed with Tabby long enough to have learned what her madge was for, but he, being a kindly fellow, did not press her but turned again to rallying with Tabby.

Then came the noise of the horses' hooves on the gravel, and we had to run to the bath room with water, for the men would be there directly, Tom said – as indeed was true, for no sooner had we got there and hoisted the first bucket to the top of the stand, than the bath was filled with half a dozen naked fellows of all sizes, pummelling each other, thrusting each other's heads below the water and bellowing for soap (of which there was great quantity, made from goat's tallow boiled with wood ashes in the kitchens). Rushing to and fro, I had no time to think about anything other than minding the stairs while carrying the hot water and had scarcely noticed that not only were Tom and I busy, but that the two girls also were engaged, and in the room with all the naked men were with brushes attending to their backs as they stood beneath the shower.

Finally, when only two men were left, I had time to stand for a while and saw that both Tabby and Ellen were soaked with the water, their shifts sticking to their bodies so they appeared just as though they were naked – a fact which clearly delighted one of the two men, though the other –

who was none other than Mr Haddon, whose head had not
it seemed been much cleared by his gallop – took no more
notice of them than, I suppose, of his horse. But his
companion, a large-boned man in his forties with a great
thrusting of black hairs upon his chest, did not hesitate to
show his admiration of the girls in the standing of his sugar
stick, which rose like a great shaft from below his belly. Far
from wishing to conceal this, he rather brandished it like
some proud marshal's baton.

When he grasped at Tabby and fumbled her, she showed
no distress, though Tom, near me, looked as though he was
face to face with Bonaparte himself, and would be happy to
dispatch him. Then Mr Haddon passing to leave the bath,
the other fellow was forced to let Tabby go while she lifted a
towel and handed it to his companion, and she going with
Haddon to open the door for him, he turned to Ellen. Seeing that she shrank from him, he lifted his hand and with
one stroke tore her shift from her. She coloured, and one
hand went to her small breasts, while the other sheltered her
man trap – at which he took her by the arms and stretched
them wide, so that she was open to his view.

I, who had never seen a man act so with a woman, made
to move towards them but felt Tom's hand on my arm, and
he shook his head. So I stood while the fellow, cursing
because she was not forthcoming, pressed her against the
side of the bath and then placing his hands upon her shoulders, forced her down until he could press his tool to her
face and force it between her unwilling lips, then thrusting
with his great bottom until, in a short time, such was his
excitement, he shouted in pleasure and drew away, while
she scooped water with her hands to wash her face and
mouth.

'Next time, girl, be willing – 'twill be more pleasant!
More water, there!' – turning to us.

We went to fetch more water, Tom explaining as we did
so that the fellow was Sir Walter Flount, a merchant of
immense riches, from whom My Lord had from time to
time borrowed much money, and who therefore was free of
the house though admired by none. Tom was then

summoned by Mrs Tickert, and I was left alone to take the water to the bath room, where Ellen stood silently, with her eyes full of tears, in a corner. I hoisted the water, and she stood to control the flow as Flount lifted his fat self from the water to stand beneath it, the water coursing over his fleshy shoulders and breasts like a woman beneath the veil of hair, then over his belly to where his lobcock now swung heavily.

I left them alone, taking the soap with me (for, I thought, it was a valuable commodity that deserved husbanding). How it came that a piece of it fell to the step outside the bath room is a mystery. However, it cannot be denied that it must have been through my carelessness that one of Sir Walter's bare feet came upon it as he left the bath, when sadly his arms were too wrapped in the towel which Ellen had folded about him for him to be able to save himself from falling down the ten stone steps to the floor of the kitchen passage, where his roars brought most of the servants to his assistance. He was carried cursing to his room and a surgeon sent for, who declared a leg to be broke. The screams as it was laid between two boards and bound reached the ears of Lady Elizabeth and Lady Margaret in their rooms, who sent to enquire the reason for the noise. Mr Caister despatched to explain the happenings and returned to order me to go to their Ladyships' rooms, for they wished to see me.

Chapter Four

Sophie's Story

My father's announcement that I was to be married came upon me with the force of a thunderclap, for I had never heard of such a thing; as with Shakespeare's Juliet, it was an honour that I dreamed not of. But, he said, it was time I was coupled, and when I enquired to whom I was to be shackled, he was mysterious, and said only that I should hear of it soon enough.

I could not console myself with Frank, for he had been locked in a room at the top of the house, the only way to which lay through my father's bedroom, which itself was locked. And I had not seen Spencer since our discovery, nor did I feel he would be sympathetic, for he had latterly seemed to disapprove of Frank's and my closer friendship with Andy. So I went to my bed, and there cried myself to early sleep only to wake in the dark night and lie thinking of my fate. Would my husband be a handsome fellow? That seemed the last thing my father would consider, money above all, and rank next, being the two first. The pleasures I had enjoyed with Frank and brother Andy had given me a taste the flavour of which was still with me, and as I felt my person it still seemed warm with the delightful friction of the afternoon. I began to think I could reconcile myself to any husband possessed of sufficient spirit, and that with one such perhaps after all life would not end within the next month.

But then a strange something stirred in the black air around me, something between a smell, a taste and a sound, and after a while concluding it was the latter, I stole from bed, and opening my door felt my way to the stairway. As I went the sound became clearer, and recognisable: it was the harpsichord in the drawing-room, upon which someone was playing Mr Tomkins' *What if a day*. Its melancholy words fell into my mind as I listened:

> *What if a day, or a month, or a year*
> *Crown thy delights with a thousand sweet contentings?*
> *Cannot a chance of a night or an hour*
> *Cross thy desires with as many sad tormentings?*
> *Wanton pleasures, doting love,*
> *Are but shadows flying.*
> *All our joys*
> *Are but toys . . .'*

It could only be Mr Ffloyd, for no one else in the house save himself and me ever touched the instrument on which I had so often heard him play the same piece. Stumbling in the dark, I made my way to the door, outlined by a dim light, and stole through. At first, he did not see me, sitting at the keyboard with a single candle set upon it illuminating his long face as he played. But as I approached, with a great start he descried my presence and stopped playing. Once near him, I saw that there was a tear upon his cheek and asked the reason, whereupon he said that he had been dismissed that day, since neither I nor Frank would be more in need of a tutor.

'Are you then so sorry to leave us?'

'To leave *you*, Miss Sophie,' he then said, falling upon his knees before me, 'for you must know that of all ladies you are the sweetest!'

Amazed, for I had never suspected these feelings in him, I stepped forward, whereupon he threw his arms about my waist and held his head to my breast. I had not thought to put on my day-dress, and was wearing only my smock of best thin cotton, and his arms being about me, his hands fell upon my lower parts, the warmth of his palms being so pleasant that I could not help responding to it by taking his head in my hands and pressing it to my bosom. The ardent emotion of his whole body, indeed, now communicated itself to me – he seemed to be almost in a fever, and to discover whether his skin was burning to excess I placed my hands inside his shirt, at the back, where it hung loosely from the collar, and felt his shoulders. They were pleasantly warm, but not to my relief morbidly so. Yet my action had a powerful effect upon him, for he immediately rose to his feet, drew me yet closer to him, and placing his lips upon mine made as though to suck my soul out through them.

It was the first real kiss I had experienced, for neither Frank nor Andy had shown any wish to use their lips except upon those other parts where pleasure lies. I was amazed at the pleasure which flowed from Mr Ffloyd's lips and felt a new excitement when his tongue slid, limber and liquid, into my mouth, playing upon my own, running upon my teeth and the inside of my cheeks.

By now we had sunk to the floor, and I felt his hand lift my smock to draw it to my waist. I pushed it away and standing lifted the garment over my head and dropped it at my side. His face was a study of mingled delight and surprise as he looked up at me, then raised himself to place his hands upon my hips and plant a kiss upon my nether lips. Bending, I seized his shirt and lifted it over his head, while he loosened his breeches and drew them off.

He was eager to be at play but I reached and took the candle from the harpsichord and held it so I could see his body – the first of a grown man upon which I had set eyes, my brothers being mere boys. I felt immediately the difference between youth and maturity: the limbs were altogether firmer and stronger, though by no means hardened by toil; upon his breast fine hairs grew in a dark mat, not thick enough to hide the fine shape of that manly platform, but as a garnish upon a delicious dish, and below in fan-shape tapered down his small belly to grow in more profusion where his handsome instrument stood ready to hand, set between two fine thighs, themselves fluffed with hair like the haunches of a brave young animal.

Seeing my admiration, he lay for a moment and let me look, then impatience overcoming him gently took the candle from my quivering hand and set it down at our side, and turning me upon my back began an exploration of my body – not like a squirrel examining a nut (whose curious innocence Frank and Andy had counterfeited) but like a groom attending to a fine steed, trying each part for its excellence. I was soon all liquid with pleasure, and simply content to rest inanimate as his eyes devoured and his fingers played with me, until myself too impatient for further delay I drew him on top of me and felt with indescribable felicity his great part enter into me and move with a reposeful action like that of my maid when brushing my hair, then slowly increasing in speed and pressure until the sparks of delight were struck faster and faster, soon seeming to set light to my whole lower person, then of a sudden bursting into a flame which for a moment seemed to destroy me. My cries would have waked the house had not Mr Ffloyd had the foresight to place his hand over my mouth. He took it away to kiss me again but to my astonishment his movements, though again they had slowed, did not cease.

Now, though there was a certain soreness, the pleasure was of a different kind – a delightful tickling and general glow. I passed my hands over his naked shoulders and arms, down his back, hairless until it swelled to those two charming flexures, covered as it felt with a light down, and moving gently beneath my hands. Grasping these, I pulled them towards me, my hands slipping between, as I did so, to feel a growth of coarser hair. At this he gasped suddenly and began to move again with vigour, until once more I felt the keener pleasure mount and this time as it reached its apogee, I perceived him also to shudder with glee, and within me a warmth that indicated that he had spent that substance which seems to be the liquid core of man.

We lay together for some time, our bodies now so damp with sweat they seemed to be glued together, until lifting himself from me, he took his shirt and wiped my breasts and belly, and with tenderness near to tears kissed me upon the cheek and fixing his great dark eyes all the time upon me drew on his breeches and silently held my smock while I slid into it. Taking my hand then, and the candle, he led me to the door and stood at the bottom of the stairs, still without a word, holding the light high while I made my barefoot way up to my room.

At breakfast next morning I saw him pass the window, carrying his bags, and heard his footsteps upon the gravel path as he left. I opened my lips to speak, but a look from my father – whose single wish it was to keep his eyes upon me the whole of my waking hours – quietened me before I could do so.

I was instructed to ready myself for a journey by two o'clock, and nothing I could ask would elicit the reason, nor the destination. I still had no sight of Frank, nor did my mother appear. Though previously, when she discovered any naughtiness and reported it to our father she had always been ready to pacify me after any punishment he saw fit to inflict, now her absence was marked, and I could not understand it. When I asked my father whether I could not see her, his reply was simply a short 'No, madam, you may not!'

At two, my father led me from the house to where our horses were ready and we set out upon the highroad for some miles to the westward, where in due time we came to a small village on the outskirts of which was a large timbered house, set a little back from the road in the midst of a tangled thicket which had once been a garden. Here we dismounted and knocked upon the door, which was opened by a slatternly maidservant.

My father giving his name, we were ushered into what no doubt was called the parlour, but which was dirtier than any stable at Alcovary. The furnishings were poor and old-fashioned, the hangings threadbare and ancient, and a thick dust was thrown upon everything like a grey snow. I opened my mouth but a glance from my father silenced me before I could speak. Soon a shuffling was heard in the passage outside and, the door opening, a tall, thin man appeared, clad in old-fashioned dress, with thin grey hair atop a sallow face upon the left cheek of which was a great, hairy mole.

I stood and made a curtsy, whereupon he bent his back stiffly, as though it was not a custom with him to bow to anyone.

'Sir Franklin Franklyn?' he asked, and without waiting

for an answer approached and stretched out his hand to me. Reluctantly, I took it; it lay within my palm all bony and limp, as though the flesh had long gone.

'And Miss Sophia,' he said, and bowing pressed dry lips to the back of my hand.

'Mr Nelham,' said my father.

'Delighted, Sir Franklin, delighted,' said the old man – for 'old man' I considered him, yet he may not have been more than forty and five. 'I am most pleased that you should suddenly have acceded to my request. My dear,' (turning to me) 'we have not met, yet I have heard much of your beauty and accomplishments, and I trust our close acquaintance will bring us equal pleasure.'

Close acquaintance! I had clung to the hope that perhaps this man had a son, to whom I was to be married, but clearly he was to be my bridegroom. My senses shrank at the thought, and I turned to my father. He stood implacable and silent, and I knew no mercy was to be sought from him, or if sought was not to be granted.

'And may I ask when . . .?'

'The sooner the better,' said my father. 'Call the banns when you like!'

In short, it was arranged that we should be married three weeks the following Friday and without more ado, we left, the old man's eyes following my every movement with what I now suspected of being a lascivious pleasure. No sooner were we out of hearing than I appealed to my father with all the strength I possessed to free me from my fate, but he simply sat impassive on his horse looking neither to left nor right, and was indifferent to my pleas.

On returning to Alcovary, I lost no time in seeking out Frank, but sought in vain, for in my absence he had been sent from the house, whither, I could not discover, the servants either knowing nothing or having been so frightened they would not disclose it. That evening my mother joined us at the supper table but sat with lowered eyes and said nothing. Next day, I was able to speak with her alone, but all she would report was that my father was outraged at my behaviour with my brothers and had decided upon an immediate marriage as the best solution to the problem, 'for what,' she said, 'if you found yourself with child?'

Here was something which I had not thought of, for no one had explained to me that playing the beast with two backs could bring about the seeding of children; I do believe that somewhere an instinct connected the two events, but not from knowledge. Now, under pressure to explain, my mother revealed that the white substance that came from a man's tool contained the seed of a child, and that when it entered a woman's privy place, a baby sometimes grew from it.

What? I enquired. But surely it could not be that the penalty for a single night's pleasure could be so heavy?

Yes, replied my mother, all too often that was so – though not invariably, which I was glad to hear, for it was plain that either of my brothers or Mr Ffloyd could have seeded a child in me. Asked whether this could not be prevented, my mother (who now the subject was broached, became informative) said that while not every passage of love produced a child, it was possible to make the event less likely by the use of what she called a *cundum*, resembling a little hat or cape made of the gut of a sheep placed over the man's affair, when it was fully extended, to prevent the milk from being spent within her. Asking whether my father made use of such a machine, she replied blushingly that he did not, but that they had now no such connection. I did not enquire further but wondered that my mother at her age could have had a lover to show her such things.

The next three weeks only more firmly sealed my fate, for preparations for the marriage went ahead with or without my assistance. I could find little more about my husband, but that he was a respectable man and a great scholar, reputed also to have a great fortune, though of a miserly disposition. Nothing ill was known of him, though also I could discover nothing good. I caught my mother regarding me with pity, as I thought. My father displayed no emotion, but I soon ceased to appeal to him to release me from a bonding I had not sought nor could delight in.

The marriage was held before breakfast one morning at

the church just outside our gates. The Rev. Fumbling, whose living was in my father's gift, performed the ceremony – not without, I thought, some incredulous glances at the groom, who appeared in a creaking suit of finery which cannot have been less than twenty years of age and had clearly been well-used. Not that my own dress was to be spoken of, for nothing new had been contrived for me, my father setting his face against any public show. Present in the church were only myself and my ancient groom, my father and mother and the parson, together with an aged crone from the village as witness.

After the wedding, and without further ceremony, my husband and I mounted a small coach and made off upon the road to Cambridge, some two hours distant. The road was bad, with many holes, and before long I was sore and shaken. My husband comforted me by producing a packet containing some bread and meat, all dry and tasteless, and a flask of water, and suggesting that I sleep! From time to time we passed through small villages, and once by a pair of splendid park gates through which I caught a glimpse of a long avenue of elms leading to a distant house. But of interesting conversation we had none, let alone endearments one might have thought natural between a new-married couple – for which, however, I was grateful, for the thought of being fumbled by those dry, bony hands was abhorrent to me. My husband throughout the journey buried his head in a book, only raising it as we rattled into Cambridge city – a sight interesting to me, who had never before seen even a large town.

We drew into the yard of the Red Lion Inn, at the very centre (as it seemed) of the city. Galleries ran around its sides, upon which maids were hanging linen to air, boys were rushing hither and thither on errands only they knew the details of, and I was handed out of the coach by a handsome fellow with the air of a host, who also greeted Mr Nelham with respect.

We were shown to the first floor, to a fine sitting-room and bedroom with a great four-poster and furnishings of the first order, my husband taking little notice of me or my small baggage, but continually warning the servants to take care of the bundles of books which were unloaded from the back of the coach. These were placed all anyhow about the floor, quite spoiling the appearance of the room, but I did not know how to protest, nor how to ask whether we could not eat, for after the journey I was sorely in need of sustenance.

Happily Mr Nelham, having assured himself that all his belongings were now brought up, ordered the servant to bring 'some food', and when asked what he required merely answered that it mattered not so long as it was palatable!

While waiting for the food I went into the bedroom and, removing my upper clothing, was wiping my body with some cool water that stood there when without ceremony the door opened and Mr Nelham appeared. I clutched the cloth to me, being unhappy that he should find me unclothed and think it an invitation to that love-making which I was not eager for. But he simply walked to the bed and picked up a book which lay there, returning with scarce a glance at me to the outer room – which gladdened me, but I was surprised that he should have shown no interest in the goods he had so recently acquired.

In some minutes, a boy came with new baked bread, some cheese and a dish of coffee, to which we sat, Mr Nelham only complaining at the expense of coffee when a dish of milk (he said) would have been sufficient. After which, he took his leave without announcing when he would return, and left me.

Recovered now from the journey I was anxious to see the town, and shortly set out to walk the streets, which were crowded with a great variety of people of every class including high-spirited young men dressed in knee-breeches and white stockings, whom I took to be students. I walked, and walked, interested by all the sights and sounds, the traders crying their wares and the people buying them, the serving women about their business and the gentle folk simply walking, it seemed, for pleasure – especially upon the paths by the swan-full river lying below some of the wonderfully handsome college buildings which I now saw for the first time.

Returning to the inn, I found that dinner was under way and since there was no sign of Mr Nelham, sat down to boiled and baked meats, pies, tarts and dishes of fruit and sweetmeats and a good bottle of Madeira, after which I lay upon the bed and fell into a sleep from which I awoke only with the return of my husband, who announced that he had taken rooms in a house by Trinity College, in whose library he had much work to do. He then settled once more to his studies, having called for a servant to remove the remains of my meal, upon which he seemed to look with disfavour.

It was a wearisome afternoon, for he did not stir and I did not like to move, not being wishful to fall out upon my first day as a wife. In due course came supper time, at which Mr Nelham ordered up merely a dish of soup and a piece of fish, which he ate in the old-fashioned way with his fingers (we had had forks at Alcovary, as long as I could remember) and washed down with ale.

Now was come the time I dreaded – bed time – and I retired first, undressing to my shift and creeping quietly between the sheets. Before long, Mr Nelham came, drew off his breeches, and in his shirt and drawers came also to bed. But he snuffed out the candle and fell immediately into a snoring sleep, while I lay awake feeling that though I did not wish for his attentions it was strange for a woman just that day married not to have knowledge of her husband, especially since she did not seem so undesirable that other men kept altogether clear of her.

After an hour of lying wakeful, I slipped from the bed and went into the next room for a drink of ale, which stood still in a tankard upon the table next the window. Outside, the inn yard was now empty and there was only some noise from a distant room where a party was still at eating and drinking. As I lifted the ale to my lips, I looked across the yard where a light stood in a room opposite and there into view strode a fine, naked fellow bearing a girl, similarly bare, in his arms, whom setting on her feet he kissed soundly, as she him, the candle-light flickering over their bodies in a warm glow and surrounding them with, as it were, a golden nimbus of light. As I looked, he slowly bent, or slid as it were down the length of her body, his head disappearing below the window as it declined to her waist.

She, throwing her head back, showed now all the signs of pleasure, her mouth open and her eyes sparkling while he was at that occupation I could only guess at. But as she threw back her shoulders and her breasts lifted in an ecstasy, the light beneath them bathing their full roundness in a rich aureate lustre, I could not help clutching myself to counterfeit the pleasure, and with the movements of my fingers bringing about a dim shadow of the joy I could see she experienced as she slowly sank towards her lover and out of my sight.

I took another swallow of ale, but it had now lost its savour. Disconsolate, I fumbled my way back to bed, and in time fell into uneasy slumber.

Next morning early we moved to the rooms Mr Nelham had taken and which proved no more handsome than I expected, cramped and dirty and ill-furnished as they were. I begged that at least I could have a maid to clean and serve, and he grudgingly agreed as long as she did not cost more than two shilling a week – to which the daughter of the house, Moll, agreed, being a slovenly creature but better than nothing, and I put her immediately to work to clear the rooms of some dirt, while I attempted to set out to best advantage the few comforts I had brought with me.

The bedroom looked out over the river and the end of the library where Mr Nelham evidently meant to spend most of his honeymoon. By ten o'clock – for we had risen at seven, and were installed by nine, at which time the library opened – a splashing revealed that just below our windows was a place where the students were wont to bathe when the weather was hot. I incautiously put my head out, and was rewarded by a display of naked young manhood in which I must admit to have taken some pleasure. Yet I was somewhat discomfited when I was seen, and far from modestly hiding themselves several of the boys (for they were of age between fifteen and twenty) grasped their persons and, as it were, offered them to me, whereat I was bound to laugh, but withdrew.

Having set the rooms to rights – or lifted them to as bare an elegance as I could command – I found myself each day with nothing to do except walk out and wait for Mr Nelham's return; this soon palled. Then out of curiosity one day I opened a book I noticed he carried always with him, and found it to be Mr William Lilly's *Christian Astrology*, published some one hundred and sixty-five years earlier and of some reputation. I had not previously looked into such matters but now with time at my hand speedily taught myself what was needful to command some scanty part of the subject, and was delighted to recognise its truth. For instance, the pictures of my father (that he was of the nature of the Sun, 'Arrogant and Proud, disdaining all men, cracking his Pedigree, Pur-blind in sight and judgment, troublesome, domineering, a mere vapour . . .') and of my dearest Frank (of Venus' nature, 'very fair Lovely Eyes, and a little black; a round face, and not large, fair Hair, smooth and plenty of it, and of a light brown colour, a lovely mouth and cherry lips, a Body very delightful, lovely and exceeding well shaped . . .') were nothing short of absolute portraits, so that I determined to study the subject fully, though without informing Mr Nelham of it – whom I soon discovered from the book came under dominance of Mercury. His looks were described there, most particularly his 'straight, thin spare body, high forehead and somewhat narrow, long face, long nose, thin lips and long arms', and his manner, 'his tongue and pen against every man' (as I soon discovered), 'wholly bent to fool his estate and time in prating and trying nice conclusions to no purpose.' But the final end, that he was 'given to wicked arts', I did not yet know, but was soon to discover, to my cost.

The discovery of his interest in the black arts came a week after we had set to live in our rooms, where he unexpectedly returned – having forgot a book – to find me looking from the bedroom window at the bathing students and exchanging a word or two with the more familiar of them. At this he first looked displeased, then sitting me down asked me whether I was not surprised that to that date he had not offered me the familiarity of a husband.

I admitted that I had wondered at it, whereupon he said

that it was to his purpose that I should remain virgin for the time, but that I should soon know why. Indeed he said that the coming weekend was to see what he described as my 'deflowering', at which I knew not whether to laugh or cry, not knowing the meaning of half the words he employed, but only guessing at them. But I maintained a solemn face, so he called me a good girl and left me. I heard nothing more until the Sunday following when in the evening, just as I thought of preparing for bed, he told me to dress, for we were going out.

In some confusion I put on my outer clothing and we descended to find a coach waiting, into which we climbed and rode for half an hour to a hill outside the city, indeed right into the country, for there was no light to suggest any human habitation when we got from the coach. In the light of a full moon which whitened the fields, my husband led the way across a field and into a wood whence we emerged eventually into a clearing. There in the moonlight stood perhaps a dozen men and some women, waiting – and waiting for Mr Nelham, so it seemed. He led me silently into the centre of the clearing, where was a grassy hummock or table, and nearby some vessels from which my husband sprinkled some substances – I knew not what – upon the ground, muttering beneath his breath as he did so.

At a signal from Mr Nelham, the dim figures gathered in a circle around the grassy mound, and I saw to my astonishment that they wore upon their heads masks formed like the faces of animals – foxes, dogs, a lion, a wolf . . . My husband led me to the hummock and, reaching out, to my astonishment not only threw my cloak from me, but began to remove my shift. I held to it but he insisted, and finally rent it in twain, so that I stood naked before the company, the cool air raising bumps upon my skin.

In silence, the circle closed. The four people nearest the altar threw their cloaks to the ground and were disclosed as handsome naked youths, who then began to embrace each other lasciviously while Mr Nelham, dropping his cloak, was revealed in what seemed to be a priest's cope – yet was strangely embroidered with serpents and with signs and symbols which were unknown to me. As he turned, I saw that beneath it he wore nothing, his thin body veiled only with sparse grey hairs. He laid me on the grassy mound, upon which I now saw to my horror stood a crooked cross, my face up to the full moon. I lay, shaking in every limb, while from my husband's lips fell a series of strange sentences in which I recognised Latin words, but in an order which seemed entirely without reason even to my small knowledge of the language. The congregation responded with grunts and animal howlings. Reaching behind him, Mr Nelham produced two black candles, one of which he placed in each of my hands, at which there was a positive shriek, and the animal-headed worshippers threw their cloaks to the ground, and nakedly embraced each other. Beside the altar the two pairs of boys were now at the game, two of them bent over with their hands resting near my head and my feet, while their companions, with wild moans of pleasure, held their hips and thrust into them from behind. Meanwhile Mr Nelham continued to recite his gibberish, then bowed himself to kiss between my legs. As he did so the watching figures drew apart and to my astonishment began to piss upon the ground, at the same time chanting Latin words which I recognised to my horror as Our Lord's Prayer, but said backwards. As it ended, my husband called forward a tall blindfold fellow in a cloak, which as he stood above me he threw back to disclose a magnificient figure, a great chest and arms above a slim waist, and a member so large as to make those few with which I was then familiar appear slender indeed (and to be truthful, in my subsequent experience, which has not been small – as the reader will discover – I have never seen a tool so great, being, it seemed, as thick as most men's wrists). Standing behind him, my husband placed his hands upon his shoulders – to which he could scarcely reach – and guided him (for he was still blindfold) to the altar, where by the use of his hands he placed himself between my legs, whereupon he thrust into me with such violence that I shrieked – my cry echoed by the vile congregation, now coupling upon the grass before me.

Mr Nelham – for can I truly describe him as my husband? – placed his hands upon the giant's buttocks as they thrust at me – and despite my terror, which rendered me incapable of movement, I could not but be aware of the pleasure such a lover could convey, nor was it possible altogether to deny that my body responded to his own, for despite myself I felt my loins lifting to meet his as I gripped his shoulders, partly to prevent myself being stifled by his weight, and partly, I confess, in passion. Beneath the fingers of my left hand, I noticed the red scar of a wound which had only recently been inflicted – under, I wondered, a similar circumstance? After a short time, the man raised his head, the black cloth still across his eyes, and shouted 'Now!' as he exploded within me. At which to my amazement my husband thrust his hand between us at the point where our privities were joined and I felt his fingers scrabbling. Withdrawing, he looked at his hand for a moment, then administered a violent smack to the giant's buttocks, who raised himself, whereupon Mr Nelham positively drew his hand across my mound, sore as it was, and again examined his fingers. I saw, even in the moonlight, his face darken with anger. Turning to the congregation, he shouted: 'It is a fault! He will not come!' and without more ado strode from the circle.

My lover, in evident confusion, rose and tore off his blindfold but, without looking at me, groped for his cloak upon the ground; one pair of the youths at my side also broke away, and gesturing at me in distaste made off (though the others were too far gone in pleasure to take notice of the confusion, and continued their congress, as did some of the couples who still lay clasped in each other's arms upon the grass).

I rose and gathering my clothes put them on as best I might in their torn state and found my way back to the road, where Mr Nelham was standing silent by the coach. He handed me into it roughly and without a word; nor did he speak on the way back to our rooms, where he discarded his cloak and the cope beneath it, and threw himself naked into bed.

After a while, I followed him, confused almost to death, and cried to him to let me know in what I had disappointed him.

' 'Twas all flim-flam!' he cried. 'Your father lied – you are no virgin!' – and was silent again.

I was no further informed, for I knew not the true meaning of the word – no one had explained it to me, nor if they had would I have understood that a husband should consider it important that no other man should have lain with their wife before themselves. Did they require, after all, that she should not have kissed another man, or eaten with him, or perhaps even spoken to him? Now, of course, I know better, but then I was innocence itself. Nor did I suspect what I now know, that Mr Nelham had needed a virgin not for himself but for the rite with which, in Black Mass, he hoped to raise the fiend, in concert with his Cambridge friends, many of them students of Dr Dee and readers of his manuscripts on converse with angels and devils which my husband had studied in the library of Trinity College.

So I lay for a while silent, and then perhaps hoping to console him in his disappointment stretched out my hand and laid it between his thighs, but all there was cold and limp, and moreover he struck my hand away with such violence that I let out a cry and thereafter lay quiet and still as he through a long night.

Towards morning I fell into a restless sleep, and woke to find Mr Nelham gone from the bed and in the next room packing his things. I asked if we were leaving, but got no reply, and thinking that this must be so began to pack my own few belongings. But when he had done, he turned and threw a few coins at my feet saying, 'Go, woman, back to your father, or to the D---l for all I care. I divorce you!' and seizing his packets, strode from the room. Desperately, I followed him, pleading to him to stay, for what should I do in a strange town where I knew no one and no one knew me, and did he mean me to starve in the gutter? But he repeated that he cared not, and went from the house only to be speedily lost in the traffic of the street.

I returned to the room and picked up the coins, which amounted to only fifty shilling. Would this be sufficient to hire a coach to return me to Alcovary? And would my father and mother receive me there? Certainly they had been aware of my state before they gave me to Mr Nelham, but this did not mean they were any more happily disposed toward me – indeed, perhaps the reverse.

Below my window the sound of cheerful voices announced that the students were at their morning baths. I looked out to where they were at play, laughing as they ducked and splashed each other, without care or thought.

I wept.

Chapter Five

The Adventures of Andy

It was with some trepidation that I made my way through the dining-room and long gallery towards the rooms occupied by the Ladies Elizabeth and Margaret, upon whom I had never yet set my eye. I feared that Mr Caister must have told them I was responsible for Sir Walter's fall, and as I went it seemed to me that the brow of every pictured Rawby in the many paintings upon the walls was bent upon me in admonition.

I opened the door which Tom had pointed out to me as leading to the ladies' apartments and entered. It had been explained to me that one never knocked at any door in the Hall before entering; servants were considered as furniture, and having one enter even if one of the ladies were upon the close stool was a nothing to them – no more than being observed by a table or a chair.

However, nothing untoward met my eye on this occasion; the two sisters sat side by side upon a couch, facing the door, each fanning herself with an identical fan, and both made the same beckoning gesture to me to come and stand near them. I have never seen two human beings more similar; but that one was dressed in blue silk, the other in pink, one would swear they were matched in a mirror, the one's fair hair dressed in the same way as the other, one's cold blue eyes the counterfeits of the other's, the same slim figure and upright carriage to be seen in each.

'So this is the fellow who is so adept . . .' said one, '. . . at handing the soap,' completed the other.

I bowed.

'A most unfortunate accident,' said the first, 'but one,' went on the second, 'that was after all but accident?'

I bowed again.

'No doubt you were concerned,' said the lady on my right, 'to prevent a misfortune in the bath room . . .'

'. . . by removing such a dangerous commodity from the floor,' completed the lady on my left.

Another bow.

And so, in turn completing each other's sentences, they continued to play with me, but entirely without malice. It was sad that Sir Walter was discommoded, for the women servants would not now have the pleasure of his company abed; such a cause for concern that he was now suffering acute agony and would not walk for several weeks; so tragic that his carriage would have to be sent for to take him to town next day. But they were sure that my care in the matter had been exquisite, and that the fact that a small piece of soap had escaped my hands was no fault of mine. I was not to feel in any way that the family attached blame to me, and I was to be assured that My Lord, though Sir Walter had complained bitterly, had been told by all that I was in no way to blame.

I was of course much comforted, and my bows were now accompanied by a real feeling of pleasure.

'We trust,' said one of the ladies, 'that little Ellen . . .'

'. . . has conveyed her gratitude to her hero?'

'Or that at all events . . .'

'. . . she will shortly do so.'

I made no reply.

'Well, you are a fine fellow . . .'

'. . . but a quiet one. What age are you?'

'Sixteen, my ladies,' I replied.

They nodded in unison, like two toy creatures on a toy couch, and eyed me up and down. I stood feeling like an animal at auction, being measured for my attributes by someone considering a purchase.

They turned to each other, and nodded again. Then one of them picked up her reticule, and fumbled in it, and something dropped from her hand to roll almost to my foot. I bent to pick it up. It was a gold guinea. I made to place it upon a table.

'Ah, what have you found there, young Andy?' she said.

'I think,' said the other, 'it is a piece of soap which fell from his pocket.'

'What a dangerous thing,' said the first, 'you should really . . .'

'. . . keep your possessions more safely about you.'

'That will be all,' the lady in blue said. I bowed again and left, somewhat bewildered but by no means displeased. Later, Mr Caister explained that Sir Walter had – mm – always been viewed as an unpleasant and unwelcome guest by everyone in the house – in particular by the female servants, among whom he took his choice. So did many guests in the house, though often with kindness and always with generous gifts, but Sir Walter had been always boorish in affection and mean in reward. Lady Elizabeth and Lady Margaret had hated him since he had first encountered them, when they were scarcely older than I, and he had rudely assaulted them – something for which My Lord had almost shown him the door, except for the financial hold he had upon him.

'Well, you – mm – you have set your foot well upon the stairs to – mm – advancement,' said the steward. 'Perhaps in – mm – thirty years you may aspire even to my position!' – and placing his arm about my shoulders, he laid a smacking kiss upon my cheek, then patting me on the rump sent me about my business. My delight at the thought of spending fifty years as a servant was limited, for my relative freedom at Alcovary had taught me that the gentle life offered more prospect of pleasure than a lifetime in service, and I had even then, though without conscious planning, laid an ambition to make my way into a class far different to that to which I was born.

I had just time to go to the room I was to share with Tom and hide my golden guinea beneath the mattress of my truckle bed before it was time to prepare the tables for supper, into which trooped My Lord, accompanied by the two ladies and the guests, all of whom were men. When I expressed my surprise at this to Tom, he explained that it was rarely that My Lord's friends brought their wives to the Hall; that some of them had an eye for the maids here, and others sometimes brought doxies, two of whom were even now upstairs, eating their food from trays taken to them from the kitchens, for they were not of a rank to eat with the family.

The meal, though not a remarkable one for the Hall, amazed me by its grandness – or rather by its profligacy, for the manner in which it was taken was far from grand. At Alcovary supper had been consumed in polite silence, with little conversation, Sir Franklin presiding with a noble mien. Here My Lord was deep in conversation with his cronies at one end of the table, while his daughters were equally surrounded by gentlemen whose conversation was no less lewd for their presence. The talk turned particularly on the Prince Regent and his unfortunate wife, every aspect of whose character and person was explored with the utmost frankness, and whose behaviour (if one-tenth of the particulars were reported correctly) reflected the morals of an alley cat.

As to the table, it creaked under beef, venison, geese, turkeys, etc., with Burgundy, champagne (white and rosy), Hermitage, red and white, Constantia, Sauterne, Madeira and punch. Every other breath issued forth a toast, drunk in bumpers, and long before supper was over, which was not until well past midnight, many of My Lord's companions were under the table, though he – not the least assiduous in consumption of drink – remained apparently sober (and Tom told me, in an undertone, that he had never been seen drunk). We had little to do other than bring more supplies of viands and then to stand attentively by – and after the day's activities, I was by then almost asleep, and more than once my shoulders touched the wall and I awoke with a start from a half-slumber. This was despite the most interesting thing to me, which was an orchestra of ten men who played music throughout the meal – to which no one listened. Tom, again my informant, told me that My Lord spent no less than three hundred and fifty pound a year on this band, which he had set up in rivalry to that kept by his distant relative Lord Chandos; it included viols and flute, and an Italian with a guitar, who sometimes played alone (though no one heard him). He, Tom hinted, was a tutor to Lady Elizabeth – 'and not only of music,' said he with a grin.

At last the evening came to an end, the reeking room was cleared, and we were free to go to bed up one of the two stone staircases which led one to the men's rooms, one to the women's. There were doors to each stairway which Mrs Tickert locked with one of the bunch of keys at her waist – a sight which somewhat dismayed me, since it seemed to promise a more monastic life than that which the situation at first had appeared to promise. However, Tom's only reply when I remarked upon it was a wink, and soon we were in the small room beneath the roof which we were to share. We shrugged off our jackets and small-clothes – glad to be free of the constriction – and yawning, I fell upon my bed. But Tom said, 'Not so quick to doze, young Andy!' – and when I looked a question, led me to the window, which he threw open.

There was a half-moon, throwing just enough light for me to see that a parapet or platform ran below the tilt of the roof above the eaves, and what was my surprise when Tom bent to crawl out upon it, beckoning me to follow. A tree-climber since I was a little fellow, I was nothing loath at the height and narrowness of the platform, nor for the cold, though I now wore only my drawers, for the night was balmy and we had been for some hours in a close and smoky atmosphere. But it seemed a strange exercise for a time when I would have been glad to be a friend to my bed.

We crawled for perhaps twenty feet, at one point flattening ourselves to the parapet as we passed below a window inside which I heard men's voices, and supposed they were those of the other footmen. Then we came to a low wall over which Tom skipped and I followed, and in another five or seven feet to a window below which Tom gave a low whistle. It was immediately thrown up, and I followed Tom through it to find myself in a room the exact counterpart of the one we had left, but occupied by Tabby and Ellen who, clad in the lightest of shifts, threw their arms around us and gave us welcoming hugs. From beneath her bed, Tabby produced a bottle, and dry from the evening's fug, we were all quick to imbibe – by which time Tom and Tabby were embraced upon her bed, his hand upon her breast while hers explored beneath the band of his drawers. Sitting by Ellen upon her bed I was uncertain how to proceed, for her natural modesty and the unkind behaviour she had received from Sir Walter Flount made me think that perhaps any offer from me would be unwelcome.

But soon, watching as Tabby drew Tom's drawers from him and threw off her shift, and they fell to play, I grew amorous, and began to kiss Ellen, who replied with an embrace no less pleasant, after which it was little time before we too were in a state of nature. The room was lit only by a single candle in a corner, but even by its low light it was interesting to see the contrast between the bodies of the two girls: Tabby, round and plump, her breasts swinging as she kneeled over Tom's recumbent form, and her ample thighs quivering as he playfully thumped them with his fists, encouraging her to lower herself upon him, and Ellen, her breasts small and round, her waist slim, and her thighs fine and lithe, though strong. As she lay, I bent my head to take her nipples between my lips, gently tweaking them with my tongue and tenderly nibbling with my teeth until I felt them harden and her body began to quiver beneath me. I threw one of my thighs between her legs, and my prick, now standing eagerly, lay upon her belly. Her hands slid over my shoulders and down to my waist, then under, and I lifted myself to let her reach my standing part and caress it gently, then pointed it to the delicious quintain at which I aimed.

As I slipped into heaven her arms tightened about me, and as I began to move the candlelight struck deep yellow sparks from her eyes. A few feet away, Tabby was panting as she rose and fell upon Tom's body. Ellen threw out a hand to take her friend's hand, and we all laughed low and pleasant together as we reached the top of our delight.

After a while, we fell asleep, all tangled together; woke to love, and slept again; and finally I was shook to full wakefulness by Tom to see a dim pink light announcing the dawn, and we barely had time to return to our own room before Fred, the oldest footman, knocked upon our door to call us to work.

The days passed pleasantly enough. They were long, but the work not unduly arduous, and the four of us – Tom and Tabby, myself and Ellen – were together as much as we might be, not only at night, but during the day time. In our free hours we walked in those parts of the grounds which were open to us and plunged often into a little lake in a remote corner of the park – which we were very glad of, for we were forbidden to use the bath room, and the days were hot in that summer.

In the meantime, I had come to know Signor Giovanni Cesareo, the guitar player, who had come originally from Piedmont, whence he had fled because, he said, at the courts there they now favoured only French musicians. So he had travelled to England for employment, and was happy at Rawby, where he taught Lady Elizabeth the guitar and the lute. Seeing that I was interested, he not only gave me some lessons, showing me how to finger the instrument and strike its strings, but, saying I had a natural bent, lent me an old instrument of his own that I could practise upon. Soon I became quite adept, at first fingering without the music but then learning from him how to read the notes – not, to me, more difficult than words upon a page – after which in a short time I was able to play some easy pieces, to the great delight of Tabby and Ellen and, I think, somewhat to the jealousy of Tom.

It was one afternoon at the end of June or the beginning of July – I remember the time because My Lord that day called the whole household together to hear the great news of the victory of Wellington at Waterloo – when the four of us were lying upon the grass after swimming, gently toying with each other, that I saw a white face between the trees, and a dark form. I started to my feet with an oath.

'What's that?' demanded Tom, and when I replied that there was a spy, replied with a laugh, 'Oh, 'tis only Beau Rust!'

This was Henry Rust, the father of the late Lady Rawby, an old man who had passed almost all his life in Bath, was thought once to have been a curate but later gave up Holy Orders for his attachment to the ladies, and was known as Beau Rust for the manner in which by his example in elegance and the care of dress he had been the descendent of his great precursor Beau Brummell, the arbiter of fashion in the town. Now, at an age no one was certain of – but certainly of seventy years, for he talked of travelling in Poland when Poniatowski was elected King in the year of '64 – he lived in rooms above his granddaughters and could be seen like some shadow, always dressed in black, moving silently about the house and gardens.

' 'Tis said,' Tom reported, 'that he spends his time with books, and is upon some great project, but nothing as yet has appeared.'

His meals were taken to him by one of the ladies' maids, and he employed no servant of his own, but lived like a recluse. I had no idea of a closer acquaintance but a week later, as I was passing along the gallery, I was plucked by the arm and found a little old man all in black, an old yellowing wig perched on his head, at my shoulder.

'Boy!' said Beau Rust. 'Boy, come now to my rooms. I have a question to put to you – yet ye shall not minish ought from your bricks or your daily task (Exodus five, nineteen).'

Having spent some time in persuading Mr Caister that I was no twiddlepoop, but one for the girls, I was concerned that Beau Rust had designs on my person, for he being my ladies' grandfather 'twould probably be difficult to excuse myself. But I followed him up a narrow stairway beyond my ladies' rooms, thence into a corridor, and into a room so busy with objects that it dizzied me; it was a litter of books, papers, boxes small and large, pieces of clothing, with not a chair nor a table that was not piled high.

Throwing a small pile of books to the floor, Beau Rust sat himself down and looked up at me.

'Now, boy, I am at work.'

I said nothing, there being nothing to say.

'I am at a great work, and this work goeth fast on and prospereth in my hands (Ezra five, eight). I am to restore

thy nakedness (Habakuk two, fifteen)' and rummaged among the pile of papers at his feet to find one which he had marked.

It being so strange a situation, both Tabby and I found it a cold invitation enough, but hustled out of our things as we were asked, and stood somewhat awkwardly in front of the Beau, protecting our privities with our hands as best we might. He gave a croak.

'Hah! Not as I've seen you many a time up by the lake, my young beauties. Never mind – here, take this –'

And handed me a drawing, which was of the lower parts of a man in congress with a woman, but with her legs at a strange angle to his own.

'My vision – hah! – is that she was lying upon her back, her legs thrown over his shoulders. Kindly adopt the position. When – hah! – you are ready,' he added drily, staring at my gaying stick, which was of no size or movement, and which, because of the oddity of the moment, refused to budge when I handled it. Tabby next turned her attention to it, but not even the warm mumbling of her lips had its effect.

'Hah!' said the Beau, standing up and looking around at a loss. 'I failed to predict such a situation. Hah! The spoiler is fallen (Jeremiah forty-eight, thirty-two). Well, cast your eye upon these,' and handed us a book, which when opened proved to show some lascivious drawings which indeed after a while warmed me to some display, but not sufficient to improve the hour, for by the time Tabby had taken up her position and I mine, Jack had drooped once more.

But then the Beau tripped his way to a corner of the room and, coming back with a box, lifted out what appeared to be a room from a dolls' house – yet furnished with dolls no mother would give her daughter, for they were all beautifully measured wax figures of men and women embracing – upon the couches, the floors, the chairs, the tables. With a grinding sound, and an explosion of dust, the Beau wound a key at its back and pressed a switch – and lo! While from the inside of the box came the tinkling sound of a gavotte, the figures began to move. The chevalier with the flowing black locks pressed his loins against the backside of a large woman who with her lips was ministering to the person of a man in cardinal's robes, which parted at the front to show the distended tool at which she was busy. He in turn grasped in one hand the prick of a young footman, his wig all askew, who had his hand deep in the *décolletage* of a young lady sat with her back to him rising and falling upon the knees of a young man whose hands were raised in astonishment at the size of the prick of the negro servant, upon whose enormous instrument was balanced a cup into which tea was being poured by the mistress of the house, seated proudly at the centre of the picture, turning her head from tableau to tableau in happy approbation.

The lifelike appearance of the figures together with the enthusiasm of Tabby speedily restored my senses, and in a moment I had thrown her once more upon her back, and lifting her legs had dived beneath them to bury myself up to the hilt in her warmth. With a chuckle, Beau Rust seized his drawing paper and set to work. It occurred to me, simply, that perhaps we were expected to prolong our ecstasy so that he could take his time with delineation of our pose, but we were both too far gone in pleasure to attend to his wishes, if so they were, and we spent together in a copious explosion of pleasure. Upon which, panting, I turned to the Beau to find that his drawing had tailed off to an inconclusive scrawl, while he had fished his ancient equipment from his small-clothes and had that moment persuaded it to void up a small dribble of juice, though accompanied with a loud squeal of pleasure.

'Hah! Not had the joy these twenty years!' he said. 'Behold, it cometh, and every heart shall melt (Ezekial twenty-one, seven). My children, thank'ee – and, you see, the drawing – well, the – hah!' Not even the artist himself could pretend that the work of art he had produced was worth the two guineas he handed to us, tucking his clothes back into place the while. Tabby curtsied, all naked as she was, and I placed my gold piece between my teeth while I persuaded my still lively prick into my breeches.

Beau Rust waved us away.

'I shall send for ye again,' he said, 'to complete the next pose.'

We made our way down the staircase and past my ladies' rooms to find Tom at the corner of the long gallery, leaning against the door and looking grim.

'So,' he said, 'how was the Beau? Did he enjoy you both, or did you only enjoy each other?'

Tabby coloured, and saying nothing passed on, but Tom grasped my shoulder and spat: 'I take it unkindly, Master Andy, after the service I've been to you, that you should betray me in such a way. You may look to yourself, for I'm no longer your friend.'

Chapter Six

Sophie's Story

My fit of weeping did not last long – I am not a creature greatly given to self-pity – and soon the ringing of bells all over the city reminded me that 'twas Sunday morning, whereupon I decided to dress myself and walk upon the river bank at the back of the colleges beneath the shade of the willows and consider my position. Indeed it was a less than happy one, my husband of a mere few weeks having left me with only a little money, far from my home and parents, and they unlikely to welcome my return there, even should I wish it.

Half an hour later I left my rooms and turned down the alleyway which led to the river. As I rounded the corner, the noise of laughter greeted me and I realised that the young men were still at their bathing, and in the way in which I was to walk. Nevertheless, I walked on; many times had I seen Andy and my dear Frank bathing in Alcovary park, and they had never shown anything but pleasure that I should witness their sport. I had no distinct knowledge that other young men might disapprove or be ashamed at being seen in a state of nature, besides which these had signalled to me in high-spirited approbation when they saw me at my window. I certainly did not realise that only women of small repute frequented this alley, long claimed as a bathing place for the students, at a time when they were known to use it.

The latter fact perhaps accounted for the ribaldry which in the first instance greeted my appearance as I reached the river and found myself on a sort of platform upon which piles of clothes lay, and below which four youngsters were sporting.

'Come, Moll, dip!' was the cry, followed by 'Ay! Doff

thy bonnet and breeks, and plunge in!' But one of the boys clearly recognised me from my former smilings from the window, and swimming to the piles below the platform, reached up with one brown hand to lift his powerful shoulders above the water while he greeted me politely, waving down the grins and shouts of his comrades.

'Forgive us bathing below your window, ma'am,' he said, 'but it has been a custom here always.'

I assured him that I was not at all disturbed, and that but for the dirt of the river – into which all the latrines of Cambridge poured their waste – I would be tempted to join them.

'Ah!' he laughed. 'I admit 'tis no great pleasure, for we must wash again when we are at home. For real joy, there are other places outside the town where the water is deep and fresh. You are a swimmer, ma'am? For the ladies of Cambridge in general are not greatly given to the sport.'

I told him I had been used to swim every day, in the summer, at my father's house, whereupon he called to his friends to inform them of the fact, and they too came to the bank to talk – and to cut the tale short invited me to go with them that afternoon by punt to Grantchester, there to eat a meal and to swim, if we so chose. Unaffectedly, they pulled themselves up to the platform, and I must confess that while I seemed to avert my eyes from their nakedness, I could not but admire their forms as they shook the shiny drops of water from them and hustled into their clothes, or rather their rags for, as my first friend, whose name he told me was Jack, informed me they wore only old things to the river which would otherwise be soiled by the filth of the water. I wrinkled my nose at this and Jack said that indeed, but for custom, he at least would be disinclined to immerse himself in that part of the river, but custom at the university died hard. Moreover, in the heat of summer it was the easiest way to be cool.

After some bread and cheese and a glass of ale at home, I went at two o'clock to the river bank just above Queen's College – passing the great chapel, whence the sound of singing came sweetly on the summer air – and there met my friend Jack, with two other boys of perhaps eighteen who I had seen at the bathing-place. One, Coln, was a dark-haired Irishman, and the second, George, a slim boy not unlike my Frank. They handed me into one of the wooden boats known as punts which are propelled by poles like Venetian gondolas upon the waters of the Cam, and there we sat waiting, it seemed, for another member of the party. But when I looked a question, Jack explained that we paused for a college servant, Will, from Trinity, who hired himself out as a puntsman for those who did not wish to expend their energy too freely.

'And here he comes, himself!' cried Coln, and in a moment the punt rocked as a large young man of perhaps thirty years leaped in from the bank and pulled a forelock. I felt, as I set eyes on him, that he was familiar to me, and when with a nod of deference he peeled off his shirt to seize the punt pole, I was in no doubt. I had surely seen him before, for he was none other than the giant who had been led to ravish me upon the grassy mount where Mr Nelham had hoped to raise the Devil, the previous night.

My embarrassment the reader will understand! I was forced to lie facing the puntsman, and could do nothing but study those limbs with which I had so lately though briefly been covered! Though a blindfold had veiled his eyes, there was no mistaking the angry, red, recent scar upon his right shoulder which I had clearly seen in the moonlight, nor the shock of brown curly hair which fell to his shoulders and had tumbled over my face, nor – I fancied – the shape of that enormous machine which I now seemed to see bursting at the seams of his small-clothes, and which had come near to bursting me!

Jack and his friends seemed not to notice my preoccupation, for they chattered gaily on about their life at the university, which seemed in the main to be composed of sporting, gambling and wenching – though they complained that too many of the local wenches were poxed, a circumstance they set down to over-willingness on their parts to 'fuck anyone for fourpence' ('begging your pardon, ma'am,' said Coln with a blush).

Soon, in the heat of the afternoon, I simply closed my eyes and surrendered myself to the gliding motion of the punt as it slid over smooth water out of the city and away to the south. The boys, too, fell quiet and seemed to doze (though Jack, nearest to me, fell to gently fondling my foot and lower leg, in an indolent manner). Only the trickle of water from the punt-pole as it was lifted from the water to be plunged in once more disturbed the quiet for a while. Then came a sudden explosion of sound as we rounded a corner and came to a bathing-place at Grantchester Meadows which, George explained to me, was sacred to the dons or teachers of the university and, it seemed, to their catamites. Through lowered lids, for I did not wish to exhibit my curiosity, I saw indeed a cluster of bodies lying upon the bank, some of which seemed to be immodestly entwined, though, Jack explained without my asking, it was in the grove beyond that the more intimate embraces were said to take place. And as I watched a beautiful, fair-haired, naked youth indeed broke from the grove followed by a plump, pale, elderly fellow, white stomach swinging uneasily as he trotted towards the bank, then, seeing me, turned his back to sit upon the grass scowling over his shoulder while his erstwhile companion plunged into the river only feet from us, causing a wave which rocked us dangerously for a moment.

On we went, between rows of poplars, sometimes passing below the branches of a willow so low that they threatened to sweep our polesman into the water, and which patched us for a moment or two with a shade dappled with round circles of light like the dots on the old rocking horse in the nursery at Alcovary. In an hour or so we passed Grant-chester and a little further on tied up where a bank held back a deep, dark pool of water under the grateful green shade of some trees.

This, Jack told me, was known as Byron's Pool, for 'twas here the poet used to come to bathe when he was at Cambridge only ten years before, sometimes bringing with him the handsome boy chorister Eddleston, who was his favourite. We climbed onto the bank – the giant, Will, offering me his hand to steady me. I clasped it, my arm lying along the length of his, and the meeting of our flesh did, I confess, send a thrill through me, for his muscles made it – as I clearly recalled – hard as iron.

The sun beating down upon the punt had warmed us, and without delay we threw off our clothes and plunged into the pool, the sudden shock of the cold water delighting us, though soon it became merely a pleasant coolness as our bodies grew used to the flow of the water around them. Soon the boys were diving to swim between my legs, or vanishing beneath the water some distance away, suddenly to appear behind me. Before long they began to grow familiar, and as they passed beneath me I would feel a hand slide over my thigh. Then Jack, his head emerging from the water at my side, enquired whether I was not cold and applied his palm to my breast in order to discover whether such was the case.

After a while I made for the bank and climbed out, dropping to the grass beneath a tree. I looked around for Will, but he had vanished. Meanwhile Jack, Coln and George were also climbing to the bank, and fell to the ground at my side, George producing from a bag he had been carrying some bottles of ale which he opened and handed us. We drank as the warm breeze played over our limbs and the beads of clear water gradually evaporated upon our cooled bodies.

I lay back in the warm air while the three boys reclined at my side, seeming to admire my form, which I had no thought of covering. I looked, indeed, at their figures with a similiar interest, for my acquaintance with the male figure was still somewhat limited. Coln, as I have said, was not unlike Frank in form, save that I saw to my distress that he seemed to be somewhat deformed, for at the end of his tool the skin, rather than forming a pouting cover, was drawn back in some way, exposing the red tip in what seemed an almost provocatively naked manner. (I later discovered, of course, that this was an appearance some men's instruments had, as the result of an operation more common among the Jewish race, and called circumcision.) Jack and

George were more conventionally formed, George the slimer of the two, with an almost feminine build, Jack more muscular; he was, I learned, a great athlete.

After a while I fell into a doze, and was awakened by a tickling at my right breast, which I soon found was caused by Jack, who was leaning over me and applying the tip of his tongue to my nipple, while the other two boys looked on with interest. I could not fail to notice from the corner of my eye that their tools, while not fully extended, were now considerably larger than they had been under the influence of the cool waters – lying upon their thighs in tumid pride rather than being shrunken between them – while I could feel Jack's nuzzling at my hip like a puppy searching for comfort. I reached down and took it in my hand, which the other two took as a signal of consent, for in a moment George was applying his hand to my other breast, feeling its texture like a market woman examining a pear, while Coln's tongue entered first my navel, then traced a moist path downwards into the hair below, and I felt his fingers part my lower lips so that it could seek out the little bud which is the seat of woman's pleasure.

Soon, they were jockeying each other for position, one no sooner lodged between my thighs than he was nudged away by another, until we all fell into a fit of laughter. At this George rolled over to reach into his breeches for a coin, which they tossed, and they reckoned as a result that Coln should take precedence and George next pride of place, while poor Jack must be content with what he could find.

And so it was that a few moments later George was sitting with his back against a fallen log while I kneeled before him, bending to take his tool between my lips. At my back Coln applied his fleshy sword to its proper scabbard, while Jack, with a muttered *sauve qui peut*, sat at George's side, and reaching for my hand placed it upon his tool and the pendant globes beneath, now drawn up into a tight pouch with pleasurable anticipation.

I could not but think of the stricture of that flaybottomist Mr Gutteridge, that 'three into one won't go', for while the sensation of Coln's tool – whose squab vigour was more delightful than his slim body had promised – gave me much pleasure, the hard ground was discomfortable to my knees. And while the saponaceous lubricity of George's gaying-stick slid with exquisite nicety between my lips, seeming to knock sometimes at the very back of my throat, was far from unpleasant to me, it was uncomfortable indeed to rest my entire weight upon one hand in order that the other could occupy itself in Jack's lap, who nevertheless was first to reach full delight, for a fine gush flooded my hand and fell to the grass at George's side. And only a moment later, at almost the same time, I felt rather than tasted the essence of George's own joy, and the warmth of Coln's luxury within my lower belly.

The three boys almost immediately fell into lethargy. George slipped to one side, his head falling into Jack's lap, while Coln drew himself away and fell upon his back. I sat back upon my haunches and at that moment, seeing a movement behind a bush a stone's throw away, recognised rather than his full figure Will's enormous tool, vigourously massaged between his own palms.

Suggesting that I should wash myself, I rose to my feet and strode towards the bush. Thinking perhaps that he was unseen, he remained where he was until I placed my hand upon his shoulder and laying my finger on my lips, seized his arm and drew him to his feet and after me towards the river bank where without further ado I fell to my knees before him and took between my lips his huge piece, reaching around to grasp with my hands his massive buttocks, covered in an animal mat of hair (in contrast to the smooth bums of my three friends, each no downier than a peach).

The truth was that the discomfort of my physical position had been such that even the lively ministrations of young Coln had not brought me to my apogee and I was ready for more vigorous attention. And soon, feeling him move yet quicker, his belly panting against my forehead, I fell upon my back, and in an instant he followed me, and I felt that mingled joy and pain I had felt the night before as that mighty prick – so large and round that an observer would not have thought it possible that it could make its way within the slender portals now distended by it – penetrated into my most secret part. Within six thrusts of those strapping loins his whole body vibrated, while he threw back his head in pleasure, presenting me with a view of the great column of his throat. And at the same time I too spent, with such relish that I would have shrieked aloud had I not buried my open mouth in his shoulder, biting it with sufficient force to make him wince, and, drawing my lips away, I saw a ring of tooth marks on his brown flesh, small dots of blood marking the trace just beside the red mark which had identified him to me.

He would have spoken, but I laid my finger once more upon my lips, rose, and made my way to the river, where I bathed my limbs, now all over sweat, in the black water.

When I returned to my three friends, I found them all asleep as they had fallen: George with his head still on Jack's thigh and Coln with one arm flung over the former's calf, their bodies now relaxed and their formerly eager tools so shrunken and diminished (it seemed) they could not harm the mildest maid. I lay myself down by them, and also fell into a doze.

Later, we woke and dressed, and I was led to a public house nearby, close under Grantchester church and looking over a bend of the river, where in the garden we sat ourselves down to more ale and a cold rabbit pie and salad. The boys showing some interest, I told them the story of my life, which they greeted with no less surprise than sympathy. They had heard, they said, that in reading the manuscripts of Dr Dee some Cambridge scholars had expressed themselves interested in occult matters, and Coln – the only one to have read in the manuscripts themselves – described how the doctor and his familiar Mr Kelley used to converse with a spirit-child, a pretty girl of seven or eight years whom they called Madimi, until the girl ordered the doctor to share his good wife with Mr Kelley for carnal purposes, whereat the said wife had taken exception and the partnership had broken up.

'But,' said Coln, 'then the angelic conversations ceased,

for Madimi herself never more appeared to them.'

'Was not Dr Dee an astrologist?' asked George, and Coln said he was, but that the matter had been put down by Mr Samuel Butler in his poem *Hudibras,* wherein he wrote of William Lilly:

> *Some calculate the hidden fates*
> *Of monkeys, puppy-dogs and cats,*
> *Some running-nags and fighting-cocks;*
> *Some love, trade, law-suits and the pox;*
> *Some take a measure of the lives*
> *Of fathers, mothers, husbands, wives,*
> *Make opposition, trine and quartile*
> *Tell who is barren and who fertile . . .*

But, I interrupted, Mr Lilly was a sensible man who used astrology to its true purpose, as anyone could see who read his *Christian Astrology . . .*

'Aha!' cries Jack. 'We have a white witch among us!'

No, not at all, said I shortly, though witch enough to venture that he had a birthday soon, for 'twas the end of July, and clearly the Sun had been in the sign of Leo at his birth, as could be seen by his great mane of yellow hair, his fine upright carriage, ease of manner and natural leadership.

'But how did you know this?' asked he, whereat I said nothing, but enquiring the day of his birth informed him that he had been born at a quarter of three in the afternoon ('tis a trick easily learned from Mr Lilly's book).

Nothing now would do but that I had to tell the other their birth days, which luckily (for the thing's not infallible) I did correctly, Coln being born under Libra (his charm being no less manifest than his romantic notions, to which he was even then giving bent by tenderly taking my hand), while George's Sun sign was Aries, which I had guessed by his celerity in completing the act of love, Ariens being notorious for their speedy accomplishment of all things, and their motto 'I shall come first!'

It was amusing to see their faces at this, for they doubted

it was anything but black magic until I explained how the matter worked, and how Mr Lilly and those before him had used the science of astrology to help their fellow men, whereat Jack was entirely sceptical, but Coln grew quiet and thoughtful. We finished our meal and strode back to the punt, where Will was lying asleep, having no doubt recovered his small-clothes from the bush where he had dropped them before we took our pleasure. As he woke and sat up there was general laughter, for Jack pointed to where on his shoulder were all too clearly the marks of my teeth.

'Ho! A dark horse, young Will!' he said. 'A girl in every village, old scamp!'

Whereat Will said nothing, but smiled slowly and took up the punt pole, and once, as we slid back down the river towards the city, swans swimming at our side, he caught my eye and moved his hand upon the pole in an unmistakable manner bringing, I must confess, a blush to my cheeks which happily none of my companions noticed.

We parted all good friends. 'Thank 'ee, ma'am,' said Will as he handed me out onto the bank, as warmly as if I had given him a sovereign. The others embraced me, and Coln made an excuse to whisper in my ear that he would come to see me the following day.

And sure enough, just before twelve midday, there was a knock at my door and the girl announced that there was a young gentleman to visit me. It was Coln in black gown and cap, which he threw off to show himself clothed not in the simple shirt of yesterday but as one might expect of a fashionable and wealthy man, with a finely cut coat and nankeen trousers. He greeted me with a little bow, and would have offered no further familiarity had I not given him my cheek to kiss. Sitting, he made small talk until I asked outright why he had come, expecting, I must confess, a profession of love. However, he asked whether I really had command of astrology and could use it to solve a question of his, whereat I replied that I would do what I could, but first, I must know the particulars of his birth – the date, the time, the place. He told me he had been born in Dublin on October the seventh in the year of ninety-seven, at precisely midday, whereupon I sat down with Mr Lilly and completed my calculations to draw up the chart of his birth. Then I asked him what his problem was.

His father, he replied, had a factory in Dublin which made fine china, sent out to all the world, and was anxious that when he had completed a university education he should return there and run the factory in partnership with him, taking particular care of the designing of the china. Coln was not averse to the idea but had doubts whether it was work for a man or whether he could be successful in it for his friends, hearing of it, were inclined to mock at him.

I was able to reassure him that indeed he would do well to follow his father's plan, for not only did his Libran Sun suggest that he had a bent for all things artistic and would thrive in a partnership, but the sign of Sagittarius had been rising over the eastern horizon at the moment of his birth, which gave him a bright and lively intelligence and willingness to study. Moreover, the Moon was in Taurus at his birth, which promised financial success; Venus was in the sign Scorpio, which would give him assurance in business dealings; Mars in Virgo allowed him the capacity to take great trouble over small things and gave a practical ability, while Jupiter in Aries made him practical and forward-looking.

It was, I opined, Mercury in Libra with the Sun that made him doubt his abilities, for that planet within that sign often persuades a person to procrastinate, to look all round a decision seeing all sides of it, and sometimes doubting on which side to come down, while Saturn in Cancer could draw his spirits into a certain timidity, and it was my view that he must be particularly careful in financial dealings with his family. I did not inform him that the fact that Venus had been in Scorpio when he was born gave him all that passion with which he happily pleasured himself on the river bank the day before, nor that Sagittarius, when it rises, offers an inquisitive inventiveness in all matters of loving!

His face, as I told him this, was a picture of agreeable surprise. I had, he said, painted his picture to the life, and much that I had said offered a confirmation of his own feelings. Whereupon he took a guinea from his pocket and placed it upon the table, saying when I remonstrated that it was the least tribute he could pay, and moreover asking whether I had not thought of becoming a professional advisor to people in their difficulties, from which he felt sure I could make a good living.

It was something I had not thought of, but it was certainly something that *might* be thought of! Coln rose to take his leave and embracing me could not but throw his hand into my bosom, at which I was by no means displeased, for I had taken a great liking to this pleasant young Irishman. But he drew back, saying he must go to a lecture, but that if he might he would call upon me again shortly and thanking me once more for my words, he withdrew.

I spent the afternoon working out, then lettering in my best script, a placard offering advice in all matters of the heart, or of finance, or of business, by one well tutored in the movements of the Sun, Moon and Planets, given at a moderate cost at these rooms. And copying it thrice, took it to the Red Lion and two other inns, where for a shilling (which I could have ill afforded except that I now had Coln's guinea) they promised to exhibit them, with the result that within three days I had had five persons call upon me who, satisfied by my words, left me with varying amounts of money. I determined to take from each according to their means rather than charging a general fee, and had from one wealthy shopkeeper (who wished to know was his wife unfaithful, whereto Mr Lilly's formula offered a negative reply, which delighted him) no less than two guineas, and from a poor girl whose lover had left her, five pence to know whether he would return or no.

And so I proceeded for the better part of a month, satisfying myself that I could aspire to a good living if not to absolute wealth, when one morning to my door came a man all in black with an ill visage who asked whether I could tell if he would be promoted to high office or no, and when I concluded no, revealed himself as a local Presbyterian and puritan who threatened to report me for fortune-telling, for which, he said, I could be put in prison. This frightened me, especially when Coln – to whom I went in my trouble – consulted a law student friend who confirmed that the law was indeed an instrument which could be used against me.

I was then at my wits' end, for what else could I do? I walked for a while in the streets, as was my wont when I wished to think, and coming to Midsummer Common found a fair, with a stage and some coarse country play upon it, posing exhibitions, dancing saloons, swinging and riding machines, and a tent in which a pretty woman of not many years more than I was telling fortunes for two pence a time, reading the hands of anyone who cared to pay. Crossing her palm with two pence, I offered her my hand, and to my surprise she said:

'Ah, my dear, but you have the gift – yet you have trouble!'

I could not but agree.

'You are one of us,' she said, 'the far-sighted ones. I can tell you nothing you could not tell yourself, except that your danger could be averted if you came with us.'

'With *us*?'

'Ay, with the Gypsies, for I am one of a band going from place to place and living as we can but living free as the air. I see it here,' she continued, tapping my palm with her finger, 'I see a partnership twixt you and me . . .'

At this, I could not but tell her my position and ask whether the church and the law did not fall upon her as it seemed it would fall upon me.

'No, they but rarely touch us,' she said, 'for fear of our curse, which is still powerful – though not as powerful' (and here she winked) 'as they may think!'

So why did I not pack my things and come with them? I could share her stall and tent, the money was plentiful, the life varied and good, and her brothers and sisters true people of the land, who would be glad to call me one of them.

I gave her a fair answer, and returning home, consulted the book. Mr Lilly said that a journey would be most positive, especially one to the west and south and my new friend having told me that the band was to leave the following morning towards Southampton, I hesitated no longer, but that night packed my few things, wrote a quick note to leave for Coln – the only person I left with regret in the city – and by seven next morning made my way again to the Common. An hour later I was seated upon the front seat of a wagon behind a good strong white mare, my new friend, Rosanna, at my side, making out along the Trumpington Road.

The light was poor, for the sky had darkened for a shower of rain, yet as we left the city a strange vision disturbed me, for I saw three students walking along the pavement towards the city, and one of them who lifted his face to look towards our procession of vans as it passed was the image of my dear brother Frank, so much so that I almost leaped from the seat to run to him. But common sense held me there, for was it possible that he should have been in Cambridge all this while and I not seen him? And so I stayed, and as morning wore on we continued on towards Royston, to camp outside the town upon Therfield Heath where, Rosanna told me, I would have to pledge my allegiance to the band.

Chapter Seven

The Adventures of Andy

'Tis impossible in a servants' hall to be free of one's companions, and so we rubbed along together despite Tom's displeasure, which he took every opportunity of showing not only to me but to Tabby, who from time to time appeared with a bruise upon her arm or (on one occasion) her face which she would not account for. And though I suspected it was inflicted by my former friend, and was eager to visit my disapprobation upon him, she dissuaded me, saying that she had fallen or that Mrs Tickert had taken her too strongly by the arm, or some other excuse. Our pleasant nights were now no more, for Tom threatened if I were to leave our room he would inform upon me to Mr Caister and that would be the end of my situation. So Tabby and I were only able to meet when it was possible for us both to escape the notice of the others – among whom the most vigilant was Tom himself – and go into the park. This was agreeable enough in summer, but what when winter came?

Poor Ellen was at a loss to know what had gone forward; she knew that Tom and I had fallen out, but Tabby did not tell her the reason, and Tom himself held short – no doubt through pride – of explaining the circumstances of our quarrel. Ellen hung about my neck at every opportunity, but I think did not miss our love-making which now was at an end, but merely wished me a friend, which I was glad to be to her. For myself I was somewhat pleased that I need no longer go to bed with her, for after Tabby she was as skimmed milk compared to cream.

It was a fortnight or so after our first summons to Beau Rust's chambers that he again skipped to me one morning as I was cleaning silver, and once more summoned us. Nothing loath, for here was an opportunity of enjoying ourselves in comfort if not in privacy, we made our way to his rooms at three in the afternoon, which allowed us two hours before we must attend to preparing the tables for supper at six. We found the Beau sitting at his table, this time with pen in hand and in front of him a book all in Latin, the title of which I saw was *Sonetti Lussoriosi de Pietro Aretino* first published, the Beau remarked, some two hundred years ago in Italy, but most of the copies were burned by the Holy Inquisition, so that the drawings by one Marcantino Raimondi had all perished, only the verses themselves surviving.

'I have been Englishing them,' said the Beau, 'and intend to publish when I have completed the task, and the drawings with which you are helping. Here –' and he flourished a drawing of a man with a woman's leg thrown over his right shoulder, '– is the one we are to essay today, and it accompanies the following verse . . . Hah!' He cleared his throat, picked up his manuscript, and declaimed the following:

Throw your leg, dearest, on my shoulder here
And take my throbbing piece within your grasp,
And as I gently move it, let your clasp
Tighten and draw me to your bosom dear.
And should I stray from front to hinder side
Call me a rogue and villain, will not you?
Because I know the diff'rence 'twixt the two,
As stallions know how lusty mares to ride.
My hand shall keep my iron dart in place
Lest it may slip and somehow get away,
When a swift frown would darken your fair face.
Your lovely arse delights me, but they say
Only the rider can enjoy that race,
Whilst the front gate gives pleasure every way.
So let us buck and spend, and spend and buck,
For ne'er two lovers more enjoyed a fuck.

He was clearly pleased with his effort, for he thumped the table with his fist as he ended, scattering several papers to the floor, and grinned as though he had been given a hundred guineas. Tabby was blushing, for though always pleased by the game, she was not accustomed to have it spoke of in such open terms, while I knew not what to say, for to tell the truth these seemed to me to be but limping verses. However, I bowed and smiled, and the Beau was too content with his own pleasure to notice any lack of admiration in me.

'And now – hah! – to it!' he cried. 'We ourselves also will serve divers lusts and pleasures (Titus three, three),' and he gestured to us to prepare, whereupon we were not slow to divest ourselves of our clothing, while he swept more papers from the desk and prepared paper for his sketches. But he was in some difficulty, for he kept searching about and finally, as we stood all naked waiting for his direction, he told us that he had left his drawing materials in the library and must fetch them.

'Hah! – warm yourselves – hah! – until I return. But not to excess, not to excess! My lord shall delay his coming (Matthew twenty-four, twenty-eight),' he said, and left us. The library being at the other end of the house, there was some little time before he could return, so we lay upon the pile of cloths he had now provided to make our little platform more comfortable and fell to toying with each other. But as I lowered my head to salute Tabby, my eye caught a curious chink of light in the floor by the edge of the platform, where one of the boards of the floor seemed loose. I bent to examine it and found a knot-hole where a finger could raise one of them and beneath, in the plaster, a neat hole had been made, through which I could see light from a window in a room below. Then a movement caught my sight and I applied my eye to the hole. The first thing I saw was a naked bottom, busily rising and falling in the unmistakable action of love, and looking further I saw my Lady Elizabeth's face turned up to me, her eyes closed in pleasure, and the dark head of her lover buried in her open bosom. I was looking down into a drawing-room occupied by My Lord's daughters, and by the black hair curling at the nape of the neck and the peculiar olive complexion of the skin I recognised the man pleasuring the lady upon her proper couch as Signor Cesareo, her guitar player, one of whose instruments was indeed giving her acute delight, while the other, its strings silent, lay upon a chair nearby.

Tabby, meanwhile, was growing curious and nuzzling at my shoulder. Holding my finger to my lips, I moved aside to allow her to see, whereat she giggled and closed her hand upon my own instrument, which, while it may have lacked the experience of the older man's, was nevertheless ready to play its own tune. Pushing her aside so that she fell upon her back, I thrust into her willing parts, whereupon she gave a little squeal, for no doubt I was somewhat rough in my urgency, being excited by the view beneath. Finding that as I lay upon her I was still able to see through the hole in the ceiling, I found myself without intending it mimicking the movements of the man below as he continued to pleasure My Lady – but as I looked he with a final fillip reached the height of his pleasure and lifting himself fell to his side, his piece still distended, red and throbbing, with a gleam of love's liquid upon it. My Lady Elizabeth was by no means content, for looking aslant, she seized his hand and conveyed it to her lower part, where he continued to rub with his fingers as she wriggled beneath them.

Meanwhile, another figure appeared, the unclothed person of the Lady Margaret who had clearly been observing them from some nearby place and now squatted down at their sides and began mummutting at his slowly diminishing affair. From this I hazarded that her sister had drawn the first chance in the game of love, and she feared that she would lose upon it which, from the expression upon the face of Signor Cesareo, whose instrument was clearly for the moment totally unstrung, was inclined indeed to be so.

Meanwhile Tabby and I kept it up, for the liveliness of the view had entirely taken from me any remembrance of the purpose of our meeting, and our mutual rapture was now incapable of restraint. Before we knew it, we spent together in a happy gusto just as Beau Rust reappeared, for the noise of a bundle of pencils falling to the floor announced his presence just as I fell exhausted onto Tabby's flushed and panting breast.

In brief, the Beau was not pleased at our betrayal, though fortunately, rolling over somewhat painfully upon the floor, I was able to conceal the displaced board and then edge it back into its position before he could guess at its displacement and thus the reason for our excitement. But my shrinking prick he could not fail to see. 'How is the mighty fallen, and the weapon of war perished (Two Samuel, one, twenty-seven),' he remarked pointedly.

'But come, come, at your age it should take but a moment to recover!' he went on. 'Why when I was a young colt at Bath, my mistress had not to wait but five minutes before I could renew the attack. 'Tis all the same with youngsters today, ye're too quick at play and too slow to revive – is that not so, my dear?' he said turning to Tabby, who indeed looked at me with a gleaming eye that showed her ready for another pass. Then leaning over me and lifting my stones with her hand, she gently nibbled with her teeth at the skin between them and my fundament, a delicious play which in a moment caused my nodding head to rise, whereupon the judicious application of her lips rendered it swiftly as sturdy as before.

The Beau this time set Tabby upon her back, and placed her left leg so that the knee fell over my right shoulder while her right leg was stretched out, and when I entered her – as I was now again very ready to do – a clear view was offered to the artist. He approached so closely to observe the play of my piece at its work that at one moment, as my pleasure increased and my movements became less susceptible of control, I actually struck his forehead with my hip, setting his wig all crooked and causing him to cough with such vehemence that our crisis occurred without his observing it, at which he somewhat lost his temper for, he said, it was his belief that the muscles of the male buttock altered their configuration at the moment of relief, which was something he much wished to observe.

'However,' he said, ' 'tis now time that I returned to my studies of the Italian text, and will summon you again,' and patting me on my naked rump, he added, 'Let her breasts satisfy thee at all times, and be thou ravished always with her love (Proverbs five, nineteen),' and once more placed two gold coins in our hands. We made our way from the room having pleasured ourselves, been of assistance to the Beau in his historical studies, and added to our small store of gold, so that we were well pleased.

At the bottom of the stairway we were making our way very quietly past the door of our Ladies' rooms, when suddenly there was a great noise within the door, a sound as of something falling, accompanied by the shrieking of voices, and in a moment the door opened and out came a great cloud of dust, in the midst of which was Signor Cesareo all naked save for a shirt clutched to him. He came up short on seeing us, but then ran away down the corridor. We were in some doubt what to do but hearing continued shrieks from within, entered to see the room covered in white dust as with snow, and at its centre a pile of sticks and plaster with a black figure – or rather one once dressed in black, but now all white with plaster – lying between the two unclothed figures of my Lady Elizabeth and my Lady Margaret, from whose lips were still emerging weaker cries of amazement.

We went forward, and while Tabby was assisting the ladies, I gathered up Beau Rust in my arms and laid him upon the floor, thinking him to be dead. But in a moment his eyes opened and he clapped his hands to his bald head and cried 'Me wig! Me wig! Bring wool and flax to cover my nakedness (Hosea two, nine),' then fainted again.

It was clear that after we had left his room he had raised the boards to watch his granddaughters at play, whereupon the floor had collapsed under him, precipitating him upon them and their paramour who, together with the rugs upon which they were lying, had broken his fall. I fetched some water from a jug upon the dressing table and applied it, whereupon once more the Beau's eyes opened and he began crying for his wig, which I found in the wreckage upon the bed and placed upon his head. Lifting him in my arms – for he was of small weight – I carried him up to his rooms and placed him upon his bed, whereupon he fell into a sleep or an unconsciousness and I returned below where now the two ladies were wrapped in loose gowns and were quiet, having drunk the best part of a bottle of sherry between them.

The Lady Elizabeth enquired after the Beau, who I said was resting, and should I send for a doctor? Whereupon she shortly replied that he was 'tough as boots' and would doubtless recover by his own efforts, from which I suspected that she realised the cause of his sudden descent. I must admit that her dishabille made it difficult for me, looking at her, not to remember the lustful enjoyment upon her features as she lay below the thrusting body of the Italian musician. At which, as though she read my thoughts, she said, stammering somewhat, 'Ah – do you see – ah – another person in the room?', looking about as if she expected the musician to emerge from some hiding place. Her sister was less reticent:

'Signor Cesareo,' she said drily, 'seems to have left his guitar here – for I suppose he has left?'

I bowed.

'He was not injured?'

'Not in any visible part, my lady,' I could not help but reply.

Lady Margaret seemed almost to smile.

'Thank you, Andrew, and thank you – ah – ?'

'Tabby, ma'am – my lady,'

Lady Margaret nodded.

'You work in the kitchens here?'

'General maid, my lady.'

'Thank you for your assistance, Tabby. We must see more of you. You need not, neither you nor Andrew, noise the accident abroad. Perhaps you, Andrew, would send Mr Caister to me before supper, and we will arrange for the ceiling to be mended, without troubling My Lord to hear of it.'

I bowed and we left.

A few days later Mr Caister gathered all the staff together in the great hall – a surprising occasion the like of which the older people among us said had never been seen before – to announce that in a week's time there would be held a great ball and buffet to celebrate the victory at Waterloo. There were to be present many members of the aristocracy and their ladies, and it was My Lord's ambition that his hospitality should equal, if not outshine, anything the county had ever seen.

The following days were so filled with incident from dawn to dusk that we had no time for anything but cleaning and polishing, fetching and carrying, sewing and patching; the kitchens were busy with food to be stored in the icehouse, or in the cellars where ice must be fetched daily to cool and keep it fresh.

In the middle of the week, the footmen were called to Mr Caister's room to be lectured upon the manner in which we were to behave to the guests: how the eldest sons of the dukes of the blood royal were to take precedence over the marquesses; how the marquesses and lay dukes being equal, the dukes' younger sons came before viscounts but after earls; how the Knights of the Garter, if commoners, came before judges of the high court; how the younger sons of viscounts came before the younger sons of barons . . . But as to how we were to recognise them, nothing. We were to address dukes as 'my lord' or 'your grace', marquesses as 'my lord marquess', earls and viscounts and bishops and barons as 'my lord'. We were to stand ready at all times to hand food where requested, to be of assistance when required, but on no account to offer it if not required . . . All this until our heads were bursting.

Then Mr Caister threw open the doors of a large cupboard to disclose rows of splendid liveries, ordered, it was said, for the time of the late King's coronation, the last time when a grand assembly was held at Rawby. Mr Caister took down a pile of beautiful, pale doe-skin breeches and told us all to try them on. I seized a pair that seemed of likely size and, removing my small-clothes, started to pull them on.

'Mm – oh, no!' cries Mr Caister, 'mm – you must remove your undergarments, for they will show beneath the doe-skin, which can on no account be – mm – permitted.'

So I threw off my underclothes, which at the best of times were sparse, and pulled on the breeches, which indeed fit like a second skin, and I had to tuck my privates down between my legs so I resembled a girl. A thick extra layer of skin lay in a flap before the breeches which, pulled up and buttoned, held in place to disguise the male appendage and to prevent the dark hair from showing through to alarm (or excite, as Tom said) the ladies.

Shortly, we were all attired in breeches and in coats bearing My Lord's arms and so much aged and dirty gold braid that my heart failed at the thought of cleaning it all and stood in a row before Mr Caister.

'Mm – turn about!' he cried, and we turned, displaying a row of fine buttocks all tight as drums under the doe-skin. Tom wriggled his bottom in an affected, girlish way, whereupon Mr Caister fetched him a thwack with his stick which made Tom cry out.

'No – mm – nonsense, young Tom!' he cried. 'This is serious business. Turn about!' And we turned again, whereupon he walked along the row, pausing only in front of James, a whacking fellow the front flap of whose breeches was incapable of disguising the organ beneath it.

'Find some way of – mm – disposing of your engine, James!' said Mr Caister.

'But sir!' protested the unfortunate James, 'I know not how . . .'

'Well, either you find some way, or you do not serve,' said Mr Caister, 'for we cannot have you looking as though you are about to ravish the ladies, much though – mm – some of them – mm – well, at all events, draw yourself in, man, or stand behind the door.'

So we stripped again and took our new finery away to be cleaned when we had time to do it, which was little enough, the work continuing day and night.

On the morning of the ball itself the household was awake at dawn and we were out gathering greenery to decorate the saloon and great drawing-room, which had had its carpets lifted and was to act as ballroom, with a platform at one end of it for the orchestra. The musicians were placed for the occasion under the direction of Signor Cesareo, My Lord believing him (and with justice) to have more knowledge of fashionable music than his colleagues. And so they sat, while we decorated the walls, practising dances, with the Signor directing them from the keyboard of a new grand pianoforte especially bought for the occasion at the cost, we heard, of no less than fifty guineas, and brought on a great wagon from Cambridge. Signor Cesareo insisted to My Ladies that no fashionable ballroom in London was without such a thing, the harpsichord being now quite out of date as an instrument for dancing.

By five o'clock a great quiet had fallen upon the house; everyone was in his room preparing. A few of the gentlemen had made use of the bath room and were now decking themselves, while the ladies had not been seen since they broke their fast, so intent were they on their toilette. We, below the stairs, were cleaning ourselves as best we might, every maid in the house readying herself for service, while we footmen wriggled into our breeches and checked each other's coats for perfection.

At seven the first carriages began to appear, and My Lord and My Ladies took up position in the great hall to receive his guests, who soon were coming so thick that Mr Caister had it hard to repeat their names to My Lord as they entered: 'His Grace the – mm – Duke of Hertfordshire; My Lord Marquess of Scrimmage; My Lord Bishop of – mm – Nunquam; My Lady Marchioness of Taciturn; Viscount – mm – Talland and the Hon. Frederick Shake; My Lord the Earl of Readymoney and Fume . . .'

In half an hour the saloon was so crowded it was almost impossible to move; I stood at the door between it and the great dining-room and at a quarter to eight precisely, at a signal from Mr Caister, threw open the doors. The crowd pressed through, as though escaping from a fire, to fall

upon the long tables laden with boiled turkeys in celery
sauce, pigs' feet and ears in jelly, tongue and *fricandeau*,
saddle of mutton, roast woodcocks, sweets and wild-fowl
in an oyster sauce, roasted beef and bacon, *raqout à la
Française*, and on a side table walnuts, raisins and
almonds, apples, cakes, pears and oranges and all manner
of other fruit.

Though used to lack of ceremony at table, I had never
seen men and women so near to fighting over their food or
so intent to fetch the champagne from the bottles, which as
soon as they were empty flew across the tables as though
they were alive, to break against the wall. Though it seemed
we had prepared food for twice the number of guests, in
scarcely ten minutes the table was as bare as before we
had set it and everyone was making again into the saloon,
carrying their glasses with them, where they continued
to drink, for each table in the house was laden with
bottles which were replaced as speedily as they were
emptied, My Lord having ordered cases enough to fill his
large cellar.

At half past eight, again at a signal from Mr Caister, the
doors to the ballroom were thrown wide and a great gasp
went up, for though it was yet light outside a burst of
brilliance like sunlight was to be seen in the ballroom, so
bright that only the press behind forced the nearest guests
against their nervous will through the open doors. The
orchestra was in its place and already playing, but above
their heads and at intervals around the room stood tall
poles on which lights burned with dazzling brightness. My
Lord had sent to London and had installed the new gas-
making mechanism, and for the first time in England (or so
'twas later said) a private house displayed the new lighting
which had only been recently seen for the first time in the
streets of the metropolis, and still did not light the provin-
cial cities, for many people regarded it as the work of the
D---l. Indeed had I not seen the workmen testing it, and
been shown the retorts set up in the cellars, with the
condenser, heater and purifier, thus making the whole
display less mysterious, I would myself have been appre-

hensive of the power of so astonishing an approximation to sunlight.

In a while the wonder wore off and the dancing began. We were then able from our posts about the walls to examine the guests and con their persons as they trod the figures of the dances, marked out in chalk upon the boards.

The room made a fine picture; the men were all at the height of fashion and there was scarce a wig to be seen except that of old Beau Rust, who had sufficiently recovered from his fall to attend, nodding his head in a chair next the orchestra. Now the men wore their own hair and since it was known that, despite My Lord's strenuous efforts, no member of the Royal Family was to be present, many were in the new loose or frock coats, and a good number even in pantaloons rather than breeches.

The women made a sight so ravishing that from time to time only the tightness of our borrowed breeches prevented our admiration taking visible, nay tangible form. Their dresses were cut so low that it was impossible that most of their bosoms should not be pressed upon the attention of even the least curious observer, while the high belts of many lifted and displayed their bubs as though offering them to the lips of the beholder. Just as we had been ordered by Mr Caister to eschew any underclothes, it was quite clear that few ladies wore anything of consequence beneath the diaphanous muslin of which most of their dresses were made. And on more than one occasion, as a more vigorous partner swung her about in a quadrille, the swirling of a skirt gave a tempting view of quarters which only a husband should, in strictness, set eyes upon. One or two wore skirts so short that they would only a few years previously have been considered scandalous, and it was clear – so closely did their dresses cling to their bodies – that they had wet them before wriggling into them.

At one moment, one woman – and not of the youngest – threw off the upper part of her clothes altogether and appeared in the ballroom stark naked to the waist, explaining, when My Lord sent one of his daughters to remonstrate, that the Princess of Wales, the year before, had at a ball in Geneva appeared dressed *en Venus* – or rather not dressed, further than the waist. My Lord was not impressed by this explanation and required that the lady's large and unstructured bosom should nevertheless remain covered on this occasion.

Late in the evening when the reels, the minuets, the country dances and the quadrilles were exhausted, Signor Cesareo introduced the new German waltz which (he had told me) Lady Jersey had brought into society at Almack's only this season, and which had generally been condemned (even by Lord Byron) as a dance which no truly modest woman would indulge in. Even in London society the most fashionable of ladies would not perform it unless another lady, or at least a blood relative, were present. Indeed it is a most lascivious measure in which man and partner are forced to embrace as though making love to each other in public. One or two of those present notably turned their backs and left the room, but others were clearly excited by the spectacle and one lady, the daughter of my Lord Bishop of Bellanach, in Ireland, was so overcome that as she stood by me she seemed like to faint, and to help recover herself put out her hand, which fell upon my backside, whereupon she started and passed her palm freely over my haunches before coming to herself.

It was three in the morning and past before the evening ended, and that with more food and yet more wine, so that many of the guests staggered as they met the fresh night air and had to be assisted into their carriages by the only truly sober men in the company, we servants. I will not say that as we did so we did not avail ourselves of the opportunity to support the more beautiful ladies with an enthusiasm more than we showed in pushing their consorts up after them, many stinking of vomit or worse as a result of their excesses. Indeed by the end of the evening, aided by the heated bodies after exertions of the dance and the additional warmth of the gas lamps, the stench which arose in the crowded rooms, composed of sweat, vomit and the farts emitted from bowels overladen with rich food, was such that it was almost impossible to breathe with freedom.

Some of the guests of the house sat around for another hour or more before they made their way to bed. In the meantime the orchestra was almost dead of exhaustion and we footmen were tired enough on our feet, though we had for the most part done nothing but stand about or fetch more bottles up. But Mr Caister was pleased enough with us, as his smiles told when he dismissed us. Tom and I were last to close the doors of the ballroom and the saloon but as we turned to make our way down to the kitchen then to our room – for the clearing up of the mess was to wait until the morrow – a servant approached who had been eating with us and whom we knew to be attached to someone staying in the house.

'My mistresses' compliments,' he said, 'and I am to bring you to them.'

'And who might they be?' asked Tom, who was less disposed than I to take things as they came.

'The Honourable Misses Glaistow of A'Mhoine, in Scotland,' said the man, 'the sisters to My Lord the Earl of A'Mhoine.'

'Hah,' said Tom, 'and what have we to do with them?'

'Ask rather what they have to do with you,' said the man. 'But if you are not geldings, are happy to jock and not averse to a gold piece, you will do well to attend them.'

At which he turned and began to make his way towards the east wing.

Tom and I looked at each other, then followed.

'Look here,' he whispered, 'I'm not your friend, but I'm not for throwing gold away, so it's each for each in the venture, d'ye see?'

I nodded.

In course we came to the door of one of the guest bedrooms, which the fellow opened, standing back for us to enter. Sitting by the bed were the two sisters, perhaps of eighteen and twenty years, one dark and the other brown, and I recognised them from the lowness of their gowns as two of the ladies who had most enjoyed participating in the waltz, and who had shown such attention to their partners that I wondered that they had not lain down in the middle of the floor and gone to it in regular fashion. Their dresses were of the lightest and their rosy nipples peeped above them, at once forward and blushing to be seen.

'Thank you, Edward,' said one, 'and goodnight.'

'My Ladies,' said the fellow, and left.

'Well, now,' said the dark lady, coming towards us, 'what fine fellows My Lord has to serve him, and in what fine uniform. But it interests my sister and me that he should employ eunuchs,' and she stared at our lower parts, where indeed the natural evidence of manhood was disguised by the cut of the breeches.

'Remove your jackets, so that we may examine your figures more closely,' said the brown girl peremptorily. We did so, and they came towards us and turned us about, the dark girl placing her hand below my belly and sliding it down to see what she could feel. By now I was in great pain through the distension of my natural parts beneath the restriction of the breeches, and so by his wincing was Tom, upon whom the brown girl was pressing similar attentions.

The girls looked at each other and laughed.

'I fancy,' said one, 'we have two men in disguise, not eunuchs at all. Shall we see if we can tempt their manhood forth?'

Whereupon they stepped back and at the same time raised their dresses over their heads and dropped them into the bed. Their figures were the most beautiful I had yet seen, fuller than that of Ellen, less full than that of Tabby. Perhaps my dear Sophia, at Alcovary, would have been the nearest in beauty had I ever been at more leisure to view her. I was so roused by their regular, spherical bosoms, their slight waists, jutting hips and firm thighs, that my agony was almost insupportable and it was with relief that I saw Tom, at my side, throw caution away and unbuttoning his breeches thrust them to his knees, his manhood, released, springing up so that all could hear the thwack with which it hit against his belly. The girls showing nothing but pleasure at the sight, I prepared to do the same, but the dark girl came forward, knelt and with her own fingers undid the buttons and drew down the flap at the front of my breeches, then passed her hands down over my hips to draw the doe-skin from my body, reaching to hold my tool and raise it wonderingly to her eyes, laying it on the palm of a small hand so that its head rested above her wrist.

'Look, Annie,' she said, 'what a splendid toy is here to be petted!' and leant forward to kiss its tip with soft lips.

Stepping out of our breeches we were led to the bed, where the two ladies drew our shoes and long stockings from our feet and lifted our shirts over our heads, then laid us on the mattress and began to minister to us with such tender attentions that speaking for myself it was only by thinking desperately of other things – trying to calculate the number of bottles drunk that evening, and the total cost to My Lord's estate – that I was able to maintain myself a man. Indeed, when my lady took my yard between her lips and began to suck upon it with a long, slow motion, the hair falling over her face to conceal my whole middle part, I attempted to draw her head away, fearing that I could no longer contain myself, but she held my hands at my side and, no longer susceptible to control, my whole privities thrust themselves with a life of their own into her face as my life flooded forth. Even then, she continued to suck upon me ever more gently, so that in almost a swoon I lay enchanted, only half aware that a foot away, upon the same bed, Tom was suffering the same glad death.

We both lay still for what seemed an age while the ladies kneeled above us. Then, almost as at a pre-arranged signal, they changed their places and with a gentle but strong motion encouraged us to turn so that we lay upon our fronts, when we felt them begin to stroke our whole bodies, beginning at the neck, their fingers trailing down our backs, over our buttocks, down our thighs to our feet, then up, passing between our legs and the inside of our thighs and up our backs again. After a while this became unbearably delightful and I lifted myself as I once more began to swell with pleasure. When, passing her hand through my legs, my fair partner felt the renewal of life, I was made to turn again and she lifted herself to kneel above me. Taking my staff in one hand, she drew aside her flesh with her other and introduced it to its proper place, sinking upon me so that her dark hair met my lighter hair as snugly as though 'twere woven into a single mat. At my side, Tom and his friend were in the same motion and the sisters twined their arms together, their hands on each other's shoulders as they began slowly to rise and fall, their movements gradually increasing in velocity as their desire mounted and their emotions grew more intense. This time we were more ready to restrain our outpouring and indeed I might have lived longer had it not been that at the moment when her bosom and face flushed with joy, my partner reached down and caught one of my paps between her fingers, pinching it with such fervour that the pain of it joined with the pleasure in my loins to release both emotions in a spasm of delight which almost threw her from her seat. At my side Tom, only a moment later, gave a shout as he too died beneath his tormenter's administrations.

The two women lifted themselves together and without a word descended from the bed, where they threw gowns over their shoulders and, without giving us a moment to resume our clothes, opened the door and ushered us into the corridor, along which we hastily raced clutching our breeches, shirts, shoes, stockings and coats, reaching the stairway to the kitchen with no one seeing us. Indeed, the house was now quiet and, without ensuring that we were upstairs, Mrs Tickert had locked the doors to our room.

Tom's comments upon the ladies could not have been repeated in their presence, but reflected my own feelings towards them.

'Though,' he concluded, ' 'twas as fine a clicket as I've had since you stole Tabby from me,' (he looked unfriendly at that). 'We must hope they've not given us the burner,' and went on to say that he wouldn't mind if I got the burner, as it might quieten me down, for I was far too randy for his liking, especially with other men's wenches.

But I was far too tired to worry about the clap, or to think of Tabby or what Tom thought or believed or would do. I was too tired even to wonder at the freedom with which the two ladies, having entertained us as though we were the dearest of lovers, had dismissed us as the most menial of pimps. Though we must spend the night upon the harsh rush mats before the embers of the kitchen fire, I lay myself upon them as though they were the softest swan's-down and slept a sleep as deep and dark as velvet.

Chapter Eight

Sophie's Story

As we rode out of Cambridge, my companion – whose full name, I learned, was Rosanna Vanis (the name of her husband was well-known among the tribes of Egyptians) – told me how they lived their lives. They were not, she affirmed, the thieves and villains popular legend supposed, but existed for the most part on the proceeds of legitimate buying and selling of horses and donkeys, though they were much harried by the constables, for every theft which took place in a neighbourhood where there was a Gypsy encampment was visited upon them. Indeed very recently a man of their tribe, one Stanley, had been falsely accused of housebreaking, and would have been executed had not all his friends met together and gathered a considerable sum to prove an alibi which had resulted in his gaining his freedom.

She had never, she said, known cases of thieving among them except in the extremity of poverty and despair, which she admitted sometimes occurred. In one case a child who had been scalded to death had had to remain unburied for many days until his father, driven to it, stole some wood from a carpenter to make up a coffin – which was unfortunately discovered but the carpenter, being a humane man, informed the constables that he had given the wood, and so the situation had been saved.

With these sad and some more high-spirited stories the journey was enlivened. Rosanna also assured me that wherever there was a fair there was also an opportunity to make money at fortune-telling and that with my superior manner and dress I would be sure to do well. This I was not sanguine of yet hoped to be the case for to be honest, charming though my companion was, I was not entirely persuaded that the company of the wandering Egyptians was something I cared to prolong further than was necessary, and an accumulation of funds would enable me to free myself, grateful though I must be for this present escape.

As we went, I came to know some of Rosanna's companions. Her horse, though willing, was old and proceeded at only a walking pace, so those who were not mounted – even the children – had no difficulty in keeping up with us upon the way, and from time to time several of them would gather to walk alongside us and exchange banter. The pretty children, with bare feet and almost naked bodies, would jump up to ride upon the shafts of the cart so that I was continually in a fear that they would fall beneath the hooves of the horses or the wheels of our equipage.

The band was indeed scattered over the road like a flock of sheep. Two other wagons with luggage kept within sight, but many women and children and men wandered along the length of the procession to keep their eye upon the whole. One in particular, who could not escape my notice, was a magnificent creature with jet-black hair and a face which, though swarthy, was remarkable for its strong features and piercing black eyes. A ragged shirt did little to conceal the magnificent shoulders from which depended sinewy, strong arms baked in the sun to the colour of mahogany, with which he controlled the reins of a fine nag. Pointing him out to Rosanna, I asked who he was.

'Ah, you've an eye for a *rincana mush*,' she said. ''Tis *Derai* Bovile, and he is our *dimber damber*. You will see much of him, later,' with which she turned taciturn and would say no more.

Here I should say that much of the language in which Rosanna and her family and friends conversed was more foreign to me than Greek, being the language of the Gypsies which, she assured me, was spoken the same throughout the world. In my time with the band I was able to commit to memory only a few words, learning, for instance, that *rincana* was 'handsome', and *mush*, 'man', while they called their leader their *dimber damber*. 'Woman' was *mannishee*, 'boy' *chau* and 'girl' *chi*. Having tied up their *gry*, or horse, they set up their *tanya* or tent, and settled then to a meal, more often than not of roast *hotchawitcha*, or hedgehog. I was able to note, with my little knowledge, that some of the words approximated to those in other languages: for instance their word for 'eye' was *yoc*, which in Latin is *oculus* and in Italian *occhio*; they say *pomya* for 'apple', which in the Latin is *pomus* and in French *pomme*. But I lack the knowledge of more than a few common words in those languages, and cannot make a true comparison. Each person I met, moreover, even the small children, used their own language freely among themselves but was able to speak English to my perfect understanding, if often with a strong accent – though to tell the truth, when they wished to converse without my following them, they would fall into the Gypsy language, to my ill-temper.

On reaching the heath high above the small town of Royston, there we set up camp, Rosanna busying herself with tethering and feeding the horse, then with putting up a tent. She was aided by Sam, a boy whom I took to be her son, but who was introduced to me as her *derai*, or master, which the women call their husbands. He could not, I thought, have been more than twenty, whereas she was perhaps in her middle thirties, but I was to learn that age was not much taken into account among them, the present head of the whole sect of Gypsies in England, said to be into his nineties, having recently taken a wife of sixteen who had already borne him a child.

Their tent was of considerable size, much larger than many cottages I had seen when visiting the poor near our house. In the middle was a space open to the sky which served as kitchen, a fire being built there, and at the two ends were separate sleeping spaces. In this tent lived, I learned, Rosanna and her husband, and his sister who was a girl of about my own age, Anna, whom I now met and with whom I was to share one of the sleeping spaces.

'But you will not need it tonight,' Rosanna said mysteriously, whereat Anna laughed, and set upon the fire a great pot into which she threw various vegetables and herbs, a fine and savoury smell soon mounting from it. And by the end of the afternoon we sat down to a good meal of some meat whose nature was undisclosed, but which was supremely nourishing. Rosanna and her husband then set to discussing how I should be best put to work – something I had thought I might be consulted upon, except that I had no idea how to set about it. Their view was that I should have to myself one of their best tents, and that they should go into the town to tout my presence to anyone who seemed likely to show an interest, and that I could ask half a guinea for a consultation. Sam also believed that it would be best for me to be as divorced as might be from the tribe itself for, he said, I was of appearance no Gypsy and the connection, if known, might result in fewer people approaching me, for though many believed Gypsy women to have 'the eye', many also associated them with the black arts and would not for that reason come near them.

By this time it was evening and the light was beginning to fail, whereupon Rosanna and her sister rose and asked if I would go with them to the stream to bathe. It being a thundersome day with hot air and close, I was glad to do so and must say here that the cleanliness and sweetness of the Gypsy women and the men too would put to shame some of our aristocrats, whose bodies are so often astink with rank sweat and old perfume slapped upon it, while the Gypsies were in the open air for much of their lives and took advantage of the running streams to cleanse themselves. Upon the heath a shallow stream running through a copse or spinney offered an ideal bathing room where we were able to strip and scrub, the water being cold but no colder than I had often been used to in the pool at Alcovary. I was cautious, half expecting some of the Gypsy men to burst in upon us. But they take great care, it seems, to show their women deference and politeness and would no more dream of purposely coming upon them in private moments than some of our men would think of not taking advantage of such a circumstance – another example of the superiority of their manners to our own.

When we had bathed, we returned to the tent and I put on

the only other dress that I had – the white muslin in which I was married. The two other women were dressed too in something approaching finery and they led me out to a clearing between the other tents where most of the band were now met, among them the impressive figure of their leader *Derai* Bovile, around whom the others cleared a space as they saw us approach so that he stood alone, still in the black breeches and torn white shirt in which he had formerly appeared.

With a whispered word to do just what I was ordered, Rosanna and her sister-in-law retired, leaving me standing before his commanding figure.

'What name do you wish to take among us?' he asked.

Bemused, I could think of none but my own and muttered 'Sophia' in an undertone, which I had to repeat, for he had not heard it.

'Then repeat after me,' he said – and I was led in the following oath:

> *I, Sophia, do swear to be a true sister, and that I will in all things obey the commands of the great tawny prince, and keep his counsel, and not divulge the secrets of my brethren.*
>
> *I will never leave nor forsake the company, but observe and keep all the times of appointment, either by day or by night, in every place whatever.*
>
> *I will take my prince's part against all that shall oppose him, or any of us, according to the utmost of my ability; nor will I suffer him, or any one belonging to us, to be abused by any strange abrams, rufflers, hookers, pailliards, swaddlers, Irish toyles, swigmen, whip jacks, jarkmen, bawdy baskets, dommerars, clapper dogeons, patricoes or curtals; but will defend him, or them, as much as I can, against all other outliers whatever. I will not conceal aught I win out of libkins or from the ruffmans, but will preserve it for the use of the company.*

After which Bovile stepped forward, seized me and, kissing me thoroughly, then swung me with little effort under his arm and carried me off, to a rousing cheer from the assembled company.

Before I retail what happened to me next, I must admit that much of my oath was meaningless to me. Rosanna later translated it and it meant, in effect, total loyalty to the band, together with some niceties such as that I must preserve to the common use any money I was able to make, and be prepared to defend as best I might my fellow Gypsies.

It was clear to me as Bovile broke through the entrance of his tent that my first duty was to be to him and, from the manner in which he set me down none too carefully upon a mattress there, then stood to look at me as he stripped the remnants of cloth from his upper body, then put his hands to his belt, that that duty was naught to do with food and drink but more to do with other bodily appetites.

I must confess that I was not ill-pleased, for I had been some days without the comfort of a man's body, having had no connection since the last visit of Coln to my rooms in Cambridge, and that, since he was somewhat the worse for liquor, had been unremarkable. Besides which, Bovile, I now saw, had a figure which would have brought any woman to a state of readiness. It was clear from the brown skin which stretched unshaded from neck to waist that much of his time was spent in the open air and without cover, while I was unable not to fix my eyes upon his essential manly part which, though not yet fully extended, promised to be of admirable proportions, both as to length and thickness. His body was as hairless as those of my brothers, though he was much their senior – indeed, this was the first time I learned that all men did not have hair upon belly and thigh, where all was smooth and white as woman's flesh, a generous, startlingly black thicket at the base of his tool being the only counterpart of that mass of pitchy curls upon his head.

He stepped forward to bestride me, smiling with pride as without the touch of my hand or his own his yard jerkily rose to its full pride.

' 'Tis not only the gentry that have fine tackle!' he said. 'Or that can swive like true Britons.' Whereupon he reached down, with one movement lifted my clothing above my head, and raised me so that my middle section was clasped between his thighs and I lay supported thus as he drew my dress over my head. I was naked as he, and as ready for the fight.

It was evident that this stallion was not interested in the niceties of polite behaviour, for having carried me off like a piece of property, he used me like one, simply dropping me onto the pile of rugs which formed the bed and throwing himself upon me entirely without ceremony so that had I not, knowing what was expected of me, spread my legs widely apart, he would clearly have forced me perhaps to my pain and peril. There was no attempt at tender caress or endearment, but simple fornication such as I had seen the animals perform in the fields – except that it was prolonged far beyond what the goat or horse achieved. His hands were placed upon my shoulders, but though his chest was lifted from my own so that my breasts were free for him to nuzzle, he at no time bent his lips to them but simply and unrelentingly thrust with his hips, ploughing the furrow with force and vigour. He had raised me no less than three times to the ultimate throes of pleasure before he himself spent with a great roar, his body continuing to plunge, though with less and less power, until even he seemed for the moment exhausted, and I, my heart beating as 'twould burst, opened my eyes at last to see his wicked own peering deeply into mine as though he would read my soul – and to my astonishment and no less confusion, behind his head the eyes of four or five men of the tribe whose duty it was (as I later learned) to witness the subjugation of each new female member.

'*Bona kom-kista!*' cried Bovile, waving away these witnesses, who vanished silently into the night. His words meant, literally, 'A good love-ride!' and the meaning was quite clear, if the words were not, and I could not deny him a smile, which in return brought a broad grin to his face which I found irresistibly charming. Though without doubt to have been ravished in such a manner of a sudden, and if one misliked the ravisher, would have been a sorely disturbing experience, his person was so handsome and his power so impressive that few women but would have welcomed his attentions – which now, after the shortest time of relief, began again. Once more, there was no ceremony but the great storm having ceased, 'twas only a minor tempest was aroused in his loins. However, this time he was all eyes, looking deeply into my own, regarding my heaving breasts with what I believed was approbation, and sometimes raising himself so that he could see how his great yard disappeared, appeared and disappeared again within my willing cleft as we rocked like two boats in a swell until once more we came to a happy berth. Upon which, without further ceremony, he simply fell asleep between my legs; after a while his weight became so burdensome that with a great effort I heaved him over upon his back, and myself curled about him, a leg thrown over one of his massive thighs, and fell into a sleep.

I awoke, he still sleeping, to find a woman standing over us with a bowl of water and early morning sunlight showing through the cloth of the tent. With a somewhat surly air (no doubt provoked by jealousy) she set the water down and left us, and I was glad after the exertions of the previous night to lave myself as best I might. As I dried my body in a cloth which she had laid beside the bowl, I felt rather than saw his eyes upon me, and indeed as I turned their twin beacons struck right into my heart – for power and fixative quality I never knew their like. He regarded me kindly and with a smile, then rising picked up the wet cloth and handing it to me represented that I should bathe his limbs with it. I was happy to do so, wiping his broad back and massive shoulders, fine chest and arms, and then, as he stood, the thighs like young tree trunks, finally reaching between them to refresh those parts which had taught me, a few hours before, the height to which animal man could aspire at the top of his bent and which even now were impressive. His instrument, even relaxed, seemed of the same length and thickness it had been when extended so that wonderingly I held it in both hands and bent it this way and that, amazed that while it had such size it was still not hard nor stiff enough to perform a loving function.

It soon became clear from a growing resistance that I was rousing it to its practical state and had not he laughingly struck my hands away and pulled on his breeches, I might once more have felt its power – not that I would have repined at that but he seemed eager to encounter the new day.

Rosanna greeted me with a knowing look, while her sister asked whether I needed any plaisters after the night's activities, to which I was able to reply that I was uninjured, and that indeed had rarely felt in better health, which was received by them with smiles. After we had broken our fast frugally with bread and fresh, clear water, Rosanna and I set out to walk into the town, where at its western end I found to my surprise a small tent already erected, in which Sam was just setting up a small table, and indeed it looked not unattractive and a small group of townspeople had already gathered. Sam had, I learned, on Bovile's instructions employed a small boy to cry me through the town as a master astrologist. I asked whether an advertisement could not be placed in the local sheet but the silence which greeted my words was interpreted by me as meaning that none of the Egyptians could write and I hesitated to show my own superiority by offering to set out a notice for them (or rather, for myself).

However, it was soon clear that no more notice was needed than word passing from mouth to mouth. At Sam's suggestion, I made no charge for the first two people who came to me; one came to know where was a purse of money that had been stolen from him on the day before, whereupon I was able (with Mr Lilly's help) to tell him the thief was a tall, fair man who had hidden the purse under ground in a direction west from the spot where it was stolen – whereat he went off to trace the steps westward from his house, to find what he could find; and another to ask whether her husband should be cut for the stone, and if so, whether he would recover, which I was able to tell her would be successful and that though ill for a time he would soon be a whole man again.

Within an hour after these two, there was a line of people

outside the tent which continued for most of the day as a result, I believe, of the novelty of the situation, for though many almanacs were sold in the town there had not been an astrologer there for many years. The people were of all sorts, both men and women, and of all qualities, some serving maids in poor clothes, some women in what passed for fashionable dress in this small town – kerseymere spencers and white cambric gowns. Many wore straw bonnets, but some neat caps, a few even of Honiton lace, and some younger women had hair curled in ringlets. I was happy that while my dress was now somewhat untidy and badly in need of replacement, it was at least more fashionable than most, which seemed to impress my female visitors.

As to the men, most were still in breeches and wore stocks, but a few wore pantaloons and some the new cravats of muslin. One tradesman, who I learned kept a shop in the town's main street, appeared in a curled wig with a dress coat and vest, knee-breeches and buckles, cotton speckled stockings and square-toed shoes with large, shining buckles – he wished to know whether his business would continue to prosper.

The questions were many and varied, from those concerning stolen goods to whether wives or husbands were unfaithful, whether a woman would consent to be wooed or a man consent to marry his mistress with child. By five o'clock in the evening I was tired almost to sleeping, having paused only for a dish of meat at mid-day, and had gathered no less than seven pounds and fourteen shillings – more money than I had seen together in one place before.

So it was in high satisfaction that I walked back with Sam and Rosanna to the encampment, leaving a man to guard the tent until the following day, for Sam was of the opinion that the tribe should remain for at least another forty and eight hours 'to milk', he said, the remaining enquirers. For there was no need to wait for a *waqqaulus*, or fair, when I on my own could command more than a whole range of fortune-tellers or lucky-card numberers together.

As we came to the tents, Bovile strode out to meet us and held out his hand for my purse, which I handed to him, thinking he wished to see how much money I had taken. But he simply seized it and strode off with it without a word to me – at which I must have looked blank, for Rosanna asked what ailed me. When I asked when the division of my spoils would take place, she reminded me that I had sworn to give all I earned to the tribe – something which I had not taken seriously, but which it was now all too plain was to be the case. I asked whether they did not think the system unfair, but they wondered at that and asked whether I would not be content that we should share everything in common? For those who lacked the capacity to earn money would live in comfort by the aid of those who had it, while those who earned should be pleased to share what they had with those who had it not.

I could not but feel there was somewhere a flaw in this argument but felt it best not to pursue it, especially since I was tired to exhaustion. After a good meal from the cauldron which seemed to be everlastingly on the simmer – and with each hour to become more delicious – and some good ale, I felt much recovered, and in an hour or so was looking forward to the consolation of another term of passion with Bovile whose figure haunted my thoughts to the exclusion even of my memory of the money I had made, and lost, that day.

But there was no sign of him, and when Sam came from the sleeping-tent to the fireside, and bending down to Rosanna and placing his hand on her breast whispered to her that it was time to go to bed, my face must have expressed my disappointment, for she asked why I looked so sour. And when I wondered whether Bovile would not come for me, she replied that it was 'not my night'.

But what did she mean, I enquired?

'Why, you do not think he has the same *com* ever night?' she said. '*Mag* goes to his *tanya* tonight; you are not for his *wuddress* except when your time comes. So you might as well *auriqqu* and to bed.' At which Anna, also by the fire, smiled at my puzzlement and explained that Bovile had his pick of the women of the camp and to avoid the ill-nature which might otherwise arise, took them to his *wuddress* or bed in strict order. I would have some twelve or fourteen nights before it would once more be my turn to wait upon him. This explained the ill-temper of Mag, the woman who had brought us water that morning, whose turn had been delayed for twenty-four hours because of my arrival.

But did not the husbands and lovers of the women complain, I asked, at their leader's making love to their women?

Sam looked as though he might have something to say upon the subject, but Rosanna laughed and asked me whether the complaint of any lover would be likely to prevent me from going to Bovile's bed when my turn next came, at which I was silent, for though indeed he was a man the power of whose loins was mightily attractive, I could imagine myself, if beloved and beloving of some other, not being entirely happy at being at his beck and call whenever the timetable showed it.

But by now Sam had drawn Rosanna to her feet and they had nodded a good night and gone into their sleeping-tent, and Anna too got to her feet and was stretching, then beckoning.

Within our half of the tent I found a single pile of rugs upon which we were both to sleep and was so tired that without further pause I removed my dress and shift and lay down upon them. Anna stood between me and the fire as she lifted her dress over her head, and the flickering light outlined her body to me which was, I must confess, extremely beautiful. I had not, at the bathing place, considered it closely; now, however, in the romantic light and the unaccustomed closeness – for I had never shared a sleeping room with another woman before – I could not but admire her. She was perhaps three or four years older than me, her body more fully formed, slim but firm, the upper curves of her breasts declining to where at the tip they turned slightly upward, the curve below the nipples heavier and more spherical. Then came the small belly – all the women I had seen at the bathing place had been slim and muscular, partly through the hard work they did each day and partly, I guessed, through healthy and unfattening food – above thighs as devoid of fat as a healthy boy's, yet a backside plump and proud.

Naked as she was, she came and stood for a moment before lying at my side, and after a while raised herself on an elbow and whispered to ask whether I was not sad at not being with Bovile instead of her.

I was bound to admit I was, when to my surprise she placed her hand upon my breast and, bending closer, asked whether she could not console me for his absence. Never having received such an offer from someone of my own sex, I replied that I was glad of her friendship.

'Only of my friendship?' she asked, and when I was silent took the lobe of my ear in her mouth and nipped it sharply with her teeth. Then I felt her tongue tracing the curves of my ear and reaching inside it – a sensation new to me, and astonishingly moving.

I was startled by this, but at the same time warmed by it, and was entirely unable to resist as she knelt and drew my sole garment from me – even unconsciously raising myself to make the action easier for her. In the dim light I felt rather than saw her lower herself until she could take one of my toes into her mouth, sucking it like a baby at the teat, while her hand edged up to my knee, then my thigh and, as I opened my legs to accommodate it, between them to my softer part, where she began a stroking which was more tender and comfortable than the action of any man I had yet encountered.

Leaving my feet, I felt her tongue follow her hand up the inside of my leg until she was nibbling at the soft flesh of my thigh and then her tongue followed her fingers and traced the twin lips of my lower mouth, then actually entering me, slowly moving, then quickening to flick lightly at the centre of emotion. A quick shudder ran through my body, at which her action quickened still further, her fingers meanwhile busying themselves about my breasts, teasing them until they seemed about to burst with the pleasure of it, which was no less delicious – though quite different – to that I had experienced even in the arms of Mr Ffloyd, so far by a long way the gentlest of my lovers.

Now, I felt Anna's body shift so that after a while she was lying with her lower parts near my shoulder, then lifting herself so that she was kneeling above me, her lips still pleasuring me, while her knees were on either side of my head. Lifting her hands to her person, she drew her flesh apart with the obvious intention that I should offer to her the attention she was paying me.

And so it was that for the first time I applied my tongue to the lower parts of a woman; to my pleasure, she was sweet and clean, only a slight musky taste falling upon my palate as I found the ultimate seat of her pleasure, hard as a small hazelnut.

Flicking it with my tongue in just the way she was exciting me, I at the same time was able to weigh her charming breasts in my hands, rolling the nipples between my fingers until they were as tight as my own, when at almost the same moment our bodies tensed with ultimate pleasure, and she tightened her thighs upon my head so that I seemed almost buried within her. Then she collapsed upon me before lifting herself to turn so that she could lie with her head in the crook of my arm, our hands between each other's thighs in a comfortable warmth which after a moment or two lulled us into slumber.

I awoke some hours later – for the fire was almost out, only a dull glow indicating the embers – to feel a movement of her fingers and once more, but this time with a slow, casual quiet which produced an equally intense but lazy pleasure, we gave ourselves to each other. And early in the morning, as cold light began to show, for a third time she devoted her tongue to pleasing me, while herself declined the attentions I now felt almost too tired to give but in politeness felt bound to offer.

I was truly astonished at the luxury of the dissipation we had enjoyed. Later, when I had an opportunity to discuss it with her, Anna told me that she had always preferred women to men, and that while she had made love with men on numerous occasions, the experience had never compared in depth with what she had experienced with her own sex. She had always felt, she explained, that men regarded the act of love as a battle which they must win, and the urgency of each occasion much diminished the pleasure she could find in it, while with a woman there was more ease, less haste, less urgency. She had never failed to reach the height of pleasure in such a manner, while with men 'no sooner are they up, than they're down; no sooner hot, than cold; no sooner on, than off,' she said. Moreover, man was too soon exhausted, while with woman there was no reason to conclude activity but the coming of morning!

With what reluctance I rose from our couch, the reader will understand. I was perhaps even more tired than I had been after my encounter with Bovile, for though he had been immeasurably more febrile than my female companion, the centre of my pleasure had not been so roused as by this night's encounter during which Anna had seemed to touch every chord of pleasure within me, so that the ultimate height of my enjoyment had been higher and more intense than on any previous occasion. Perhaps it was true, I considered, that men were always more concerned with their own pleasure than that of their companions.

But I was able to rouse myself, if not until Anna had fetched cold water to splash upon my body, for she seemed instantly to have recovered herself to her normal vigour, while even after I had clothed myself and made my way out to where Rosanna and Sam were breaking their fast, my eyes were still heavy, a fact which brought a blush to my cheek when Rosanna seemed to look questioningly between me and her sister-in-law. However, she may not have guessed what passed between us, while Sam seemed only concerned that I should eat my bread and drink my water and go with him to the tent where, once more, I would make money to be placed in the general coffers of the tribe – an activity about which I was less enthusiastic than he.

As we left the camp, I saw a woman's figure leave the tent I knew to be Bovile's, and as she lifted the canvas I thought I glimpsed for a moment his naked frame behind her. One thing of which I was confident was that if I was not to be summoned to his bed for another two weeks, he would certainly be waiting to receive my purse that same evening.

The day was unremarkable; another procession of the good folk of Royston invited my advice and rewarded me liberally for it, and as I expected, Bovile indeed met me on my return to the camp and seized my purse, nodding in approbation as he weighed it in his hand.

'You do well, *arincana* Sophia,' he said, smiling. I returned his smile only faintly, I fear, and made my way to our tent where Sam and Rosanna had food ready for me.

I retired early to my pile of rugs and was almost asleep when I heard a pitiful moaning outside the tent walls and, rising, put on my dress and took myself out, where I saw Sam and another man supporting a third as he staggered past. His shirt was torn and bloodied and blood streamed from his nose and one ear, while one of his arms dangled uselessly at his side; at each step he grunted and groaned.

Anna was at my side, having come to see, as I had, what was the trouble. She merely nodded grimly, and turned back. As I followed her into the tent, her sister-in-law asked, 'What goes forward?'

'Ah, 'tis only Rafe again,' Anna replied, and when I later asked her what had happened to the man, she replied that he was recently married to a beautiful girl of the tribe, a favourite of Bovile's. The latter had no right to object to the match, since the girl and he were not related, but having shown his disapprobation before the contract, he had insisted ever since on enjoying the girl each time her turn had come round as was his inalienable right under Gypsy custom, which had the force of law.

She had first entreated him then even tried to hide from him when her time came. Once before, Rafe had tried to protect her within their tent and Bovile had beaten him severely before taking her and forcing her to his pleasure. Now, once more, the unfortunate young man had tried to reason with the Gypsy leader not to claim his rights with the *chi* but Bovile had insisted, and when Rafe had once again tried to protect her, had again beaten him and broken his arm, such was his superior strength. The couple's tent stood close by ours and for most of the night I had to suffer his moans of physical injury as much as mental anguish at understanding what pain and humiliation Bovile was at that moment visiting upon his wife. To my surprise, Anna showed no sympathy at all for him and even at one time cried out to him to 'hold his noise' or she would come and break his other arm. I hoped that I would never myself be in need of sympathy from her or the other members of the tribe, for while they evidently took great pleasure in their animal instincts, it seemed that the human emotions of pity and compassion were foreign to them.

Chapter Nine

The Adventures of Andy

The adventure of the night of the Waterloo Ball did not, alas, result in an improvement in relations between Tom and me. On the contrary, for in relating to the other footmen our encounter with the Misses Glaistow, he was quick to magnify his part in the orgy while diminishing mine so that for a time I was known as 'Handy Andy' on the supposition that, my manly part being incapable of maintaining its rigidity until My Lady was content, I had had to bring her to satisfaction by means of the application of my finger – a proposition I was quick to deny, but which afforded the others far too much opportunity for country humour than it was easy for me to sustain.

Tabby only made things worse by stoutly defending me, even to claiming that Tom was not half the man I was. He took this extremely ill and as often as was possible got in my way when I was serving at table, making me appear clumsy and maladroit, so that on one or two occasions I received a stern look from My Lord. Fortunately Mr Caister saw what Tom was about and made allowances for me, though far from knowing the cause. Although he was indifferent to the fact that any guest in the house could summon one of the female staff to his bed without anyone raising an eyebrow, he would by no means have taken it easily had he known that any of the male servants provided a similar service for the female guests, much less for their fellow servants. I cannot guess at the reason for this, unless it was rooted in his own proclivities, but at all events it was the case and Tom dared not reveal to the butler the cause of his ill temper with myself, for he too would have felt the brunt of Mr Caister's undoubted anger.

Tabby and I were able, in our spare time, to continue to provide Beau Rust with the means to illustrate his great work – though I must confess to doubting, from time to time, whether there was not more pleasure taken in the simple sight of our love-making than in the provision of illustrative material for his book, for his powers as an artist were sketchy in the extreme.

During the hours we spent with him, we gradually grew to know more about him, for at the end of our activities he would regale us with memories of his youth, from which we ended with a clear view of how he came to leave the church and become rather a man of fashion than of the cloth. In the suspicion that his account of himself might interest the reader, I take the liberty of appending it here, though with his usual exclamations and quotations from the Scriptures excised, no less for reasons of space than of tedium.

Beau Rust's Account of Himself.

'Twas in the year of 'fifty-nine when half the world was reading M. Voltaire's *Candide* and the other half mourning the death of Wolfe at the victory of Quebec, that I for the first time set foot in the city of Bath. I was then, I must tell you, eighteen years of age, and placed by my father in the hands of the Bishop of Exeter as a curate. My elder brother having entered the Army, and my next elder the Navy, there was nothing left for me but the Church, to which indeed I had no reason to believe I was unsuited for my father was gravely religious, severe upon the Non-conformists and Wesleyans, keeping daily prayers and raising me to be entirely ignorant of such pleasure as music or the stage or the company of women. My mother having died at my birth, I must have had a nurse, I presume, but have no memory of her for at the earliest possible age I was plucked from the breast and offered to the less tender mercies of a tutor who taught me verses from the Psalms before I could with confidence stand upon my feet. My brothers, on their rare visits to the ancestral hall, took great care not to outrage my father's susceptibilities (hoping for his purse strings to remain firmly tied until their succession) and kept to themselves any amorous adventures their travels may have afforded them.

However, in my eighteenth year, by which time my piousness was a legend throughout the cathedral close and my knowledge of the Bible positively encyclopaedic, I developed a troublesome complaint of the skin which declined to repair itself despite applications of the concoctions and decoctions of the Exeter doctors. There was nothing for it but to dispatch me to Bath to take the waters there in the company of an elderly clergyman of impeccable decorum. He, alas, fell ill and died promptly upon our arrival at the Royal Crescent, and I was left to take myself off to the baths as best I might.

My shyness was inordinate and it can be conjectured with how particular a shock I discovered that men and women visited the baths together, and frequently in a state of nature. I, of course, retained my shirt as I paid my threepence and entered the waters of the King's Bath, considered most efficacious for the treatment of troubles of the skin. Indeed, though the water was filthy and the condition of the bodies of some of the other visitors made it difficult for me to contain my disgust, within a day or two my own skin began to clear so that I felt able to go on to one of the other baths where the water was less vigorous in its curative efficacy. The bath I chose was the Cross Bath, simply because an attendant at the King's recommended it as being patronised by all the quality. Again I entered the water in my shirt and again found I was the only being there who was so covered, both men and women flaunting their nakedness. But, as I became soon aware, it was a more attractive nakedness than that of the poor sufferers I had earlier seen, for here were no pustules and putrefication, no scorbutics or lacquered hides; all was rather softness and whiteness, the bodies shapely and appealing, reminiscent more of the Song of Solomon than the Book of Job.

The Cross Bath was indeed a curious sight for one more used to the cloister. The ladies positively displayed their beauties in wanton dalliance, their languishing eyes darting killing glances and before them, often, floated japan bowls in which they kept sometimes fine perfumes, sometimes confectionary. The men, when not hanging by their arms at the sides of the bath viewing the whole, paid court to the ladies of their choice, openly toying with their breasts and sometimes, I suspected, with other parts of their bodies, for often a couple would positively embrace for a length of time, only their heads and shoulders, closely in proximity, to be seen above the somewhat muddied waters.

The great Beau Nash, orderer and king of all Bath, was still living then, though rarely seen, and society was still of the brightest and most colourful, and I spent many hours, in my dark clothes, considering the evil proclivity to plea-sure with which the town reeked. The streets, from dawn to dusk, were crowded with sedan chairs for no one ever seemed to walk anywhere, and the place was ruled by the chairmen – stout, brawny fellows, their muscled calves encased in white stockings. Monarchs of the pavement, they gave way to no man, pushing aside anyone unfortu-nate enough to come in their way. In fair weather smiling and obsequious, when rain fell and they were in demand they became surly and presumptuous, purse-proud and arrogant.

Harrison's and Thayer's ballrooms, to which I took myself on Tuesday and Friday evenings in order to store up for my superiors in Exeter observation of the execrable ungodliness of the city, showed such scenes as I had never imagined. The ladies' dresses were an assault on the senses – black velvet embroidered with chenille, white satin embroidered with gold, green paduasoy embroidered with silver – and the gentlemen were no less handsomely dressed, some in coats lined with ermine, many in velvet, some in silk. The balls began at six o'clock precisely when a single couple led off a minuet, and the same dance con-tinued for two hours, until each couple in the room had for some moments danced alone before the rest.

After the minuet came the country dances, one of the most spirited being 'Hunt the Squirrel' in which the woman fled and the man pursued her – a pursuit which sometimes ended outside the ballroom, and in what activity we were left to conjecture. Young girls were handled, and in public, with much familiarity, and much use was made of a lascivious step called 'setting', which was the very reverse of 'back to back', so that the man's and woman's bosoms brushed in a most wanton fashion. On the very first occasion I was at Thayer's, a young man bid the fiddlers play a dance called Mol Patley, and after capering ungraciously, seized his partner, locked his arms in hers, and whisked her round cleverly above ground in such a manner that I, sitting upon one of the lowest benches, saw further above her shoe than I could ever had believed to be possible.

You may properly conjecture that on more than one occasion I was conscious of a troublesome warmth in my under parts, which previously had visited me only during sleep so that I had awakened with my member erect, and only an application of cold water from my washing bowl would reduce him. At Harrison's and Thayer's however, hot punch was more readily available than cold water, and often I had to remain in the warm waters of the baths for some long time before my body was in a fit state for me to remove myself.

It was at the Cross Bath that I finally met my undoing – or my salvation, depending on how you view it.

I was in the habit, now, of going to the bath as soon as it opened, for thus one took the advantage of clean waters, they being changed each night. Standing one morning immersed to the shoulders in the tepid water with only three or four other people around me, I saw two ladies enter at the far door. Both were wrapped in the large towels which were provided for our covering as we walked from the changing room to the bath; one was a matron of middle years and generous proportions, the other a young girl whose features took me immediately, for she resembled nothing so much as an angel, her fine face framed by yellow curls which seemed to gleam even under the low light of the morning. I watched with peculiar interest as they came to the bath's edge where they would (I trusted) throw off their coverings to enter the water (you see that I was already captive to the flesh, though I still nightly prayed for forgiveness for my concupiscence, which only took the form of imaginings and, when my amorous propensities were particularly stirred, of self-satisfaction). The older woman undraped, revealing a body generously corpulent with pendulous breasts, a belly which rolled as she descended the steps, and thighs which would have provided ample support for a beast of burden. She seemed, however, a pleasant soul, and turning to her companion smiled and beckoned as she entered the water.

The girl looked about her almost in fear, but then allowed the sheet to slip from her shoulders – and ah! It was at that moment that I lost my heart, for she was a ravishing example of her sex, the perfect proportions of her breasts, teasingly sweet, balancing above a frame not one ounce too liberally endowed with flesh, where the fall of her hips and thighs in one sublime line seemed to me as lovely as any in picture or poetry. It was but for a moment that I was allowed a glimpse of her beauty for she slipped into the water like some bird into its aerial element, scarcely seeming to disturb the mirrored surface.

She and her companion remained at the other end of the bath, the older lady laughing and joking, the girl smiling and more thoughtful, but clearly of a pleasing and cheerful disposition. I must confess that I slowly began to make my way towards them for I was eager at least to examine the younger lady more closely, being of too retiring a disposition to hope for an acquaintance.

Slowly, more people arrived at the bath, including among them a young officer whom I had seen at a ball the night before at Harrison's, drunk and importunate with the ladies until he was invited to leave by the attendants there, who were finally disposed to expel him by force. A surly fellow, he clearly believed himself irresistible to female susceptibility and had contrived to offend many of the ladies during the evening by his mock-courtesies, which they properly regarded as insults.

Now, he strode into the bath, barely keeping hold on the towel about his waist, which he threw to the ground almost

as soon as he entered, striding to the edge of the water quite
naked and with the air of someone who believed his person
to be a *sine qua non*. And indeed he was powerfully built,
muscular and bronzed, and were it not for the head set
awkwardly upon the trunk, with a sardonic look upon its
face, he might indeed have been considered an attractive
figure.

He descended with a splash into the waters, causing a
disturbance in them which made the girl and her companion gasp as for a moment the waters rose to their chins. He
saw them at once and was all eyes for the beauty of the yonger
creature, and without hesitation he half-strode, half-swam
towards them, greeting them with a low salutation which I
could not properly hear.

She turned her head modestly aside, at which he reached
out and roughly took her chin, turning her face back
towards him. Her companion's jaw dropped at the audacity. The girl however retained an astonishing calm, and
made a retort which somewhat abashed him, for he
released her and bowed shortly. However, he remained at
their side, from time to time making some comment, and
eventually once more grew rough, bending down and saying something into her ear which brought a blush to her
cheek and at the same time, I suspected, placing his hand
upon her waist below the water, for she drew back from
him. He took a step forward, however, and with the utmost
audacity bent to place a kiss upon her shoulder. She gave a
little scream – which was enough for me, my temper
already roused by what I had seen.

Less than two yards away, I threw myself towards the
party and seized the officer by the shoulders from behind,
pulling him back so that his head disappeared beneath the
waters. He reappeared, spluttering, and with his face red as
a turkey cock's took on a sneering expression as he saw the
youth who had assaulted him, and raised his hand to
deliver a blow. which, had it landed, would perhaps have
been the death of me. However, with self-preserving
instinct, rather than shrinking back I ducked in beneath his
guard and reaching out beneath the water, grasped his

manhood in one hand and wrenched at it with all my
power. His raised arm fell, his face contorted, he let out a
bellow which echoed around the walls and he doubled up
and disappeared again beneath the waters.

By now, the commotion had brought the attendants,
who recognised the source of the trouble and leaping in
(as they were always ready to do), rescued him from the
bath – for he was entirely unable to stand – and carried
him out.

Myself much shaken by the incident, I had almost forgot
the ladies, but a voice at my ear reminded me.

'Sir, we are much indebted!' said the older woman.
'Sarah, your thanks to the young gentleman.'

The girl half-curtsied in the water, which had the charming effect that as she rose again the rosy tips of her breasts
for a moment broke the surface.

'As my aunt remarks, sir, we are much indebted,' she
said. 'That officer has been troublesome before, and I fear
followed us here with the intent to be impertinent. I can
only offer you all my gratitude.'

'Please, ma'am, say nothing of it,' I protested. 'Perhaps
you will allow me to take a dish of tea with you in the Pump
Room, when you are ready to retire?'

She looked at her aunt, who nodded, and shyly half-
curtsying again turned to mount the steps out of the bath,
revealing as she did so a back quite as ravishing as her
front, the gentle curve of her shoulders and waist hanging
upon her spine with a lovely aspect, and the fall of her
posterior below, in two charming globes, resembling a ripe
peach. Her aunt, following her, displayed no such beauty
as she rolled forth, but since she was clearly well disposed
towards me I was prepared entirely to admire her ample
proportions, if they did not rouse my passions in the same
way. I followed the ladies from the water, turning to the
wall as I reached for my sheet, to conceal the fact that my
admiration had begun to take corporeal form.

We met a quarter of an hour later in the Pump Room, an
imposing setting for the fashionable and beautiful where a
woman stood at the pump dispensing King Bladud's water,

which aunt and niece were drinking with no enthusiasm together with an old duchess of eighty and a child of four. I took a glass but it was very hot and mineral and it was easy to persuade the ladies to join me, instead, in a dish of tea, while the orchestra played and the company walked up and down, not minding the music, but in a continual buzz of conversation – though at the end of each tune they clapped their hands, not knowing what for.

My seraph was introduced to me as Miss Sarah Wheeler, the daughter of James Wheeler, Esq., a merchant of Bristol, and was in Bath to take the waters under the guidance of her aunt, Mrs Hester Muster, the widow of a major in the Guards. Miss Wheeler was now dressed in a handsome gown, its high waist and *décolletage* provokingly displaying her beautiful breasts, the white roundness of which would have raised passions in a statue. Her aunt wore a voluminous gown of green satin with sufficient material about it to have dressed a positive crowd of younger and slimmer ladies, but her humour was so placid that no one but could have liked her, and my own liking was increased by the suggestion that I should walk her niece back to their lodgings in the Centre House in Pierpont Street. Doubtless her gratitude for my assistance was amplified by the sight of my canonicals in which, my figure being slim and, dare I say, elegant, I must confess I looked handsome enough.

Miss Wheeler – although I could already only think of her as Sarah – had quite overcome her shyness, and as we walked through the streets, crowded with gentlemen in breeches, stockings and cocked hats and ladies in superb pelisses laced with gold cords round them, with great tassels of gold upon their sides and reticules hanging at their waists, she chattered of her enjoyment of the season – how there was a run of balls, parties, concerts and masquerades without end, how Catalini was singing her best songs here, how Kemble was coming to perform at the theatre, how Lady Belmore's masquerade was a great success though three or four others took place the same night, but Sir William James thought Lady Belmore's the most brilliant. And she related how one of her aunt's gentlemen acquaintances had gone to the whole, making a change of dress for each masquerade, and had told her there were better dresses and more lively masks elsewhere and certainly a much better supper.

'But,' she remarked, 'I suppose, sir, that a gentleman of the cloth can have no interest in such affairs.'

On the contrary, I told her, I was most interested by the goings on, of which I had had no previous experience. She was astonished at my innocence and when I asked if I could attend her at Harrison's Rooms for the ball that evening, was pleased to acquiesce, at which, we by now being at Pierpont Street, I kissed her hand (though looking enviously at her lips) and bade farewell.

You can imagine with what a beating heart I waited at Harrison's Rooms at six o'clock that evening, when the minuet began without Sarah's appearance. However, after half an hour, she and her aunt arrived and greeted me with every sign of pleasure. We danced the minuet, after which Mrs Muster, seeing a dew of perspiration on her niece's face, asked if I would not take her into the gardens for some air. I needed no second invitation, nor did Sarah demur at taking my arm and walking out to where a path over a lawn led under some trees. Here the lights shone only fitfully through the still branches and the balmy night air, while it cooled our faces, did nothing to cool my ardour, which had been almost unendurably roused by the proximity of so much fairness during the dance.

At last we came to a seat in a quiet corner of the gardens, and I handed Sarah to it and sat beside her, daring to take her cool hand in mine. You young blades of today would have thrown yourselves upon her, and no doubt the young doxies of today would throw up their skirts to accommodate you, but it was some time before I dared to bend forward and plant a kiss upon her lips – a kiss which was delicately but not unkindly received, so that returning it again I raised my hand and let it fall upon the upper part of one of those alluring breasts, which rose and fell beneath my palm with what seemed like fervour. I dared to slide my palm downwards below the edge of her dress, feeling for the first time the strangely exciting small round bud of womanhood under my hand.

By this time the whole pressure of my eighteen years was ready to discharge and it was at this moment that Sarah unconsciously dropped her hand, which had been resting upon my shoulder, into my lap, so that it fell upon my distended but still imprisoned manhood. No doubt the peculiar swelling in my breeches intrigued her, for she softly grasped and squeezed it, at which with a low moan I felt my manhood flood from me, and almost fainted away at the pleasure of it.

Concerned, she drew away and asked if I was not overcome by the exercise of the dance. I could scarcely explain the true reason for my lassitude but instead fell upon my knee and made an immediate declaration of passion, to which she responded by leaning to kiss my lips and to reply that she, too, felt the power of love – and for the first time in her sixteen years!

Imagine my rapture as once again I clasped and kissed her, my manly vitality almost immediately returning. But I was conscious of extreme discomfort below and thinking quickly explained that I had to return to my lodgings, where I was expecting a communication that evening from my Bishop. But could we not – I implored – meet at some time later in the evening? In short, we agreed to meet in that same place at nine o'clock, which hour, she assured me, she would await with the keenest anticipation.

Sarah then returned to the dance, promising to give my regards and explanation to her aunt, and I slipped out by a side entrance and hailed a sedan chair, in which I returned to my lodging, cleansed myself and exchanged my small-clothes for fresh dress.

Back at Harrison's, I saw with some disquiet Sarah dancing with an elderly man in Army uniform. I went straight into the garden and sat upon the seat to wait and even a little before the appointed time a figure in white flitted silently through the trees to join me and without hesitation sat upon my knee, threw her arms around me, and kissed me. There was no question that Sarah's passion matched my own; later, I was to hear that she, like myself, had been kept from the world, and had never had the slightest communication with a person of the opposite sex. So it was that as her touch inflamed my senses, so mine ignited hers. In a few moments I had unloosed the neck of her gown and was planting my kisses upon her heaving bosom, while she had lifted my shirt from the band of my breeches and was stroking the flesh of my back.

I rose and, lifting her in my arms, carried her deeper into the garden to where bushes provided a more sheltered and private place, where I placed her upon the grass and bent to lie beside her, once more applying my mouth to a swelling breast, and at the same time lifting her skirt to reach upwards – waiting, I must own, for her to cry out or invite me to hold. Far from doing so, she responded as hotly and I felt with increased delight her hands fumbling to undo my breeches, which she found difficult because of the tightness of the buttons. Pausing for a moment in my ministrations, I loosed them myself and drew my clothes from me, while at the same time, to my delight, she slipped her dress from her. In the dim light reflected from the sky, I could see only a blur of white, but what my eye could not discern my hands discovered, and we made a mutual exploration of each other, myself astonished to feel for the first time a mist of hair between her legs (for it had not occurred to me that the ladies could possess such), while she gave a gasp of amazement at the nature of my parts – the size and inextensibility of my prick, the weight and roundness of my cods. Her handling of my parts almost again drew me to the supreme moment so that I removed her hands, and myself began to explore her lower parts, whose sensibility to my touch clearly rendered her equally delirious, for as I kissed the fleshy lips beneath their down I felt her whole body shiver, and she in turn reached down to pull my head by the hair so that I could not reach her.

By now neither of us was prepared to terminate our pleasure without experiencing the final crisis; that instinct with which the Creator provides us all guided me (for I had had no teaching, I need not say) so that parting her thighs I placed myself between them and with little difficulty, its head being slippery with those juices which prepare us for the assault, slipped my instrument into her irresistible person. There I seemed to meet with an obstruction but I was in no mood to temporise, and for a moment losing control of my natural politeness, gave a strong push – at which to my concern Sarah gave a cry of pain, when I made to withdraw, but she threw her arms about me, placed her hands upon my arse and pulled me into her; upon which again with that blessed natural instinct I began to move in the manner of which you know, and after a while felt her body move beneath me as naturally as the waves move to the pressure of a vessel.

It took but a moment for my pleasure to acuminate and as my joy was released, so I felt her arms tighten about me, and she sighed with the same satisfaction.

With a common consent we lay still, close in each other's arms, and such was my youth that my member remained upreared, filling the natural cavity in which it was encased as though constructed for the purpose. Beneath me, I felt Sarah's breathing quieten, and slowly her hands began to stroke my shoulders and back with such tenderness that I felt, for the first time in my existence, that I was the beloved object of another human being rather than a simple thing to be sent hither and thither with nought but impatience and scorn.

In a while, my body again seemed by itself to move and once more, but more slowly, we performed that special act of adoration with which man and woman alone, of all creation, celebrate their union – for I now realised with what completeness my soul was engaged in my body's actions, and with what closeness these united us.

It was without a word that we roused ourselves, put on our clothes, and walked, arm in arm, back towards the light. As we reached it, I noticed traces of red upon her dress, which you will of course know was the sign of her lost maidenhead. Fortunately, she had a shawl which, claiming to be cold, she draped around her, and pleading a sudden sickness, Mrs Muster (who was too occupied with her own pleasure) happily agreed to my escorting her niece back to Pierpont Street.

But as we walked towards the doorway, two figures strode towards me. For a moment, I did not know who it was – merely I saw two officers in dress uniform, one of whom appeared to be for some reason angered. Then I recognised the scowling face of the man whom I had encountered at the baths. He came to attention before me, and without a word brought up his hand, slapped me in the face with his glove and threw it to the ground before me, then turned upon his heel to stride from the rooms.

The second officer clicked his heels, and said: 'Sir, allow me to present myself; I am Major Constant Hawtry. Major Willoughby Fawcett's compliments, and he will be pleased to meet you at Duncan's Fields at dawn tomorrow.' Upon which he clicked his heels again, turned upon them, and left the room. A buzz of conversation broke out, which almost drowned the faint cry which Sarah gave as she fell, unconscious, to the floor.

I was left in no doubt that what was proposed was a duel. Mrs Muster went so far as to congratulate me upon it, as though 'twere some victory, and introduced me to one of her friends, a Captain Dawkin who, she said, would be my 'second'.

'My second what?' I innocently enquired, at which he found it necessary to explain the etiquette of duelling to me while Mrs Muster took her niece, now quite distraught, back to their lodgings.

It can be surmised that I slept not at all that night. Captain Dawkin produced a sword, the property of his father, which he said I was welcome to borrow. He spent most of the hours before dawn explaining Major Fawcett's prowess as a swordsman and saying that he was, however, much disliked and that if I could contrive to wound him before he overcame me, Bath would be delighted – and after all, he might only wound me. He then produced the day's papers and read me the accounts of duels which had took place that week, including one between Ned Goodyear and Beau Fielding at the Play House in Drury Lane, and one between a captain and a young man of fashion in Warwickshire, one of whom now lay in the earth, and the other in Newgate Prison. All this comforted me much.

As dawn broke I waited, cold and shivering, with Captain Dawkin upon Duncan's Fields until out of the morning mist emerged the two Majors, gruff as dragons. Fawcett produced his sword, I drew mine, we crossed, Major Hawtry struck the steel aside, and we began.

While by no means a swordsman, I had at least some knowledge of the art for as a boy an uncle of mine had taught it me with foils, saying that I had a natural ability and could become a great man if I was inclined. Indeed I had some inclination but my father dispatching me at an early age to the care of the clergy, I had never held sword more until that morning. I managed to block two strokes and parry a third. Then, reaching forward in an ambitious pass, the Major's foot fell into a great turd of cow dung which he had not noticed; he slipped forward and positively threw himself upon my sword, which passed through his body without the least resistance, being torn from my hand as he fell to the ground devoid of life.

The result was the best possible for me, for both his second and mine were in agreement that his death was an accident. So that while under severe censure from authority for participating in a duel, I could not be charged with the Major's death but was none the less a hero to Bath, which was thrown into a positive passion of pleasure at the Major's death, he having insulted half the ladies and offended half the men of the town.

Mrs Muster was moved to admiration; Sarah to renewed ardour. I was now in a desperate predicament: I could not think of leaving my love, yet I must now return to Exeter and the cloister, for the time allowed for my treatment was past and messages daily arrived at Bath inviting my return to the jurisdiction of my Bishop. Had I money of my own, I would have known what response to make, but I had none and if I were to resign from the clergy and marry my mistress on what could we subsist?

In the end, after a leave-taking, stolen one evening while Mrs Muster was at bridge with her cronies, when many tears fell from each other's eyes onto our respective bosoms, I left by the mail coach and within a day was once more immured far from the sight of the girl I had come to love. As for her, she was silent, for though I had given her an address to which she could send a loving message, she sent none and after a week's silence, then two, I was reduced to cursing the duplicity of women. My thoughts, rebellious to the command of my mentors, stubbornly declined to soar to heavenly matters, and remained below.

One morning eighteen days after I had left Bath – I marked the days with melancholy thoughts – a fellow student knocked at the door of my room (which indeed was no more luxurious than a monk's cell) and announced to me that 'my boy was come'. This I took to be a joke, for while several of my companions were indeed accompanied by boy servants to care for their bodily comfort, my father made me no allowance for such a luxury, and I looked after my own linen, the cleaning of my room, *et cetera*. But my friend insisted that a boy had come who claimed he was sent to serve me, and wearying of the argument and willing to be fooled if that was the wish of the joker, I told him to send the lad to me. He retired and a few moments later, after a timid knock, a small figure dressed in the black cassock worn by the servants of our house made its way in; he had a close-cropped head of fair hair and blue eyes which somehow reminded me . . .

And yes – you are ahead of me; the boy ran forward to clasp me in his arms, and as he did so I felt the warm pressure of two breasts beneath the black cloth. It was indeed my Sarah. Pausing only to lock the door, I fell with her upon my hard bed and within moments we were joined in that activity which had haunted my every waking moment since we had last parted.

When the storm had sunk, and risen, and sunk again, she told me that she had determined at Bath that we would not be parted and that if I could not stay with her, she would come to me. Making the excuse that she wished to say farewell to a female friend, she had concealed what small store of money she had, eluded the unfortunate Mrs Muster, and taken the Bristol coach. Then she travelled on to Exeter where she had for forty-eight hours watched my comings and goings and those of my friends, and seeing that some of them were served by boys whose bodies were covered by loosely-cut cassocks, had decided that this was the way she should be able to stay with me. First acquiring a cassock by bribing one of the cathedral caretakers, and persuading a friendly barber to crop her hair, she had found no difficulty in passing as a boy to the gateman and then to my friend. The looseness of the cassock was such that she had not even to bind her breasts, which were free beneath it, as I had now discovered.

Though my mind misgave me, for there were sure to be drawbacks to such a crazy scheme, I was too overjoyed at her presence to demur. And for several weeks there was indeed no difficulty. There was in fact only one moment of peril: returning from a day's study during which I had had no opportunity for time with Sarah, I ran up the stairs to my room and threw my nether garments from me, pausing only to lift her cassock (under which she generally wore no clothes, it being still very hot weather, and the rooms stuffy) and throw it over her head, turned her so that she was bending over a table and supporting herself with her hands, and plunged into her from behind (though lawfully) and was bucking with all the enjoyment and vigour of eighteen years when I heard a step behind me. I turned and saw the Dean of the Cathedral – a corpulent and good-humoured man – at the door, which in my hurry I had omitted to close!

'Oh, my dear fellow!' he said. 'Use your pretty lad gently or he will not be able to sit comfortably at table!' and closed the door behind him as he left.

Sarah lifted the cassock from her head and grinned and though I was quite crestfallen from the shock, I laughed too. Mr Runciple was well-known to look with a kindly, nay envious, eye upon the boy servants of the house – most of whom indeed were kept to serve their masters in bed as well as at board – and being used to turning a blind eye had seen no good reason to interfere with my pleasure. Sarah found, however, that he was now given to patting her thoughtfully upon the head, or the rump, whenever he had the opportunity, and took every precaution never to be caught alone by him lest he should attempt her and discover all.

It was a fortnight later that a less sympathetic figure, the prebendary in charge of the house itself and its running, who for that reason possessed keys to all the rooms, let himself into mine in the late evening (for what reason I never discovered, but suspect treachery of some sort). In this case there was no disguise, for we had just concluded a passage of love and were lying side by side as God made us upon the bedclothes, and it would have been a blinder man than the prebendary who did not notice Sarah's pouting and thankful breasts, or the fact that she did not possess the appendage which decorated my own loins.

I was summoned next day to the library of the Dean, where Mr Runcible was prepared to be severe; the long tradition of boy-love within the church was one thing, he explained; to allow women within the sacred precincts was another. But here was news which made condign punishment unnecessary.

What could this be? I wondered. He told me that my uncle had died and left me all his fortune, amounting to no less a sum than four thousand pound a year, which would allow me to live comfortably where I chose and with whom I wished. Pausing only to resign my connection with the church, I ran back to my rooms, where Sarah was sorrowfully preparing for exile, and within the week we were man and wife, with the reluctant permission of her father who, himself having a small fortune, believed he might one day be reliant upon mine.

There is little more to record: we lived together happily for over fifty years and had one daughter, who married My Lord and by him had my two grandchildren with whom – my dear wife and our child, alas, dying within months of each other some five years since – I now live, occupied still, as you know, with those delights I first discovered in Bath so many years ago, though now in recording rather than performing them.

And with that, Beau Rust closed his account, and we left him.

Chapter Ten

Sophie's Story

My disillusion with the Gypsy band had begun with Bovile's calm appropriation of all the money I was able to make, without indication that I would ever see a penny of it. His treatment of everyone under him continued it, for while he was always smiling, and though brusque never outwardly cruel, he acted as though every person and thing connected with the tribe was his personal property and moreover everyone in the tribe accepted this.

As the days passed into weeks and we moved on from Royston through Baldock and Gravely, Dunstable, Wendover and Princes Risborough in the direction of the western coast, and I came to know more of the Gypsy customs – partly through experience and partly through conversation – my discontent grew. The men, certainly, had not such a bad time of it as long as they fell not foul of Bovile who was unregenerate in his treatment of anyone who crossed him. But the women were no more than chattels, and though only Anna complained, they all fell under the same interdicts and were regarded with the same lack of consideration. It was no surprise to me that they bore the brunt of most of the hard work of the train for so it has ever been; that we should be expected to fetch and carry, to cook, to look after the packing and unpacking of the tribe's few possessions, was nothing to me. But in the matter of their family life, I was appalled at the severity of the standard applied to them, and not only by Bovile but by all the men of the tribe.

Except that she was, the moment she became a woman, subject to the desires of the *dimber damber*, every woman was expected to eschew the company of men until she was married, and once married was expected to remain faithful only to her husband until her death – again, with the exception of her ministrations to Bovile. If she was unfaithful, her husband was wont to strip her naked, cut off all her hair and chase her from the camp. This had been done, within the past year, by one of our men who now awaited his wife's return, which could only take place after her hair had grown back to a length of at least five inches.

Men, on the other hand, were never punished for their infidelities (as Anna told me with a laugh) though they feared to make love with the wife of one who was absent or to have dealings with a prostitute, lest they should be subject to the *mokadi*, or taboo.

This was, Anna explained, the only weapon a woman possessed but it could be a strong one, for she was at certain times and under certain conditions capable of contaminating the men of the tribe by a single touch and his falling under *mokadi* would expose him to strong magic and evil. Though the younger girls and the older women lost this power, those who were of years to interest men most strongly had the power also to affect them by magic by simply touching a drinking vessel or a plate in a particular way, by merely walking over a stream of drinking water. In some cases food could be 'poisoned' by being touched by a dress and so a white apron was always worn while food was being prepared.

Anna failed, however, to explain just how this magic could be raised, though she promised to do so if ever I should need to use it. I doubted whether this would be possible, for since I was not of the Gypsy stock, how could I use their magic? None the less, I was interested to hear about it and many hours of otherwise tedious travelling from place to place were enlivened by stories of the strange customs of the people, none of them, after all, stranger than Mr Nelham's idea of raising the Devil.

The more that I saw of the life of the people in the villages and small towns through which we passed, the more I realised the power that could be held over them through playing upon their superstitions. However slender the knowledge I had been able to acquire at Alcovary, at least my father and mother had always been at pains to keep me from the superstitions of the few country people I met, rebuking the maids for talking to me of pixies and elves, and Mr Ffloyd too had been strong against those who believed in what he termed the irrational. But the people we saw as we passed throughout the countryside were almost at our mercy, for they so believed in the capability of the tribe to influence them by means of magic that they were ready to do anything to keep on good terms, from providing food to giving what money they had, on threat of being cursed.

But all was not entirely bad, for Rosanna was one of the women who had a powerful knowledge of medicinal herbs and other cures. Some of these were unpleasant – the drinking of potions made from saliva, urine or excreta, for instance, to expel a devil from a body by inflicting him with nausea. Sometimes small bags were given containing spiders or woodlice which were to be worn until they died, for as they did so, so the affliction would leave the body of the sick man or woman. I once saw her treat a woman for the wheezing of the breath by catching a trout, making her breath three times into its mouth, then throwing it back into the water – and indeed the woman was much relieved. In the same way, a roasted dormouse will cure the whooping cough and a concoction of bacon fat, pepper and vinegar, the croup.

Sometimes a neighbourhood which proved unreceptive could be reduced to hospitality by the simple means of leaving magical charms on doorsteps – elderberry branches and growing bushes to protect evil from entering the house of the kindly, a horse's skull or animal bones to introduce ill into a house. Whether by luck or by magic, the denizens of the house seemed plagued by ill-luck on the introduction of these charms, and would sue for peace.

My own case was a strange one for, far from relying upon strange incantations or charms, my own art was drawn from an ancient study which had for centuries been respectably practised throughout the civilised world, as Mr Lilly explains in his book. Though it was clear that I had connection with the Egyptians, I was in a sense separate from them, not least in my appearance, for I had declined to dress myself in the old clothes they begged from any passers-by or cottagers but had insisted that I should buy good dresses to wear from some of the money I brought the tribe. Bovile had at first strenuously argued against this but in the end had listened to sense, and seeing how I brought the money in had grudgingly afforded me sufficient funds to purchase fashionable clothes. As I appeared either in the best of their tents or, sometimes, in a room of a private house, or one hired for the purpose, this helped to attract the better class of enquirer, able to pay more for the privilege of consulting me.

I must confess that I found the celibate life I was expected to lead between my regulated visits to Bovile's bed extremely tedious. Having had my passions ignited, as it were, at so early an age, they needed regular feeding. While Bovile himself, though I grew increasingly to dislike him, had a physical power capable of satisfying any desire, few other men of the tribe attracted me and in any event they were too terrified of their leader to consider making an approach to me or responding to any I might make. Anna remained attentive but, sensitive lover as she was, my tastes were towards the masculine sex, of whose ministrations I was now starved.

It was at Winchester that I embarked upon an adventure which might have cost me dear. We were encamped upon the outskirts of the town but I had taken a room at the Coach and Horses Inn, not far from the cathedral, for my consultations and a steady train of townspeople had come there to ask me the usual questions. Near the close of the second day a young man appeared mysteriously wrapped in a cloak (though the weather was hot) and with a hat pulled well down, neither of which did he throw off until the door was closed behind him, when he was revealed as a handsome fellow of twenty years or so, well dressed, with auburn hair neatly tied.

His name he declined to give but he was the son of a local alderman, a tradesman, who wished to marry him to the daughter of a rich merchant of Canterbury. This was a pleasant but unattractive maid whose company, upon meeting her, he had enjoyed, but who he felt might pall as a wife – 'For,' he said, somewhat stuttering, 'to be honest she is more than somewhat plain, and of a figure less than handsome.' Could I tell him whether their union would be a happy one?

He being able to supply me with the particulars of his own birth and that of the lady, I set to work while he sat nearby to wait. The charts being prepared, I saw immediately that here was an amiable girl enough, ready in conversation and free in pleasantries, but likely to have a small bodily appetite so that, as I told him, while he would not find daily intercourse with her unpleasant, their bed-life would not be likely to be fiery.

Clearly he had not expected to hear a woman talk to him upon such matters and while his face fell as he heard my words, his eyes sparkled more than a little and I felt that they played more than a little around the neck of my dress, which was fashionably low, so that the globes of my breasts were certainly not concealed from view.

My study told me, I went on, that he was a young man of virility and high passions and if not supplied with material for their satisfaction at home, would seek them abroad – was this not the case?

It was, he replied, and had been since he was a schoolboy.

He was now shifting somewhat upon his seat and, bending over in guise of consulting my charts, I stole a look into his lap where I fancied I could see a strong member struggling to be free of its bonds. The sight somewhat roused my passions and I had not been unaffected by proximity to such a handsome fellow who would not, I felt sure, be unwilling to assuage that appetite which had over a week been starved in me. But how was I to broach the subject without being unladylike?

I need not have concerned myself for in leaning over, my dress had fallen away to an inflaming extent and he leapt to his feet, caught me by the shoulders and drew me to him, exclaiming that no woman had previously understood him so well and that had Betty – his proposed wife – been so well-formed, no problem would have arisen. Almost before the last word fell from his lips they were pressed upon my own, while his arms gathered me so closely to him that I could feel his manly part like an iron bar against my thigh.

'Oh, sir!' I cried, as soon as I could free my lips. 'Pray release me – the door is not locked!'

It was the work of but a moment with him to stride to the door – and discover that it had no key, whereupon he simply lifted the table at which I had been working and placed it against the door in such a way that it would at least delay the entry of anyone approaching. He then turned and began to unbutton his shirt as he walked slowly towards me.

I felt a pang of pity for the unfortunate Betty whose sensibilities were so blunted that she could not appreciate such a packet of pleasures. His curled hair fell low over a wide forehead and a quizzical eyebrow, bright eyes and lips which were strong and sweet. His frame, as the shirt slipped from his shoulders, was slim but powerful, the shoulders broad, the chest tapering to a narrow waist from which, as I looked, he slipped the breeches revealing a standing device as stalwart as I had imagined.

'Now, madam,' he cried as he stood before me, 'I have shown you the way; surely you will not deny me an equal view?'

Needing no encouragement, I was out of my gown in a trice and for a long moment we stood regarding each other with a pleasure soon to be keenly enlarged. As he took a step towards me, I fell to my knees before him in wondering delight, taking him in my hands to examine that part to which every woman must sometime, surely, pay the tribute of admiration. In this case, it was not only strong but beautifully shaped, smooth as polished ivory and decorated at its base with a scheme of curls each of which might have been individually fashioned by a hair-dresser, so decorative and well arranged were they. Below, in their dependant pouch, hung twin orbs whose weight decreased as I held them in my palm, for while they swelled in appreciation of my tender attentions, at the same time they drew themselves up in admiration, nestling at the base of their superior companion.

Pausing now only to plant a kiss upon the tip, where a small bead of liquor stood in tribute to the passion to come, I raised myself to be clasped once more in strong arms and laid upon the single couch which stood in the corner of the room, where for a while he was content to graze upon my body, his fingers running lightly as butterflies over my shoulders and breasts, across my belly and thighs, until they came to rest upon my mount of love where, as he bent to kiss me, they insinuated themselves to smooth the way.

My feelings were now near to overflowing but his ardour was wonderfully controlled, so that when I was at what seemed the apogee of my emotion, he raised me still further by the tender moderation of his touch. Parting my thighs he at last slid between them, but palpitating my nether lips with his fingers he placed the very tip of his instrument only between them, moving so that I merely felt it jostling, so to say, at the entrance. Then, still raised upon his arms to afford us the clearest view, he slowly descended so that first the purpled tip, then the lip of skin below, then the fine, strong shaft slid gently in, and my cap of golden hair met his auburn curls in their own embrace.

He then began to move with a peculiarly graceful, slow motion, as though gently riding upon a rocking horse, his hips and buttocks swinging so that his instrument moved into then out of my privities smoothly and without violence, all the time supporting his weight upon his extended arms and regarding my charmed body with the keenest interest and admiration. Then at almost the same moment we were transported with delirium, his teeth fixing upon his bottom lip and nipping it, while a rosy glow flooded over my body, the brown rings about my nipples enlarging so that the engorged tips stood proud within them as witness to my pleasure.

It was at just this moment that the door rattled and the table against it moved and before we could but draw apart, with a hefty blow the entrance was clear and Bovile strode into the room. He stood with his hands upon his hips as I reached for my dress to pull it over me, while my companion coolly drew himself to his feet with a composure unusual in one so young and stood proudly confronting the newcomer, not even troubling to cover his tool, still upstanding and too obviously humid with the juices of our love for us to pretend that we had not been very recently in congress.

'Clothe yourself!' said Bovile shortly, and without a word my cavalier picked up his breeches and drew them on, then buttoned his shirt upon him, all the time facing Bovile without any sign of fear.

'This is your husband?' he asked me, not turning but inclining his head.

'Indeed not!' I replied indignantly.

'Then there is no reason for complaint, sir, and I will bid you goodday,' he said, taking a step towards the door.

'Ah, but there is, *chau*,' said Bovile, 'and I shall take pleasure in splitting your *noc* before you leave this place!' – and tapped his own nose to leave no doubt of the threat he was offering.

I was now in a state of apprehension for the boy, though wiry and strong, could be no match for the brute, and should he be dangerously injured what would be my position in the ensuing trouble?

But now Bovile in turn took a step forward and suddenly swung a punch at the boy's head. The latter, however, with a motion quick as thought, eluded the blow, then seeming to move through the air without the least preparation, caught the underside of Bovile's chin with his head. The Gypsy's own head sprung back with an audible crack, and he fell to the ground like a dead thing to lie unmoving. My lover turned to me and bowed.

'I did not understand that you were one of the Gypsies, ma'am,' he said, 'and I am sorry to have destroyed your – ah – master, but at public school one speedily learns to deal with those stronger than oneself. And now, with your permission, I will take my leave.'

But he must have seen from my expression that I was not at all dismayed by the fate Bovile had suffered, for he came over to me as I still sat, hugging my dress to my middle parts, and bending down planted a kiss upon my raised hand, then upon my lips, and left – turning at the door to say, 'And thank you for your advice. I fear my future wife's beauty will never be a match for your own but if my marriage must be, it must be, and I shall simply be kind in concealing wherever I may have to take my pleasure.'

As he descended the stairs, Bovile groaned and opened his eyes, then sat up, and shook his head, and in a moment was, somewhat shakily, upon his feet.

'Where is he, young puppy?' he cried, and I saw that for a man of his strength a blow which would have put another in bed for a week had only a few moments' effect.

'Gone,' I said, 'and whither, I know not!'

'Then I must satisfy myself with you!' he said, coming towards me with arm raised.

'Whatever you wish!' I cried with a sudden flash of inspiration. 'But I am *mokadi*!'

He paused.

'I have had my menses upon me.'

'I saw no blood,' he said, suspiciously.

'It ceased yesterday,' I said, knowing that after her menses a woman was *mokadi* for at least a week even to the slightest touch. He could not so much as beat me with a shoe without rendering himself unclean and incapable of ruling the tribe until he had purged himself by fasting and travel.

His anger was almost ungovernable, but his superstition greater. He said nothing and left, forced even to leave me the money I had received that day which, since I had touched it, was also *mokadi*. I dressed and, going downstairs, ordered myself a meal and some wine, which I consumed with much pleasure before returning to the camp, where Anna heard my story with great amusement though, she said, she was aware that my menses were not due for at least ten days.

'Be careful,' she warned, 'Bovile never leaves a grudge unpaid.' But she was nevertheless unable to conceal her pleasure that I had outwitted him and I was pleased not only with that, but with the gold I concealed carefully among my few possessions.

The day after, as we were on our first day's march out of Winchester and deep into the country, just as dusk was falling Rosanna clutched my arm as we sat upon the board of the cart. I looked at her questioningly.

'Did you not hear it?' she asked – and held up her finger for silence. In the distance, through the gloom of the falling night, came the call of an owl.

'It is the sign of a death,' she said, shivering, and would say no more. Twice, in the night, I woke to hear the melancholy cry, and though I determined to shrug off such superstitious nonsense, the strange sound could not but affect my spirits. Next morning as we rose, Sam came with the news that an old woman who was familiar to me as a half-deranged creature, muttering on the outskirts of the camp and too infirm to walk, had died in the night and that preparations for her funeral were already in train. Bovile had sent into the nearest village for a *Gorgio*, or non-Gypsy, to prepare the corpse for burial, for all Gypsies have a strong aversion to touching the dead bodies even of their nearest relatives. It was to be washed all over in salt water by the *Gorgio*, and properly dressed for its journey through the next world with particularly strong shoes and a head-scarf over the hair. Since the dead woman had been among the poorest of the band, the other women had come together to give of their best clothes, it being considered an honour to dress the dead.

All her worldly goods were to be packed into the coffin about her, the clothes carefully turned inside out so that she would be too ashamed at being so oddly clothed to return to plague the living.

For two days a vigil took place beside the coffin, the two relatives she had – a son and a daughter – being careful neither to wash, nor eat, nor sleep during that time. Meanwhile outside the tent some members of the tribe were always present, chanting in a low voice some words in their own language, which meant nothing to me. Their purpose was, Rosanna explained, to convince the dead of their sorrow for her departure, so that she would not visit them during the long winter nights.

The funeral itself began with a walk from the camp to the nearest church – a distance of about two miles – behind the coffin which was carried by four of the men of the tribe. The local priest conducted the funeral service, which to my surprise was according to everyday rites, though the Gypsies themselves did not normally attend the church except on this one occasion. Afterwards, the coffin was opened and everyone filed past it to say a parting word and to throw a few coins into the box. As she did so, I heard Rosanna mutter: 'This I throw to thee, so that thou canst pay thy fares and custom duties.' When the final spade of earth had covered the grave, Bovile stepped forward with a jug of beer and poured it down, to provide liquid nourishment for the journey of the dead.

It was to my surprise that everyone at the funeral wore white rather than black, or if they had no white clothes, wore at least a band of white about them. And I was equally surprised to see that only artificial flowers were strewn upon the coffin, carefully made from coloured papers by the women. This was because they wished nothing as quickly perishable as live flowers to be laid on the grave, though the dead woman's son planted a bush upon it before we finally left the area.

Back at the camp, we made preparation to move on. As I asked a question about the dead woman's belongings (which I had seen being piled together upon the ground outside what had been her tent, and which were to be entirely consumed by fire) Rosanna quickly stopped me and warned me never on any circumstance to mention her name, or if I inadvertantly did so, to pray immediately that she forgive me for pronouncing it, for if I did not do so she would think I was summoning her from the grave. I was also told not to wash myself nor comb my hair for one week from the day – an injunction which, I must confess, I disobeyed, not being inclined to consult such superstitions.

During the next ten days the men of the tribe were forced to abstain from any connection with their women and it was on the very day that this injunction terminated that it was my turn to be summoned to Bovile's tent, where the combination of his deprivation together with his desire to revenge himself upon me was sufficiently potent a medicine to persuade him to fall upon me with an even more voracious appetite than usual, and a force so terrible that only my determination not to show him that he had the ascendant over me prevented me from crying out at the pain of his assault. He performed the act no less than four times during the course of the night, but I was wholly excluded from enjoying any pleasure in it. Next morning, upon waking, he pinned me to the ground once more and ravished me with great indignity, forcing me finally to kiss his arse before leaving the tent which, having no alternative, I performed, vowing at the same time to be revenged in my turn.

One thing which perplexed me at the time when I entered the tent was that he was sitting with his hands in a pail of water to which he had added the best part of a pound of salt. I mentioned this to Anna, who nodded sagely and said: 'Ah, then he is preparing for a bout,' and when I asked of what, she replied that from time to time, if the purse offered was sufficient, Bovile would offer a bare-fist fight with some opponent or another. He was, she said, a powerful and skilled opponent, the suggestion being made that he had learned at the hands of none other than the Jew Daniel Mendoza, of whom I had never heard tell, but who Sam, overhearing the conversation, informed me had been the greatest fighter of his time and had a school of fighting at the Lyceum in the Strand, in London.

Sam had heard, he said, that a purse of a hundred guineas had been offered for a combat between Bovile and Sergeant Hardy, a former Army man now working as a butcher in the village of Itchen Abbas, which we would come to next day. Upon my asking how the salted water came in, Sam scornfully asked if I did not know that bare-fist fighters pickled their hands in such manner in order to harden them, both so that they should not be injured by striking, and that they should be capable of inflicting the utmost injury on an opponent.

Two days later the entire tribe together with a number of villagers attended in a field outside the village where a square 'ring' had been marked out by ropes. Bovile was already there, attended by Sam and another man of the tribe. He made, as I must confess, a noble figure, sober and upright, serious and without apprehension. At length, with great noise and cheering, the local champion, Sergeant Hardy, was carried to the ring on the shoulders of his fellows – a big man, of more weight than Bovile, though as he removed his shirt, I believed to be less hardy and more fleshy. Both men prepared by stripping to brief cloths knotted about their loins (Anna whispered that she had attended several fights fought naked, as the ancient Greeks did, but she seemed not specially regretful that this was not now to be so).

The combatants stood at the centre of the ring – Bovile slightly taller, but Hardy more stoutly built – while a man who Sam had said was a local squire recited the rules of the game to them. These were simple: they were to fight until one fell to the ground, when there would be a pause for recovery. The match would be won when one of the two fighters could not come to scratch – that is, stand at the centre of the ring – or by other means admitted defeat. Finally, he summoned into the ring a servant who held a bag from which came the chink of coins – one hundred pounds in gold. The fighters then retreated to opposite corners, and in a moment by means of a stone beat on the side of a metal bucket, the fight began.

Evidently hoping to win the battle before it properly began, Bovile strode to his opponent and delivered a prodigious blow to the side of his head, which staggered him, and then followed with a blow to the breast. But Hardy was made of sterner stuff than one blow could fell and in return smote Bovile mightily below the right eye, where immediately blood poured. Enraged, the Gypsy smashed a fist into his opponent's face, bloodying his nose.

There was little parrying, or what I might call avoiding the blows. I, who had never seen such sport, had nevertheless imagined that half of the skill would be in defence, but in this case it was all attack, the fighters scorning to prevent the opponent's fists landing on their person, but rather determined to show that no amount of punishment could hurt them. All seemed for some time even, until Hardy with two quick blows made Bovile stagger back, and, catching his heel in a turf, fall to the ground. The bucket was immediately smitten by the stone and the men retired to crouch on their heels while their assistants bathed the blood from their faces and shoulders; not only was this evidence of the battle, but bruises were beginning to show upon Hardy's whiter flesh, while upon Bovile's brown breast a cut had laid the flesh open above the left pap.

When the squire had counted to one hundred, the signal was once more heard and they went to it again with no less force. Though I was ill-prepared to mourn for Bovile's hurts, and had been prepared to watch with interest, I was now sickening of the affair – no less for the injuries the two men inflicted upon each other, than for the crowing of the crowd, upon one side or another, at the landing of a blow. It was as though they were cheering not simply for their man, but for the pain he was inflicting upon the other – which, I must remind the reader, they had never seen before that day. The women, I shame to say, of whom there were a number, were not backward in urging on their man, and some with a satisfaction which made me suspect their motives – which I was more conscious of when Anna took my hand and conveyed it to her nether parts, while I felt her wriggling with satisfaction.

There was much I would do for one hundred pounds in gold, but to inflict such pain upon another human being I would not be party to, yet all I could do was close my eyes, for the press was such that I could not escape. In a moment a great roar went up, and opening my eyes I was in time to see Bovile, having evidently received a great blow, stagger back into the path of the squire – also in the ring, to see fair play – so that he fell to the ground. And while he was getting to his feet Bovile sprang forward and with the utmost deliberation punched his fist into the lower part of Hardy's stomach, at which the man collapsed to the ground and lay in agony as the 'round' (which must have lasted ten minutes) ended.

Bovile was perhaps the more tired of the competitors, but the ex-soldier now found it difficult to stand, though the aspect of his face was such that he clearly intended to repay the Gypsy fully for his last blow – which, Rosanna explained, was one not allowed by the rules of pugilism.

At the signal, the fighters rose again to their feet and slowly approached each other. They were both very much bruised, and both with shocking cuts all over their faces and eyes, and bodies too. The battle had lasted in all almost forty minutes. Hardy opened with a blow as low as could be to Bovile's body – at which the squire shouted an admonition. Bovile was rocked upon his feet but, recovering, smote Hardy on the throat, and then before he could recover cuffed him again upon the temple and again upon the ear, and as he almost fell forward, brought his knee up to meet his body, and smashed a fist down with enormous force upon the crown of his head. The larger man fell to the ground as though every bone in his body was broken and remained there while the squire counted off ten seconds, at which he stood forward and raised Bovile's arm in signal that he was the winner. His servant placed in the exhausted man's hand the purse – quickly seized by Sam, who vanished with it amid the tumult which followed as half of the people fell to recovering the loser and half to hoisting Bovile upon their shoulders, where he was carried to the camp, blood all the while streaming from his nose and mouth onto the shoulders of his bearers. Five or six women, of whom I was chosen to be one, attended him in his tent, stripping him and washing his body which was torn and bruised as though he had fought with ten men. The gashes were such that one would have thought them inflicted by some more adamantine instrument than the human fist. Among his injuries we were astonished to find that three teeth had been knocked from his mouth, for we had seen no sign of this at the time, and it subsequently appeared that he had swallowed them rather than reveal to Hardy that he had been hurt.

It was a remarkably short period of time before Bovile was up and about as though he had experienced nothing more serious than a brush with a gamekeeper, though some of his injuries took a time to heal. The gold which he had won had vanished and when I questioned Sam about it he was silent. I gathered that it was an impertinence to question upon any ground what the *dimber damber* did with any money belonging to the tribe for it was considered that all gold was held in common, though I saw no sign of much expenditure on anyone's behalf – even, I must confess, on Bovile's, who appeared always in the same clothes, ate the same food, and was in no way favoured more than the rest of us. We moved on from the place of the fight within a few hours, for though the men of the village had applauded Bovile's courage, it was generally considered that he had not fought fair and there was talk of revenge. Within a day or two we set up camp again, at Walderton, a few miles north of Portsmouth.

Here, after two days during which I had been little able to interest the villagers in my astrological forecasts (for their condition was so low that indeed they had nothing to look forward to other than a quick encounter with some village lad under a hedge, followed by marriage, the bearing of children, and death). At dawn on the third day we were rudely awakened by the sound of shouting and commotion and as we dazedly roused ourselves, men roughly broke into our tent and, barely giving us time to clothe ourselves, we were pushed into the general area of the camp where the whole of the band was gathered, surrounded by constables with weapons drawn. When Bovile was produced as leader of the group, he seemed to me to be a very different man from the one who had won the prize fight, or lorded it over us. He was instead polite and agreeable, even servile, this springing, I am sure, from a fear of authority which had once imprisoned him for some days in the Fleet prison, an experience dreaded by every man but perhaps most of all by a Gypsy, whose natural habitat was the open air.

It seemed that a boy child was missing from a house in the neighbourhood and that hearing there was a camp of

Egyptians in the area, it was the natural and first thing to do to search it, for there was and remains a suspicion that they are prone to child stealing, and indeed I would not like to swear that it never takes place.

As the tents were searched and we were questioned, I noticed a young man standing apart with a sad expression upon his face and, making opportunity to approach him, asked him what he knew of the affair. Surprised at the gentility of my address, he confessed to being the father of the child who, he said, had been playing happily in the garden of his house the previous afternoon, but had then disappeared. And was there any true reason to suspect the band, I asked? No, he replied, except that the constables informed him it was most likely we had something to do with the affair.

Would he accept, I asked, that if the child had been brought to the camp, I would know it, and that since I did not know it, there could be no question that he was here?

Somewhat hesitatingly, he agreed to take my word, and summoning the chief of the constables instructed him to call his men off, which he could do being, as he told me, a magistrate of the area. Enquiring his name and address, I made a careful note of it in my mind, and thanked him respectfully as he left. Bovile was brief in his acknowledgement of my intervention, merely wishing to know why I did not do it earlier. I had expected no more, but invited him to consider whether it would not be worth while to arrange for the band to hunt for the child, for if we succeeded in finding it the neighbourhood, hearing of it, would be sure to be more hospitable to us. He shook his head, saying that we did not need their hospitality, but when I added that I doubted not that Mr Finching, which was his name, would be generous in the matter of financial acknowledgement, he immediately became more enthusiastic and within half an hour had organised four bands of our company, each led by a man who was an acknowledgedly good hunter – or poacher – and who could read the signs of the countryside.

We made our way as quietly as possible to the house Mr Finching had described to me, which lay but a mile distant, and there spread out and began our search, each bush being thoroughly beaten. Meanwhile, I managed to separate myself and entered the gates of the house, intending to look around the grounds, for while its owner might not welcome a band of Gypsies there, he would be less likely to object to my own presence, especially upon such an errand.

The grounds were not extensive but were beautifully modelled; I had not been in such a place since leaving Alcovary, and here was a pool very like that in which Frank and Andy would bathe, which brought tears of recollection to my eyes. At its side was a small hut or barn from which, as I passed it, I seemed to hear a small sound of discontent. The door being shut but not locked, I pushed it open with little effort and the noise became louder, and in a while, upon a search, I discovered it to come from below an upturned boat kept there, and to be the unhappy cries of an infant who, from his appearance, had been there for some time.

It was, as the reader has by now inferred, the missing child and what were the scenes of joy when I walked to the house with it mewling in my arms – joy only interrupted by strictures upon the servants for not having searched with sufficient diligence. One servant indeed claimed to have searched the lakeside hut, and suggested that I had stolen the child and was now, in fright of my offence, returning it, but I am happy to say that Mr Finching disbelieved, or at least discredited it. He offered me a dish of tea and asked my story, for, he said, it seemed I could not have been raised in the company of the rascals who now commanded me.

Affected by this sudden display of sympathy, and alone with Mr Finching and his wife, I broke down into tears and revealed the whole story of my life, omitting, it will be guessed, the more intimate descriptions with which I have favoured the reader.

Both Mr and Mrs Finching were affected in turn by my narrative and were as one in suggesting that I must stay with them until the band had departed the area. If I simply failed to appear Bovile would believe that I had made good my escape, for had I not made it plain that I despised their way of life? This was perhaps not entirely true, for I had been too afraid to speak openly against him or his manner of commanding the troop, but nevertheless I welcomed the opportunity of escape and was taken immediately to an attic room, whence a kindly servant brought hot water with which, for the first time for many weeks, I was able in leisure and privacy to attack the grime which now seemed to engrain my skin.

As I was halfway through this process, I heard footsteps below and looking cautiously out saw on the gravel path Bovile, Sam and Rosanna and some other members of the troop, who for some time talked with Mr Finching at the door. I could not hear what was said but later learned that they had reported that they had learned a rival band of Gypsies had stolen the child and made off with it towards London, and expected reward for the information. Mr Finching greeted this by indicating his wife who stood in a nearby window, the child in her arms, and bidding the band be gone. The discussion then became heated, and Bovile threatening, but Mr Finching was evidently firm, and then summoned two of the house servants with cudgels. At this Bovile called Sam forward, who had been skulking in the background, and something seemed to change hands, whereupon my erstwhile friends retreated, grumbling. Nothing had been said of me and I could only imagine that it was thought I had returned to the camp.

That evening before supper Mr Finching presented me with a purse containing twenty guineas which, he said, he had extracted from Bovile as my due, threatening him otherwise with prosecution on several grounds, from stealing money from me to attempting to extort money from him by giving false information. I could only conclude that, knowing Mr Finching to be a gentleman and magistrate, Bovile thought him cheaply bought off at what seemed to me then to be a small fortune.

So, having thanked my benefactor, I sat once more at a civilised table, eating with knife and with fork, drinking from a crystal glass, and almost overcome by being treated again as a lady. Mrs Finching indeed acted to me as a sister might act, and Mr Finching as a brother, and at last I was returned to my room, with a warning not for the time to set foot outside the grounds. I had no notion to, for here was a bed dressed with clean white sheets which I slid between, finding them as welcome as any lover and much more conducive to slumber. Indeed in no time I fell into a deep sleep, in which all my dreams were of happy past times, and friends so long absent.

Chapter Eleven

The Adventures of Andy

It occurred to me as the Lady Elizabeth was loosing the waistband of my breeches that perhaps I had been at Rawby Hall for quite long enough.

Not only was I weary of a footman's duties, these being extremely repetitive and boring and the hours long, but to the physical weariness inflicted upon me by the work was added that which was the result of my having to make love with Tabby who now expected my attentions not only as a concomitant of the commissions of Beau Rust, but also as that of my supposed adoration. Ellen too from time to time required solace, besides which, Mr Caister was more and more pressing in his attentions, summoning me again and again to his pantry to insist that my breeches needed refitting, and making me change and change them in front of him, though offering no affection being, no doubt, afraid of the pillory and the rope, the penalty for backgammon players. And now, it seemed, I was to be pressed into service in My Ladies' rooms. Perhaps it was time to be away, and somewhere else.

During my spare time – though there was little enough of it – I often took myself to Signor Cesareo's rooms, where we played the guitar together. Giovanni was a pleasant enough fellow and though his English was rather poor, he was an excellent player and a no less excellent teacher, so that in time I was a dextrous performer upon the instrument. It happened that the Signor's rooms were close enough to those of Beau Rust for him to overhear our music, and he must have reported our dexterity to the ladies, for I am sure that Giovanni did not do so, being of continental temperament and thus jealous of his intimacy with our employer's daughters. However, be that how it may, one afternoon we received a command to attend the ladies with our instruments and in course made our way to their rooms, where Lady Elizabeth and Lady Margaret were at ease, leisuredly fanning themselves in *déshabillé* upon the twin couches which stood between the two tall windows of their drawing-room.

'We hear –' said Lady Elizabeth.

'– that Master Andy is now almost as adept upon the strings as yourself, Signor,' said the Lady Margaret.

'And we wish to hear –'

'– an example of your duetting.'

Setting up our music stands, we played an arrangement Giovanni had made of some Mozart dances, following this (in tribute to England) with some music of Mr Handel's. The ladies expressed themselves delighted and told us to play on, whereupon we engaged in some earlier pieces. So intent was I upon acquitting myself well at this, my first public performance, that I scarcely noticed – or if I noticed, thought little of – the ladies rising to their feet and moving about the room, until I felt a soft arm slipped around my neck and a hand diving into my shirt and falling upon my bosom.

At this, perhaps unsurprisingly, I ceased to play but noticed that Govianni continued his part, despite receiving a similar attention from the Lady Elizabeth.

'Pray continue, Master Andy,' said the Lady Margaret, and as I did so I felt her lips pressed to the nape of my neck. I found it increasingly difficult to keep time and the black notes danced before my eyes as, leaning over me, she unbuttoned my shirt, then slipped it over my shoulders, which she caressed with her lips, her long hair falling about me like a shawl. It was not that the lascivious emotions aroused in me were so new as to preoccupy me entirely, but a mixture of apprehension, shyness and even modesty was the result of amorous attentions being pressed upon me by the daughter of an earl! I had certainly travelled far from the wattle and daub hut in which I had been born!

Somewhat to my relief, I became conscious that

Giovanni had ceased to play and, glancing aside, I saw that the Lady Elizabeth had now slipped his shirt quite to his waist, trapping his arms to his sides, and that pulling aside the neck of her gown she was offering one breast to the excited Italian's lips, who was gulping at it with no less enthusiasm than he had been paying to the work of M. Lully, upon which we had been engaged.

My own guitar fell with a soft clamour of strings to the floor as the Lady Margaret, whose every action seemed to mirror that of her sister, drew my own shirt to my waist. Following Giovanni's example I did not attempt to free my arms, while an exquisitely white breast fell to my lips, and as I pulled gently at it I felt her hands at my waist, working at the buckle of my breeches.

It was at this time that the thoughts recorded at the beginning of this chapter swiftly flew through my mind, though not, I confess, for long, for by now my waistband was free, the flap of my breeches was opened, and an instrument as tightly strung as the highest string of my guitar was in the loving hands of one who offered to play upon it with no less dexterity than the finest of musical performers.

Acting so in unison that our figures seemed to mirror each other, Giovanni and I were drawn to our feet by our partners who, falling to their knees, released our lower persons from the trammelling clothing and paid us the tribute of a kiss before leading us to the couches and disposing us upon them. Standing back, they then disrobed, revealing bodies as like as two eggs and more beautiful than any upon which I had previously set my eyes.

I have, it must be said, no strong feelings in the matter of society, taking the view that any woman may be as good as any other; nor do I wish to cast aspersions of a derogatory nature upon Tabby or Ellen, or indeed upon my dear Sophie. However it must be said that the figures of the two ladies as they stood before us were of another breed altogether, marking the difference between a sturdy working pony and a handsome racing filly. These ladies were, it is true, more mature, their figures fuller and more generously endowed. Their breasts, heavy with promise, were like rich fruit, peaked with brown tips eager for our mouths; their haunches were portly but firm, enhanced by enchanting dimples; their bellies too, without being gross, were ample, the navels deeply marked, while below delightful sprigs of velvet hair barely masked the dark outlines of their cunnies.

It need scarcely be said that by now any weariness I may have felt at the prospect of connection had vanished and I was all eagerness – eagerness which was deferred, however, for first the ladies must explore our bodies, moving their fingers and palms with an enchantingly careful diligence, playing upon us with every bit as much care as any musician upon his instrument. First, they laid us upon our bellies, and covered every inch of our backs with kisses and caresses, coming at length to our back sides, upon which they lavished attention, smoothing and kneading them with their hands, then drawing the cheeks aside to tickle with a finger the entrance to that aperture in which, I had thought, only a madge cull could be interested. The sentiment this courtesy arose in me was beyond expectation delicious and I was unable not to squirm beneath her hand so that, my prick rubbing against the couch, I was within a moment of the ultimate excitation when she ceased and, first planting a kiss upon my double jug, turned me upon my back. I had noted carefully the responses of the Signor, who had, I knew, been here before, and as he lay still beneath the ranging fingers – save for his tool, which as the Lady Elizabeth played upon it involuntarily vibrated like one of the strings of his guitar – followed his example, taking care not to move despite the exquisite nature of the sensations invoked by the Lady Margaret who, having pleasured every other area of my body, now came between my thighs and began to stroke my almost insanely ravenous piece with her fingers, rousing it if possible to an even greater extension, so that the ring of skin beneath its head bid fair to burst with the pressure upon it. And, as she lowered her head to run her tongue from the base to the very tip, all control left me and with only the presence of mind to throw the lady's head to one side, I died, jet after jet of sap rising high in the air to fall upon my body. As it did so, I remember that my eye fell upon a black dot in the recently repaired ceiling, which led me to suppose that Beau Rust's eye was still able to observe what went on below; a fine display he had of it, that afternoon!

I feared My Lady's anger – except that recovering from the delirium which had resulted in, I believed, too speedy a resolution, I saw that on the neighbouring couch Signor Giovanni was in a similar state. I later learned from him that he had been accompanied in similar orgies by two other footmen and that the sisters had by some alchemy always succeeded in rousing the two men to their culmination at precisely the same moment!

The ladies now handed us fine towels with which to wipe ourselves and rang the bell; not long after, one of their maids – a girl whom I had only seen once or twice, for their ladyships' maids were kept in their own establishment – entered with a tray of tea, showing not the slightest sign of surprise at the presence of two naked men in the room.

For the half of an hour, or perhaps a little less, we drank tea, all in a state of nature. Giovanni picked up his guitar and played a little, while the Lady Margaret congratulated me upon my expertise with the instrument, though asserting that I had come too quickly upon one of the pieces, which I took to be a joke, since they both laughed at it. However, I saw nothing to laugh at since in the last duet (or rather, quartet) in which we had played a part, Giovanni and I had reached the end together – a fact at which, when I asserted it, the ladies also laughed.

In a while, setting down his guitar, Giovanni rose and took the Lady Elizabeth by the hand, leading her to one of the couches – whereupon I did the same, and in the manner they had ministered to us, so we attended to them. I was for the first time entirely conscious of the beauty of a woman's back and even ceased to wonder, as I had previously done, that any man should wish to swive at a tail. However, Giovanni not making that offer, I thought it best not to attempt it, contenting myself with insinuating a finger into the passage, which from the shudder it invoked, gave some pleasure.

Of the joy I took in caressing My Lady's handsome bubs, I need not prolong description; their springy resilience beneath my palm was an irresistible invitation so that I could not but climb upon her, my knees beneath her arms, and place my whorepipe between those delicious spheres whereat, though surprised, she eagerly clasped her breasts with her hands and closed them upon it, moving them in such a manner as to give me great delight. There was a pleased cry from the Lady Elizabeth, and I saw that she encouraged Giovanni similarly to mount her and treated him in the same way. (I was later to learn from him that they had greeted with the same pleasure some new and lascivious tricks which he had learned in Italy and which were not commonly performed in our country.)

It was in no short time that, placing her hands upon my shoulders, the lady persuaded me to lower myself and throwing up her legs invited me to enter her, which I did with no less pleasure. Through the intensity of the delight she had earlier given me, I was able to prolong the ride until she had twice cried out in pleasure before, seizing me about the waist and plunging to meet me with the virility of a girl, brought me off to my own and her satisfaction. I need not say that at the moment when I experienced the apogee, I saw from the corner of my eye an expression of intense pleasure upon the face of my fellow musician, marking the fact that he too had concluded his performance.

We were then bidden to resume our clothes, and picking up our instruments were dismissed with the wish that we should perform again within a few days. Before we left the room we were handed a purse which, examining in the corridor, I found to contain two gold sovereigns, which Giovanni assured me was a usual result of such a connection.

I was none the less still of a mind to leave the Hall and the next day told Giovanni so, who himself having been itinerant in his own country recognised and applauded my instinct for, said he, youth was a time for experience; time enough to settle down when one was twenty. He now assured me that I was of sufficient skill upon the guitar to make a living by playing upon it, in one way or in another, and gave me the name of a merchant in Southampton who had once offered himself a position in his household. He was, Giovanni said, eager to impress his neighbours, and only two months ago had heard him play when My Lord had taken him to Cambridge to perform during dinner at some meeting of mayors and aldermen, and offered him a position.

Back in my room I counted my hidden store of gold which, with the contributions of Beau Rust and the money given me by visiting gentlemen to whom I had been of assistance, now amounted to no less than sixteen pound – almost a year's wages for a labouring man and sufficient to keep me for several months. I went that day to Mr Caister and told him that I had received a message that my mother was ill and should need to go to her. He was suspicious, asking how I had heard. I said, from a passing tradesman by whom word was sent, and took the opportunity to lay my hand as though by accident upon his thigh as I bent to ask him for leave, whereat he could not resist but to take my hand in his and, squeezing it, said he would make all right and I could leave that very day, if I wished to do so. I settled to serve that night at supper and to leave the next morning.

I am sorry now to record that I lacked the courage to inform either Tabby or Ellen of my going, and perhaps fortunately – for though I was at that age resilient, my afternoon's work had sapped my amorous energies – neither requested my presence in their bed that night. I slept soundly, rose before even Tom was awake and, having surreptitiously packed my few possessions the night before, crept from the room and by five o'clock had begged a ride upon a tradesman's cart, to Cambridge.

At Cambridge I learned there was a stage leaving for Southampton at seven o'clock that evening and I determined to use the time to make myself more presentable to any prospective employer. I took myself off to a tailor who by midday had turned me out in a dress both fashionable and hardy: a good broadcloth coat, pantaloons – for I was tired of breeches – hessian boots and a satin waistcoat, plain but elegant. On presenting myself at the Red Lion Inn, a distinctive hostelry from which the coach was to depart, I was welcomed as a gentleman of sorts and ate heartily in preparation for the journey, watching my fellow travellers as they prepared themselves: a squire and his wife and daughter, plain but good-humoured; a parson, blustery and overbearing; a tall, thin woman accompanied by a servant and two small boys at the sight of whom I was glad I had taken an outside place for they were noisy and ill-tempered and the other passengers looked already abashed at the thought of spending a night in their company.

Just before seven, having changed back into my poorer clothing and packed my new dress into a box, I and my fellow travellers boarded the coach, the others crowded to suffocation inside and myself seated beside the driver, divided only by a narrow, low rail from a fall directly onto the road. There was nowhere to place my feet, so that I clung with some attention to the rail as the coach dropped into, then climbed out of innumerable pits and hummocks in the surface as we rattled out of the town.

The first stage ended at Dunstable, in Hertfordshire, where the driver took a tot of liquor. The second was completed at Reading, where he took another and I descended to stretch my legs and ease the soreness in my lower limbs, for I had been incessantly cuffed and bumped by the jolts and jumps of the coach, up hill and down dale. My condition however was nothing to that of those unfortunates travelling inside, for both boys had been sick within and without the coach, and from the door as it opened came a wave of foul and rancid air.

Mounting again, the driver by now inattentive of his charges – which fortunately seemed to know by heart the road to Winchester – we rattled on at a pace which, while not great, due to the badness of the road was sufficiently terrifying. With the greatest care, I climbed from my place into the midst of the luggage piled upon the roof of the coach itself and, inserting myself into a cranny among the parcels and packages, wedged myself into position and disposed myself to a semblance, but little reality, of sleep.

It was nearing dawn and we had just passed (I was later to hear) the hamlet of Popham and were jolting through Micheldever Wood, five miles from Winchester, when I was rudely shaken to my senses by the loud neighing of one of our horses and a sudden jar as the coach came to a halt.

'Down, driver, and all out from the coach!' came a commanding voice, accompanied by a scream from the squire's wife. Cautiously I roused myself as the driver descended and the passengers began to climb from the doorway, to see a couple of feet below me the mounted figure of a masked man, holding in his hand a cocked flintlock, pointed now at the head of the parson, whose bluster had evaporated into a remarkable subservience. Indeed, he was already removing his purse from the pocket of his greatcoat.

With great care to make no noise, I removed myself from the shelter I had contrived and without thought launched myself at the highwayman's head, landing square upon it. As we both fell to the ground I heard an explosion, which at once frighted and heartened me, for if the charge had involuntarily exploded the gun could not now be dangerous. In any event, the situation was safe for, landing on top of the man I had winded him and was now almost winded myself by the driver, the squire and the parson, all of whose bodies landed on top of us.

After some confusion, however, the muddle was resolved and the fellow bound and unmasked. He was revealed as a young man not much older than myself, with a thin starved face, who had not – by his appearance – been too successful in his trade. Though invited to give his name and explain himself, he maintained a desperate silence and was hauled to the top of the coach where, his hands behind him and his feet bound, he was placed between the driver and myself as we made the short remaining journey to Winchester.

Dawn was breaking as we entered the town, and at a crossroads just on the outskirts of the town we passed a gibbet from which swung a cage occupied by fluttering rags and a miscellany of bones, the skull still imprisoned within its steel frame. I could not but glance at our captive who gazed without emotion at his fate (for he was surely for the morning drop) except that as he lowered his eyes, he remarked in a low voice, 'I hope you're satisfied, cunning shaver!' I did not reply, for I could not but pity the man who no doubt had been reduced to thieving by the distresses of poverty. I dared not enquire whether he had wife and family, for my heart would have misgiven me.

There was a delay at Winchester while the constables were sent for and the man handed over. The parson, as it turned out, was a native of the place and served at the cathedral and his evidence was considered in itself sufficient to condemn the thief, so that after hearing my story and congratulating me, the constables were content to let me continue my journey. In the meantime we had all taken grog and eaten, and as we entered Southampton were in a buoyant mood, increased in my case when I learned that my fellow travellers had taken a collection among themselves and now presented me with three guineas in earnest of their gratitude for my saving them from losing their valuables (no doubt worth considerably more).

At the Chequers Inn I prayed for a room in which to refresh myself – a favour granted without charge, for I was for a moment the hero of the time – and there washed myself and changed into my good clothes, at which the landlord was more than a little surprised, now addressing me as 'sir' rather than 'princox'. And when I asked for the house of Mr Harry Grose he was yet more impressed and directed me with courtesy to a handsome building two streets away.

Mr Grose was a man of great dignity in Southampton; formerly a yeoman's son, he was now an esquire, having been not only mayor, but justice of the peace and sheriff of Hampshire. He was a merchant, collecting tallow from all over the south of England and selling it throughout the world. He imported indigo, cochineal, logwood, woad and other dyes from the Indies and the Middle East; flax, tow, madder and whale-fins from Rotterdam; alum from

Hamburg; wine, cherry brandy and prunes from Bordeaux; he dealt in tea, sugar, chocolate and tobacco and he sold grindstones. His wealth and influence was such that he had recently obtained a coat of arms and decorated his house in the finest modern style, setting his wife and daughter in the best society of the town, yet remaining himself distinctly rough in manner.

In the style of his house he vied with the first of the nobility, in his table, furniture and equipage; his wife had her tea and her card-parties and he had kept for many years a tutor for the young madam, though now at the age of eighteen she was considered to know everything it was advisable for a young woman to know and all his energies were concentrated upon finding a suitable husband for her – who would have, as I subsequently learned, to be at least of the person and rank of an archangel.

I knocked at his door at an opportune moment, for the day before Mrs and Miss Grose had been to an evening party at the house of a fellow merchant at which a harpsichord player had performed throughout the evening, and were sorely distracted that they had no such attraction to offer when the invitation must be returned. Indeed, Mr Grose had been driven almost to distraction throughout breakfast by their importunings, and no sooner did he hear that I came recommended by Signor Cesareo than I was engaged at a wage of one guinea a week, my keep being provided, which was more than I had dared to hope for. I was also to be provided with a room and, having made my bows to the ladies, asked to be shown to it, for to be frank I was almost dead with fatigue after the joltings and adventures of the journey. A footman led me up four flights to a small attic room, sparsely but reasonably furnished, where I fell upon the bed in my finery and instantly into a deep sleep.

By the time I was awakened in the early evening, news had reached the house of my adventure in the coach and I was somewhat a celebrity; indeed so much so that when, after having enjoyed a good meal, I was summoned to the drawing-room, I was greeted by a polite round of applause

from Mr and Mrs Grose, Miss Grose, and five or six of their
neighbours (no doubt those they wished most to impress).
They smothered me with congratulations upon my bravery
in fighting, singlehanded, with so dangerous and vicious a
fellow, armed as he was with two pistols and a sword! I am
shamed to say it was a picture of which I did not strive to
dim the colours and contrived to delight the company by
playing a few of the numbers at which Signor Cesareo had
said I was most adept.

I was determined to become as skilful at my playing as
possible and daily set aside time for practice in my small
room, performing exercises Giovanni had shown me for
improving the dexterity of the fingers, and learning new
pieces – some of which I purchased in sheets from a
counter in Bar Street, the fashionable quarter of the town,
where I was cordially received, my feat having been noised
abroad by Mr Grose in terms which showed me off as a
fellow fine as the Iron Duke himself! But fame fades, and
within a month or so I was no more regarded than any other
household servant.

My work was not arduous; only, of an evening, to play
for the family and friends, who gathered almost every night
in the drawing-room, where Miss Grose worked at her sam-
plers or made covers for footstools, led her younger friends
in spillikins, commerce and cribbage, or propounded rid-
dles and conundrums. Her mother and the older ladies and
gentlemen sat at whist or played brag, speculation or *vinqt-
et-un*. Mr Grose was rarely present on these occasions, pre-
ferring to take himself off to a drinking club whence Bob,
the footman, escorted him home at three or four in the
morning, often incapable of climbing the stairs to his bed.
Nevertheless he was invariably up at seven the following
morning, and apparently with a head clear enough to outdo
most of his rivals in business.

Mrs Grose was a kindly, middle-aged woman who, conscious of the comfort in which she lived, readily forgave her
husband for his absence. Unlike him she had no pretence to
grandeur, but being in every way amenable accepted his
views in everything and adopted them as her own. Miss

Patience Grose, however, had pretences to even greater things than her father and had so far scorned the young men of the town presented to her by her father as possible spouses. 'She's waiting for royalty,' said Bob, 'but she may wait too long, for she's getting long in the tooth and she's something scare-crow, and one bub's partial, for Rose seen them often and says the left one's higher than the right. If she don't get a man in her mutton sharpish, she'll die an old maid!'

I did not for a week or two feel the lack of female companionship; there was in the house only a cook and a housemaid, the one an old woman of fifty, and the other a girl with a face like a flat-iron, and as demure as an old whore at a christening. However, after a while I began to be proud, and in need of a good strapping. When I enquired of Bob, he said that I was to come with him late that night to Buss Street, near the churchyard, and we would see if we could find a public ledger – by which I understood a common woman or prostitute.

So after the last guest had gone and I had finished my last piece, I made my bow, went to my room and changed my clothes, then meeting Bob (himself out of his livery) we set off through a close and sultry night. We were not two yards inside Buss Street when we were approached by a cockish dell, who enquired whether we would dock with her. Upon Bob expressing that he had no desire to lie with a buttered bun, she went a few steps down the street and gave a low whistle, at which another ladybird appeared. On my asking whether they would take us to their rooms, both they and Bob laughed. 'We'll give 'em green gowns in the churchyard!' he said, for it seemed that that was the place of all, in this as in every town, where the mutton-mongers met to go about their business. Indeed we had to go about for some time between the tombstones before we found a place which was not within touching distance of a grunting pair.

Without more ado the two girls laid themselves down upon the stone slabs of twin tombs – still warm from the day's sun – and throwing up their clothes disclosed that they wore nothing beneath their skirts. Though I had hoped for more comfortable rogering, I was not slower than Bob at dropping my breeches and finding the place, for I was more than ready for the fray. But my entry was accompanied by a loud peal of thunder and scarcely had I made five thrusts than with another peal a bright flash of lightning struck the church tower and heavy rain began to pelt – at which with a wriggle my girl clutched at my cods and manipulated them so exquisitely that, though hoping for a longer passage, my bolt was shot, whereupon she drew herself up and demanded five shillings, which without enthusiasm I paid her, the rain now being so great that all I wished was shelter. Bob at the same time had risen and with a wry grin also paid his term, and we ran for shelter of a tavern, where we consumed several tankards, and he promised me a fuller passage next time. However, I resolved that there should be no next time, or at least not in such conditions, for now that I was spent my mind circled wonderfully on the question whether my girl had been poxed or not and whether I was for the Covent Garden ague, as Bob called the clap. Several days elapsed before, closely regarding my plug tail for signs of the disease, I concluded that I was lucky in avoiding it.

I was very happy, for the space of five or six weeks, to enjoy the relative quiet of my daily life with Mr Grose and his family. My work was so light as to be almost nothing, I had time during the day to wander about the town and familiarise myself with it, and while I lacked the pleasures of female companionship, an occasional bout in the churchyard (for which purpose I availed myself of a cundum or sheath of skin – a notorious protective against the pox – bought at no small cost from a doctor in the next street) satisfied my animal instincts at a very reasonable charge, at the same time teaching me some tricks with which I made no doubt I could impress future conquests.

One day, the household was all agog at the arrival of a gentleman said to be coming from London to court Miss Patience Grose. Bob had this news from the maid, who had it from Miss Patience herself. He was, she said, the son of a lord, whose interest her father had secured by the simple expedient of helping his family from bankruptcy by the promise to purchase at an exorbitant price an interest in a coal mine in the north of the country which, it was generally believed, was exhausted of coal. His eagerness to provide a noble husband for his daughter had been allowed to outweigh his normally sharp business sense.

'But,' said Miss Patience, 'be he a very Adonis, I shall not wed him at my father's behest, for I count myself as particular in the matter, and shall not chain myself to a man at the nod of any head.'

At the first sight the young man seemed extremely pleasant: not of remarkable features, but of some elegance of manner, and a kindly disposition, and on being introduced to Miss Patience he made a low bow which she received without special grace, but not unkindly.

It being quite understood by all what was the purpose of his visit, the conversation at supper was somewhat low and consisted on Miss Patience's part of an almost complete silence, and on her father's part an excess of enquiry about the visitor's family's history, responded to in as short a manner as was concomitant with politeness, so that had I not provided quantities of music by Dowland and Purcell there would have been prolonged periods of complete silence. After dinner, we retired to the drawing-room, where again I played quietly while our visitor – whose name, I must not omit to record, was the Hon. Frederick Mellor – and Miss Patience, left alone in order that they should cultivate each other's acquaintance, sat wrapped in a discouraging hush at the other end of the room.

Finally Mr Mellor, leaning forward, addressed Miss Patience in a low tone, which none the less was audible to me.

'Ma'am,' he said, 'you cannot but be aware that our parents have brought us together in the intention that we should wed. For myself, my brief acquaintance with you has furnished me with ample proof of your delicacy of manner and your exquisite poise and grace, to say nothing of that natural beauty which no man could but regard with approbation. May I now enquire whether you are so good as to find in me qualities which would not entirely disqualify me as your husband?'

'Sir,' she replied, without a moment's hesitation, 'I have no intention of putting myself forward to you or to any other man for the purposes of breeding, much less of supplying my father with noble relatives. It would be best if our intimacy should proceed no further than an acknowledgement of our relative virtues, in the acquiescence that neither of us shall look forward to any further familiarity than a cordial but distant friendship may afford.'

Such a speech could not but dampen the ardour of any swain, let alone one as lacking in force as Mr Mellor. With a look of sorry surprise he bowed coldly and shortly afterwards made an excuse and left the room, whereat Miss Patience rose with something like a sneer and marched after him, leaving me, if I would, to play on for my own pleasure.

Bob, who was sharing his room with Mr Mellor's servant, confided to me the following day that Mellor was in despair over his rejection, for if he should not acquire Miss Patience's consent to their marriage and the arrangement should fall through, Mr Grose would withdraw from his business association with his father and the family would be ruined.

This, needless to say, did not concern me – what had I to do with the fortunes of a family of which I knew nothing? But I must confess, in my slight boredom with the sameness of my daily life – lacking as it did in so many respects the small excitements of the Hall – I began to toy with the idea of helping brother Cupid to bring the two together, the sheer impossibility of the task providing a challenge which, after a few hours, was almost irresistible to me.

Next day I found myself leaving the house for my usual morning walks to Bar Street, where I took chocolate and watched the quality walking and talking, at the same time as Mr Mellor, who himself seemed in an idle mood. He greeted me kindly, and invited me to walk with him, and it being a fine morning we took a turn in the park which lay between us and the heart of the town. After a while I asked: 'You prolong your stay in Southampton, sir?'

'Not for more than a day or two,' he replied. 'My business here is, I fear, concluded.'

'You will forgive me if I am impertinent,' I said, greatly daring, 'but it is, I believe, the case that you seek the hand of Miss Patience in marriage?'

He looked for a moment abashed that a mere servant should raise such a topic with a gentleman but, as I had suspected, in his dejection was eager to confide in almost anyone.

'That is so, Master Archer. But I fear the lady has a firm natural aversion.'

'If you will allow me, sir, the problem is I believe one of coolness.'

'Of coolness?'

'Yes, sir. You will not be aware of the fact, which indeed is not generally known, that contrary to her appearance and behaviour Miss Grose is not without passion.'

He raised his eyebrows and I wondered whether my impertinence in speaking of his host's daughter would be too much for him. But I went on.

'You will forgive me, but my interest in what would seem an ideal match persuades me that I should speak out. Miss Patience is of a naturally fiery temperament, warm and affectionate; her maid has often spoke to me of her mistress' desire to be wooed, for she is not one of those ladies who will respond to a cold declaration of interest. She is a great reader of Mr Fielding and Mr Richardson and awaits a hero who will sweep her into his life without a thought that she might refuse him.'

'You mean,' he said, 'that she awaits corporeal evidence of my passion?'

'Indeed, sir.'

We walked for a while in silence.

'Mr Archer, we must speak more frankly. If I understand you, Miss Patience has – ah –'

'Yearns to be clasped to your bosom, sir.'

'To my bosom? To *my* bosom?'

'Indeed sir, for her maid has indicated that she regards you with the utmost admiration. She has spoken, it seems, with approval of your face and figure, and regretted that you have not saluted her with vigour.'

'So it is your belief that were I to –'

'Yes, sir, you should lose no time, but sweep her from her feet. Any tribute a vigorous man may pay to a lovely woman will be greeted with delight, and I am sure that a match will follow.'

He wrung my hand.

'My dear Mr Archer, I am greatly your debtor, greatly your debtor!' he said, at which I found it necessary to excuse myself, on some ground of necessity to call upon a friend, and left him a new and hopeful man. It was now necessary for me to prepare Miss Patience for his assault.

I found her sewing in the drawing-room, and surprised to see me, for we only had the slightest acquaintance and almost never met except when my instrument was needed.

'Forgive my intrusion, ma'am,' I said, 'but if I may have a word with you?'

'Certainly, Andrew,' she said.

'Forgive my impertinence, ma'am, but I feel under the necessity of speaking to you about Mr Mellor.'

'About Mr Mellor?' she said coldly. 'I believe that you can have nothing to say upon that subject which could fall with any degree of propriety from your lips.'

'Ma'am,' I said humbly, 'I speak only as a man who has suffered the despondency of unrecognised love.'

She looked up with some interest at this, partly, no doubt, as one who doubted whether a servant were capable of the emotion.

'Mr Mellor's man, ma'am, has spoken to me of his master's despair . . .'

'Despair?'

'At your rejection of his addresses. If I may so express it, his senses are so overcome by the apprehension of your beauty that they are dizzied by it, and he is made so faint that he has been unable to offer you the tribute he would wish to pay.'

She sat silent but clearly not unimpressed.

'He is known, it seems, as one of the most fiery and

attacking of lovers; his conquests among the London notabilities are legion, and the ladies to whom he has successfully paid his addresses are counted among the most fortunate.'

'Indeed?' she said, with more than a glimmer of curiosity.

'Indeed, ma'am. If you will forgive a certain coarseness, his physical attributes are said to be consumedly impressive, so much so as to be almost unendurable . . .'

'I have not noticed it.'

'But now, for the first time finding himself in love rather than merely wishing to make another conquest, he is tongue-tied and incapable. Knowing this, ma'am, I felt it no less than my duty to make his apologies to you – without, of course, his knowledge or approval. Having myself felt all too keenly the biting cold of a lady's disdain, and knowing the genuineness of his passion, I could not but wish to appraise you of the true situation.'

'Thank you, Andrew,' she said thoughtfully, and more warmly than she had ever previously addressed me. I made my bow and left, and that evening was careful to arrange a screen at the end of the drawing-room, behind which I could play without being seen, but contriving that a gap at the hinge should be so placed that I could observe the rest of the room.

Throughout the meal Mr and Mrs Grose as usual made most of the conversation, but I was aware that the two young people were eyeing each other with a new interest. I noticed that Miss Patience had attired herself in a low-necked dress less modest than any she had previously worn in Mr Mellor's company – one which had previously been reserved for wear when she was with her female friends, when it caused some laughter and giggling should I enter the room. However, since I was but a servant, the generous display of bosom it offered was of no consequence.

I was for a moment dismayed when her father and mother – no doubt assuming that there was nothing else to be hoped for in the affair – seemed about to accompany them to the drawing-room, but I was able to take Mr Grose apart and appraise him that Mr Mellor was to make one more attempt to gain his daughter's hand.

'Fat chance!' he muttered, but led his wife off to another room, and soon Mr Mellor and Miss Patience were in their chairs, while I established myself behind the screen and began upon a carefully selected programme of love-sick lute pieces.

Within a moment, Mr Mellor had fallen to his knees and, taking her hand, declared himself as irremediably attached to Miss Patience – upon which he planted a kiss upon her palm. For the first time in her life, I dare swear, a blush spread across her features.

'Mr Mellor,' she said, 'I fear I have perhaps been mistaken in my view of your virtues . . .'

'Oh, ma'am!' he cried, and bending forward transferred his lips from hand to bosom, at which the flush upon her face deepened – certainly not with displeasure. It may be that my words about her lover's physical attributes came to her mind, for as his lips explored the vale between the twin white peaks, she allowed a hand to fall into his lap, where it seemed to discover something of interest, for they both drew away from each other and their eyes met. Then without pause they clasped each other and in a moment she was unclothed to the waist and his hands were appraising the suppleness of breasts more handsome (I must confess) than I would have imagined Miss Patience to possess.

I may have struck more than one disproportionate chord during the next few minutes, for I confess my own discomfort grew as I was forced to observe the scene of passion before me, while my hands were engaged in continuing the music. Though it was clear to an experienced observer that Mr Mellor in fact had little competence in love, as the speed with which he reached satisfaction showed, Miss Patience's innocence made her unconscious of his inexpertise and her delight first at the sight then at the touch of his not unhandsome body knew no bounds. Before they had done aught but explore each other, handling here, kissing there, and no sooner had he caressed with his fingers her love-bower, than with a cry his soul flew forth – to her great interest, who had clearly no apprehension of the culmination of man's amorous play. Clasping his hand within her own and directing it, in a moment her own joy was accomplished – and without the discomfort of the disposal of her maidenhead; which would now wait for their marriage night. Indeed, with one more kiss they hastily clothed themselves and made off to find Mr Grose and appraise him of their intention to be wed as soon as the banns were approved.

I am happy to say that my contentment that I had achieved the impossible in bringing two such apparantly irreconcilable people together was made the keener by the approbation both of Mr Mellor and Miss Patience, who independently and without reference to each other rewarded me not only with their verbal thanks but with a gift of gold which I was able to add to the store in my room.

Chapter Twelve

Sophie's Story

I note that I have so far given no description of my benefactors, Mr and Mrs Charles Finching, of Gauzy Hall, near Walderton in the county of Hampshire. Mr Finching was a young gentleman of perhaps twenty-five or twenty-six years, but though mature was flexible and open in his attitudes and behaviour, as was his wife, Mrs Lettice Finching, his junior by only two or three years.

The Hall, though a manor house of small proportions with eighteen rooms, was nevertheless perfectly impressive and set in elegant grounds of delightful proportion. Mr Finching had inherited the estate from his father and, both his parents being dead, kept up a style of life which, I learned, had subsisted at the hall for centuries, for the place had been in his family for as long as records could recall. He was tall and slim, and made a handsome figure in the fashionable clothes which he affected even when at home; his face was long but good-humoured, his black hair carefully cropped, his dark eyebrows seeming to comment humorously on the world about him, while his mouth was full and generous.

A magistrate, he sat at the local court whenever required, but otherwise spent his life in his library, or riding abroad to administer the estate (which included farming land of a few hundred acres only); he led a life which might be said to consist of leisurely but careful preoccupation with duty.

His wife shared his interest in books; most evenings found them in the drawing-room, he reading aloud from the pages of Sir Walter Scott or Miss Austen, or from the poems of Mr Crabbe or Mr Wordsworth, while she tatted or embroidered chairbacks. It had been made clear to me that it would be unwise to leave the house until Bovile and the tribe were thoroughly moved on, something of which Mr Finching constantly expected news, and also that I was welcome to stay with them for as long as I desired. I was also pleased to spend some time in a tranquillity which had been foreign to me since I had left Alcovary.

If tranquillity was the word I at first applied to my stay at Gauzy Hall, the word which I would soon have applied to it, I fear, is 'boredom'. Perhaps because my life had been so crowded with events since I left home, I soon opened my eyes to the day ready to contemplate enormities or face trials, only to find that the most exciting incident I could expect of the coming hours was the taking of tea with the wife of the local rector, a walk with Mrs Finching to the village with a basket of cakes for some poor person, or a reading of chapter seventeen of *Waverley* which, admirable narrative though it no doubt is, scarely brought the blood to my cheeks.

But perhaps that is not entirely true, for soon I found myself waiting with more or less eagerness to hear of the latest adventure of Edward, the excellent hero of Sir Walter's romance, and on hearing of his love for Rose Bradwardine could scarcely forbear from voicing my scorn that he should love such a poor creature; were I to be clasped in those strong arms, I told myself, Miss Rose would have no chance of holding her lover. The fact was, as I gradually recognised, that as the days passed into weeks and still I sat at the Finchings' table (now in the main for want of anywhere else to go), I found myself increasingly in want of that robust male company to which I had been used. Why, lying awake at night, I even thought of Anna and the manner in which she would comfort me in the absence of Bovile, and would on many an occasion have welcomed even her with open arms.

There were few servants at Gauzy Hall, and without exception they were unprepossessing; the single footman, John, was a mean, thin and gawky young man who could never have been a hero to any woman, while the boy who was his general assistant was too young and innocent for me to consider as a possible lover, though no doubt he was only a year or so younger than I!

My loneliness was exacerbated by the marked devotion of Mr and Mrs Finching whose bedroom was just below mine. In the late summer days, when the windows still lay open, I heard from time to time the low, gasping cries of satisfaction and pleasure which suggested that they were enjoying those marital pleasures to which, no doubt, they looked forward during the long evenings. Despite my host's obvious attentions to his wife, I found myself in time regarding him with an admirer's eye and even believing that perhaps he eyed me with approbation. Could any man, after all, be truly content with the attentions of one woman, however handsome? And Mrs Finching, though in all respects a lady, was not particularly beautiful. Nor, if my instincts were correct, was she so addicted to the game of love as to be much capable of lascivious invention, for she seemed rather sentimental than romantic.

In short, I determined to attempt to seduce my host, and to employ to that end the hour before supper when he made use of the room on the top floor of the house which had been set aside for bathing. There, just down the corridor from my bedroom, a large metal hip-bath lay, to which John brought hot water for the use of anyone who wished to bathe themselves. Mrs Finching had led me there in the course of explaining the hall and had made it clear I was to use the room whenever I wished, which I did. Mr Finching occupied the room every day without fail at the hour of seven o'clock and I had glimpsed him, wrapped in a soft towel, making his way from the bedroom on the lower floor, and had heard a splashing from inside.

So one evening, as dusk was falling – for the evenings were now drawing in – I undressed myself to my shift and waited until I heard the soft footsteps and the closing of the door which indicated that Mr Finching was in the bathing room. Slipping out of my shift, I then wrapped a sheet around my person and made my way down the corridor. Hearing the noise of water within, I breathed deeply, took hold of the handle of the door and turning it, strode in. At the sight which greeted me I gave a cry of surprise and, lifting my hands to my glowing cheeks, let go of the sheet, which fell to the floor leaving me naked as I had ever been.

Though of course my action was contrived, I had not too much to equivocate for the sight that met my eyes as I entered was indeed a delightful one. Mr Finching stood in the bath facing the door, soap in one hand and cloth in the other. A film of suds covered his body, their whiteness only something whiter than his flesh, which was pure and unsullied as a girl's, only a sprig or two of dark hair curling upon his breast, where his paps were small, dark and delicately tinctured. The soap between his thighs almost concealed his manly person, which would however be seen nestling, as it were, in a cloud of white.

My acted distress was not mirrored upon his face; he seemed to take in my figure coolly and while clearly not finding it ugly, was not moved by it, for he simply turned his back upon me, with a simple 'I beg your pardon, ma'am.'

I stammered something about not knowing he was there, while at the same time drinking in the sight of his delightful back, broad shoulders and tapered waist, and below, two globes of a handsome, tight plumpness so enticing that almost without knowing it I took a step forward –

But no, 'twas impossible; he simply stood, not so much as glancing at the dish I so clearly offered – for an intelligent man could clearly not but have been aware that my presence was no accident. I bent to pick up the sheet and, wrapping it about me, excused myself and left. No word was said about the incident to me – nor, I think, to Mrs Finching – but it was to my chagrin that later that night I heard from the bedroom below prolonged sounds of amorous congress which suggested that Mr Finching was presenting his wife – unknown to her – with the outward signs of a passion he had concealed from me.

Next morning I woke to unmistakable signs that the summer was indeed waning: I saw from my window a park hung with mist, with here and there the tops of trees appearing above it like the sails of great ships becalmed in a fog. By ten o'clock, however, the mist had lifted and the sun appeared; it was clearly going to be a fine day and I made my excuses to Mrs Finching, saying that I felt sorely in need of exercise and would take a long contemplative walk for, apart from stretching my limbs, I must think of my future – I could not be their guest for ever.

She answered with words so kind that I could not set them down without the tribute of a tear, and I was especially tenderly inclined because of the wrong I should have done with her husband had not he been steadfast in his affection to her. She charged me with a basket for a sick old woman on the outskirts of the village and I took some food for myself wrapped in a kerchief, and set forth.

Having delivered the basket – and without thanks from the cantankerous old party who took it as her right rather than a charity – I left the village and struck into the country, and after perhaps an hour's walk came to a field where a single man was engaged in binding the last products of the harvest, and there sat down upon a loose pile of warm yellow straw, and ate my food. Meanwhile the man continued his work, gradually approaching the corner where I sat. He was shirtless now in the hot sun, and as he grew closer I saw him to be a giant of a man, with shoulders and arms stronger even than those of Bovile. Having no doubt worked in the open all summer, his body was darkened to the colour of mahogany and shone like polished wood as the sweat poured off him.

He seemed to be regarding me with interest, and eventually when his work brought him within a few feet of me touched his forelock and enquired whether I wanted a drink. Surprised by the courtesy, I replied that that would be welcome – which indeed was nothing but the truth – whereupon he dived into the shadow of the hedge and reappeared with a straw-covered bottle, the neck of which he wiped on a piece of rag he took from his breeches pocket before handing it to me. It contained a delicious but strong cider; even after only one pull of it, a delightful warmness seemed to spread over me.

The farmhand had meanwhile sat down beside me, and it

could not escape me that his eyes seemed to be upon my
bodice, which since I had loosened it for the heat showed
rather more of my breasts than I would have displayed
except in ballroom or bedroom. It was not, I admit, unconsciously that I leaned forward to place the bottle at his side,
offering him an even more comprehensive view.

I had begun to wonder in what way I could suggest to this
man that a bout with him would not be unacceptable, when
looking me straight in the eyes he offered the opinion that
he saw that my apple dumpling shop was open, and enquired
if I wanted a 'buttock ball'. His intention seemed clear if his
words were not and my reply was simply to remove my
dress; while it was over my head he climbed with equal
celerity out of his breeches, revealing haunches solid as
those of a horse and, rising from a positive thicket of sweat-
soaked hair, a tool which in its size matched his other limbs.
I knelt as he came towards me, ready for amorous play, but
there were to be no soft words or gestures for he simply
pushed at my shoulders as I fell backwards and, lifting my
legs upon his shoulders spat upon his hands to anoint his
instrument. Then, as I waited for the delicious sensation of
his giant limb filling my proper vent, to my horror he presented it at quite another breach and forcefully rammed
home. This was the country custom, as I later learned, of
those uxorious men who wanted to enjoy carnal congress
without the risk of enlarging their families.

The pain was excruciating and did not diminish as he
continued to batter me so that his cods slapped audibly
against my lower back. I shrieked aloud so that birds rose in
clouds from the branches of the trees and horses stirred
uneasily in the nearby meadow, but he evidently believed
my cries to be of rapture for he continued to swive, despite
my attempts to push him away – which were quite fruitless,
for his body, now ringing wet with perspiration, was so
slippery that I could get no hold and even if I had, he was so
strong that I would have failed to move him.

Happily, as is common with the lower orders, he was not
long before spending and with a grunt he withdrew and let
me fall with relief to the ground. Pausing only to wipe

himself with a handful of grass he crammed his parts back into his breeches, took a swig from his bottle and pulling his forelock again thanked me kindly, and made off leaving me lying naked upon the ground – sore, pained, distraught, angry, buggered and still unsatisfied.

Back at the hall, whence I made my way with some discomfort, I found Mrs Finching in a state of great excitement, for the mail had brought news of a visit from her elder brother, who was passing through the county on his way to London and expressed the intention of staying for a week or so with his sister and brother-in-law. Mr Finching seemed for some reason less enthused than his wife, but perhaps I mistook and he was simply preoccupied with some problem of his own.

I had by now determined that I must leave the hall within a week or two but I must confess was eager to see this paragon, as Mrs Finching described her brother; a man, according to her, of all the virtues.

My first view of him as he dismounted outside the hall two days later supported her fervour. Though somewhat stocky, Mr Edmund Weatherby was well-proportioned with handsome, virile features, a fine head of hair and a manner immediately impressive, for having positively lifted his sister from the ground, swinging her off her feet with the joy of their meeting, and having wrung Mr Finching's hands, he turned to me asking for an introduction, upon which he took my hand and bowed low over it. That evening at supper he paid me particular attention, listening to my story (or such a part of it as could be related without impropriety) with the utmost interest and sympathy. He was also kind enough to beg the loan of one of Mrs Finching's horses so that I could ride out with him into the country. We rode sometimes accompanied by Mrs Finching, and sometimes alone, when he acted always with sensitivity and humour so that I grew more and more to admire him, for apart from my host – my relationship with whom, perhaps inevitably, had a flavour of uneasiness about it since my interrupting him at his toilet – he was the first complete gentleman with whom I had spent much time.

One day Mr and Mrs Finching were invited to dine at a neighbouring house and asked whether they should send across a message requesting that Mr Weatherby and I could be of the party. But he declined, on the ground that he would find a visit to these neighbours – whom he had met on a previous occasion – more boring than was concomitant even with the obligations of brotherhood. And he begged that I might remain with him to pass the evening in some agreeable game: 'Perhaps,' he said with a smile, 'you play piquet, Mrs Nelham?'

I replied that I did, and would be delighted to have a game with him.

So my host and hostess made their way, and Mr Weatherby and I sat down to a supper of fowl and salad and some white wine, at the end of which we were in a good humour with ourselves and the world. As we finished eating a peach from Mr Finching's garden, my partner leaned towards me.

'I think we understand each other, ma'am, and need not equivocate. It is my cordial wish to taste the delights of your body and my belief that you would not be dissatisfied with those pleasures I could offer in exchange.'

Though surprised at the directness of his words, I was ready with a response.

'Sir,' I said, 'we *do* understand each other. I shall be delighted to offer you the tribute of which you speak, and to receive what offers in return you are ready to make.'

Whereupon, without delay, he took my hand and led me upstairs, but to my surprise passed the first floor, upon which his bedroom was situated, and went on up the stairs.

'Sir,' I began to protest, 'my room is small and bare, and –'

But he put a finger to his lips, and at the stair-top turned right rather than left to open the door of the bath room, where I found hot water and sheets had already been brought.

'I have become accustomed,' he said, 'to wash myself before a passage of love which, when one can perform the rite in the presence of the loved one, becomes in itself a part of the ritual of pleasure.'

So it was that within a moment or two we were stripped and standing together in the bath, which happily was a large one. Taking a cloth and anointing it with soap, he began to wash my body with the utmost attention and delicacy, passing over my bosom with an expression of delight, reaching around so that as I leaned against his broad breast he could wash my back and buttocks, and then crouching to attend to my nether lips, which he opened with his fingers even to smooth the pink rose within.

Then passing the cloth to me, he stood smiling while I sponged his hard limbs – the chest like the lid of some elegantly carved box, the back like that of a magnificent wild beast, the small, powerful, tapering thighs and finally a male instrument which rose, during my administrations, to a fine power, and seemed as I handled it to be of the imperviousness of polished wood.

By this time I was ready for the battle and even passed one leg about his own, pressing my lower body against his and feeling the expectantcy of his loins against my tenderer parts. But, smiling, he merely wrapped me in a cloth, lifted me in his arms, and strode from the room and down the stairs.

His bedroom, set aside for guests of the house, was of course grandly furnished, with a fine four-poster bed, beautiful furniture and a large mirror upon a stand, which I noticed had been placed next the bed. Dropping me upon the covers, he whisked the sheet from me and, naked himself, allowed his eyes to feast upon me. He stood for what seemed an age, one arm, a cord of muscle running up it, raised as he grasped the curtains of the bed and his body inclining forward so that he seemed to offer it to my view – and indeed my impatience was barely contained, for I too was happy to let my eyes rove over his body, the very sight of which fed my senses almost to repletion.

After a moment I rose to my knees and, taking his sturdy device in my hands, drew back the fleshy veil from its dome and gently slid my lips upon it, delighted to feel by the tremor which ran through his body that he was pleased at the tribute. As I fed upon him, I felt him turn somewhat, and from the corner of my eye caught sight in the mirror of a scene the like of which I had never seen: a fine and handsome man standing quite naked while a beautiful woman, kneeling before him, was ministering to him with her lips, one hand upon the inside of his thigh nuzzling with its fingertips his hanging pouch, and the other clasping with vigour one of the globes of his backside. The reader may find it difficult to credit but for a moment I forgot that that woman was me, and the man the accommodating Mr Weatherby, but the inspiration of the sight warmed me even more so that I redoubled my efforts, my head positively bobbing and butting his stomach in my eagerness, so that after a while he took my head in his hands and drew it away.

'My dear Miss Sophie,' he said, his voice perhaps a little uncertain, 'I must dissuade you for a while from your attentions if my power is not to desert me before I can pay proper tribute to your beauty,' with which he sank upon the bed, taking me with him, and held me close in his arms, his whole delightful length pressed against mine, the bristles of his chin harsh against my cheek. After a while he began to move his hands softly upon my back, stroking me as he might stroke a favourite beast, but with at the same time the most endearing words of praise for my beauty, the softness of my skin, the shapeliness of my limbs.

I was able to reciprocate with the greatest honesty, for he showed a combination of strength and tenderness, of hard and manly comeliness, with an almost feminine concern for my comfort and content that was wholly admirable. I was utterly at ease with him and felt there was nothing I would not do, no action I would not perform, were he to command it. It was a pleasure not only to graze upon his body, but to apprehend his pleasure as my tongue played about his paps or the delicate whorls of his ears, around which his hair curled with a delightful springiness, or as I took a finger into my mouth to suck gently upon it, or transferred my lips to that other, more turbid spur, all eagerness and readiness, which trembled and jumped as I touched it. So much delight did I find indeed in devouring him with my lips that he had again to draw away from me, begging me to lie back so that he could pay me the compliment of his adoration.

He did this with all the courtesy and care I could have hoped, his hands firm and soft about me, preparing the way for his lips until, drawing me to the edge of the bed so that my thighs lay over it, he knelt between them and lifted me to another dimension of pleasure as he proceeded to smooth with his tongue my most intimate parts, first with a very rapid and tickling motion, then with soft gentle kisses followed by long laps up and down the length of the cleft, at the same time gently rubbing with his hand my belly and breasts until I was unable to restrain my joy any longer and with a glad cry curled my legs about his shoulders as I gave up my soul.

Then, conveying his body to the bed, I placed myself astride his hips, lowering myself onto his colossal piece, and with my lower parts milked and milked him, watching, the while, our two bodies moving together in the mirror at the bedside, his hands the meantime busy smoothing my breasts and thighs until both he and I rejoiced in a joyous and simultaneous culmination.

I feared, now, that Mr and Mrs Finching might return but even if they did, he said, there would be no reason for anxiety, for they would simply conclude that we had ended our card game early and retired. So, for two hours or more, we luxuriated in each other's company – and no less in the enchange of confidences than caresses – until finally I fell asleep with my head upon his arm and my leg thrown over his own, to be roused only at dawn, my hand unconsciously curled, in sleep, around his member which, while he slumbered, had grown to a renitent and impressive mass. I cautiously released myself from the grip of his arm about my waist and, leaning, attempted to wake him to a gradual consciousness by running my lips along its length from the coarse hair at its base to the smooth and polished curve of its head. And when after some moments he had still not stirred, looking in the mirror I saw his eyes open and his lips smiling, reluctant to confess to wakefulness lest I should cease my ministrations! At which I laughed, and continued until for the last time that precious night I felt the tremor at the root, and from the tiny slit crept a thin gruel – a tribute to the generous spending of the previous hours, exhausting the reservoirs of his handsome cods.

I crept back to my own room after a final kiss, and we met at breakfast with due ceremony, though I could not but exchange a secret smile with him as I handed him the bowl of chocolate which was his usual pleasure at that hour.

During the next few days we met each night in his room – on one or two occasions almost betraying ourselves to our hosts by my too hasty departure from my own room, so that I almost met Mr or Mrs Finching as they made their way to their own rests. But all too soon came the Saturday before the morning on which he was to ride on to the north. There was, upon that day, a bull-baiting to be held in the village and Weatherby, hearing that I had never seen such sport, invited me to witness it with him. His brother-in-law remonstrated, saying that 'twas a cruel sport and no sight for ladies, but Weatherby replied that Mrs Nelham had not so weak a stomach as to be distressed by a little blood. Though disturbed by his words, I would not be seen to be less adventurous than my lover thought me and so we took our way at three in the afternoon to a field just outside the village, where a large crowd had already gathered around a space by the river bank in which a fine animal was tethered by his nostrils to a rope chain fastened to a post set in the midst of the water. Mr Weatherby explained that this was to add to the amusement, for as he was tormented the bull would often take a new direction in which to try to escape, and the rope then sweep a number of people into the river.

After a while a cart came upon which were three dogs kept in cages and their owners began to take bets upon which would cause the bull most injury, or which might or might not be killed in the adventure. Weatherby, looking about him, found a place for me upon a hummock of ground, and making his excuses went off to place a bet. The press of the people was such that I could no more make my way to him than he to me; nor indeed could I escape from the sight that followed.

The first dog was set on by his owner, and being practised sank his teeth immediately into the bull's nostrils, from which blood immediately began to pour as the wretched, tormented animal raised his head and the dog with it, waving it to and fro until the dog loosed its hold – or perhaps a piece of flesh gave way between his teeth. The dog was thrown several feet into the crowd, which scattered lest its members should be attacked.

The bull, freed for a moment from pain, backed away and, feeling the constraint of the rope, turned in a wide circle towards the water, which indeed as Weatherby had predicted caused two small boys and a woman to be thrown into the river, where the woman and one boy were almost immediately drawn out, being near the bank, but the other child, a smaller boy, was swept away by the current and out of view – a circumstance which was much enjoyed by a quantity of spectators, who made no attempt to ascertain whether the little creature would be saved or not. There was nothing I could do but watch as the second dog was released and immediately gained purchase on one of the bull's ears, the animal letting out a bellow of pain which was echoed by a cheer from the crowd at the sight and sound of more torture.

Sickened by the entertainment, I tried to turn away – and immediately met the eyes of a fellow who was frankly staring at me from only a foot away. I recognised him immediately as my stalwart friend of the straw field. Meeting my eyes, he gave me an enormous wink, and leaning forward, said, 'Tes no sport fur women, ma'm – best come away for another strum!'

At this I leaned forward, and under the shadow of those around, placed my hand upon his thigh and gripping his member, squeezed it affectionately – then saying,

'Certainly, sir – but you must release the bull first.'

His eyebrows were raised almost to invisibility beneath his ancient hat, and he asked, 'What?'

'Release the bull,' I said, 'and I will meet you at the field you know of.'

He stood silent and surprised, then nodded, and turning

forced a way with his great bulk through the crowd in the direction of the space where the bull had just succeeded in dislodging the second dog and was attempting to strike it with a foot, while the smaller animal danced and dodged to the cheering approbation of the crowd. After a moment the dog's owner nipped forward and attempted to recover his animal, receiving in the attempt a blow from one of the bull's feet which seemed from the crack and cry of pain to have broken a limb. For a moment the crowd's attention was on the agonised man, and at that moment I saw my friend dart in, and I glimpsed the flash of a knife as with one blow he severed the rope, eighteen inches from the bull's torn nostrils.

For a moment the animal was not conscious of its freedom; then shaking its head, it lowered its horns and charged straight at the crowd, cutting through it like a scythe through corn. There were cries and shouts, bodies flew through the air, others fell to the ground; a great wave seemed to move through the field as the watchers attempted to escape from the maddened animal's path, and indeed it soon had free ground in front of it and made off through a gap in the hedge, leaving a scene of utter carnage behind.

The crowd had cleared from the river bank, where around one side of the circle where the bull had been tethered lay the bodies of those who had been unable to escape its passage. Some had been trampled, others tossed; all were injured and some perhaps dead, for at least twenty bodies lay upon the grass, some utterly still, others moving, a few climbing uncertainly to their feet. There were shrieks, cries, groans, both from the injured and from those who now returned and sought their companions. I had not thought that such an action might cause so painful a scene, though I could not help reflecting that the injured had brought their pains upon themselves by attending such a horror and inflicting such agony upon a defenceless creature. As I moved towards the injured, however, I came upon a child lying unconscious with an arm dangling at a strange angle from its shoulder, and as a weeping mother watched while a man lifted the small body in his arms, I reflected that perhaps I should have paused to consider the consequences before setting my erstwhile companion on to his sudden action.

Slowly, the field began to clear, one body being carried forth on a hurdle, blood colouring the side of its head, another slung upon a broad back, a brutal and bloodied slash torn in the breeches, no doubt by the horn of the maddened bull, and I began to look about me for Weatherby, whom I had not seen since he left me. Soon, I saw him coming towards me, his arm – I was concerned to see – slipped within the breast of his coat, and he white and dishevelled, his back covered in mud and a graze upon his cheek and the side of his head.

'Ah – you escaped injury!' was his relieved cry. 'I had feared you might have suffered in the outrage. Happily, they have caught the rascal!' – and he gestured behind him, where at the centre of a knot of enraged men I saw the implement of my act, his arms twisted behind him as he was hurried along, while some hurled blows at him with their fists and others attempted to strike at his face with switches plucked from the hedgerows.

'Oh – poor man!' I involuntarily exclaimed, and then felt myself redden as Weatherby looked at me with amazement.

'Poor man' he exclaimed, 'when he has caused such injuries?'

'But no doubt he was moved by pity for the bull,' I said.

'What absurdity is this?' said Weatherby angrily. 'The man is no doubt a revolutionary – he will be whipped and pilloried, and well he will deserve it! But come, Mrs Nelham, you are distraught. We must get you home and to your bed.'

We rode back in silence, which he ascribed no doubt to shock, while in fact I was wondering how I could save the farmhand from his fate, for it had been entirely my own action which had set him on. I could not explain this to my companion, who even if he believed it, rather than ascribing it to ill-conceived pity would certainly have done nothing to gain the man's relief, much less his release. I found myself strangely roused by his anger and disdain at my pity both for bull and for man; his humour and tenderness had been replaced by an implacable sternness which set his jaw and caused his eyes to shoot forth not loving looks but cold reproaches. Yet I could not but be moved by his manly carriage, as women have ever been moved by a strict demeanour and a commanding port.

When we had arrived back at Gauzy Hall, and Weatherby had left me at the door of my room, I rang the bell and sent a message by the maid imploring Mr Finching to come to me. And in a while, hesitating only at the door – I suppose to ensure that I was fully clothed (whereas nothing was further at that moment from my thoughts than seducing him) – he approached. The reader may imagine with what hesitation I explained my predicament, omitting only the carnal scene in the fields, but I finally persuaded him that I had exercised feminine wiles to persuade the man to release the bull from its rope.

He nodded thoughtfully, conceding that he himself had many times attempted to persuade his fellow magistrates that bull-baiting in such a manner was a peculiarly cruel sport, unworthy indeed of the name, and should be forbidden by law.

'I shall see what I can do,' he said, informing me that he would at that moment start for the village. I implored him to allow me to come with him and succeeded, though he attempted to dissuade me.

We heard a noise of shouting and disturbance as we approached, and as we rounded a corner by the one inn the place boasted, and came to the small square by the bridge, saw that we were too late to have prevented my unfortunate admirer from having been hoisted up to the pillory where he now stood, his head and hands through the cross board, while below him stood a rabble of men and women hurling mud, rotten eggs, the entrails of animals (brought in a steaming pail from the butcher's slaughterhouse), dirt from the ground and even stones, so that the man's face was a mat of muck and blood.

With a cry of horror, Mr Finching sprang from his horse

and in a moment had pushed his way through the crowd and mounted the base of the pillory, appearing so suddenly there that an egg meant for the prisoner smashed upon his shoulder and the mess ran down the length of his fine black coat. Equally suddenly, the crowd was stilled.

'Friends,' he cried, 'this man has not been tried – at least allow him to come before the magistrates before punishing him so!'

There was a general outcry at this; 'We seen him!' – 'Ay, and my wife's broke her arm 'cause of he!' – and other similar remarks roused the mob again to full cry, but once more Mr Finching raised his arms and appealed for justice. A young fellow to whom, he later explained, he had done some good, joined him in his appeal, and after a few moments during which the argument could have gone either way the crowd reluctantly began to be still, and Mr Finching was able with the help of two constables to release the man, who was led away supported by the two officers, his head drooping upon his breast, and taken to the lock-up where he would await an appearance before the magistrates. I managed, for shame, to keep my face turned away the while.

As we rode home Mr Finching explained that my man would be tried within the week, and suggested that in exchange for getting him the most lenient sentence, he hoped to persuade him to keep my name out of the affair, and therefore it would be wise of me to leave the neighbourhood within the next day or two. He enquired too as to Weatherby's part in the affair, being outraged that having insisted on taking me to such a show, he should then have left me alone.

Back at the hall, raised men's voices were heard in the drawing-room and when that night – somewhat to my surprise – my door quietly opened to admit Weatherby (to whose room I had not thought of taking myself) it was first that he might inform me coldly that he indeed left next morning at dawn, and second that he might take me voraciously and almost in the style of one inflicting a punishment. Despite the pain in his arm he would allow me no tender caresses but fell upon me as though to teach me subjugation, which at first annoyed and then excited me so that I could not protest, his vigorous and almost painful attack raising flames in me that despite myself excited my utmost ardour. And while he voided himself without any concern for my feelings, I none the less felt a satisfaction difficult to disguise.

I bade him a farewell in which regret was married now to a certain contempt, for his behaviour seemed to me to reveal an entire disregard for any emotion other than the merely animal, and his previous tenderness merely as a means of winning consent and regard for his powers of making love, which indeed were considerable.

Her brother leaving the hall, Mrs Finching was not positively condemnatory but certainly no longer greeted me with special warmth, something I could understand, and could not condemn. Mr Finching came to me at midday that Sunday and presented me with a letter, explaining that it was one of recommendation to a cousin of his, a Miss Jessie Trent, who kept a school for young ladies in Southampton. She was always looking for assistant teachers, he said, and would no doubt be able to offer me at least a temporary employment.

He suggested, though not unkindly, that I should leave the next morning upon the coach which passed through the village at nine o'clock and understanding his predicament – for he adored his wife and I had no wish to be a bone of contention between them – I promised to do so, and would have embraced him but that he took my hand and, bowing, pressed his lips to its back as he took his leave. I went to my room to begin to get my few things together, and to start once more upon my travels.

Chapter Thirteen

The Adventures of Andy

Finding myself in possession of a considerable sum of money, I decided to allow myself some entertainment and, curious as to the pleasures offered by the ladies of a certain establishment in Southampton which, because of the necessary expense, I had not previously visited, determined to pay it a call. I asked Bob whether he would care to be my guest for, though I was beginning to feel my way towards a position in society which would preclude my keeping company with the poorer kind of servant, he was a pleasant fellow enough, good-hearted and a friend to me. He accepted my invitation with enthusiasm.

Our visitations to the mutton-mongers of Buss Street, whom without exception we possessed in the relative discomfort of the graveyard nearby, were short, brutal and to some degree expensive, for Bob himself had on one occasion been accosted by a swaggerer who accused him of seducing his wife, stripped him of his belongings, and beat him before sending him home through the streets without his shirt. However, he had persisted in re-visiting the place, not having the means to visit a bawdy house.

Bob led me to a street not far from the centre of the town and to a fine-looking house with a door guarded by iron spikes. We knocked and a face appeared at a small opening and a raucous voice enquired 'Who goes there?'

'Friend,' replied Bob, whereupon the door was narrowly opened and we were allowed in, one by one. Then the door was slammed shut and an enormous key was turned in a lock, an immense bolt slid across it, and a claim clamped home.

From a room off the corridor inside a great noise came

and when we came to the door, we saw a crowd of men and women, some standing upon chairs or tables, watching a bitter fight between two women, their clothes mostly torn from them, their breasts bare, their faces running with blood. This was a contest such as was mounted once a week, Bob explained, for the pleasure of those who liked such sights. Bets were placed and some trouble was gone to ensure that the competitors were bitter antagonists who would not pull their punches.

Neither Bob nor I were much inclined to watch, and Bob invited the man who had let us in – a massive fellow whose mission it was to protect the house from unwanted visitors and to deal with any trouble which arose within – to give us two tankards of sky-blue and take us to the ladybirds. Two handsome tankards of gin were soon pressed into our hands, and we were led upstairs, where a lady abbess presided over a company of nymphs who lay around the room in various undress. Bob, bowing to the abbess, who was an elderly, plump, kind-faced woman, sedately dressed, made straight for a sofa on which reclined a handsome girl who eyed him with admiration and reached out to take his hand, drawing him into an embrace.

My eye fell elsewhere, for I saw to my interest that one of the girls was black – the first black girl I had ever been in a room with, though I had seen them in the streets of the town, especially those down towards the docks. But this girl was exceptionally handsome with a little, round face, dancing dark eyes and pouting lips, and a figure whose voluptuousness was enhanced by the white dress she wore; one delicious breast was free from all encumbrance and hanging like a ripe pear ready to be gathered, while the skirt was cut to the waist so that one leg from bare foot to fine thigh was completely open to the view.

Bowing in turn to the abbess, I made my way over to the girl and taking her hand kissed it – somewhat to her surprise, I believe, for no doubt she was used to rougher greetings. She lowered her eyes prettily and, rising, asked if I wished to accompany her, to which I gladly assented. She then led me up some stairs to a small but pleasantly furnished room, the furniture consisting merely of a bed, some chairs and several large mirrors, one fastened at a tilt on the wall above the bed. There, she helped me to undress, unbuttoning my shirt and lifting it from my shoulders to fold it carefully and place it upon a chair, then unbuttoning my pantaloons and drawing them from me. Somewhat to my embarrassment and no doubt because of the strangeness of the situation, the originality of the company and – I must confess – my slight nervousness, I was not as yet showing my admiration of her in that part where she might properly have expected to see it. Catching my eye, she smiled shyly and passed her hand gently between my thighs before releasing the shoulder strap of her dress and allowing it to fall to the floor, revealing a body of great beauty, its handsome curves enhanced by the almost purple bloom which lay upon her otherwise jet-black skin.

Taking my hands, she guided me to the bed where, as she drew her length along my own, I saw to my delight our bodies reflected in the mirror – her dark skin making mine seem whiter than it were possible to imagine it. Ah, what transports then ensued! Such indeed, that I can now scarcely record them without putting myself into a passion, for she was in command of every lascivious trick, her fingers playing upon my body, enquiring at every orifice whether pleasure lay within, pleasuring every projection with a smooth and light touch which brought me to the very precipice of delight, her lips sucking my own, drawing upon my tongue like a teat, and conferring upon my now positively resplendent tool such caresses that it seemed likely to burst.

I too took the utmost pleasure in exploring her body as one might a previously unknown land. Her breasts were somewhat longer, or so it seemed to me, than those of our native girls, their extremities coarser and in erection harder and less sensitive so that even a nip from my teeth seemed to give pleasure rather than pain. And below a long undulant belly deeply marked by the dint of an angular navel, the lips of her cunny were large and of a deep crimson, veiled by tightly curled, harsh, black hairs, while between them projected something akin to a little finger, shaped like a tiny counterfeit of a man's instrument, from which, when I stroked it, she evidently received most pleasurable sensations, for a cry of delight seemed to bubble in her throat.

Raising myself I sat upon her thighs, my cods nestling upon the pad between her legs so that I could view the country as 'twere from on high. She wore an expression of friendly pleasure – always the mark of a good whore, for one should always be able to believe that she too is taking pleasure in the encounter, however untrue that may be. She gave me a smile of singular sweetness as I allowed my eyes to relish her delightful body, while her hands, laid gently in my lap, played lightly with my masculine parts. It made an interesting sight, the black fingers of one hand upon the white flesh, running up the length of my instrument, tickling with the most delicate touch its every surface, while she inserted the other beneath, palm uppermost, to pinch with a firmer grip the very base as it projected even below my now tight and almost painful cods.

As I looked, my emotion overflowed and with all the force of a pent stream, I gushed forth the vital liquid, which rose so that it almost struck me upon the chin, then fell glistening upon the dark flesh of her body.

'I's sorry, mister,' she said. 'My fault!'

I assured her that *I* was not at all sorry, except that I had perhaps deprived her of the pleasure – if pleasure it was – of receiving my seed within her. She asked if I would stay longer but, reluctantly thinking of the money I had brought with me, I declined, whereupon she assisted me to rise and with a clean towel wiped my body, lingering especially over those parts which, in the heat of our encounter, were damp with amorous perspiration.

As she was thus ministering to me I was dimly conscious of an uproar below, imagining that it was connected with another fight. But in a moment the girl lifted her head in concern as there was the sound of footsteps on the stair, then in the corridor – and suddenly, as she was still upon her knees before me, the towel in her hand, the door burst open and three men came into the room. They were in the uniform of the navy, one of them an officer, and without so much as a word they dashed forward and took hold of the girl, throwing her upon the bed while they gripped me by the arms. Without allowing me time to seize my clothing and paying no attention to my protests, they hurried me from the room and down the stairs, where a coat – someone's coat, and certainly not my own – was thrown to me to cover my nakedness before I found myself in the street, manacled and marching between two columns of sailors, my bare feet grating upon the stones beneath. Just ahead of me I saw Bob, similarly clothed only in an old coat – but his a short one, so that his sharp buttocks showed beneath it – being hurried along.

I was in no doubt what had happened to me: I was in the hands of the press gang, of which I had heard – nay, been warned. Mr Grose, when the subject was raised, was hot upon the necessity of getting men for the Navy, by force if necessary, though when I had demurred he asserted that no officer would dare touch one of his servants (a fact now contradicted by my present predicament).

Our march to the docks was accompanied by jibes and insults hurled at the officers and men by passers-by, though notably the few men who dared show themselves were chary of joining in the outright condemnation of the women, no doubt for fear that they should find themselves among the captives.

We seemed to march for miles – though perhaps the condition of my feet, by now lacerated and bleeding by the condition of the roads, made the way seem long – before we reached the quayside, and were crowded into two boats. The first man declined to descend the ladder (for it was low tide) and was taken and thrown down some six feet or more, when he landed with a dreadful cry on the bare boards of the craft and fell silent, whereupon the rest of us followed meekly. I found myself next to Bob, who whispered to me to keep my pecker up for he had been pressed before, two years ago, when he had been able to smuggle ashore a note to Mr Grose, who had come to his rescue, and was now confident he could do so again with the promise of reward for the fellow who would carry a message to our master.

Bumping across the waters (to the distress of my stomach, for I was never a good sailor) we came to a craft, the sides of which seemed to rise sheer, like cliffs, above us – it being now too dark to see outside the ring of light shone by the lanterns carried by the ruffians who commanded us. At a cry from one of them, a rope ladder was thrown down and we were forced to climb it one by one – much laughter from our guardians being directed at Bob and me, as, clumsily climbing it we, having no breeches, revealed our privities to them.

As I climbed over the rail and onto the deck of the ship my heart gave a great bound of hope for there, in the light of a lantern upon the deck, stood the figure of an officer – and a figure I knew, for above the white starched shirt and the severe collar was the face of Spencer Franklyn – the elder son of my old patron, Sir Franklin Franklyn, of Alcovary!

'Mr Spencer!' I cried, taking a step forward. I am sure I saw a look of recognition cross his face but almost instantly I felt a blow upon the side of my head as a seaman nearby, I suppose believing I was about to attack his officer, struck me with a stout wooden baton he held in his hand, and I fell unconscious to the boards.

When I came to my senses, I was in almost complete darkness, conscious only of the press of many bodies around me and of a fearful reek of sweat and vomit, gin and urine. My head was in the lap of my companion, Bob, who again assured me that we would simply have to live through that one night and then we would be released, he was confident of it. After a while, utterly weary, I fell into a fitful sleep, to wake when the dim light reached us through the single window and I saw myself to be in a small room, which Bob told me was a part of the hold of a naval vessel. As the light strengthened, I saw that we were but two of about twenty fellows more or less disreputable, who were also, like us, the subjects of one of the gangs of men sent out to press men into the service. After a while, a trap opened above us and a bucket of water was lowered, from which we all drank in turn, mutual sympathy lending a certain compassion even to the roughest of us – especially towards one boy, a plump lad of perhaps only fourteen years of age, who cried bitterly at his fate and enquired again and again 'how his mother would do without him', which after some time so preyed upon the nerves of his companions that one man offered to throw him overboard if he did not hold his tongue.

Some hours passed, then the trap opened again, a ladder was lowered, and two seamen descended with a container of rank bread which was to serve us as lunch. One, particularly brutal, took pleasure in kicking and spurning any of us who got into his way and, coming to the youngster, reached out to take his face in a gigantic fist and cry: 'Here's a buxom Miss Molly for us, Jack. Hold up, boy, we'll call on you tonight!' while his companion picked me out, throwing up my coat to display my naked lower parts and crying: 'Here's another – and ready for you, Bill!' reaching down to give me a blow upon the privities which well-nigh took my senses away.

When they had gone Bob looked grave and told me – which I had already guessed – that these were fellows who, deprived of the comfort of their whores by long confinement on board, thought to play at rantum scantum with us. This had happened to him, he said, when he was similarly captured. He, however, had been taught by another fellow how to bear it, which was, he said, not to resist but to loosen the hinder parts so that there was no impediment to the invading tool when, he said, though not pleasant, such a venture at least inflicted no injury, whereas resistance would only increase the invader's passion and bring a resultant anguish.

This, the reader can believe, comforted me but little during the hours that passed. The gentle rocking of the boat confirmed that we were still at anchor and Bob said that this meant we would not be released until the ship (whose size and kind we could not even guess at) had

sailed – a fact which concerned him, for on the previous
occasion he had been able to get his message ashore only by
making a contact with a fellow upon deck as they were
allowed to take some air before sailing from harbour. It
seemed as though there was to be no such chance upon this
occasion.

After a while, I took the opportunity to explore our
surroundings, which were plain enough; we were in a
simple box, with no furniture but merely the floor. The
single window or port was too high to reach and was pretty
narrow, though I thought that perhaps I could squeeze
through it, unclothed as I was, could I but reach it. But
then, how far from shore were we? I could perhaps appeal
to Master Spencer but the look I had received from him
promised little; then, it seemed I could not reach him until
the ship had sailed, when it would be too late for me to be
released even should he have the influence to assist me, or
care to use it.

I sat in gloom, as did we all, until once more the light
faded when, the trap opening, the two fellows we had
previously seen appeared once more with a lantern and a
bucket from which a smell arose promising food of a kind
none of us would have been glad to eat but for our
circumstances. The men did not withdraw, however, but
placing the bucket upon the ground, came forward and
seized the youngest of us and pulled him towards the corner
furthest from the glimmer of light which they had placed
upon the floor. The boy began to whimper, whereupon
there was the sound of a blow, followed by muffled
sobbing.

'Remember the toss, Jack!' cried one of the men. 'I'll
hold this one for you, then we'll find the other. Come now,
boy –' and there was a sound of clothing being rent, and
thereafter a violent cry of pain, muffled (no doubt) by a
hand being thrown across the mouth of the victim.

I was now desperate to escape my fate. Throwing off the
coat which was still my only covering, I made as quietly as
possible for the side of the ship below the single port and
began to scrabble at the timber walls, but there was no

purchase. I looked around; the men in the dark corner were intent upon their business. I glanced appealingly at my fellow prisoners. I believe that my desperation struck a chord in them, and that they realised that I was the only man among them slim enough to make an attempt at the port, for Bob and another came forward, linked hands, and made a step from which I was able to grip the opening, pulling myself up and getting my arms, then my shoulders, through. Wriggling forward, I found myself hanging in the dark, how many feet above the water I could not know. Now my hips had caught, and for a moment I was unable to move. Then, by twisting my body so that my hips were diagonally fitted to two of the corners of the port, I felt them beginning to move again and, throwing my arms forward, and feeling a pain as the wood tore my skin, I was at last free and falling through the dark air for what seemed minutes before I struck the water and sank down, unprepared for a dive (since I had not had the presence of mind to fill my lungs with air before being immersed). Happily, the drop could not have been great, for I quickly felt myself beginning to rise, and was soon able to take a gulp of cool air.

Though the splash I had made must have been a noisy one, there was at present no reaction from the ship, which I could see dimly outlined against the starry sky. There was no moon, which happily would make it difficult to see me were the alarm given, but equally made it impossible for me to see the shore. I struck out towards what seemed to be the nearest light, trusting that it was from land rather than from another vessel. My bathing in the rivers and pools of the land were no real preparation for essaying a sea-swim, but the waters were not rough, nor was the distance too great, for within perhaps twenty minutes I was drawing myself up onto a small beach, cold and shaking. Behind me, at last the alarm had been given, and I could both hear and see (from the lights appearing on deck) that preparations were being made to launch a small boat to attempt to find me.

I had thought myself alone, but as I staggered up upon

the beach a light suddenly came into view along with two figures – a tall, elderly man with a young girl – who, before I could make my presence known to them, began to converse:

'If by my art, my dearest father, you have put the wild waters in this roar, allay them,' said the girl. 'The sky it seems would pour down stinking pitch, but that – but that –'

'But that the sea,' said the man.

'But that the sea, mounting to the welkin's cheek dashes the fire out. Oh, ah – ah –'

'I have suffered,' put in the man.

'Oh, yes – I have suffered,' said the girl, 'with those that I saw suffer . . .'

But at that point she saw me – no doubt a dark and menacing figure – and broke off with a cry.

'What is it now, girl?' asked the man, impatiently; then, when she pointed silently at me, put his hand to his waist and half drew a sword hanging there.

'Oh, sir,' I said, coming forward into their light, and attempting to hide my privities from the young lady with my shivering hands, 'could you perhaps direct me to some hiding-place? The press gang . . .' and I pointed out to sea, where now there was clearly the sound of rowlocks, and a small lantern could be seen bobbing shorewards, carried by a small boat in which, none the less, were several large men.

Happily, the elderly man was quick of apprehension.

'Quick,' he said to the girl, shielding the light sea-ward, 'off with your shift.'

'What?' she enquired in understandable surprise.

'Off with your shift, and into it, young fellow. You, miss, up to the inn.'

Somewhat unwillingly, I guess, the girl shrugged off her only article of clothing, rendering herself bare as I was to the cool night air and, handing it to me, vanished. I drew the article upon my body, and the man looked critically at me. 'Your hair could do with being longer,' he said, 'but if sufficiently ruffled . . .' and reaching up, pulled it forward over my eyes, then reaching out his arm drew me to him – I somewhat unwilling, this time, except that he said, 'Fear not – I am not of *that* persuasion. Remember, you are my daughter . . .' And so saying, he began to walk calmly, leaning upon me, towards the edge of the sea where even now the keel of the rowing-boat was cutting home into the sand, and the men leaping out, led by a rough fellow who came straight to us.

'Who be you, sir, and where be the escaped ruffian . . .?'

My friend drew himself up, though still leaning heavily upon me – which indeed gave me excuse to bow my head somewhat under his weight.

'We have seen no ruffians, sir,' he said, 'except yourselves.'

The sailor looked suspicious.

'What be you doing upon the shore so late in the evening?'

'And who are you, sir, that you have the cheek to enquire?' asked my friend, who was old enough to address even the press gang with impertinence, not being of an age to be of use to them. 'Watch your manners, man, or you'll find yourself arraigned before your betters!'

The man paused for a moment and looked, I thought, suspiciously at me.

'And this girl? She's remarkably silent for one of her sex?'

'Sir!' said my saviour, drawing himself up to his full height. 'Shame upon you that you should refer in such a way to one who has suffered! My daughter has been deaf and dumb from birth; that the heavens should have seen fit to place such a burden upon her and her loved ones is one matter – that some impertinent nazy mort, fresh no doubt from the nanny house, should add to our insupportable sorrow by such rude words . . .'

But by now the fellow was backing away, positively fawning, with 'Ah, sir – no, sir – my regrets, sir, for the inconvenience – he must have put ashore at some other beach . . .' And he made his way back to his mates, where after a short conversation they all leaped once more into the row-boat and pushed off, my benefactor standing staunchly all the while and watching them.

When they were safely out of earshot he turned to me and said: 'Now, sir, your name.'

I gave it him.

'And your condition?'

I told him.

'Then you must come first to our rooms and warm yourself, before we see you returned to your employer's house!' And he strode up the beach, and a hundred yards from the pathway which led down to it we came to a small tavern from the upper window of which issued the noise of singing. This was, as I later learned, the single tavern in the village of Calshot, near the mouth of Southampton Water.

'My companions are so noisy tonight,' said my friend, 'that Cynthia and I took ourselves off to read through Prospero and Miranda on the beach, it being yet early . . .'

And indeed, though I had had no means of telling time, and thought it perhaps to be past midnight, it was barely ten o'clock. But what could these people be? What was Prospero, and what Miranda?

Of course the reader will be before me but must remember that I then knew nothing of the drama, and could not connect those names with Shakespeare's drama of *The Tempest*, nor guessed that the company was one of actors.

However, they soon introduced themselves to me: a company of twelve, including the girl who had so kindly given up her shift and who now stood none too demurely clothed in another garment. At first she was inclined to be short with me, but when I had kissed her hand and begged her pardon, she smiled upon me sweetly – and the more so when my predicament was explained to her. Her friends were equally cordial, though at first they greeted my appearance with many a catcall and ribald joke against Mr Higgens (as my friend was called, and who was the leader of the company) such as 'Turned buttock bouncer, old Sam!' and other niceties, at which he grinned good-humouredly.

'Some gigs from the basket for young Andy' (for I had introduced my name to them) he said, and a young fellow of my own age, introduced to me as David Ham, promised assistance and took me off to the next room, where I was quickly out of my shift, and rubbed myself down roughly before climbing into a pair of breeches and a shirt he produced for me from a trunk.

When we were back in the main room I had to tell to the full my night's adventures, whereupon there were many murmurings against the whole business of the gangs, one elderly member of the company asserting that in one day, in 1802, three hundred men were pressed in Yarmouth – though two hundred and fifty of them were later released by the order of the mayor. Another man said that he had seen a group of fishermen seized in broad daylight while spreading their nets, at South Denes, and David, who came from the extreme west of England, said that he had heard from his father that only twenty years ago at the news that the press gang was coming all the men of Newlyn, in Cornwall, would flock up the hills and away to the country as fast as possible, hiding themselves in all manner of places till the danger was supposed to be over.

They were full of praise for my escape, and shared my anxiety for Bob for, they said, it was now likely, since I would certainly carry the news back to the town that respectable servants were among the drunkards made captive, that the ship would sail before dawn. I felt, too, for the poor boy who was being ill-used as I escaped, but whose predicament I had not fully described in the presence of ladies – for besides the young creature whose dress I had temporarily borrowed, there was also present a lady of more advanced years.

I learned, in my turn, that this was a company of actors who had been appearing in Southampton – 'In,' my friend announced, 'a selection of classical pieces including productions of *King Lear* and *Hamlet*, in which the leading parts are played by myself and my lady wife' – and he introduced himself as Samuel Prout Higgens, and his lady as Esmeralda Plunkett Cope – 'Famous, sir, for her Ophelia!' The young woman was his niece, Cynthia, and I learned the names too of the others, though did not at the time commit them to memory.

The company was interested to hear that I was a musician and thereupon produced a lute, which they invited me to play. Treating it as a guitar, I managed to produced some fair numbers from it, so that we sat and drank and sang for some time, myself carried forward by the excitement of the evening, until a sudden exhaustion came upon me, and I scarcely remember being half-carried to bed, where I awoke next morning to find myself beside young David, sleeping like a babe though the light outside announced broad daylight. I leaped up and ran to the window, which as I thought commanded a view of the Solent clear over to Gosport; but not a single ship lay within a mile. Poor Bob, I feared, together with Lieutenant Spencer Franklyn, was by now in the Channel, heading for God knew where.

I got myself up and awoke Higgens, saying that I must go to Mr Grose's house to let him know what had happened to me.

'One moment, Mr Archer,' said the actor. 'I was most impressed by the tunefulness not only of your fingers upon the instrument, but of your voice last night. Our lutenist left us a se'enight ago, but we must have music for our plays. We start tonight towards Bristol, performing at various hostelries upon the way. I can offer you an emolument commensurate with your skill, together with not unpleasant company. Your work would not be great, and with your musicality, my dear sir, the experience would be invaluable – I can see you upon the London stage, young man, gathering plaudits along with guineas! What do you say?'

Almost before he had ceased to speak I was determined to agree. I had been in one place long enough, for my adventures had endowed me with a wanderlust. I would pause only long enough, I said, to apprise Mr Grose of the facts, fetch my guitar (and my gold, though I said nothing of that), and would meet them just outside the city, on the Salisbury Road, at midday.

It was the work of but a few minutes to rouse David, who

was glad to escape the tasks of packing in order to ride with
me on the back of one of the company's horses to Mr
Grose's, where fortunately the merchant was at home –
though the whole house was at sixes and sevens, for the
marriage of Mr Mellor and Miss Patience was to take place
in two days' time and great preparations were under way.
The merchant was at first disposed to be angry, for he had
assumed that Bob and I had simply fallen into drunken
company, or decided to leave our employment without
notice. But he was outraged to hear of the events which had
carried us off – needless to say, I did not say where we
had been taken, but that we had been seized in the open
street (as so many men were) – and professed that he would
take the whole matter up with the Admiralty and that
someone's back should burn for it. None of this, however,
would be of immediate use to Bob.

Mr Grose acquiesced somewhat unwillingly to my departure, at first being disposed to insist I should stay to play at
the wedding, but since Mr Mellor was bringing a small
band of musicians from London (for which the merchant
was, naturally, paying) he agreed to my leaving, especially
when I offered to forego the wages he owed me for the
past week. In my room, I recovered my small store of gold
and my guitar, which I wrapped in a cloth I had cut for the
purpose. I then made my farewells to the family, and was
wished well in handsome fashion; I had not informed them
in what company I was to leave the town, for they would
not, I am sure, have much approved of my becoming part
of a band of players.

My few belongings were not a great extra burden for the
horse, and before midday David and I were waiting outside
the city at the appointed spot, where in due course the
procession of my friends approached – four wagons, upon
the first of which in state sat Mr and Mrs Higgens, both of
whom bowed to me gravely as they rattled past. The wagon
immediately behind paused, and I mounted it to sit
between Cynthia Cope and a somewhat saturnine young
man, Nathaniel Grigson, while David joined the last
wagon, behind which he hitched our horse.

The way to Salisbury was enlivened by details of the life of my friends, who comprised a party of theatricals who during the winter played in a part of London known as Fulham Park, while during the summer they toured some part of England; two years before they had been in Wales, last year they had turned north-east to Norwich, and this year they were to end their current expedition in Bristol before returning to London to prepare for the autumn season. They took with them costumes for several plays, but scenery was improvised from whatever they could beg, borrow or contrive in whichever inn or yard they played.

Miss Cope carried, it appeared, the parts of young beauties and heroines: Miss Hardcastle in Goldsmith's comedy of *She Stoops to Conquer*, Maria in *The Citizen*, Bizarre in *The Inconstant*, and was about to essay the part of Miranda in *The Tempest*, in which Mr Higgens was to play once more the part of Prospero with which, I was told, he 'positively paralysed' the audiences at the Theatre Royal in Drury Lane, in the year of '89.

Mr Grigson's parts in general comprised the villains (it being, he said, his fate to be dark, whereas the British public preferred its heroes to have yellow hair and – he added – a stupid expression, which I took to be a gibe at some other member of the company). Mr Grigson was not taken by the parts he was at present assigned by Mr Higgens and longed to surprise the public, he said, by his Sneerwell, his Iago, his Macheath. But Miss Cope asserted, in my ear, that he would never be happy, were he to be offered the part of Hamlet with a supporting cast consisting of John Philip Kemble, George Frederick Cooke and Mrs Elizabeth Farren! None of these were familiar to me, but I took them to be the current kings of the stage. And so we rattled on, my new friends exchanging story upon story of their adventures, most of which consisted of narrowly escaping ruin by some trick played upon an innkeeper or local dignitary, and the four hour journey to Salisbury passed quickly indeed in such pleasant company.

The Bell at Salisbury was almost in the shadow of the great cathedral which though familiar, I make no doubt, to all my readers, was new to me, so that its majesty and grandeur made an indelible impression upon my mind, being so much grander (it seemed) and imposing than any building I had heretofore seen. The inn itself was an old one, with a gallery and open yard in which, it was said, we were to perform; in exchange for the proceeds of which, we were to be given free accomodation and a division of the moneys our efforts brought in. Our beasts were quartered in the stables and we unloaded the seven large baskets which contained costumes for the plays and placed them too in the stables, in a disused stall. Then we were shown to a large barn where sheets had been stretched on lines to divide the space into a number of small compartments in which mattresses had been placed, and to which we were assigned in order of seniority. Once more I was to share a bed with David, which did not disturb me since he was a pleasant boy, and much preoccupied at the present time because he was shortly to be allowed to play his first large part upon the stage – that of the spirit Ariel in *The Tempest* – and spent much of his time laboriously conning the pages of the play, and asking someone to interpret the print for him, for he read but uncertainly.

After we had had supper and a drink or two, we repaired to our barn, where after a while the noises attendant upon our preparing for sleep quietened, and David and I began to fall into a doze. But I was not yet asleep when I seemed to feel a nudging at my side, and in the pitch dark (for no lights were left on, the place being dry as tinder and likely to flame) I felt in a moment a hand upon my shoulder, which slid down until it held my hand. For a moment, half asleep, I thought it was David's, either in sleep or in want of comfort, but soon realised that it was on the other side of me, and that it must come from someone in the next compartment, stretching out beneath the sheet which was all that lay between us. Moreover, I imagined from the lack of sinew and of hair that it was a female hand, and from its slightness guessed that it was that of Cynthia.

Not caring to offend her, and by no means without gratitude for her quick agreement to my rescue the night before, I turned and passed my own hand up her arm until it encountered a shoulder, then a willing bosom whose alertness seemed to signal a willingness to endure more than mere touch – for she took my hand and first pressed it to her bosom, then conveyed it lower, where a willing moisture suggested compliance with more radical action.

Carefully, so as not to disturb David, I rolled from my bed, and moving cautiously slid beneath the sheet until my body was alongside the softer, willing frame of my accomplice, whereat in a moment she had seized me with a surprising strength and lifted me upon her, throwing open her legs with such willingness that almost before I knew it my ready sword was sheathed to the hilt.

I must confess that at this moment I was inclined to wonder whether Cynthia had not previously entertained a man, for it seemed to me that the manner in which she twisted beneath me, the seeming familiarity with which her hands played about my backside and prised between our bellies to seize my cods, and the assurance with which her tongue plunged between my lips, seemed to hint that she was not entirely unfamiliar with the practices of love.

Our frenzy was conducted in utter silence (though the snores and gurglings proceeding from the next compartment, where Mr and Mrs Higgens lay in complacent slumber, would no doubt have drowned any noise we had made) until the sharp pain of a bite upon my shoulder with a shudder of her body beneath me hinted that she had reached her meridian, whereat my senses, encouraged by her satisfaction, also accomplished their crisis. A quick kiss and she lifted herself so that I rolled off and with the same movement back to my side of the intervening sheet.

With great care not to awake young David, I crept between the blankets; but in a moment his lips were at my ear: 'You've been welcomed into the company in the old way,' he whispered. 'She gives it to everyone on the first night – but now you'll have to fight for it. Me, I'm too young, for she regards me as a baby – which I am not, and could satisfy her more than she might think!' – and to prove it took my hand and thrust it down to where, between his thighs, there was indeed a tool sturdy enough to give any girl occupation. I attempted to remove my hand, but evidently in the throes of an unsatisfied passion he retained it by a gentle force, and in pity I let it remain, moving it in compliance until with a sharp-drawn breath he spent, whereat he whispered, 'Thanks – and I'll do the same for you when she turns you away – as she will!'

So, finally, we slept.

Chapter Fourteen

Sophie's Story

My arrival, clutching my few belongings, at Miss Trent's school for young ladies in Southampton resembled nothing so much, I imagine, as a convict's arrival at her prison; for though I have not, as yet, had experience of such a penitentiary, it could surely be no more securely guarded – by high walls and stout doors and windows – than the former establishment.

Upon ringing the bell, there was after a pause the sound of approaching footsteps, and then a thin voice made its way through a small grille in the door, asking my name and business. On my giving it there followed a great noise of locks and bars being withdrawn, and eventually the door opened for the distance of one inch or so, when I was inspected by an eye applied to the crack and, appearing respectable, and nothing like a maurauding thief, the door swung sufficiently far open to admit me to a stone-flagged corridor, where I was told to wait.

As I stood in the cold, I seemed to hear in the distance the chanting of some kind of choir, which abruptly stopped, and in a moment I was invited to follow the small, sallow maid who had greeted me, and found myself at last in Miss Trent's study, a room furnished chiefly with a large table upon which stood writing implements, some handsomely bound books and a cane. Behind the table stood Miss Trent herself, a tall, severe looking woman dressed in dark blue, her greying hair cut in a masculine style almost to the root – *à la Titus*.

'Yes, ma'am,' she said, 'your business with me?'

Handing her his note, I explained that I came with a recommendation from Mr Finching, and hoped she might have temporary employment for a teacher.

'Ha!' she exclaimed, having read the brief missive. 'My cousin tells me you are adept in music – and indeed we are in need of a lady to give instruction in the harpsichord, the minuet and the country dance. You consider yourself capable?'

I said that I would do my best.

'I am of the opinion that that phrase in general is the mark of the person whose best is rarely of a high standard,' said Miss Trent ominously. 'However, I am prepared to keep you for a week, after which we shall see. You can read, write and figure?'

I began to explain that my reading and writing was of a sufficiently high standard.

'We teach the use of the goose-quill here,' Miss Trent interrupted.

'Arithmetic is not, however, strong with me,' I went on.

Miss Trent shook her head.

'A sad dereliction on the part of your teachers, Mrs Nelham,' she said. 'But I myself impart the usage of numbers, and though an assistant in that area would have been welcome, will clearly have to continue to do so. By the way, what of your husband?'

I said that he had, alas, died within two months of my marriage, and dabbed an imaginary tear.

'Leaving you, I trust, with no child to encumber you?' asked Miss Trent unsympathetically, and when I replied, no, remarked that that would certainly have been a bar to my staying, for squealing children were worse than squealing young women.

'Very well,' she said finally. 'You will not of course expect any payment until we are satisfied with your work, but your meals you will take with us, and we will review the matter in a week or so.' So saying, she rang the bell, and almost simultaneously the little maid appeared, who during her working hours made it her business to follow her mistress around like a pet dog, ready to be useful at any moment.

'Dolly,' said Miss Trent, 'show Mrs Nelham to the dormitory.'

Whereupon I was taken up three flights of stairs to a long room constructed under the roof, containing eight beds, and one at the end about which a curtain could be drawn, and which I was informed was my own. I learned from Dolly – who stood moving uneasily from foot to foot, eager to return downstairs in case her mistress required her – that a former assistant teacher had left a week ago, since when Miss Trent and a visiting emigrant priest, M. de la Cuisse (who taught French and a little Latin) had been the only instructors.

I was prepared to unpack my things and settle into my small space, but Dolly insisted that Miss Trent would require my presence in the schoolroom immediately and so, only pausing to take off my bonnet, I followed her down to the first floor where from a large room, no doubt once a drawing-room, came the sound of chanting:

Five ones are five
Five twos are ten,
Five threes are fifteen,
Five fours are twenty,
Five fives twenty-five,
Five sixes thirty . . .

I opened the door and walked in.

Miss Trent stood in front of a class of eight young ladies, each clad in dresses of neat while muslin with necks cut remarkably high, sitting at desks in two rows of four while Miss Trent conducted them with a cane, which upon seeing me she brought down upon her own desk with a brisk *thwack*, at which the girls instantly broke off.

'Young ladies, stand!' she commanded, and beckoned me to the front of the class.

'This is Mrs Nelham, who will be aiding me in your general education.'

I inclined my head, and the girls bobbed a curtsy.

'We will now have our brief pause for refreshment, after which I shall leave Mrs Nelham to conduct a class in English literature,' Miss Trent said, and swept from the room. Giving the young ladies an uncertain smile, which they greeted with blank stares, I followed her downstairs to her room while a subdued chatter broke out behind me.

'You will find,' said Miss Trent, as we sipped our tea, 'that you must keep a strict watch upon the girls, whose natural propensity to un-Christian behaviour breaks out all too readily.'

She picked up two books and handed them to me.

'We use here Dr Bowdler's editions of Shakespeare and Mrs Trimmer's Bible. As to the first, there are, as you will be aware, many passages in the original which must be kept from tender ears, and which indeed I would be sorry to hear that you have read. Personally, I would be inclined to deny the whole work of that person (who for no good reason has come to be regarded as our national author) to the eyes of all women, but sadly parents seem to expect it. The unbounded licentiousness of this age has made it almost impossible for young ladies to come anything towards years of discretion without such a knowledge of vice as must render them incapable of a proper command over their imaginations. But we can at least attempt, here, to keep the news of the world from them.

'Kindly remember that if any word or expression is of such a nature that the first impression which it excites is an impression of obscenity, that word ought not to be spoken, or written, or printed, and if printed, it ought to be erased.

'As to the Holy Book, Mrs Trimmer advises the use of only some half of the text, omitting those portions which refer to that function which if freely performed leads to the procreation of children. There are many passages in the translation allowed by King James which include terms not now generally made use of in polite society, and in Mrs Trimmer's edition these passages are either omitted or the expressions altered. That prudent woman, while she admired the beauties of the sacred writings, was convinced that, unrestricted, no reading more improper could be permitted to a young woman. Many of the narratives can only tend to excite ideas the worse calculated for a female breast; everything is called plainly and roundly by its name and the annals of a brothel could scarcely furnish a greater choice of indecent expressions. In fact I have this evening to inflict punishment upon Sarah Burtenshaw who not only had in her possession an unexpurgated edition of the Old Testament, but was discovered reading passages from' – she shuddered – 'the Song of Solomon to her unfortunate fellows!'

She pushed the two volumes towards me.

'Here, then, are Dr Bowdler and Mrs Trimmer, from whom you will perhaps now instruct the class in reading, paying particular attention to intonation and clarity.'

Finishing my tea, I took myself upstairs, where the young ladies quieted to an uneasy hush as I entered, and settled to the dullest and most pedestrian readings of the more innocuous portions of the Letter of St Paul to the Thessalonians, which they performed one by one, and very decently, except for one poor, pale girl who stuttered her way through her portion as though she could scarce see it. When I asked her name she announced in an almost inaudible voice that she was Miss Sarah Burtenshaw, at which I assumed she was concerned for the hours of copying out of passages from the Good Book which would no doubt be her punishment for having explored those portions of it considered improper by her mistress.

Excusing her from further participation in the lesson, I told her that she might if she wished go to her bed to rest but, clearly terrified, she said that Miss Trent would not permit it, whereat I announced that I would be answerable to Miss Trent, and after much hesitation and with a wan smile she disappeared. The other girls now seemed disposed to be pleasant to me and we went on splendidly until the end of the lesson, when a bell ringing below took us to the dining-room – a bare, cold place at the back of the house – for a meal of boiled mutton and potatoes, the only one of the day (I was told), apart from some biscuits in the middle of the evening.

As the day went on an unaccountable tension seemed to grow, so that none of the girls could concentrate on their lessons and made a sad showing when I attempted instruction on the harpsichord. Finally I gave up attempting it and passed the time playing some of the pieces I loved best, at which they cheered up somewhat – apart from poor Miss Burtenshaw, who had reappeared for lunch, and now once more sat silent and pale.

The reason for such apprehension over what could surely only be a light penalty was not clear to me until eight o'clock, when, as I sat with the young ladies over the sewing which occupied (they told me) most evenings at the school, a bell rang and we were led by Dolly into a back room on the first floor, which had the appearance of a bedroom. Indeed it was the room in which Miss Trent slept, except that its centre had been cleared and there stood a remarkable erection, the like of which I had never seen before, consisting of three strong pieces of timber fixed together as a sort of pyramid, with cross-pieces to ensure its stability. Completely silent and overawed, the girls trooped into the room and stood in a row by the door, which in a moment opened to admit Miss Trent, bearing in her hand a bunch of birches.

To my horror, I realised that she must be first cousin to that notorious flaybottomist Mr Gutteridge, who had so beaten us at Alcovary.

Miss Trent took up her station facing us.

'Miss Burtenshaw, step forward,' she commanded.

Poor Sarah took a step forward, looking as though she would faint at any moment.

'Miss Burtenshaw, you know your offence?'

'Y-yes, Miss Trent,' she said.

'Recall it to me?'

'I was reading from the Bible, Miss Trent.'

The mistress thwacked her thigh with the birches.

'You were reading from a forbidden portion of the Bible, girl!' she said. 'You know perfectly well that that work is omitted from *our* Bible, lest in the fervour of youth it give too wide a scope to fancy, and interpret to a bad sense the spiritual ideas of Solomon. The purpose of the chapters in question is to exhibit the chaste passions of conjugal life as they existed among the Jews, to whom polygamy was allowed, but their reading cannot be recommended in families, let alone in organisations as chaste as ours. Had I not discovered your impertinence, you had been in the way of corrupting all your companions by admitting them to notions which could only lead in the end to a life of sin which would disqualify you all from participation in decent society. Miss Burtenshaw, prepare yourself.'

The poor girl gave a look of entreaty, which was met only with a cold stare, and reluctantly lifted her dress to her shoulders, revealing her naked back to all. She then stepped forward and, turning to face the wooden structure, leaned against it, clasping her arms around it and bending her belly across the horizontal support so that her fair, plump buttocks were extended.

Miss Trent, as slowly as possible, inspected the bundle of birches and carefully chose one, making it whistle through the air – at which everyone in the room, I believe, shivered.

'Nelly Morrison – apply the mark!' she then said, handing the birch to one of the other girls – one who was, as I learned, Sarah's particular friend. Nelly reluctantly took the birch, went to the fireplace (which contained only a few cold ashes) and taking from it some charcoal, darkened the birch. Then she approached her friend (taking the opportunity, as I saw, being on the right side, of whispering a word of comfort in the poor girl's ear) and laid it tenderly across her buttocks so that a horizontal line was marked upon the backside. She then handed the birch to Miss Trent, who whistled it once more through the air, and took up a stand behind and somewhat to the left-hand side of her victim.

'I have ascertained,' she said, 'by counting them – without of course reading the matter – that there are sixteen verses in the chapter of the work whose indecencies you were so diligently conveying to your friends; you will therefore receive sixteen strokes. Are you ready?'

Sarah's lips moved, but no sound came from them.

'Are you ready?' the schoolmistress repeated.

'Yes, thank you, Miss Trent,' came the weak reply, whereat the mistress raised the cane high above her head and brought it down with a sharp crack upon the bottom of her unfortunate pupil, whose whole body shook.

'One,' she announced.

The birch rose again, and with great accuracy fell upon the dark charcoal mark, now deepened by the red of the former assault.

'Two,' she cried, as great tears began to roll from the eyes of her pupil, now biting her lips in her attempt to remain silent.

'Do feel, Miss Burtenshaw, free to express your emotions aloud; we shall not be distressed – shall we girls?' she asked, turning to the white-faced class.

'No, Miss Trent,' they chorused, meekly.

By the time the birch had descended five times, specks of blood had begun to appear and Sarah had, despite herself, given out a shriek of pain. Seven strokes and blood was running freely, and the girl crying for mercy – which only seemed to rouse her mistress to more vigorous motion. With the tenth stroke the cries suddenly ceased, and releasing her hold Sarah slid unconscious to the floor. Disappointed, Miss Trent threw down her birch.

How I had contained myself, I know not. Perhaps the fact that I knew no one in the town and had no one else from whom I could command shelter, restrained me but now I stepped forward and bent to try to rouse the unconscious victim.

'Mrs Nelham!' cried my employer. 'Pray retire!'

I rose to my feet.

'It is the custom here that the friends of the punished one should minister to her, as a memorial to them of the consequences of disobedience. I ask you, on your honour, to refrain from having anything to do with her!'

She stared straight at me. Looking back, after a moment, I nodded, not trusting my voice to reply, and in any case crossing my fingers firmly behind my back.

'To the dormitory!' commanded Miss Trent, and Sarah, now once more conscious though barely able to stand, was supported by her friends and taken from the room.

'Now, Mrs Nelham, perhaps you would care to join me

for a cup of chocolate?' said Miss Trent. 'Dolly – the birch!' At which Dolly came forward, picked up the bloody instrument, and took it away to clean and replace it in its cupboard for future use.

I made, needless to say, my excuses to Miss Trent, saying that I was tired and wished to retire.

'Of course, my dear Mrs Nelham,' said the mistress, whose dark eyes seemed now to be sparkling with a vigorous and unusual brightness. She placed her arm about my shoulders and walked me to the door.

'Do not allow the young ladies to incommode you; if they prevent you from sleeping, there is always room for you – elsewhere,' and she seemed to nod in the direction of her bed, behind us.

I thanked her with what politeness I could muster, and made my way upstairs, where the body of Sarah, who was now sufficiently recovered to command her weeping, lay face downward upon one of the beds, while her friend Nelly and the others stood around, not knowing what to do to comfort her.

At first I, too, was at a loss, and then remembered how my brother Andy, after Mr Gutteridge's assaults upon me, had salved my wounds; and sitting upon the edge of the bed and bending my head, I applied my tongue to Sarah's cuts – so much more savage than those I had experienced. The salt of blood on my tongue, I felt the poor girl flinch even at so tender a ministration, but after a while, she evidently felt some comfort, for her sobbing ceased, and presently she fell into an exhausted sleep. Making sure the single window was closed so that no cold air should strike upon her, I instructed the others not to lay any bedclothes upon her body, but to allow the air of the room to play upon it, which should seal the wounds and render them less painful.

'She will be excused lessons for three days,' I was told, for this was the custom after a whipping, which took place perhaps once a month, sometimes with far less excuse than poor Sarah had given, and was often more severe. The girls had now learned somewhat to counterfeit pain and eventual collapse, to save themselves from the wilder extremities of discomfort, though they had to do so with great care for if she suspected pretence Miss Trent only laid on the harder, and it was rumoured that she had actually killed one young person, many years ago.

'At least,' said young Nelly, 'now we get some peace,' for after her display of cruel discipline, Miss Trent would then conduct the school strictly but without undue passion for at least a month, before seeking another reason to inflict a birching upon one of her pupils.

My care for Sarah had evidently endeared me to the young ladies, for during the next weeks they showed me great kindness, not only behaving prettily in class but also allowing me every courtesy in the dormitory – especially Sarah, who displayed the utmost gratitude, often creeping into my bed after dark and inviting me to hold her in my arms, which I did with pleasure, she being a dear and charming creature to whom I was happy to be a substitute for her mother. In the meantime several of the girls showed an aptitude for music and, taking the greatest care to conceal it, I was able to acquire a small anthology of poetry in the town from which I read very quietly, after we had retired, some verses from Thomas Campion, Christopher Marlowe, Sir Philip Sidney, Edmund Spenser and even Dr Donne, whose lines considerably roused our spirits.

I was permitted to walk in the town once or twice a week, but as for the girls, they were kept strictly immured. There was a small garden at the back of the house, whose high walls prevented us from seeing anything but the roofs of the neighbouring buildings. There, once a day, the girls and I were allowed to walk and even to throw a ball to each other, but that was their only exercise except on Sundays, when we walked in a column to the cathedral for Matins, led by Miss Trent and concluded by myself. The huge building was almost empty apart from ourselves; a very few townsmen and women could be seen, but the services were otherwise almost unattended. However, the outing was a pleasant one, allowing us at least to see other human beings.

The longer I stayed at the school, the more I felt that it

was unnatural and unreal that young ladies – the oldest of whom was only perhaps eighteen months younger than I – should be kept for so long periods altogether from the world of men. They talked longingly of their brothers and cousins, but of course had no notion of the carnal pleasure of congress with the male sex, and I hesitated to speak to them of it – not because I believed this would harm them, but because I believed that any description I could give, while sufficiently educative, might rouse their emotions to an ungovernable extent.

This led me into some difficulty when, in reading from works of which Miss Trent would no doubt disapprove, we came across terms with which (or so I thought) the young ladies were unfamiliar. Though now sharing confidences with me, they were guarded in their speech, and sometimes I caught them sharing a private joke or giggling in a corner. I thought their jokes to be at normal childish things, until having reluctantly taken chocolate one night with Miss Trent, who treated me now with the utmost courtesy, I came up to the dormitory expecting to find the girls asleep, but heard outside the door little cries and laughs, and on entering was to my surprise confronted with a view of Sarah, quite naked, leaning over the end of her bed, while a figure I thought at first to be a man approached her from behind, his enormous and erect instrument in hand.

The scene held still at my opening the door, whereupon the girls who had been gathered admiringly around the tableau scattered and the man, to my amazement, apparently wrenched his tool from its root and thrust it under a bed where, on my looking, I found it to be nothing more dangerous than a cucumber, no doubt stolen from the kitchen, which Nelly had been about to employ upon her friend in imitation of the act of love!

The girls were clearly terrified but when, unable to control my emotions, I burst into laughter, they too burst into uncontrollable giggling the noise of which was only with great effort repressed so as not to be heard by Miss Trent in the rooms below! It was clear that some, at least, of my companions were more educated in the difference between

men and women than I had supposed, and indeed Sarah
confessed to me that she had, one day, come upon her
brother and one of the village girls in a barn, in the posture
which she and her friend had adopted and which she
believed to be the only one a man and a woman *could* adopt
for such purposes. Nor was she, except instinctively,
cognitive of the pleasure such activity provoked, so that I
felt I should enlighten them all, and drawing them in a circle
about my bed, explained to them the many postures love
could adopt, which they begged me to illustrate. So, playing
the part of the man, though without the aid of the vegeta-
ble, and without the least difficulty persuading Sarah to
play the woman, I placed us in the various positions which
afforded the most acute sensations of congress.

They were just as amazed as I had been to learn, as I
thought fit to warn them, that one such instance of
commerce between a man and a woman could lead to
procreation, and Sarah was insistent in reproaching the
Creator for not arranging things more conveniently (which
I was bound to agree with, though I felt it my duty to
reprove her for blasphemy). However, I was able to point
out that not only the male instrument was capable of giving
pleasure to woman, asking whether some at least of them
had not found that the exploration of their own bodies gave
them some entertainment. Blushingly they confessed it, and
Sarah – who was proving herself to be nothing other than a
forward hussy, though a most attractive one – confessed to
receiving much enjoyment from mutual caresses with her
friend Nelly. But had they not also found, I enquired, that
the employment of the lips and tongue was equally delicious
to our sex? No, they replied with surprise, and invoked my
description of those subtle pleasures – which led to their
imploring me to teach them how they might best please their
future husbands in such a manner.

Once again, Sarah showed herself most forward in
wishing to know in the most detailed form how to under-
take such adventurings, and after some persuasion I persuaded myself, upon her stretching herself upon her bed,
still naked from her experiment with her friend, to apply my

lips to her breast, and then my tongue to her most sensitive part – upon which after a moment she gave a shriek so loud that we all took ourselves to our beds and lay trembling for some time, sure that Miss Trent must have heard.

However, it became clear that she had not and after a time we crept from our covers like mice and the girls all decided – driven on by Sarah, who spoke with the utmost relish of the delirium, the transport, the indescribable delight of the emotion she had felt – that they must experiment in the action I had shown them, so that in no time each bed bore two girls, head to tail, busily at work – while I strolled between them to give a hint here, or a suggestion there, which might result in a keener apprehension of passion.

From that time forward, with all the enthusiasm of beginners at joy, the young ladies I fear devoted more attention to the practice of amorous pleasure than to scholastic pursuits, much of the day being spent with yawning lips and half-closed eyes – except during those lessons in which Miss Trent occupied herself, when they contrived to appear more wide awake. I found them willing and grateful pupils, who even drew up a round-list which brought one or other to me every night for such additional tuition as I could contrive, which it was no trouble to me to give, since they were all sweet young things whose bodies were slim and attractive, and which could even – with an effort of imagination – be compared to those of young men; though one thing always was missing, which I must confess I grew increasingly aware of as the weeks passed.

It was on the fourth Sunday of my presence at the school that, as we walked through the cathedral close to service, poor Sarah stumbled and almost fell. Before I could go to her, a young man darted forward and assisted her to her feet, at which she curtsied, blushingly, and walked on. When I turned to thank the young man, he had vanished.

That night in the dormitory it was her turn to visit me, but instead of unclothing herself and climbing immediately into my bed, she sat upon its side and whispered the confidence to me that she had that day received a message from a secret lover!

The sly puss had kept this entirely from me, and indeed from all except Nelly, but hearing us whisper, her companions gathered around and insisted on hearing the story, which Sarah needed no persuasion to tell. It appeared that until three months ago she had been privately educated at her parents' home by a series of female tutors until, the last of these leaving, her father had engaged a young man to come to teach her, believing (most sensibly) that it was time she met some member of the opposite sex other than servants, and that a tutor could be trusted to behave towards her with propriety. As indeed at first he had, but he was (she said) of extraordinary beauty and before long she was drinking in his appearance and actions rather than his words. Desperate for some other attention than the correction of her recital of the conjugation of the verb *asseoir*, she had contrived to stumble while out walking, and to fall against him, forcing him to catch her, whereupon, being human and feeling in his arms this charming morsel of young womanhood, he had clasped her rather longer than the situation truly warranted. The next day Mr Burtenshaw, her father, unexpectedly entering the schoolroom, had seen the tutor pressing the first kiss upon lips which had never previously known such an impropriety.

The tutor left that same afternoon and two days later Sarah found herself at Miss Trent's school, where her spirit had been almost but not entirely subdued by the wicked beatings which that unregenerate mistress had inflicted upon her.

Her Evan (for such was his curious name) had, it seems, discovered by some means her whereabouts; some weeks ago Dolly had brought her a note pledging his love and offering to attempt to release her from the bondage of the school and to marry her. However, the maid was far too terrified to carry further messages so, taking great risk, her lover had that day taken the chance of discovery by passing her another note:

'My love, contrive to send a message to me at Mr Bobbins' lodging house in Fence Street. If you will consent to come away I will somehow engineer your release, and have employment in Wales which will support us both. Your lover, Evan.'

Of course I consented to carry a message – for it was now my solemn belief that no effort to release any pupil from the clutches of Miss Trent could be unjustified – whereupon nothing would content Sarah than that at that moment she should sit down and write a note introducing me to her lover, and confirming that she would agree to any plan for her escape that he and I could construct. After this she slipped into my bed and in her untutored affection amply demonstrated the joy she would eventually give even the least receptive of husbands.

It was not for three days that I was able to excuse myself for an afternoon and took the note from the secret hiding-place in which I had secreted it, finding (for I had not looked at it before) that it was addressed to a Mr Evan Ffloyd. The coincidence seemed too much; surely this must be the tutor who had taught me all I knew, at Alcovary? And indeed, when I had made my way to Fence Street and the appointed lodging-house, I found myself in due course face to face with my old friend, whom I had last seen making his way out of my life through the park at home.

For a moment he did not know me – doubtless the experience of the past months had marked my features with a certain maturity – but then took me in his arms and pressed my lips to his until I pulled myself away and with the uttering of the single word 'Sarah!' not only reminded him of his obligation, but instructed him that I knew of it.

Blushing, as well he might, he escorted me to a room where we could talk and I gave him my friend's note and explained to him the circumstances which had brought me to him. He was able to satisfy me that indeed his intentions were honourable, and within the hour we had made our plans, which that night I explained to Sarah and her friends.

On the following Saturday morning, I made a point of attending the weekly class during which Miss Trent examined the girls in their lessons of the week. After several unexceptional recitations of passages from the expurgated

Bible and an animadversion by the Rev. Anthony Westcott, former Bishop of Salisbury, on the subject of the true dimensions of the Noah's ark, she invited Sarah to recite the verse she had chosen that week to memorise.

Sarah got to her feet, and in the clearest voice began:

Come, madam, come, all rest my powers defy,
Until I labour, I in labour lie . . .

Miss Trent obviously did not recognise Dr Donne's poem but gradually, as the sense came upon her, her complexion became one blush, until Sarah reached the lines:

Licence my roving hands, and let them go
Before, behind, between, above, below . . .

when she gave a loud shriek of outrage and protest.

'Sit down, Miss Burtenshaw! I have never in my life heard such indecencies. Mrs Nelham, what do you know of this?'

Stammering, I lied that I knew nothing.

'Miss Burtenshaw, I have had enough of your impertinence. You will all present yourselves to me at nine this evening in my room!'

Whereupon she swept from the room, and we relieved our tension in an outbreak of stifled laughter.

That evening at nine we filed into Miss Trent's room, where the flogging-frame had been erected in its usual place, and after a while Miss Trent appeared, birches in her hand.

'Miss Burtenshaw, prepare yourself,' she said.

Sarah stepped forward, but rather than stripping herself, drew up to her height and replied, 'No, miss – it is now your turn!'

Shocked and amazed, Miss Trent at first could not reply, then raised her hand to strike her rebellious pupil across the face. But now the other girls crowded round; one seized the birches and the others clutched at their mistress' clothing, and in a little time had removed it, revealing madam's skinny body and then forcing her to the frame. In a passable imitation of Miss Trent's voice, Sarah invited Miss Morrison to 'apply the mark', whereupon Nelly applied the charcoal to a birch, and laid a black mark upon the mistress' lank backside.

The beating which followed was by no means as severe as that the mistress had inflicted upon Sarah, for though the girls applied themselves with enthusiasm, they lacked the power – and indeed the will – to draw blood. However, the indignity their mistress suffered was an additional punishment, as was perhaps the cool stare with which I received her pleas for help. Even Dolly, who had known nothing of our plan, though she cowered in a corner perhaps anticipating the end of the world as she knew it, was not displeased at her employer's fate.

Finally, tiring of their sport, the girls threw down the birch and left the room, locking the door behind us, conscious that Miss Trent, now past the power of speech, could only cry help from a back window and that neighbours were immured to shrieks emanating from this house.

Now we went to our room, where we had packed our belongings, and thence to the ground floor, where the key of the front door was kept in Miss Trent's cupboard. Breaking the lock of this, we discovered not only the key but a large selection of canes and birches of various sizes, together with books entitled *The Whippingham Papers, The Flogging Horse, An Essay upon the Whipping Block*, and several similar volumes, which appeared upon a glance to be of the utmost indecency. Removing these lest they should corrupt anyone into whose hands they might fall, I took the key and unlocked the door, and we all trooped out into the sunlight. From my small store I had given the girls sufficient money to command a chair to their homes for they all, save Sarah, came from the immediate areas of the town, and I accompanied her to Fence Street and her lover.

Mr Ffloyd had taken places in the Oxford coach though he intended, he said, to break the journey at Basingstoke, where next day he would marry his love – news of which delighted her.

Upon reaching the Pestle and Mortar Inn at Basingstoke and enquiring for accommodation, we discovered that only a single room was available, which distressed Mr Ffloyd, who had certainly intended to anticipate the joys of marriage and now feared that his design would be impeded. Upon his suggesting that Sarah and I should share the room while he passed the night in the travellers' room downstairs, Sarah demurred for, she said, I was friend enough to be almost a sister to her (we had not revealed to her that Mr Ffloyd and I had met before).

Upon his somewhat reluctantly agreeing, we were shown to our room, which had a single but large four-poster bed. It was offered to make up a mattress upon the floor, but again Sarah insisted that since she and I had often shared a bed before, there was no reason why we should not do so for one last time. After all, she could sleep between me and Mr Ffloyd to avoid embarrassment and indelicacy. And without more ado she threw off her clothes and got between the sheets. Mr Ffloyd and I carefully turned our backs towards each other while removing our clothing, and climbed into the bed, one upon each side of Sarah.

For a while we all lay still, I suppose somewhat checked by the strangeness of the situation, but Sarah then fell to telling Mr Ffloyd of the rebellion at the school and in the excitement of retailing events sat up in bed, the light of a large moon through the window illuminating the room so that the beauty of her young breasts was clearly visible to the young man at her side, who must have been made of stone had he not given way to it. Indeed in a while he raised himself with a low groan and threw his arms around his love, planting a kiss upon her bosom, in which he buried his head.

Sarah was obviously pleased at the attention, and at another less visible manifestation of his admiration, for she mouthed silently to me over Mr Ffloyd's head the information that he was 'very big', by which she did not, I believe, refer to the stature of his torso merely.

I must admit that his attention to my friend reminded me strongly of the salutes he had given me at our last meeting, and I was unable to resist passing my hand over his neck and shoulders. He may have thought this was a compliment paid by Sarah, for he redoubled his caresses, covering her bosom with kisses and – by her expression – passing his hands over her lower limbs.

Her pleasure obviously increasing, and remembering my teaching, in a while she threw back the covers and persuaded him upon his back. Wriggling downwards and first gasping with a pleasurable admiration of his manly beauty – which indeed was as vigorous and upstanding as I recalled – she applied her lips with such tender condescension that a look of blank amazement passed over her lover's face. This gave way in a moment to a tranquil delight, in the course of which, whether abstractedly or not I could not say, he stretched forth a hand to caress my breast – which welcomed his tickling fingers, for the sight of the couple's mutual pleasure conveyed most vividly to me my recent lack of male company. In a moment I was constrained to join my lips to his in a kiss which lasted so long that when I finally withdrew my lips it was to see that Sarah had raised her head and was regarding us – not with displeasure, but a simple happiness. This encouraged me to join her in making Mr Ffloyd a happy man. First – having that right by her chief place in his affections – she received him within her arms, while I merely contented myself with passing my hands over his back, or reaching to grasp with tender approbation his weighty cods to encourage the ebullient eagerness of his jogging. Then after a while she persuaded me to revive him and to allow him in turn to satisfy me – which, being young and vigorous, he was perfectly able to do.

Finally, in relaxed pleasure, each exhausted of our eager striving, we lay still, our limbs tangled in friendly repose, and fell into a quiet sleep.

Chapter Fifteen

The Adventures of Andy

Waking on the morning after our arrival at Salisbury, I found myself plunged into a day's frantic activity; first, the erection of a rough stage in the courtyard of the Bell Inn, then the sorting of costumes, and – in our barn, so as not too much to disrupt the business of the inn – a rehearsal of that evening's play *Isabella, or The Fatal Marriage*, by Thomas Southern, as altered by Mr Higgens for his small company, with Mr Grigson in the part of Biron, Mr Prout Higgens as Villeroy, and Mrs Plunkett Cope as Isabella, a part played until lately, I was informed, by the great Mrs Siddons herself. Both the latter actors, I soon gathered, were at least forty years too old for their parts, but this was common practice with them.

I was instructed that music would be needed between the acts and was told to play 'something tragic' immediately upon Mrs Plunkett Cope remarking 'Then Heav'n have mercy on me!' and leaving the stage with her child (the three-year-old daughter of the innkeeper, whose pride in seeing her upon the stage resulted in the provision of an excellent midday repast, without charge). Then I must render 'something romantic' upon Villeroy announcing, in heartbreaking tones, 'Next, my Isabella, be near my heart! I am for ever yours.' Finally, I was to play 'a merry jig, or some such nonsense,' at the end of the play, 'to send 'em home happily' – which considering the piece ended in utter disaster for each and every character, seemed to me to be somewhat strange. But 'twas not my responsibility, so I looked out some pieces and practised them quietly in a corner, while everything was in chaos around me.

I was then led off by David to a corner of the barn where

a small, squat woman, addressed by all as 'Wardrobe', was to produce a costume for me to wear 'in the style of the play', as Mr Higgens instructed. Since the players were dressed in clothes from every decade of the past two hundred years, it seemed to me to be immaterial what I wore, but again, it was not for me to protest.

'Wardrobe' was surrounded by a vast quantity of clothes and by several members of the company, ignoring the various degrees of each other's undress as they climbed into or out of breeches and shifts. David pointed out several of the costumes as having belonged to the deceased nobility, for it was still the fashion then for the relics of noblemen to give or sell their clothes to the actors. So, he said, the suit of scarlet and gold Mr Grigson was trying on had been worn by Lord Northampton upon his entrance as British ambassador into Venice, while a brown suit into which another actor was attempting to squeeze his ample form had been made for the actress Peg Woffington, whose fame and beauty, it appears, is well known, and who had worn it in the breeches part of Sir Harry Wildair, before it had come to this company through a neice of hers. Mrs Plunkett Cope was just divesting herself of a dress which she had worn (so David whispered) in the part of Lucinda in *Love in a Village* forty years since, and which now restrained only with difficulty the generous spread of her bosom.

I was provided with a pair of green pantaloons and a jacket, and without complaint took them away and placed them upon my bed, where I drew the sheet which cut me off, in sight at least, from the general press. I lay down for a rest, being somewhat exhausted by the excitements of the day, following as they did upon those of the previous twenty and four hours.

As I turned over I saw a female arm lying near to me, just falling beneath the lay of the sheet which hung between me and the bed of Miss Cynthia Cope, and thinking to be friendly, I stretched out my hand and laid it upon the wrist, whereat in a moment the sheet flew up and a positive virago attacked me. Miss Cope, though in *negligée* – for she had taken off her day clothes in order to don her costume, but at present had merely laid an excessively thin petticoat upon herself which indifferently concealed her form – threw herself upon me, striking me violently about the face with her fist. Amazed, I at first made no attempt to defend myself, and her nails caught my cheek, laying it open, before I succeeded in taking her by the wrists and restraining her.

'Unhand me, sir!' she cried. 'You think you can assault a defenceless woman! Base upstart crow, keep your dark hands to yourself!'

Whereat I unhanded her, and with a final scornful glance she returned to her mattress, drawing down the sheet with a flounce.

There was a laugh, and I saw that David had appeared just in time to see his fellow player's exit. I must have looked a picture of amazement, dabbing at my torn cheek, quite unable to understand why a young woman who the previous night had welcomed me into her bed with a sharp enthusiasm should have greeted thus what was intended as a simple mark of affection.

Laying himself down at my side so that he could whisper into my ear, David told me that Miss Cope was known not only in the company but abroad for the indelicate profligacy of her passions, which, however, she intended should remain cloaked in night. Never had she been seen to give a sign of warmth to any of her lovers while anyone else was by, but while under cover of night she would, as he put it, share cock alley with anyone near, and was as lively as any Covent Garden nun.

'Fear not!' he said; 'if you bed next her, you'll have another buttock ball before long. But remember' (and his lips tickled my ear as he spoke) 'if you are in need of a strum and she's not by, I can offer you a relish.' Whereupon he stole his hand upon my thigh and pinched it.

Though I had never before been so diligently courted by one of my own sex, I omitted to strike him as some fellows might, for he was a likable rogue, and indeed the whole company had been excessively kind to me, so that I had no wish to offend any of their number. I simply made no sign, whereupon David kissed me upon the cheek and asked me if I would 'hear him' in his small part of Sampson, servant to Count Baldwin. This meant my holding the book of the play (or in fact merely the writing out of his part, with the 'cues' which brought in his speeches) while he recited his part:

'I have no ill-will to the young lady, as a body may say, upon my own account; only that I hear she is poor; and indeed I naturally hate your decayed gentry – they expect as much waiting upon as when they had money in their pockets . . .'

And so on.

The performance that evening went well; my pieces were approved, and indeed when I left my place below the stage at the end of the evening several of those who had seen the play invited me to drink with them, which I did until past midnight, later being told that one could normally expect such hospitalty, for some people liked to boast that they were friendly with the players and their company – surprisingly enough, for it seemed to me we were a raggle-taggle lot. However, I accepted the offered ale with pleasure, in the company of some others of my new friends. Mr Grigson, I saw, left the room accompanied by a young lady dressed in the height of fashion, with a modest high-necked bodice above a dress which fitted her elegant figure so closely that she clearly wore no petticoat beneath it. I must have been looking somewhat jealous, for David – who hovered attentively near by – whispered that Mr Grigson often attracted the attentions of the ladies, and indeed sometimes of the gentlemen – none of which he disliked, it seems, as long as there was financial inducement.

That night, as David had taught me to expect, Miss Cope once more stretched out her arms and welcomed me between her thighs, with no word about the day's rejection, much less apology for the damage to my cheek (which had caused many a knowing glance, and some ribald comment). The ale had had the effect upon me, which sometimes it does, not of making me incapable of standing but difficult of satisfaction, so that the lady twice attempted to throw me off, having gained her own satisfaction. But I continued to pump away, with perhaps unaccustomed diligence which in the end roused her again to a fever, and by the time my own slow fuse had been fully burned out we were both exhausted, and I scarcely had the energy to return to my mattress. There I felt David attempting to fumble below my waist but, without even the vigour to strike his hand away, I fell into a deep sleep.

The following day we played again at the Bell – this time in Shakespeare's *As You Like It*, in which Mr Higgens essayed the part of the Ancient Duke while Mrs Plunkett Cope, crammed into Miss Woffington's well-worn brown suit, played the part of Rosalind, her general appearance being as like that of a boy as the view of an elephant resembles that of a doe. The audience was reduced by this to a regrettable levity which extended not only to the humorous parts of the piece, but the serious, and during the last Act there came from several drunken ruffians a demand for a hornpipe, which was so insistent that Mr Higgens was forced to halt the expounding of the plot while Ned Farkin, the company's comedian, came forward and performed the dance to music I hurriedly improvised.

Unfortunately, Mr and Mrs Higgens in essaying roles which displayed no regard to the reality of their age and size, often reduced audiences to extremes of laughter. The following day we moved on to Wilton and that evening gave the tragedy of *Philomena*. When we came to the part of the final Act, in which the heroine falls tragically dead at the hero's feet, and Mr Higgens struck a pathetic attitude, crying: 'What shall I do? What shall I *do*?' there came a cry from the audience of 'Fuck her while she's warm!'; which remark, though it bitterly tried the sensibilities of Mrs Plunkett Cope, whose dead corpse showed palpable signs of taking deep offence, reduced the rest of the company to an unwonted hilarity which made it difficult for us to complete the performance with any decorum. Happily, however, the people were in receipt of so little entertainment outside the tenor of their everyday lives that they were content with anything that was offered; the success of the evening was assured, and the money received on the next night redoubled.

A few days later, as we were resting in a small village between Amesbury and Warminster, Mr Grigson came to me with a pile of extremely ragged music paper, saying that they had received a message inviting some of the company to perform at a private party at a manor house nearby, the property of a Lord Shaveley. This was something they had done before and it was to consist not of a play, but of an evening of recitations and songs. These, Mr Grigson said, were the songs – perhaps I could con them in order to accompany him, Miss Cope and Ned Farkin in them that evening?

'They are,' he said, somewhat apologetically, 'a little – hah – *warm*, but a young fellow of your experience will not object to that!'

The songs indeed were 'a little warm', and what the recitations were to be I could only imagine. However, since gold was involved, I had no hesitation in setting off with a small party late that night for the manor house, which proved a large establishment in the hall of which we were to perform. It was crowded with ladies and gentlemen who had evidently enjoyed good food and ample wine, and were now ready to be entertained.

We were shown to a small room which I imagine at one time must have been an adjunct to the butler's pantry, and there climbed into our costumes. Miss Cope's, I saw, consisted of an Empire gown of the lightest clinging gauze or fine muslin placed upon her naked body. Mr Grigson wore tight-fitting breeches of stockinette, the flap covering his privities being handsomely decorated with embroidery but nevertheless obviously concealing equipment of impressive dimensions. Mr Farkin had cap and bells, in the old style, and David white silk stockings with brief trunks of black above.

When we were ready, we were announced as 'one of the Regent's most popular bands of entertainers,' and having

entered quietly and taken my place at the side of the large
but empty fireplace, where there was space for the performers, I struck up a march at which my friends entered
and without pause passed into the chorus of the first song:

> *Come, pretty nymph, fain would I know*
> *What thing it is that breeds delight,*
> *That strives to stand, and cannot go,*
> *And feeds the mouth that cannot bite . . .*

This was greeted with a roar of applause, after which
Miss Cope stepped forward and with a curtsy rendered the
old catch *Have at a Venture*:

> *A country lad and bonny lass*
>   *they did together meet,*
> *And as they did together pass,*
>   *thus he began to greet:*
> *'What I do say I may mind well,*
>   *and thus I do begin:*
> *If you would have your belly swell,*
>   *hold up, and I'll put in.'*

This proved remarkably popular, especially with the
verse:

> *She held this youngster to his task*
>   *till he began to blow,*
> *Then at the last he leave did ask*
>   *and so she let him go.*
> *Then down he panting lay awhile,*
>   *and rousing up again*
> *She charmed him with a lovely smile*
>   *again to put it in.*

At this there was a tremendous outcry, with many ribald
calls, and one man near the front of the gathering actually
interrupted the performance by stepping forward and
catching at Miss Cope's dress, for a moment pulling it

down to expose a breast, whereupon he was caught a blow upon the ear by one of his friends and restrained.

Mr Grigson and Miss Cope retired after this, and Ned Farkin gave us another prick-song. The couple returned, coverd by the same cloak – and Farkin began the song of *Walking in a Meadow Green*, and when he came to the second verse –

> *They lay so close together*
> *They made me much to wonder;*
> *I know not which was whether*
> *Until I saw her under . . .*

– the cloak was dropped and the actors fell upon it on the floor in a state of nature, Miss Cope beneath and Mr Grigson above, pressed close together as the song described. He began to move upon her with a bucking motion and when Farkin reached the lines –

> *Then off he came and blushed for shame*
> *So soon that he had ended*

– Mr Grigson raised himself, revealing his prick indeed to be small and unimpressive, whereat Miss Cope struck at it with her palm and the company expressed itself most amused.

The song continued:

> *Then in her arms she did him fold,*
> *And oftentimes she kissed him;*
> *And yet his courage still was cold*
> *For all the good she wished him.*
> *Yet with her hand she made it stand*
> *So stiff she could not bend it,*
> *And then anon she cries 'Come on,*
> *Once more, and none can mend it.'*

And suiting the action to the motion, Miss Cope applied her hands and lips to the person of Mr Grigson, whereupon his tool in an astonishingly short time rose to enviable eminence and became capable of its work, whereupon he set to, and the tragedians vigorously presented the beast with two backs to their appreciative audience. Meanwhile David capered about them administering a brisk slap here or an encouraging pinch there, set to it by the cries of the gentleman and ladies watching who themselves (as I observed) were now engaged in sundry amatory experiments, with caresses above and below the clothes and a slapping of lips almost audible above the general lubricious murmuring.

In a moment, Mr Grigson sharply withdrew himself from his position between Miss Cope's thighs, just in time to show the tangible sign of his enjoyment (which Miss Cope took upon her belly) while there was an enormous cheer from the entire company, which then for a while subsided into its own enjoyments. I played on while Miss Cope and Mr Grigson (who off the stage, David later assured me, had no regard whatsoever for each other) lay clasped in each other's arms apparently whispering endearments, in a splendidly effective play of amorous relaxation.

In a while, however, the company began to cry for new amusement. The difficulty was, however, that Mr Grigson, despite the best endeavours of Miss Cope, was unable to recover himself; whatsoever stimulation was offered, his apparatus was incapable of standing. Indeed, as the song put it –

> *At last he thought to venture her*
> *Thinking the fit was on him,*
> *But when he came to enter her*
> *The point turned back upon him*

– whereat a chorus of angry booing broke out, which appeared to me to be unwarranted, for, after all, while a woman may counterfeit amorous play at any time, if a man's body should rebel there is little he can do.

Seeing some of the audience becoming positively angry,

Mr Grigson made his escape, being near to the door, but Miss Cope, all undressed as she was, was restrained by two men, one catching each arm, while two others seized Ned Farkin. However, a lady cried – 'No, he's old meat – who would see him bare? Here's better metal!' and took young David by the arm; he was soon stripped by her and her friends, and pulled to face Miss Cope. He was in no better case than Mr Grigson (and indeed who, in the hands of an angry mob, could be expected to display an outward ardour?). Even when one of the ladies holding Miss Cope let go her grip and to the general applause of her friends fell to her knees before the boy and took his tool, small and shrunken as it was, between her lips, there was evidently no response, whereat Miss Cope remarked, 'You'll get no charge from him – he's a mere Molly, and can only tup another!'

But by then the company was in too coarse a mood to be quietened, and to my horror I felt a hand at my collar.

'Here's the fen for him, then!' cried a man behind me. 'All musicians are notorious madge culls!'

I attempted to assure him that I was in no way interested in making love with my own sex, and turned to appeal to Miss Cope, but seeing her opportunity, she had wrenched free in the confusion and disappeared.

Meanwhile, my clothes were being carelessly wrenched from me, the shirt literally torn from my back, then, my being up-ended, my breeches pulled from my legs. I found myself thrown to the floor beside David, who now looked (as I thought) far less terrified than he had formerly done. Indeed, without prompting, he rolled over to take me in his arms – his prick was stirring, for I felt it against my thigh.

'Take care!' he whispered. 'They've turned ugly, and will not let up without an exhibition. Simply lie still – I will be gentle!' And so saying, he kissed me thoroughly upon the lips, to a cheer from the assembled company and then raised himself upon his hands and knees and leaned to take my reluctant instrument between his lips. I was incapable of making any response. Though shutting my eyes I attempted to imagine that the tongue now playing about me was that of Miss Cope, or even of dear Sophia, who had first wakened me to such pleasure, it was to no effect. Gradually, however, a genial warmth spread through my limbs and I found myself able to relax somewhat, though my tool no more than slightly raised its head. Then my companion raised his own, taking care to cover me with his body, and encouraged me to turn so that I lay face downward upon the cushions which, for Miss Cope and Mr Grigson, had represented a mossy bank.

Now David began to caress and smooth my back, turning so that my head lay between his thighs, his eager prick against my cheek – which, if he or the company expected me to favour with kisses, they were much mistaken. Though it is true that by this time I was not altogether averse to his attentions, as his lips slid down the length of my spine and his hands embraced my backside, kneading the cheeks as a woman kneads bread. Then, to my astonishment, I felt him draw those cheeks apart and his tongue slide between them until it was at the doors of my fundament, when, despite the deep aversion I had always felt to unnatural acts, I could not prevent an extraordinarily reposeful fervidity invading my limbs, so that rather than clenching my buttocks against so intimate an invasion, they became loosened and relaxed, at which David slewed around and placed his hands beneath my hips to raise them slightly, at the same time moistening his tool with spittle. I felt it gently nudging, then beginning to enter the most private of bodily passages.

Fortunately, remembering what Bob had told me when I was likely to have been raped by the press gang, I did not fight against the ingress, and in a moment I felt David begin to move in the unmistakable fashion of a man mounting a woman – a strange sensation indeed for one who had so often played the man's role, but now found himself in the subservient one. I felt no pain, but neither did I feel pleasure; indeed the whole operation was one of excessive boredom – though clearly not to David, whose panting lips now expressed endearments and whose hands, still at my hips, gripped me with what was certainly no counterfeited passion.

After a while, I opened my eyes and saw before me a scene of the utmost dissipation, for inspired by the sight of we twain, the company had thrown all restraint aside. Some of the women had entirely removed their dresses, others had merely thrown their skirts over their heads, while again some of the men were altogether bare while others retained their shirts and even their waistcoats, and one impatient fellow had merely opened the flap of his breeches and, finding no spare woman to hand, was pumping away with his fist, his eyes meantime glued to our display. Right before me lay a handsome young fellow prone upon his back while a woman rode him with as much assiduity as he himself ever rode horse; and at the same time, behind her, a stout fellow rode her in the manner David was mounting me.

The sight, I confess, was a lively one, and I felt my tool striving to arise, though constricted between my body and the cushions. But gradually the familiar transport gripped me, increasing in its intensity until by simple coincidence I gave forth at the very moment at which I felt, or thought I felt, the heat of David's spending within me.

In a short time I felt his instrument relaxing, and he slipped from me, planting a kiss as tender as any woman's upon my shoulder. Throwing his arm about me, he raised me to my feet, whereupon to my amazement there was a round of clapping from the company – even those who were still at their work pausing to shout applause – and in a moment a great rattle of coins as they started throwing money towards us. Picking up my tunic from where it lay nearby, David knelt and began to collect the coins, whereupon I joined him, noting that most of them were of gold. We threw them into the jacket and when we had done folded it, whereon David made a bow and led me to the side room, where Miss Cope sat looking black as thunder and Mr Grigson and Ned looking no better pleased.

'Ah! Here come the twiddle-poops!' cried Miss Cope.

'I'm surprised, Mr Archer, that you should lend yourself to such indecency.'

I could only blush and stammer, but to my surprise David, usually the mildest of boys, strode straight up to her and cried: 'Mind your tongue, Miss Wagtail. You are scarcely free of accusation – what would your admirers at the Theatre Royal think if they knew of your enjoyment of balum rancum all over the countryside? Your chances of playing Desdemona to Mr Kean would scarcely be improved, though doubtless you'd play the biter with him to climb onto any board!'

Whereat Miss Cope fell silent, Ned Farkin laughed, and Mr Grigson enquired after the dibs, which I took to be the money.

'There's plenty of that,' said David, 'and I'll thank you to remember who satisfied the audience most, when it comes to divvying up.'

When we rejoined the rest of the company nothing was asked of our evening's activities, from which I took it that Mr Higgens and the others were entirely aware of the nature of our engagement. My feelings towards the company had somewhat altered now, but I must admit to being pleased when, David and Mr Grigson having counted up the cash and argued long and loud over its division, I was handed no less than seven pounds in gold – an astonishing sum for one evening's work, if work it can be called.

I went to bed that night with a bustle of emotions I could not balance. David made no attempt upon my body, however, either because the evening's enjoyment physically precluded such activity or because he was uncertain of my reaction; he merely kissed me upon the cheek and asked if he had hurt me. I had to reply, which was true, that he had not, but I gave no opinion upon the satisfaction I had or had not received, and he merely suggested that it was at all events an easy way to make a few guineas, to which I was bound to assent. I determined, however, to use my best endeavours to avoid such a situation in future, not only because it gave me no pleasure but because I feared that

Miss Cope, clearly a woman to bear a grudge, might betray us to the authorities, and while I could perhaps overcome my indifference to sodomy for a sufficient fee, I had no love for the gallows, to which such an activity might lead me.

At Warminster I spent a morning placing notices announcing that –

MR SAMUEL PROUT HIGGENS
late of the Theatre Royal, Drury Lane,
will play for one night only
the role of
HAMLET, THE PRINCE OF DENMARK,
in Mr SHAKESPEARE's play
of that name,
assisted by
Mrs PLUNKETT COPE as the Queen
Miss CYNTHIA COPE in the role of Ophelia
Mr Nathaniel Grigson – Laertes
Mr Ned Farkin – 1st Gravedigger
with the acclaimed company
late of London
fully and entirely costumed.
GREAT SWORD FIGHT
THUNDER AND LIGHTNING AFFECTS
FAMOUS GHOSTLY APPARITION.

The performance was greeted with much enthusiasm – though when Mrs Plunkett Cope asserted of Mr Higgens that he was 'fat and scant of breath' a great chorus of agreement went up which much disconcerted the latter – especially during the fight between Laertes and Hamlet at the end of the play, when cries of 'Four to two the fat 'un!' were heard. Upon Mrs Plunkett Cope's seizing the poisoned cup, there were shouts of 'Bring on a barrel!' and 'Free ale for all!' In general, however, all was well and the takings considerable, so that if our chief actors were disappointed in their reception, they were not so at the cash which went into the common chest.

Mr Higgens being now of the opinion that *Hamlet* was above the heads of the public in those rural parts, we gave *Romeo and Juliet* at Westbury, Trowbridge and Bradford-on-Avon, with Mr Higgens himself as Romeo (Mr Grigson becoming very vocal about his elder's inability to climb any balcony over two foot high) and Miss Cope as Juliet, whose virginal innocence was loudly questioned by David in a monologue delivered while she was upon stage but not out of hearing. This made her positively quiver with rage, which seemed to be taken by the audience for an excess of emotion, for they cheered loudly the happy ending when she and Romeo came back to life and were married by the Friar – for Mr Higgens was of the view that Shakespeare had been sadly mistaken in giving the play a tragic conclusion, and preferred to use a new ending written for him for a small fee by some literary person in London.

Eventually, we came to Bristol – my first sight of that bustling port and great city, with its Hot Well, which attracted the gentry of the Westcountry not already drawn to the place by business.

Here my first task, after we had moved into a run-down inn by the waterside, was to spread broadsheets about announcing Mr Higgens' production of *King Lear*, in which Mrs Plunkett Cope would essay the role of Cordelia (to the misgiving of Miss Cope, who considered herself by quite thirty years more suited to the part). David and I spent the better part of nine hours in that business, and were making our way back along the quayside when a hue and cry was suddenly heard behind us and in a moment came shouts of 'Stop, thieves!' and running footsteps. On looking behind me, I found to my amazement that pointing fingers accused us, and while I was for stopping to make our excuses, David shouted: 'Come off – this way!' and in a moment had vanished round a corner, while I, laggard, was in the hands of a mob all accusing us of being pickpockets.

I strongly asserted my innocence, and called on the mob to search my pockets and make themselves aware that I had nothing upon me but my own property – to which they replied merely that of course my accomplice carried the purse we had 'lifted' from the pocket of a merchant further along the quay and, in short, in a brief time I found myself in Bristol gaol.

This was the worst place imaginable – the evil-smelling hold of the press gang's vessel was infinitely preferable. Within one room barely twenty feet long by twelve broad were no less than sixty-three people, no distinction being made between men and women, sick and healthy, guilty and innocent. Eleven were children scarcely old enough to leave the nursery. To my indignation, laughter only greeting my protests, and I was placed in heavy irons, for all charged or convicted of felony were thus bound.

Though I did not consider my dress to be rich – I wore only my everyday clothes – I was an emperor to my companions who were filthy in the extreme and clad only in rags. The uproar of oaths, complaints and obscenities, the desperation of all, the dirt and stench, presented altogether a concentration of the utmost misery – a scene of infernal passions and distress the like of which few of my readers, fortunately, could envisage.

When night fell things became worse, for a scuttling arose, accompanied by oaths and occasional cries of pain which revealed the presence of rats going about to steal crumbs of food and, these being few, nibbling the feet of any unfortunate prisoner who for an instant lay still. A cat was kept in the room to prevent the rats, but no single animal could have dealt with so many. To my astonishment and something to my horror, even their filthy and horrific state, even their ill-health and weakness, could not prevent men and women from sexual congress, so that all around to the moans of pain and hunger were conjoined sounds which, when we are in comfort, are the reflection of pleasure and happiness, but which here were rather signs of a desperation which clutched briefly at forgetfulness through bodily passion.

Happily, with the light came Mr Samuel Prout Higgens in the costume he wore for Malvolio, which he believed would most impress the gaolers. And so it did, for I was released at once to a more roomy cell, and came soon before the magistrates who – the accusing merchant admitting that he did not recognise my face, and that he could not be sure that I was one of the two fellows who had taken his purse – released me in Mr Higgens' company, my having denied knowing anything about my companion.

I denied David because it seemed most appropriate; and indeed it was clear that I was right to do so, for as we walked back to our inn Mr Higgens explained to me that the boy had come to him to relate my difficulty, confessing that he had 'found' a purse which someone had dropped, and that he imagined this to have been the cause of the uproar. This seemed to me to be unlikely and when I taxed him with it, he simply gave me a smacking kiss upon the lips and handed me three gold guineas as my share of the profit, with the words – 'You'll know to be more lively next time!' – which suggested to me that his coming by the purse had been less innocent than he pretended.

Apart from this incident, which taught me to be chary of accompanying David on any excursion he proposed, I enjoyed my first freedom within a large city. Bristol then had something of the order of forty thousand inhabitants, and many amusements which I was able to taste when I could take the time to do so. A fine display of lifesized figures of departed celebrities, made from wood and wax, was to be seen at Colston's Hall; Mr Salmon's toy warehouse and exhibition of waxwork figures was on the first and second floors of a house in the centre of the town; lions and other animals were kept in cages in Parker's Menagerie on the downs; and there was Duborg's exhibition of cork models of Roman antiquities. All these took my attention, as did the astonishing display by Zerah Colburn, the calculating boy from America, able to perform any trick with numbers shouted to him from the audience, bidding fair to distract from our own performances until Mr Higgens hit on the notion of allowing Mr Grigson and Miss Cope to perform Romeo and Juliet for only one night – provided that they divested themselves of all their clothing for the scene in Juliet's bedchamber. The rumour of this built up

our takings to an inordinate degree, though upon Mr
Higgens and Mrs Plunkett Cope making their entrance as
the two lovers on the following nights, there was much
libidinous humour at their expense, and some demands for
the return of their entrance money from various members
of the audience, though others asserted that the additional
bulk of the senior actors represented more value for their
ha'pennies.

I was, I admit, by now once more eager for female
company. Miss Cope had shown no interest whatsoever in
my company since the night of our display, and of the three
other ladies in the company, Mrs Plunkett Cope was not to
my taste (though certain signs seemed to indicate she might
have been interested in a passage with me) while the other
two had their own lovers, to whom they were entirely
faithful.

There were many prostitutes in the city, not only on the
quaysides (where they were of the roughest sort) but in
almost every street, where they ranged themselves in a file
on the footpaths in companies of five or six, most of them
dressed very genteelly; there, they accosted passers-by with
'Come and have a drink!', sometimes taking one by the
sleeve or tapping one upon the shoulder. Agreeing, one was
led into one of the shops where they sell beer, where there
was a room behind and a bedroom for any repose.

David, to whom I mentioned my itch (and who was now
content to accept that I would not become his intimate
friend) persuaded me not to buy such wares for, he said, the
French disease or pox was widespread in the city, as in most
of the ports of England. But one day he came to me bearing
a small book, entitled *The Man of Pleasure's Kalender for
the Year*, in which was a list of ladies of the city who, he
said, were guaranteed to be clean and wholesome. This
indeed named a number of ladies, with their addresses and
their costs, such as:

*Miss Bearn, 14 Bow Street. This lovely nymph recently
attained her eighteenth year, plays upon the pianoforte,
sings, and has every accomplishment including the*

*amatory. Of slight stature, she has fine yellow hair, and
in bed is everything a man might desire, her every gesture
a delight. Her price, two pounds ten.*

After reading the book through with great attention and
rising interest, I fixed upon Miss Tamblin, of whom the
page spoke glowingly:

*This amorous charmer is but seventeen, and of good
family, agreeable and genteel, full of delightful conversations and a pleasure both in and out of bed. Between the
sheets she reveals a figure plump without grossness, ath-
letic without coarseness. She particularly enjoys the rites
of love in the equestrian manner, in which style she gives
great pleasure, her thighs being powerful, seating her
with a pliancy and balance which make her the satisfaction of every mount. She will converse at any hour of
the day and night, expecting a present of two or three
guineas at least for the pleasure of her company.*

And so it was that, with a purse containing three guineas
(which seemed a large sum, but for which I expected complete satisfaction), I took myself off to the address offered
and hammered upon the door of what seemed a highly
respectable house.

This was opened by a neatly-dressed maid who enquired
my business, then vanished for a moment, and returned to
assert that Miss Meg Tamblin would receive me. She
showed me upstairs to a handsomely furnished drawing-
room, where I was received by the lady herself, who
appeared the very picture of respectability, clad in a
fashionable *robe en calecon* which clearly revealed the
outlines of a fine figure. Upon my taking her hand and
kissing it, she gave a delightful smile and led me to a chaise
longue, where she sat at my side and for a while engaged in
polite conversation, enquiring how long I had been at
Bristol, and how I found the town, without at any time
asking my name or the nature of my employment, which I
found to be most tactful.

After a while, however, she took my hand and said, quite openly:

'I take it, sir, that you wish to purchase my favours?'

'I do, ma'am,' I replied, 'though rest assured that under any conditions I would be happy to pay court to so beautiful a woman.'

She smiled and bowed at this, and said that the custom was that gentlemen should contribute to the expenses of her establishment at the termination of their visit.

'Now perhaps we should prepare a tribute to Venus?' she said, taking my hand and pressing it to her bosom.

The reader can imagine that after some two weeks of abstinence I needed no second invitation, and in a trice we were both as little encumbered with clothing as our forebears in the Garden of Eden, and she was admiring the proportions of that part of me most anxious to be acquainted with her touch.

I must imagine that the tribute she paid to what she termed the magnificent proportions of my manly parts was one she accorded many of her gentlemen acquaintances, for I am not so proud as to believe myself inordinately well equipped. Moreover, I was distressed to find that my need was such that before she had for long been caressing me, I involuntarily gave way to the dictates of nature, in such an explosive mode that the essence flew perhaps two or three feet from my pulsing instrument, at which I feared she would consider our business concluded.

But no, she merely expressed approval of my vigour and the view that I had been too long without female company and, ringing the bell, bade her maid to bring some chocolate, which we drank while she talked of her life, which far from being a sad one she seemed to enjoy, able through good husbandry to live well and to visit London at least once a year, where no one (she said) knew her true occupation, and she was accepted as a lady in all the best circles.

But surely, I said, some of her friends must be coarse fellows whose only attraction was the size of their purse?

No, she said, her maid had strict instructions that she was not at home to any but those who appeared personable, and downstairs there was a stout fellow with a cudgel whose duty it was to protect the house in case of trouble. However, she was kind enough to agree that not all her friends were as handsome as myself – these are her words, and reported rather than repeated in pride – nor, she added with an appropriate gesture, were they all capable of so swift a recovery from collapse to readiness to renew the fight.

She had no need to devote much attention to my prick before it was once more, indeed, fully extended, when to my interest she took from a box nearby a little covering of transparent skin, eight inches long, closed at one end and decorated at the other by a pink ribbon which could be used to tighten it. This she drew over my standing prick – not without my fearing that her gentle touch might again have the unwonted result – and tied the ribbon at the base before laying me upon my back and mounting me to ride with a smooth and rocking motion which gave the utmost delight.

The *cundum*, for such it was, only slightly moderated my pleasure, for while the liquid embrace of an unprotected intimacy must remain the *sine qua non* of delight, the machine had the effect I believe of somewhat prolonging the period of pleasure, and certainly did not detract from the charming culmination. After this she took my friend, while he was still upright, between her fingers and undressed him by untying the ribbon and peeling back the skin, depositing it in a container nearby. She then drew me behind a screen, where was a bath of warm water and towels, and washed me and herself thoroughly, talking all the time in the most charming fashion and with a most delightful and witty air.

It was with nothing but pleasure that I placed three guineas upon the table, upon which she curtsied, and hoped I would call again – which I am determined to do, if I can, for despite the great expense the adventure was much happier than a quick stand against a wall by the harbourside, which most of my companions favoured.

Next day, as usual, I went to buy a broadsheet in which

there was to be an advertisement of our performances, and turning it to see what news might proccupy the city, came upon the following paragraph:

The brig Persephone *arrived at Bristol yesterday with news from the Meditteranean of the death at Genoa, by the fever, of Sir Spencer Franklyn, the son of the late Sir Franklin Franklyn of Alcovary in Hertfordshire. The baronetcy now falls to the second son, Sir Franklin Franklyn, whose present whereabouts is unknown.*

Chapter Sixteen

Sophie's Story

The morning blushed to find me still abed with the two love-birds, who indeed woke me by their amorous entwinings, which I regarded (the reader may imagine) with all the delight of a fairy godmother who had been instrumental in bringing them together.

In the light of day Mr Ffloyd had the grace to blush as, while he was still embraced by the limber thighs of his bride-to-be, he caught my eye and no doubt recollected the similar compliment he had in time past paid to my own beauty – to say nothing of our play on the previous evening, in which Sarah had been a not unwilling partner.

Rising and making our toilets, Sarah was melancholy at having to dress herself in the one piece of clothing she had with her. So I made our excuses to Mr Ffloyd and appointed to meet him at the parish church at eleven, then took my young friend off into the streets of the town, where we soon found a dressmaker who not only had a delightful piece of frippery which she had made up for a young lady whose wooer had sadly disappointed her at the altar, but was able with very little trouble to contrive that it fitted Sarah as if it were made for her. The latter protested at my insisting upon paying for it from my purse, but it gave me the greatest pleasure to do so, and to equip her – though in that virginal white which was perhaps not an entirely accurate reflection of her moral state – for her marriage. This went forward without hitch, and though the clergyman (notified a mere twenty-four hours in advance by Mr Ffloyd) and I were the only witnesses, it was as stylish and complete a ceremony as can be imagined.

Repairing to the inn to eat, we found all at sixes and

sevens in consequence of the arrival of a company of travelling players, led by an elderly lady and gentleman of enormous dignity and self-importance. There was a clown of a man who immediately began joking familiarly with the maids, a pert young girl with an air of 'touch-me-not' who made her way upstairs with a wiry, dark fellow paying much court to her and a young fellow carrying a guitar, who immediately vanished into a room from which soon came forth the dulcet tones of the instrument, played, I presumed, in practice.

We now considered our position. Mr Ffloyd had reserved places for himself and his wife on the coach westward, but when he and his bride asked whither they should send their news, I was quite unable to supply them with an address – and at that moment realised that I meant to go home to Alcovary. The house, and my mother – to say nothing of Frank – had been much in my mind lately, and I now longed to see them again, and was even able to persuade myself that Sir Franklin's anger might be mitigated by pleading. It is true there was the small matter of my husband, but should he prove troublesome, I had no doubt that a threat from me to reveal his practices in magic would persuade him not to insist on my living with him. In the event that I was not allowed into my parents' house, I had little doubt that my wits, together with the skills I had learned from the writings of Mr Lilly, would enable me to earn my bread.

So I attended the office of the mail and was able to take a seat east to Windsor, whence I could travel north to St Alban's and thence to Alcovary – a distance of some two days' travel only. The coaches arrived at almost the same moment and so it was that, leaning from the window of my vehicle as it began its journey, I received the farewells of Mr and Mrs Ffloyd as they made their way westwards to Cardiff and then to Llandridnod Wells, where a position as schoolmaster awaited my old tutor.

I was fortunate in that my coach contained, as inside travellers, only two people – one a plump gentleman who soon fell into a doze, and the other a young man of a markedly handsome appearance, with clear light blue eyes, an ingratiating smile, and a large brown mole near the corner of his mouth which seemed to emphasise a certain sardonic twist of the lip, rendering him perculiarly interesting. He insisted upon my lying back and placing my heels on the opposite seat, at his side, where he covered them with the tails of his coat against the cool air (though indeed it was remarkably sultry for the time of the year).

I cannot say that I was surprised, after a while, to feel his hand steal upon my ankle to caress my foot, which I had slipped out of its shoe. Nay, it crept up past the ankle, though without a change in both our positions which I had no intention of making, further intimacy was impossible. The expression of his eyes, however, and the motion of his tongue over his lower lip, spoke volumes of his desires – which I met with a steady gaze, though I admit without removing my feet from their comfortable position.

So, with this amusing game of foot and palm, the time passed engagingly enough as we drove on. At the first stage, we descended to take the air, and the young gentleman introduced himself as Mr Harry Rockwall, travelling to Cambridge to college there. When I mentioned that I had lived in that city for a while, and described the house in which I had lodged (or rather, the bathing-place below my windows) he knew it well, and seemed to have something to say on the subject. This, after a while, turned out to be a question whether I did not know 'his friend Jack', who was clearly the young man with whom I had spent such a pleasant afternoon at Byron's Pool, of which my present companion had heard tales which clearly had lost nothing in the telling, as the warmly increased pressure of his palm upon my ankle (when we were re-established in the coach) expressed.

His company was welcome on so tedious a journey and the bottle we shared brought us to a further quiet exchange of confidences, our companion being asleep. He asked whether friend Jack was not 'a pretty dog', to which I was bound to reply that he showed some of that animal's interest in continual congress! I should have met then, he said, a friend of his who had given up his studies to accompany him to his house near Basingstoke, where they had spent the vacation in cutting a swathe through the local female population. Now his friend, declining to return to the university, for he had but little interest in learning, had remained at his home as a sort of manager to the estate there, 'for,' my friend admitted, 'I am deucedly fond of the boy and would be sorry to lose sight of him – and rejected by his family he has nowhere else to go.'

The time passed in such interchange and in retailing accounts of my various adventures. He was amused, for instance, to hear of my management of the escape of Sarah and of her alliance with Mr Ffloyd (omitting, however, my own familiarity with the latter).

We half slumbered on the road to Windsor, where I awoke to find that he had transferred my foot, under cover of his coat, into his lap, where I had all unconsciously been caressing a something with which my sole had not previously been familiar. Our companion, whose snores had signalled a complete lack of interest in us which had no doubt contributed to my young friend's forwardness, woke with a start and jumped down to take, I suppose, some refreshment, while I leant from the window and looked out on the busy yard in the half-light of early morning.

The swiftness with which my skirts were drawn up and a familiar organ was brought into close propinquity with my lower back precluded all argument, and the enjoyable friction of its introduction into its proper place stopped my objection before it could find words. Gripping the sides of the window, I closed my eyes and surrendered myself to the pleasure of an early morning engagement, which reached its culmination at the moment when, opening my eyes, I met those of our plump fellow traveller below me, with a bottle in one hand and his hat in the other, requiring entrance.

I straightened up, not unblushingly I suspect, and backed away from the window to allow the man to climb into the coach, and upon turning I found my young friend seated, his coat over his lap, and apparently in an innocent sleep. Only my eyes recognised, in the squirmings and fumblings which disturbed his covering, the difficulty he had in rearranging his dress, which amused me so much that I had difficulty in not falling into a laugh.

I was only half awake when, many hours later, I looked out of the window to recognise a stretch of road; surely it was that along which I had ridden in such depression with my father when we first went to call upon Mr Nelham – how long ago it seemed! Yes, around the next corner must stand his house! I made ready to retire into the corner of the coach, lest by any chance my husband should be walking nearby. But – what was this? No chimneys were to be seen above the trees around the garden and as we passed the gate, all I could see were the blackened tatters of the outer walls of the house!

As we passed almost immediately into the single street of the village, I put my head out of the window and shouted to the coachman to stop. With a quick adieu to my friend, who was still in a sleepy half-stupor, I leaped down and caught my small bundle, thrown by the coachman, and as the coach moved off I made my way into the nearby inn.

There was no one there I knew, but when I asked the landlord after 'a Mr Nelham' who I understood was a distinguished astrologer, I was told that he had perished some three months ago in a fire, allegedly caused by a furnace which he had established in the cellar for an attempt at the conversion of base metal into gold!

'He left a widow,' said the landlord, 'but no one knows where she is, though Lawyer Cox has advertised in all the local sheets.'

Where did this lawyer reside, I asked, and being told the house, which stood nearby, made my way there with all alacrity and had myself announced as 'Mrs Sophia Nelham', which brought Mr Cox to me at a positive gallop.

I had no difficulty in convincing him of my *bona fides*, though he would need, he said, to see my marriage lines. My father, Sir Franklin Franklyn of Alcovary, had care of those, I said, and would also identify me. At this he informed me that my father had died shortly before Mr

Nelham, of a seizure – and not only him, but brother Spencer too, of some distemper caught in a foreign port.

I was more disturbed at my brother's death than my father's, but truthfully not much by either, for I was closer to my mother and to brother Frank – now, no doubt, reigning as Sir Franklin! – than the other two.

But there was more news! Frank had no more been heard of than me, having vanished from Oxford not long after I had departed from Cambridge, and his present whereabouts no one knew. Again, advertisements had been placed in all the sheets for, said Lawyer Cox, to everyone's surprise my father, thought to be improverished, had left a considerable fortune. And more – Mr Nelham, whose miserly behaviour had been a legend in the country, had in the bank no less than sixteen thousand pounds in gold, as well as a house in London, all of which was now mine! Suddenly I swooned clear away, partly from the news and partly from the fatigue of the journey, but recovered swiftly thanks to Mr Cox loosening the neck of my dress and fanning me with a collection of papers he happened to have by him.

I lost no time now in hiring a hack and making for Alcovary, riding up the familiar drive at midday to slip in through the front door and discover my mother, all in black, sitting in the drawing-room, where also sat a fat, bald, pasty-faced fellow in a tawdry brown coat, reading at a book.

After we had greeted each other with many tears, and I had commiserated with my mother on the loss of a husband and a son at the same time and she had commiserated with me upon the loss of my husband, which for both of us was a matter of form rather than of true mourning, the third party, who had been sitting by, broke in with: 'Patience, my dear, am I not to be introduced?'

'Mr Thomas Bidwell, my daughter, Mrs Sophia Nelham.'

'Aha! So I had conjectured,' said the fellow, taking my hand in his large, damp palm and pressing it. 'Welcome home to Alcovary, ma'am. You have been apprised, I gather, of the fortune of which you are now happily in command?'

I must have looked surprised at the impertinence, for my mother broke in:

'Mr Bidwell was your father's man of business in London, Sophia, to whom all our circumstances are well known' and 'we are fortunate that he has consented to stay here for a time to make sure all our business matters are in order,' she went on, without any great enthusiasm. 'There is property in London, as well as a considerable fortune, which he is keeping in trust for Frank' – and a tear sprung now to her eye – 'when he returns.'

'As he will, dear lady, as he will!' said Bidwell. 'Trust me – I shall be happy to remain in this house until my presence is no longer required, and even then would leave with reluctance, especially now that Alcovary is graced with the presence of so handsome a lady as yourself, Mrs Nelham!' – at which he directed at me a look of such plainly lascivious a nature that I almost struck him.

In a while, he made his excuses and left the room, whereat I enquired of my mother whether it was really her wish that he remain in the house? She replied, no, but there were reasons why it was impossible for her to require his departure, and on my pressing her revealed that he had suddenly appeared at the house soon after the news had been printed of my father's death, bringing with him not only information of the astonishingly large fortune of which all details had been kept from his family, but graver news, which only Mr Bidwell and my mother, in the world, knew: for my father had apprised him some time ago that while Spencer and myself were the lawful fruit of his marriage, Frank was my mother's son by a former lover! This, my father said, had been revealed to him during the course of the altercation following upon the scene which he had interrupted at Alcovary just before I had left it, when, it seems, he had discovered my mother and Andrew sharing an amorous congress.

My mother blushed at this, and would have said more of it but I longed to hear the rest of the story, and she revealed that my father had informed Mr Bidwell – at first in a letter in his own hand, which the lawyer still possessed – that he wished to change his will, entirely disinheriting Frank. But upon the very morning when the new document was to be signed, he had been stricken by the sudden flux which had killed him.

Upon hearing news of Spencer's death Mr Bidwell realised that he could now hold over my mother the threat of losing the entire estate, for while she could no doubt count upon being supported by Frank, should he be disinherited the same fate would fall to her, for the entire estate would then pass to a distant cousin of my father's who cordially disliked her, and would have her out of the house with no care for her future. However, as long as she supported Mr Bidwell in comfort, he had promised to keep the document private, and under this threat not only was he living in luxury at Alcovary, but had even insisted upon sharing my mother's bed whenever the mood seized him.

My mother having breached the dam of her confidences went on to reveal the name of Frank's father, whom I dimly remembered as a kindly neighbour who many times took me upon his knee when I was a child, and had shown a peculiar interest in all us children, but perhaps – now that I came to think of it – Frank in particular. He had not seemed to me to be especially handsome, and was certainly not particularly rich, and I must have looked my surprise at hearing his name, whereon my mother blushingly revealed that my father's interest in the fleshly pleasures had been confined to the procreation of children, and Mr Bidwell had hinted that his true proclivities lay elsewhere. Deprived of conjugal joys, my mother had yielded to the advances of her neighbourly admirer who – she confessed – had that one physical characteristic to commend him which was irresistible to all women – 'as you will one day discover,' she said.

I could not help at that moment exclaiming that our adopted brother Andy was also a charming fellow.

'Indeed,' said my mother thoughtfully, 'I remember observing your admiration of him.'

'Not more, ma'am, than you yourself,' was my reply, at which she had the grace to blush, and then to rise and embrace me, saying that we must not quarrel for I was all she had left in the world to comfort me.

Mr Bidwell, returning at that moment to find us in each other's arms, congratulated us on our affection, and himself on being so fortunate as to be living in a house graced by the presence of two such charming women.

Going to my room to change for supper, I was eager to find a clean gown, for the dresses I had were all now travel-stained and over familiar. I had grown considerably in stature since I left Alcovary, with the result that the gowns I used to wear were tight about me (my mother was of a larger frame altogether, and I would have looked ridiculous in one of her dresses). However, I managed to climb into one which at least did not constrict my movements too much, though it was I must confess like a second skin to me and Mr Bidwell's eyes, on my presenting myself at table, almost fell from their sockets, only the intensity with which he fixed them upon my bosom seeming to keep them in place.

My mother took the end of the table, myself sitting opposite Mr Bidwell, who poured much of his soup over his person, so eager was he to observe me at every point. While consuming the bird which followed, I felt his foot making a progress up the inside of my leg which, waiting until it reached my thigh, I greeted by dropping my fork, and bending to recover it plunging it with what energy I could into his ankle, so that he almost choked upon the drumstick over which he was slavering at the time. This did not disconcert him, however; he was clearly a man to whom resistence was the greatest aphrodisiac, and from the glances which my mother exchanged with him, and the disappearance of his left hand beneath the table, he was obviously paying her some attention while at the same time stroking my lower limbs with his foot.

We cut the meal as short as we decently could and then retired to the drawing-room, where my mother requested me to play the harpsichord, thus releasing me from the necessity of fending off Mr Bidwell's attentions, so that he merely sat ogling us both and booming out ridiculous compliments whenever the music ceased.

At length my repertoire was exhausted, and I rose from the keyboard.

'If you will pardon me, ma'am,' I said, 'I will retire. The day has been a long one, and I am fatigued.'

'My dear Mrs Nelham,' said Bidwell rising, 'you must indeed pay to Morpheus that tribute all beautiful young women owe if their loveliness is to be preserved. Would that my arms could receive the compliment you will shortly pay to his!' And he took my hand, raising it to his lips and kissing it with a loose-lipped motion that even included the insertion of his tongue between my fingers, so that it was only with a great endeavour that once more I commanded myself sufficiently to refrain from striking him.

'My dear Patience,' he said, turning to my mother, 'shall we also retire?' At which, coldly and it seemed to me with a despairing air, she rose, embraced me, and we all walked together into the hall and mounted the staircase to the passage where my mother's and my bedroom lay and where, to my astonishment (though I might indeed have expected it) Mr Bidwell disappeared through the door of what had been my father's chamber!

I had no sooner stripped off my clothes and fallen into bed then I fell also into a deep and dreamless sleep – but not, I imagine, for long, for I awoke at the opening of my door (which had never had means of barring it) and the glow of a candle which showed me the face and figure of Mr Bidwell. His arrival was a shock, but not a surprise to me; I had merely hoped that his attentions would be pressed that evening upon my mother rather than myself, nor did I think he would have the impertinence to appear in my bedroom without devoting at least a little more time to the seduction he hoped to accomplish.

I feigned sleep as he approached, but could not continue to do so as he sat down upon the side of the bed, which was thrown upon one side by his weight, so that despite myself I rolled somewhat and fell towards my night visitor, and in putting out my hand to save myself placed it – entirely, I need not say, without the intention of doing so – upon the hairy, plump and naked thigh beneath his shirt.

'Ah! Miss Sophie!' he sighed, and gripping my hand with his own raised it so that it was truly between his legs, where in a thicket of wiry hair I felt what I had expected to feel, though happily it was somewhat less massive than I might have expected in a man of his size.

How I resisted the temptation to grasp and twist with all my might, I can never explain, but I feared to rouse his temper, for so large a man would have been impossible to resist should he attack with all his force, and I still hoped to find a way of declining his advances.

'Make me, my dear Miss Sophia, the happiest of men!' he breathed, leaning over me and slobbering kisses over my face and bosom, while attempting to plunge his hand between my own thighs.

'Ah, sir!' I said. 'I did not believe in my wildest dreams that I could hope . . .' – at which he ceased his slobbering, perhaps in astonishment, for it must have been many years since a lady paid him an unforced compliment.

'I would have come to you, sir, but that I feared rejection!' I cried, and persuaded myself to reach for his cods and caress them, at which he shook like one about to have a seizure.

'But sir,' I went on, 'let us go to your chamber, for my bed is narrow and I fear that upon it it would be impossible for me to give you that full joy which so handsome a man merits. Nor, I think, could it support the vigorous activity of one so virile!'

He was much complimented at this and rose to his feet, taking the candle in one hand and my arm in the other, and whispered: 'Most amiable of young ladies come, then, come,' and led me forth.

Outside my door, we turned to the right towards my father's room, myself careful to take the inside path next the wall. As we passed the top of the stairs, on our left, I suddenly wrenched my arm away from his grip and, bracing the other against the wall, gave him a push with all my force. Not in the least expecting it, he did not even give a cry but staggered, missed his footing, and plunged down the dark stairway. The candle almost immediately went out but in the pitch dark I heard the continual rumble of his descent, a final crash as he reached the stone floor of the hall, and then a silence which was only broken, after a while, by the opening of my mother's bedroom door.

In the light of the candle which she carried, we could only see a dark shape at the bottom of the stairs.

'Alas, Mama,' I said, 'Mr Bidwell has had an accident.'

She said nothing but descended the stairs where, on lowering the candle, we saw our guest's head lying in a pool of blood, his face ashen white, his breast still. I was reaching for his hand, to feel for a pulse, when there was a sudden loud knocking at the front door, only a few feet away.

I looked, terrified, at my mother, and she at me. We stood in silence for a moment, when the knocking redoubled and we had no recourse but to open. Two men stood outside, one holding the reins of two horses, the other with a lantern held on high.

The man with the lantern stepped forward to take my mother in his arms. It was young Sir Franklin Franklyn of Alcovary and behind him, smiling broadly, was Andrew Archer. Frank and Andy were returned! My head buzzing, I looked into my brother's eyes for a long moment, then fell at his feet in a swoon.

Chapter Seventeen

The Adventures of Andy

We left Bristol after some five weeks, having made a very considerable sum which, when shared out between us, would amount to sufficient to keep me in comfort while I decided whether to join the company on a permanent basis. I was a little in doubt of this, for while there were many things about our life which I enjoyed, I must confess that I found many of the actors tiresome and over-full of their own importance.

Our first pause after Bristol was at Chippenham, where Mr Higgens and Mrs Plunkett Cope gave their Romeo and Juliet once more. Then, after two nights, we proceeded to Devizes, which was delighted by a performance of *Hamlet* in which Ned Farkin, who had partaken rather too enthusiastically of small beer in the company of some fellows in the taproom, was so well received in the gravedigger's scene that he declined to leave the stage, appearing in several subsequent scenes by default. When Osric came to issue Laertes' challenge to Hamlet, Ned suddenly appeared from behind the scenes and danced a jig of his own devising which much disconcerted Mr Higgens (especially since, being somewhat hard of hearing, he was not aware of Ned's cavorting behind him, mistaking the roars of laughter for roars of applause, and taking several 'calls' before the truth of the situation was conveyed to him).

From Devizes we travelled a little to the south, performing at Everleigh and Weyhill, Andover and Overton, and then received a command to attend upon Mr Harry Rockwall at his house on the outskirts of Basingstoke, to entertain at a party of some kind. I agreed to accompany the usual small group but made it clear that I was to provide music only for the occasion, and not take part in any exhibition which might be expected, my taste being, on the whole, for privacy in matters of love.

The house proved a small but capacious one, with a fine hall above which, at a height of only perhaps eight or nine feet, hung a little minstrels' gallery where I installed myself with my guitar. The party was in the way of a farewell to Mr Rockwall, a handsome young man whose beauty was if anything enhanced by a large, brown mole at the corner of his mouth. He was clearly the owner of the property, but young enough still to be at Cambridge University, whither he was bound next morning. Some twenty of his friends, men and women, had dined and drunk well and were ready for some boisterous entertainment, which began with Ned capering in an obscene dance of his own devising based, he said, upon that of an Italian jester of two centuries previously, and in which he wore a conterfeit cock and balls of gigantic proportions, with which he belaboured the ladies about the buttocks, to their great amusement.

Next, Mr Grigson delivered himself of *Love's Physiognomy*, a song he always performed before an intellectual audience, for there were many classical allusions which, he explained, enabled young ladies and gentlemen of education to derive additional pleasure –

If her hair be yellow, she'll tempt each fellow
  In the Emmanuel College;
For she that doth follow the colour of Apollo
  May be like him in zeal of knowledge.

If she be pale and a virgin stale,
  Inclined to the sickness green,
Some raw fruit give her to open her liver
  Her stomach and the thing between.

– while Miss Cope appeared cleverly disguised to counterfeit the different kinds of woman sung of. This item indeed gave much pleasure, though it was followed by a cry of: 'Now, something hotter, for 'tis almost fairy time!' So Ned gave them *Riding Paces*, pretending to be a description of a horse-ride, but in reality quite other:

> *When for air*
>   *I take my mare*
> *And mount her, first*
>   *She walks just thus:*
> *Her head held low*
>   *And motion slow,*
> *With nodding, plodding,*
>   *Wagging, jogging,*
> *Dashing, plashing,*
>   *Snorting, starting*
> *Whimsically she goes,*
> *Then whip stirs up,*
>   *Trot, trot, trot,*
> *Ambling then with easy flight*
> *She wriggles like a bird at night . . .*

Miss Cope, now devoid of cover, meanwhile mounted Mr Grigson, bare as she, and rode him to a climax which ended with the song:

> *Mane seized,*
>   *Bum squeezed,*
> *I gallop, I gallop, I gallop,*
>   *And trot, trot, trot,*
> *Straight again up and down,*
> *Up and down, up and down,*
> *Till the last jerk, with a trot,*
> *Ends our love chase.*

I must confess to admiring the remarkable control which enabled Mr Grigson to lift Miss Cope from her seat just as the last words echoed out, to show himself spilling over with pleasure at the expertise of his rider, and the applause and shouts of encouragement from the audience showed that many among them shared my surprise and admiration. The scene was by this time, as I expected, one of a bacchanalian orgy, most of the young ladies and gentlemen now divested of their dress and lying upon the rugs generously spread upon the floor, some warming their partners with caresses, others already engaged in the act. Mr Grigson and Miss Cope retired, while Ned seized a bottle and sat himself in a corner to look on – being himself, for one reason or another, unconcerned with matters of love – while David, as usual, had divested himself of his clothing and was darting among the company, stopping to twitch a lady's buttock here or a breast there, but contriving all the time to bring his loins into close contact with some part of the anatomy of their partners. Some knocked him away with an oath, while others accorded him a pat, and one or two (for, as I have heard, the universities are full of young gentlemen whose tastes are for whichever sex comes most readily to hand) offered a more intimate caress.

I suddenly became aware of a young fellow who, I guessed, had been seated directly below the small gallery in which I was perched, for I had not seen him until now, stretched out upon the body of a handsome young woman who he was enjoying with some zest. There seemed to be something familiar about the turn of his back, so that I could not help but stare (the lady beneath him believing me to be staring at her, and giving me a broad grin as he worked away upon her). After a while, having reached his goal, he lifted himself and, turning, lay upon his back at her side, whereat I found myself staring right into the astonished eyes of my old friend Frank – now Sir Franklin Franklyn of Alcovary!

In a moment I had dropped my instrument, was out of the gallery, down the narrow staircase, and had clasped him to me – seeing to my amusement as I embraced him, an extremely jealous look from David at the sight of me with a naked man in my arms! So great was our pleasure and surprise that it was some moments before either of us could speak, but then Frank covered himself with a cloak from the floor and led me up to a bedroom on the first floor where we could talk.

This is not the place in which to relate all his adventures, though he told of his short time at Oxford University, whence his father had sent him, of his meeting there with Harry Rockwall ('my companion,' he said, 'in many a jape which will amuse you when we are at leisure'), how Rockwall had invited him to pass the vacation with him at his home (where he was lord of all he surveyed, his family being dead) and how . . .

But here I stopped him, for it was clear to me that there was certain information he had not heard, and I broke to him the news not only of his father's death, but of his brother's and that he was now a baronet, in possession of whatever small fortune his father had commanded.

Though shocked at the news, his pleasure was perhaps more than his pain; though he felt for his Spencer, somehow (he said) it was not with that keenness with which a man might be expected to mourn his brother. 'But we were never close,' he said. 'Poor chap.'

He had not intended ever to return to Alcovary, believing his father entirely turned against him, and since his sister Sophia had been sent away and married to some elderly clown (which was the first I had heard of it, and was sad to hear). But now, surely, he must return to comfort his mother and to discover what estate he had inherited.

What pleasure I now felt, sitting before a fire with my old friend, upon whose familiar limbs, as he sat half-covered with the cloak, red light flickered, and whose face was relaxed into the old companionable smile I remembered! We remained talking long into the night, until we heard the noise of my companions leaving the house (doubtless perplexed at my disappearance) and with a knock at the door Harry Rockwall appeared, to be introduced to me and welcome me to the house to stay as long as I wished – 'For,' he said, 'young Frank stays here to care for my estate while I am in Oxford!'

Then, bidding farewell to Frank – for he left for Oxford the next morning – he left us and we retired to bed, still talking for a while, and then fell asleep, Frank throwing his arm about my shoulders in a gesture of friendship for old times.

My friend evidently lay awake for much of the night, for next morning he announced to me that we must leave that instant for Alcovary, not being able to bear longer to be unsatisfied as to the knowledge of his fate. Would I return with him, he asked, for now fate had thrown us once more together he would not be deprived of my friendship.

'Nothing,' I said, 'would give me more pleasure,' and while he settled to write a letter to Mr Rockwall explaining the change in his plans, I went into Basingstoke, where the latter had taken the early morning coach, and found my companions at the Mail Coach Inn. They were sad at my decision to leave them but it was not a disaster, since they were almost at the end of their tour, and Mr Higgens pleasantly handed me a small but welcome bag of gold pieces, the reward of my time with them.

'If you have need of employment, my dear Mr Archer,' he said, 'pray seek us out. We present in the new season the play of *Timon of Athens*, and need some pleasant music to lighten it; you will be always welcome upon any stage where Mrs Plunkett Cope and I take our stand.' With great condescension that lady bade me farewell, and I went off to take my leave of the others; whereas Miss Cope merely allowed me to kiss her hand, David threw his arms about me and whispered that it would be some time before he had another so pleasant a bedfellow, and seemed almost to have tears in his eyes at our farewell.

By the time I returned to Mr Rockwall's house, Frank had two horses waiting, and bade me prepare for an arduous journey for he did not intend to stop except for food and sleep and to change horses until we reached home. And indeed so it was; with little pause, it seemed no time before we were within reach of Alcovary and though the night had fallen, Frank demanded that we should press on. By the light of a lantern we made our way forward, coming in time to the gates of the house, and passing up the drive to the front door.

All was in darkness. Lifting the lantern and handing me the reins, Frank went forward and knocked. There was no answer. He knocked again and there was a shuffling from within, the door opened and who should stand there but Sophie, who looked for a moment into her brother's eyes, then fell at his feet in a swoon.

Tying the horses, I rushed forward, and together we raised Sophie from the floor and placed her in a chair. Lady Franklyn now came forward and greeted her son, and soon Sophie was stirring, and we were at leisure to consider the fifth figure in the hall – the body of a large man clad only in a shirt, who had lain all this while upon the floor (for my part I had thought he was drunk) and whose head, now we came to examine it, was broken and bloodied.

Sophie, now quickly recovered and having greeted us both with a kiss, explained briefly that the dead man was a villain who had fallen to his death as a consequence of an attack upon her virtue and that there was much more to tell us, but first the servants must be roused, a magistrate sent for, and all done in order.

When I had roused a man and sent him for Sir Ingle Fitzson, a magistrate and a neighbour and a good friend of Lady Franklyn's, we went into the drawing-room and took some brandy while Sophie and Lady Franklyn between them explained not only the circumstance of Mr Bidwell's death (whom Sophie said quite frankly she had pushed downstairs, and would be happy to do so again) but the fact that Frank was heir not only to the house but to a fortune the size of which was not precisely known, but which certainly comprised an income of not less than seven thousand a year, and property in London which included a house in Brook Street.

'So,' said Sophie, 'we are both landowners now, Frank!' And when we expressed amazement, she told us of the death of Mr Nelham and the unexpected fortune he had left. Frank immediately embraced her, and an air almost of gaiety supported us until Sir Ingle arrived, who had met Mr Bidwell and liked him as little as Sophie and Lady Franklyn. It was clear to him, he said, after looking at the body, that Mr Bidwell had risen from his bed in the dark for some purpose of his own, that his candle had gone out, that he had lost his footing in the gallery and fallen downstairs to his death. He failed to congratulate the family upon the incident, but pressed affectionate greetings upon Frank and Sophie, complimented Lady Franklyn upon their return, and took his leave.

The servants now lifted Mr Bidwell's body and took it off to an outhouse, remaining to clean the flagstones while we all went upstairs, Lady Franklyn to her own room, and we three to Sophie's, where in a counterfeit of our childish days we crept into the same bed and fell almost immediately into a sleep.

Waking, it was with great joy that I saw upon the pillow at my side the faces of my two best friends in all the world – Frank, his manly visage framed by close-cropped hair, resting in the arms of his sister, who was now one of the most beautiful women my eyes had ever fixed upon. I had paid the day the tribute, as was so often the case, of waking to it in a state of readiness for amorous combat, and it was with great difficulty that I refrained from waking Sophie with a caress, but knew not how she would take it and so contented myself by laying up against her warm body until she and Frank also stirred, and we three regarded each other in the light of morning with the affection we had shared before our last meeting. Sophie lifted her head to kiss my lips, and then Frank's – but he drew away, and when she asked what was the trouble, replied that childish affection between brother and sister was well enough, but they were now grown and should have regard for decency.

Sophie was for a moment quiet at this and then, lifting herself upon her elbow, informed us that there was something she had still to tell us, and thereupon told of the circumstance of which Mr Bidwell had been aware – that Frank, while his mother's son, was no relative at all of Sir Franklyn's.

'So I am disinherited!' cried Frank.

'Far from that!' said Sophie. 'If you are disinherited, so is our mother, and everything she has will go to cousin Bartley in Staffordshire, a greater nincompoop and swaggerer than whom I have never met, apart from the fact that he is already in possession of a fortune entirely sufficient for so considerable a ninny as himself.'

Frank was thoughtful for a moment, and then expressed himself of the opinion that it would be a pity that his mother should become a pauper on his account, and that it was clear he would have to put up with wealth in her interest. Upon which we all burst into laughter, and on its subsiding Sophie pointed out that being only his half-sister perhaps he would now allow her a kiss, for (she said) if Lord Byron could father a child upon his sister (as was put about) she had no objection to a certain degree of familiarity from her half-brother. He needed no encouragement but kissed her soundly, a kiss upon her lips leading naturally to a kiss upon her bosom, and a gradual descent until neither were in a condition to delay further from the ultimate embrace.

I lay all this time merely laying a hand, from time to time, upon one limb or another, and as they concluded their endearments was (I must confess) in the way of affording myself what comfort I could by manual application, whereupon Sophie cried out that while I might not command the blood tie of a half-brother, I was an honorary brother nonetheless, and laughingly pushing Frank aside welcomed me to her body. I was able to show that I had gained in experience since we had last been so joined and, I believe, afforded her something of the same satisfaction as I, certainly, received. Frank too (I must in modesty report) was complimentary about my amatory skills, whereupon I promised to import to him some secrets, when we were in private.

We rose in great good humour to join Lady Franklyn at breakfast, and later that day rode with Sophie to Sir Ingle's house where he sat in inquest on Mr Bidwell's body, returning a verdict of his being accidentally killed.

Back at Alcovary, in what had been old Sir Franklyn's room, was Mr Bidwell's box of papers in which we found what must be the only record of his discovery about Frank's parentage, which we had the pleasure to burn, and we also found notes of the investments and property in London which now made Frank a gentleman of property.

We set about putting the late Sir Franklin's will in order

and satisfying the lawyers, too, of Sophie's claim on her late husband's property, which resulted before long in the whole business being settled to the satisfaction of the men of law.

For seven months we all lived together very pleasantly, but when spring came the three of us – but perhaps Sophie and I in particular – began to feel restless, and I believed that I could at any event no longer batten upon the hospitality of my friends. So one evening, just when the small green buds were beginning to show, I announced that I would take myself off once more into the world.

'But where will you go, dear Andy?' asked Sophie.

'To London,' I said, 'to seek my fortune, for alone of the three of us I have nothing of my own and can no longer press upon you for my keep.'

Both Sophie and Frank were kind enough to find the statement ridiculous and when we began to argue, Frank at last cried:

'But we both have property, sister, in London, which we have not seen. We have an income sufficient to keep us in comfort. Why do we not *all* go?'

Sophie was loud in her approval but I demurred, saying that I could not live on my friends.

'Then you shall come as my steward – companion – tutor – what you will!' said Frank. 'But can you not see, dear Andy, that we will not under any circumstance be parted from you?' and they both embraced me and warmly enjoined me not to leave them.

And so it was, reader, that our life in the provinces was over and that we three bumpkins, with only the experience of life we had gathered during our rambles in the country, were now headed for the city – and the greatest of them all, London town.

MALEE

—

TIGER CLAW AND VELVET PAW

—

The erotic odyssey of Thai prostitute

The world of Suzie Wong . . .

The daughter of a Thai rice farmer, Malee is forced to leave her village and enter domestic service at the age of fourteen. Raped by her master, she flees to the nearest open door – the local brothel.

Realising that prostitution offers her only chance of survival, Malee becomes a showdancing star, devising erotic spectacles of Oriental sensuality.

She moves on from the world of the American GI to the cosmopolitan life of Bangkok and finally settles in the red light district of Hamburg.

Explicit and touchingly honest, Malee's story explores a sexual underworld of fantasy and compulsion exploited by whore and punter alike.

NON-FICTION   0-7472-3047-1   £2.50

Headline books are available at your bookshop or newsagent, or can be ordered from the following address:

Headline Book Publishing PLC
Cash Sales Department
PO Box 11
Falmouth
Cornwall
TR10 9EN
England

UK customers please send cheque or postal order (no currency), allowing 60p for postage and packing for the first book, plus 25p for the second book and 15p for each additional book ordered up to a maximum charge of £1.90 in UK.

BFPO customers please allow 60p for postage and packing for the first book, plus 25p for the second book and 15p per copy for the next seven books, thereafter 9p per book.

Overseas and Eire customers please allow £1.25 for postage and packing for the first book, plus 75p for the second book and 28p for each subsequent book.